RELEASING GILLIAN'S WOLVES

RELEASING GILLIAN'S WOLVES

◈ A LACLAND STORY ◈

BY
TARA WOOLPY

Bats in the Boathouse Press

MINOCQUA, WISCONSIN

Copyright 2011 by Tara Woolpy

All rights reserved. No part of this book may be reproduced without written permission with the exception of reviewers who are welcome to include brief quotations in their reviews.

Originally published in ebook and paperback form by Bats in the Boathouse Press 2011.

The characters and events described are fictitious. The town of Lacland and all its inhabitants exist only in our imagination, although Gillian, Edward, Sam and Maggie regularly blog with Tara at http://www.batsintheboathouse.com/lacland-news-blog.html

Bats in the Boathouse Press
PO Box 685
Minocqua, WI 54548
Batsintheboathouse.com

ISBN-10 098320330X
ISBN-13 978-0-9832033-0-8

For Jer

PART ONE

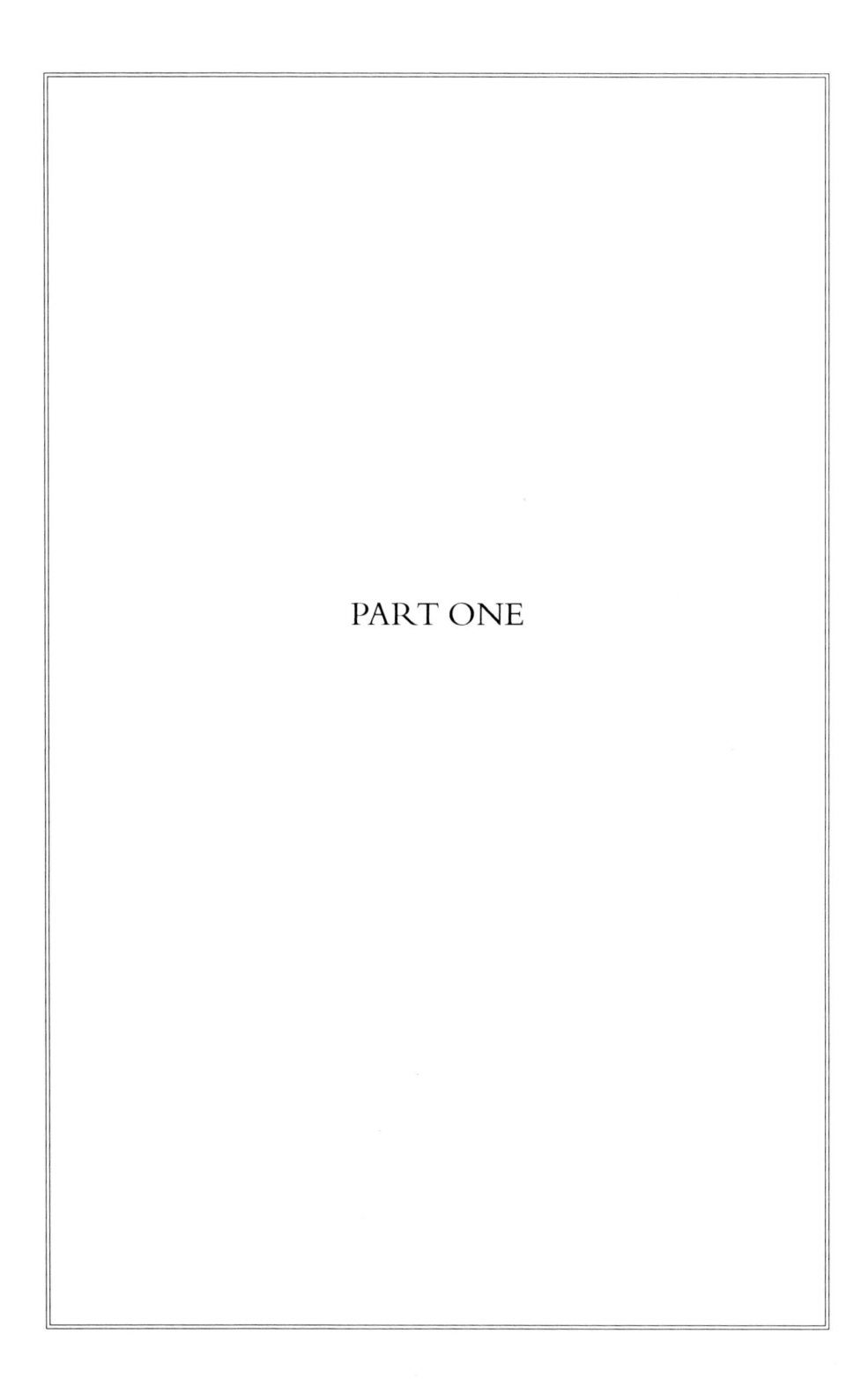

Survive Anything Double-Chocolate Brownies

Preheat your oven to 350 degrees. Melt nine ounces of bittersweet chocolate and seven tablespoons unsalted butter (most of a stick). Chop and cut the chocolate and butter so they melt easily in a double boiler (if you're like me and don't want a big double boiler cluttering the kitchen, use a four cup Pyrex measuring cup placed in the middle of a pot half-filled with boiling water). Some people melt chocolate in microwaves. You could try that. Use a spatula to keep the mixture from gunking up the sides, stir continually and when it's completely soupy set aside to cool.

    Beat three eggs in a large bowl at medium-high speed until thick and pale, it takes a few minutes. Add two teaspoons vanilla extract, two tablespoons coffee (whatever's left in the pot), a half-cup milk and a cup of sour cream (use real sour cream!). Beat until fully mixed (just seconds). Reduce speed to low, add chocolate mixture. Don't lick the spatula yet.

    Whisk one and a half cups all-purpose flour, a half-teaspoon baking powder and a half-teaspoon salt together in a medium bowl. Fold in the flour mixture. Add a bag or so of semisweet chocolate chips (this can vary depending on what you're surviving. When we visit Evelyn, I use at least two bags).

    Grease the sides of a ten by fourteen inch cake pan, using the lopped off end of the butter stick. Line the bottom with parchment paper. Cover with batter and smooth it out. Now you can lick the spatula. Bake until cooked through, about a half hour (test with a toothpick to make sure). Allow brownies to cool before cutting.

    Eat, share and repeat until everything's okay.

ONE

The moon drew a rippling arrow across the surface of the lake, exposing Edward and Sam making love on the dock. Rounding the point in my kayak, I stopped, mesmerized by the romance of the lake, the moon and two beautiful men wrapped in each other on an oversized deck chair. Good, I thought, good for Edward. My marriage is such a wreck. I silently paddled toward the next dock and home.

Not bothering to turn on the lights, I lifted the kayak into its rack. I stepped out onto my moonlit dock and breathed deeply, smelling pine and the fertile scent of decomposing lake weeds, turned and walked up the steep wooden steps toward the house.

Pausing on the landing, I could feel the muscles in my shoulders relax a little. I could see Jack working at the dining room table with his campaign manager, Mark McLaughlin. Mark almost always put him in a magnanimous mood. I climbed the last few steps, opened the screen door and passed through the kitchen into the dining room.

"Gillian, home from the sea." Jack toasted me with his highball. "Drink?"

"No thanks, I'm chilled. I think I'll make some tea. Hello, Mark." I motioned to the brochures on the table. "Are these the new fliers? They look good."

"Thanks." Mark blushed, color rising from the base of his thick neck to the top of his bald head. He didn't look at me, but that wasn't unusual. Mark McLaughlin's had a debilitating crush on me for twenty years, since Jack's first victorious run for State Assembly.

"Mark and I are going over the campaign schedule. There's a League of Women Voters meeting on Wednesday that I think you should address." Jack tapped the datebook, open on the table. "You could talk about my support for Maternity Leave legislation."

"You know I hate that sort of thing, and isn't it Family Leave legislation?"

He shrugged. "Same thing. How many men do you know stay home with babies?" He swirled the ice cubes in his glass. "Will you at least go shake some hands for me? Please?"

I sighed. "Okay. But no speech. Frankly, I don't have time to put one together. Tomorrow I'm cooking for the mailing party. I also need to drop off the dry cleaning and pick up your mother's prescription and make sure she has enough food for the next couple days and I promised Edward I'd drive with him to see his mother on Tuesday."

"Can't that new guy, what's-his-name, drive him? It's August, Gillian, I really need you here." Jack sipped his drink.

"It's Sam DaCosta, and would you subject someone new to Evelyn?" I held his gaze. "Although if you wanted to pick up your mother's prescription yourself—"

Jack waived dismissively. "I don't have time. You take care of Momma Pearl. Mark can write your speech."

"No speech. Has Jack offered you anything to eat?"

Mark smiled shyly. "Thanks, but I ate earlier. I'll take some tea if you're making it."

I turned toward the kitchen.

Jack mumbled, "Why can't she have girl girlfriends like other women?"

"I do," I threw over my shoulder. "You've just never liked Maggie."

"I like Maggie fine. But I wish you had more normal friends, like Katy Swanson and those girls."

I turned and stared at him for a long moment. Mark looked down at his hands. Finally I said lightly, "You wish I had more political junkie friends like Katy. I get plenty of politics at home, thank you. Caffeinated or something herbal, Mark?"

"Whatever's easy. I doubt I'm going to bed anytime soon."

I busied myself with the tea and with breathing through my resentment. The thought of spending more time with Jack's groupies made me nauseous. Jealous? I didn't think I could be jealous at this point, but I hated the way they fawned and he lapped it up. Breathe. Let it go. Right.

The kettle whistled and I poured, placed tea and a few cookies on a tray for Mark, and brought it into the dining room. Excusing myself, I took my own cup upstairs to our large, sparsely furnished bedroom where floor to ceiling windows overlook the lake. Pine trees on either side provide some privacy. In winter, with only a few snowmobilers and ice fishermen out there, we mostly leave the curtains open. Summer, when the lake's crowded with tourists and boats, it usually feels safer to pull them, like hiding in a tent made from the sofa, coffee table, chairs and a blanket.

Jack's blue linen jacket lay crumpled on the floor. He must have tossed it toward the bed and missed. I gathered it up, fumbling in the pockets as I walked it toward the closet and my pile of dry cleaning. One of the many things I've forgiven over the years is Jack's habit of leaving garbage in his pockets for me to empty. Crumpled receipts that his campaign treasurer would want, empty breath mint wrappers, a wad of bills – I imagined him quickly stuffing the change from some purchase in order to free himself for a firm, manly handshake —one of his half-dozen silver Tiffany business card holders and a credit card?

My stomach clenched as I stared at the black strip along one side, the directions given in words and pictures. Maybe it had been in his pocket since the last time he traveled across the district, when was that? Last week? I turned it over. The only real surprise was that the Starlight Hotel had electronic keys. I let the jacket fall, tossed his litter onto the dresser and tucked the card in the bottom of my underwear drawer.

Turning off the lights, I sat in my tree house room, watching the moonlight stripe the lake and thinking of Edward and Sam, wrapped in the hormonally charged illusions of new love. It was a long time ago, but I could remember the hot shiver of being breathlessly, hopelessly, hotly in love. Nothing to cry about. I forced myself to focus on the children, the grandchildren, told myself that in spite of everything we lived a good life, really, a good life. Tears were silly. Isn't there something about how expecting things to change is the definition of insanity?

In the dark I changed into well worn, powder blue flannel pajamas and climbed in bed. Cooking for the volunteers tomorrow, I reminded myself, and using an old trick, I menu-planned until I finally slept. I woke as Jack slipped into bed, rolled toward me and caressed my hip. Scooting close, he nuzzled my neck. I could smell the scotch on his breath. I pretended sleep until he gave up.

Maybe chicken wings, roasted peppers and a salad. I could make salsa. Listing ingredients for double chocolate brownies, I finally fell back asleep.

❧ ❧ ❧

I woke just before dawn, moving slowly so I wouldn't disturb Jack. Thirty years ago, when we first met, I'd loved watching him in this shadow light, innocent with sleep. He'd filled out from the slim twenty-two year old I'd worshipped. Still a handsome man, tall, broad shouldered, with a full head of blond hair he probably had colored during his monthly hair appointments at Illusions on Main. I'd never asked. It was always easier not to know his secrets.

I rose, and wrapping myself in a soft chenille robe so old it held stains from the blueberry pancakes I used to make the children on late summer mornings, crept silently down the stairs and into the kitchen. Filling the kettle with fresh water, I set it on the stove to heat and ground the Highlands Coffee Company beans (shipped every two weeks from a small, perfect roaster in Seattle). An extravagance, an indulgence, a consolation, the beans released a rich, pagan scent as the electric coffee grinder pulverized and I shook them into my insulated French Press. Now, that was a reason to live.

Finally, I poured myself coffee, stepped through the kitchen door onto the deck and settled into the porch swing, nesting in the cushions, and pulled my robe tightly around me. The lake sparkled an amazing pink, reflecting the mid-sunrise sky. I spent one whole summer trying to capture that scene, painted, drew and photographed it, but the results were universally disappointing. Perhaps some things were never meant to last.

I hadn't thought of that summer in a long time. Seventeen, the year before I met Jack. Hadn't that been the summer I worked as a hostess at Harriman's On the Water? Back when old man Harriman was still alive, before the Pattels bought and refurbished the place. That was the summer I spent developing my portfolio to submit to art schools, a long time ago.

The pink gradually faded from the lake. I relaxed into the pillows and listened to the birds, breathing in the rich coffee scent. I closed my eyes, pushed the swing gently with one foot and started to drift off.

Suddenly something landed in my lap. My eyes flew open as I felt a splash of hot coffee hit my thigh and a wet tongue lick my cheek. "Daphnia. What are you doing here?"

"Sorry," came a deep voice from just beyond my shrubbery. "I let him out and —"

"Good morning, Sam. Coffee?"

"Sure, maybe just a cup. Edward's still sleeping. I don't think I need to get back too quickly."

I stepped around him into the house, laughing. "I doubt you'll need to get back until eight at the earliest. Edward's never been an early riser, one of the few things about which he and Jack agree completely. I forgot, do you take anything in it?"

"Black's great, thanks."

I returned, handed him a cup and tossed a dishtowel onto the swing chair. "Let's walk down to the dock. I'm afraid I spilled coffee all over the cushions up here."

"You mean Daphnia spilled coffee. I'm so sorry. Can I help clean up?"

"It'll be fine. The cushions are waterproof and older than I am." I led him down the steps.

We paused at the landing and Sam pointed to a small cabin, nestled into the slope between the house and the lake. "What's that?"

"That's the grandfathers' original cabin." I smiled. "Do you want to see it?"

"Sure."

I led him along the dirt path, through the dense wild grass carpeting the slope to the house.

I paused at the door to the cabin. "Better duck your head, low doorway." I led him into a large, open space. The sun filtered in through lead-paned windows that faced the lake. Brightly colored throw rugs cluttered the gray slate floor. A worn leather couch, piled with pillows, and an old, red and gold rug lay angled in one corner before the wood stove. Stacks of books surrounded the couch. The only other furniture a paint splattered picnic table covered with stacks of papers, bins of pens, pencils, paint tubes and jars of brushes. An easel, with an unfinished stylized painting of what looked like it might be a landscape, faced the window. Other canvasses, in various stages of incompletion, leaned against the walls and the picnic table. The cabin smelled closed in, windows latched and everything covered in dust.

"I haven't been in here since Jack got back from Washington." I looked around. "I should get in and clean one of these days."

Sam looked around, wide-eyed. "This place is amazing." He picked up one of the canvasses. "Yours?"

I nodded and peered at the canvas in his hand. "I've been experimenting with adding collage lately. I don't think I have it quite yet, but I like the idea."

"These are great." Sam put the one down and picked up another. "Edward said you painted but I didn't think… Hey." He stopped. "You must have done the abstract hanging over the bed. I love that painting."

"Thanks." I beamed. "Pretty much all the artwork in Edward's house that isn't photography or brought back from his travels is mine. He says he loves my work but I think it's cheaper than buying real art. I'm kidding," I added when Sam began to protest.

"Do you show?"

I shrugged. "I had a few local shows years ago, but I haven't in a long time. I'm always afraid it would get billed as sort of a novelty item, you know 'Congressman's Wife' sort of stuff, or it would end up as a fundraiser or something. And I hated the openings I had, all that schmoozing." I shuddered. "So I'm afraid I decorate my friends' and children's houses and let stuff pile up here. But I don't mind, it's the doing of it that I enjoy."

Sam picked up another canvas. "Enjoy? I don't know, Gillian, it's hard to imagine 'enjoying' making this."

I laughed. "That one is dark, isn't it? I supposed scrawling RAPE across anything might make it something of a downer. Don't worry. Those aren't the ones I give my friends. Now let's get out of here and into the sunshine; it's freezing."

Sam reluctantly replaced the painting and followed me onto the path and down to the dock. We settled in deck chairs, facing the lake.

After a moment he said, "It's beautiful. Have you lived here long?"

I nodded. "Most of my life. My parents died when I was a baby and I came to live with my grandfather."

"Oh, I'm sorry, that must have been awful. I mean losing your parents."

I shrugged. "I suppose, I don't remember. My grandfather was a wonderful parent. I think he was always trying to make it up to me. It's been over twenty years and I still miss him, especially on mornings like this." I looked at Sam out of the corner of my eye. "My turn to say sorry, the coffee doesn't always come with self-disclosure, first the studio and then my life story. Jack frequently points out that my social filters don't always work as well as they might."

"Your social filters are fine. I loved seeing your studio." Sam sipped his coffee. "Your coffee's great, too." I laughed and he continued, "No really, I'm glad Daphnia got out of control again this morning. I'm having a wonderful time. And since you're Edward's best friend, I think it's my job to get to know you better, try to win your approval and all that."

I laughed. "You know, of course, I'll kill you if you break his heart."

"Of course." Sam stared at the lake for a while. He turned to me. "So was he really that wild when he was young?"

I looked at him, surprised. "Edward?" When Sam nodded, I laughed. "Edward was crazy. I was so jealous, here I was with a couple of babies and a proper, political husband, and there was Edward, thoroughly enjoying everything out there." I shook my head.

"And then?" Sam asked.

"And then it got very ugly for a while. Turns out drugs and alcohol can be addictive. Who knew?" I asked, eyebrows raised. "But later it got better."

I watched Sam, his gaze fixed on the horizon. Finally he spoke. "He went to jail, didn't he?"

"Guess he has told you everything. Yes, our Edward's the best object lesson I know for having a designated driver." I shuddered. "Those were some pretty awful times." I touched his arm. "But he's okay. Better than ever. Really."

Sam smiled softly at me. "I just don't want... So I shouldn't worry?"

"No. Edward's fine, he's in recovery as they say and he's quite the twelve-stepper now." I leaned back in my chair. "I never think of those days. Same place, but it was a different time and we were different people." I smiled at Sam. "Middle age has its consolations. I believe in redemption, don't you?"

"You mean religiously?" Sam looked at me sharply.

"I mean personally." I pulled my robe tighter. "I mean that we can't always be defined by the mistakes of our youth, even if we're stuck with the consequences."

"I guess you're right," he agreed. "But what about making the same mistake over and over?"

"Hopefully we grow up, eventually. So does that mean Edward isn't your first addict?"

Sam laughed and shook his head. "I've never been involved with someone with drug or alcohol issues. But my last relationship was, well, let's just say he put the fun back into dysfunctional."

"How so?"

He shrugged. "For starters he was married. To a very nice woman. They had three kids who thought of me as something of an uncle."

"Ouch. And how about her, what did she think?" I took a long, slow sip of my coffee, watching the sunlight sparkle on the waves.

He closed his eyes and leaned back. "I still don't know how much she knew, but she was always kind to me. I hated that."

We sat quietly for a few minutes, watching the lake.

"Eagle." Sam pointed to a large bird scooping a fish from the surface of the water. He shook his head. "I can't imagine living in one place all my life, although if I were going to, Lacland might be the place."

"I was away while we were in college."

"We?"

I smiled. "I met Jack on the second day of classes, so college was always a 'we' experience."

"Was it love at first sight?"

"Oh yeah. You've met Jack. He was as charming and even more beautiful then. One minute of that vote-getting smile and I was lost. You know the one. You've certainly seen it on the posters; sort of crooked, radiantly wholesome, with just a suggestion of impropriety around the edges. A naïve, eighteen-year-old virgin, I didn't stand a chance."

"So you went through college together?"

I shook my head. "No. Jack was a senior when we met, taking an art class to fill a general education requirement. He got accepted to law school that fall. By the time he graduated college I was pregnant with Aurora, so I married him and followed. You know, whither thou goest and all that. Oh look, there's the muskrat." I pointed to a furry brown body plowing determinedly through the water near the shore. "She goes back and forth between here and the point. I think she has a nest under Edward's boathouse. So I take it you've lived lots of places?"

Sam shrugged. "Some. I grew up in Rhode Island where both my parents taught high school, he in English, she taught Chemistry. They were great parents, but it did make high school awkward and definitely delayed my coming out. This is the longest I've lived anywhere since then." Daphnia leapt onto his lap, licking his face several times. Sam had to wrestle him away before he could go on. The dog immediately jumped down, ran the length of the dock onto the shoreline and waded into the shallows. Sam smiled, watching him. "I guess part of my inability to stay in one place is just the nature of academics. I did my undergraduate one place, my Master's another, my PhD a third, then a Post Doc somewhere else," he glanced at me, "under, so to speak, Professor Married With Kids."

"Ah."

He nodded. "And finally here for a real job and, if I'm lucky, a real relationship."

"How do you like it now that you're here?"

"It's certainly beautiful. And this has been a great year. I got tenure in the spring and now Edward." He smiled. "Although I think I'd like to be doing more research, between job security and Edward it's hard to think about moving on."

"Aren't you going on sabbatical in a month or so?"

"Yes, Amsterdam for a year, but then we'll be back."

"We?"

Daphnia ran back along the dock and again jumped onto Sam's lap, this time with a dead fish hanging from his mouth. "Daph! Shit – that stinks." Sam pried the fish away and threw it back into the water, holding tight to the dog so he wouldn't follow. Then he dumped Daphnia onto the dock, walked across to kneel and rinse his hands in the lake.

Drying his hands on his jeans, he turned apologetically to me. "Last night I asked Edward to come with me and he agreed."

I looked down into my coffee cup. "I'm glad. Really I am. I'll miss him like crazy, but still, it's a good thing." Suddenly half a dozen brightly colored fast boats rounded the point, heading for the far end of the lake. "Must be a fishing tournament today. That also means it's seven. I should go back up. Jack will want breakfast soon."

"I should get back, too. Maybe my prince is awake."

"Don't hold your breath. Come up to the house and I'll send you home with a couple cinnamon rolls." I shrugged. "They're from yesterday but I bet there isn't much for breakfast where you're going. Don't eat the cereal. When I found bugs in the box one day he said, 'protein.'"

Sam followed, laughing. "Well, he's right."

"Biologists," I shook my head. "I'm used to this from Edward, he's just a photographer and a very amateur naturalist. But you, you're a professional."

"Which is why I'll be grateful for the cinnamon rolls."

Just then Jack opened the screen door, wearing a blue T-shirt and old grey sweatpants, cup of coffee in hand. When he saw us, he smiled broadly and bounded down the steps, holding out his hand. "Sam. Great to see you."

Sam shook his hand, smiling. "Nice to see you, too, Jack." Daphnia ran past us to jump on Jack.

"And who's this?" Jack asked, leaning down to scratch the wet, but happy, Boston terrier between the ears.

"I'm afraid that's my mannerless dog, Daphnia," Sam apologized. "I keep meaning to take him to obedience training. Sorry about the mud."

Jack looked down at the dirty paw prints peppering his thigh. "It's okay," he smiled. "I was about to go for a run and get them all sweaty anyway. Morning, darling." He kissed me lightly on the cheek.

I smiled absently at him. "I'll go get breakfast started. Come, Sam, and I'll get those cinnamon rolls."

Jack put his arm around me and turned again to Sam. "Jill makes the best cinnamon rolls on the planet. You're in for a treat."

I stepped out of his embrace. "Thanks, Jack but I'm afraid these are yesterday's, so they might be stale. Still," I smiled at Sam as I opened the screen door, "they're better than bugs."

Sam laughed and turned back to Jack, who was looking out over the lake. "Beautiful place you have."

"Yes, yes, we're very lucky." Jack nodded. Then he stooped to pet the dog. "Daphnia? But isn't this a male? Or, uh, maybe that doesn't matter to your people."

Sam raised an eyebrow. "A daphnia is a type of zooplankton, a microscopic animal, a water flea if you like. When Daph was a puppy, the way he moved looked to me just like a daphnia."

"Oh." Jack stood and looked out at the water.

The two men were silent. Finally, Sam said, "Okay. I need to be getting back. I'll just grab those rolls from Gillian and be on my way."

"Fine, fine," Jack said, still gazing out at the lake. As Sam started up the steps, he added, "Give my best to Ed, won't you?"

"Sure, thanks." Sam ducked into the kitchen. "Ed?" he whispered to me as he closed the door.

I stood at the counter, a knife in one hand and an orange in the other. "It's not his fault. He's in campaign mode. Here." I pointed toward a large tray covered with a bright red and yellow cloth. On it sat a platter holding two large cinnamon rolls, garnished by one blood orange cut so the wedges opened like a flower. I made four quick cuts to the orange in my hand and laid it open beside the first. While Sam watched, I poured coffee into a thermos and set that on the tray as well. I looked up and smiled. "There you go, breakfast in bed for two."

He thanked me profusely as I ushered him out the front door. He called to Daphnia, who came bounding around the side of the house, racing past Sam and into Edward's drive.

As I returned to the kitchen, I found Jack lacing his running shoes. "That guy gives me the creeps," he muttered. "Naming your dog after bugs—"

"What are you talking about?"

"Oh, never mind. I'll be back in an hour." He banged out through the front door. I saw him glance right, see Sam, and turn left to start jogging backwards along his usual route.

I sighed, poured myself another cup of coffee, refilled the teakettle, turned on the oven and started a pot of stone ground oatmeal so it would be ready when Jack returned. I put two thick slices of homemade, seven-seed bread into the toaster, took a sleek, dark purple eggplant from the refrigerator, poked it with a fork several times and placed it in the oven on the center rack. Finally, I sat to read the paper.

Outside the sun hit the roses along the front wall. From the window facing the side yard, I could see the corner of my vegetable garden. Jack hated the tall chain-link fence. He would have preferred a quaint, British kitchen garden, even if the deer took everything.

"What do you care?" he'd asked me. "We can afford to buy vegetables. It's not like we'd starve without your farming efforts. We don't need a half-acre eyesore blighting the yard."

But I loved my garden (which actually covered almost an acre). I loved the feel and smell of the dirt in the spring and the buzz of bees on hot summer afternoons. It made me feel proud and full and self-sufficient to bring baskets of food into the kitchen. I relished the order and seasonality the garden brought to our meals. Spring spinach and pea salads, with raspberries or strawberries and cream for dessert, gave way gradually to chard and beans and tiny, early summer squash, roasted or sautéed or raw. Then the garden exploded with ripe tomatoes, melons, blueberries, fresh corn, carrots, beets and sweet onions, and finally settled back again to salad greens, as the frosts came and it was time to dig the potatoes. In deepest January, the planning began again, as I dreamed over seed catalogues and my sketchpad.

My hands itched to get into the soil. The garden needed some attention, only a few hours really. Between mulched walkways and raised beds, the garden was almost self-sufficient, but there was still purslane to weed out and my beans needed picking. Maybe if I included a bean salad on the menu I'd be forced into the garden, otherwise it could be days before I got to it.

When Jack returned I held out the paper. "You're in the news," I told him, as he stepped through the door.

"I am?" He brightened.

"Something about your work on the Energy and Commerce Subcommittee on Health and some group called American Health Conglomerate, AHC? I didn't read it closely, what's it about?"

His face darkened, then went blank. "Nothing, just some reporter trying to make a mountain out of a molehill, as usual. Don't worry about it." He stalked off to shower.

I dished out his oatmeal, placed the paper beside his plate, and left to run my errands.

Two

By nine-thirty I was trotting up the walk to my mother-in-law's ground floor apartment, carrying a large canvas bag full of groceries, a small bag from the pharmacy and an eggplant parmesan casserole. I cooked for her before she broke her hip but now, during her recovery, I tried to keep her kitchen well stocked. My hands full, I hit the doorbell with my elbow yelling, "It's just me."

A beautiful young woman with deep chocolate skin and close-cropped hair opened the door. "Good morning Gillian," she said in a melodious accent. "Come in, the mother is in the kitchen finishing breakfast."

I smiled back. "Sabah Il Kheer, Aziza"

Aziza's smile widened. "Sabah Il Noor, Gillian. Your Arabic is beautiful today."

I laughed. "Shukran. See, I can say good morning and thank you, but now I've exhausted my vocabulary."

"No, I have heard you say goodbye and good evening as well. You are practically a native speaker, although I am afraid I have given you a Somali accent, so they might not understand you in Cairo."

"That's all right, I wasn't planning to go there anyway. I think your accent is beautiful in English, so it must be lovely in Arabic as well."

"Shukran," Aziza thanked me. Taking my bags, she led me into the bright yellow kitchen where Pearl sat in a wheelchair, basking in the sun streaming in from a south-facing bay window lined with plants. Aziza began to put the groceries away.

"Good morning, dear." Momma Pearl smiled at me as I kissed her cheek. She smelled of baby powder and the light rose perfume Jack always bought for her birthday.

"Morning. What a beautiful day." I set down the casserole dish. "I brought eggplant parmesan. I thought the two of you could eat some tonight for dinner and freeze the rest. There's also a fresh loaf of bread in the bag, some nice tomatoes and a small watermelon from those organic farmers who sell out of the back of a pickup on the highway every Monday. I don't know how they get such early tomatoes. Mine are still at least two weeks off."

"Thank you, how lovely. The best thing Jack ever did for me was to marry you. Have some coffee." Pearl patted my arm.

"Okay, a quick cup. Maggie's coming to help me cook for tonight and I still need to shop. I'll get it." I held up a hand to stop Aziza and filled a cup from the automatic coffeemaker on the counter. Sitting across from my mother-in-law, I asked, "How are you this morning?"

Pearl shrugged. "The same, a bit better, it's hard to tell. That nice young physical therapist says I'm progressing, but I can't really feel it."

Aziza snorted. "You don't always think she is such a nice person when she is here and you're groaning from the pain."

"It isn't her fault it hurts." Pearl smiled ruefully. "But you're right, it's hard to like her right at that moment. It must be a hard job."

"Paid torturer?" I asked. "Probably. How's your book supply? Can you make it through until Wednesday? I'm going with Edward to visit his mom tomorrow. I'll try to stop by and check in when we get back, but the library will be closed by then."

"Oh, I'm fine, thank you. Why is Edward going up to visit Evelyn? I thought he didn't like her much."

I shrugged. "He doesn't, but what can he do? She's his mother." I regretted my words immediately.

Pearl looked out the window. "I suppose." After a moment she continued, "Jack's very busy with his campaign isn't he?"

Just because he hasn't visited you in months? I thought, but said, "Well, you know how it is this time of year." I looked at my watch. "Speaking of which, I've gotta run. Twenty hungry volunteers are showing up tonight and I haven't even started dinner. Just think, in a few months we'll officially be in an off-year and everyone can relax." Standing, I gave her a quick kiss on the cheek. "You want me to save you some brownies?"

"Oh yes please," "Yes!" Pearl and Aziza said in unison.

I laughed. "Ok, I'll bring them by tomorrow after we get back. Bye, Momma Pearl, Ma'a Salaama, Aziza." And with a wave, I left to their "Bye, dear" and "Ma'a Salaama, Habeebiti."

≈ ≈ ≈

Maggie pulled up as I was carting the last load of groceries into the house. As she emerged from the car, long-limbed and beautiful, dark curls cascading around her face, I thought (and not for the first time) this woman is too beautiful to be a scientist and if this were high school we wouldn't even be friends. But grownup life is different, I guess.

I greeted Maggie with, "Hi. There's a sack of potatoes in the back seat. Can you grab it?"

"Sure, no problem. Where's the Congressman?"

"Campaigning or something. You want food first or later?" I knocked open the front door with my hip.

"Both." Maggie followed me inside.

I laughed. "Of course. How can you eat so much and stay so damn thin?"

Maggie shrugged. "Good genes I guess. Or maybe because I'm stuck with my own cooking most of the time."

I set the groceries on the counter, started the teakettle and glanced at the clock. "All right, it's eleven. I'll put these away while you eat, then I'll start lunch and you can peel potatoes. Don't worry, I'm betting Edward and Sam show up to help any minute now. Actually, I don't expect them until noon, but by then you'll have barely started the potatoes."

"You're going to have so many volunteers tonight you need the whole crew?"

"I didn't say I asked them to come over, I just said I expect them. They've been surviving on whatever's growing in Edward's kitchen, possibly supplemented by diner food, for three days. I think Edward wants to keep Sam around, so I expect they'll drop by for lunch." I shrugged. "I'll make enough for four and if they don't show up I'll wrap up the leftovers and drop them off." I took a cake from the refrigerator, cut a generous slice, added a dollop of whipped cream and handed it to her.

Maggie nodded her thanks. "Don't you ever get tired of cooking for everyone?"

I paused, considering. "I get tired of cooking for strangers sometimes, although if the other choice is speeches," I shuddered, "I'll cook all day. But I never get tired of cooking for you or Momma Pearl or Edward, that's a joy."

"And Jack? This is good, by the way." As she spoke I could tell she was watching me carefully, though she was pretending to focus on the cake.

"Thanks." I shrugged. "Jack doesn't care about food. He only cares about how the volunteers, or whoever, like the food. On his own he'll eat anything. I think he lives on fast food, bagged carrots, breakfast meetings and fundraiser dinners when Congress is in session."

"Is it just me, or was that frostier than usual?"

"The cake?" I looked at her, puzzled.

"No, the discussion of your husband."

"Oh." I finished putting away my packages, stored the canvas grocery bags and reopened the refrigerator. I knelt and peered into the produce bin. "Since I'm making chicken tonight, do you mind a vegetarian lunch? I picked too much lettuce last night. It isn't incredibly fresh but should still taste good. Maybe sautéed vegetables in a warm vinaigrette on salad greens?"

"That all sounds great, of course. And you're right. It isn't any of my business, go on with your denial or whatever you're doing. I like a good resentment, myself, warms the cockles and all that—"

I straightened up. "Sorry, I thought I'd wait until after lunch to spoil it. I found a local hotel key in Jack's suit pocket yesterday."

"Damn. I knew it. The bastard. I'm so sorry." Maggie sprang up and wrapped her arms around me.

I relaxed into her for a moment then pulled away, wiping my eyes. I reached for a tissue. "I'm fine. You know it isn't the first, or last. I just hate these finding out times."

"God, he's a shithead."

"Yes he is. Unfortunately he's also the father of my children, a pillar of this community and I've been married to him my entire adult life. Not to mention, if I left him it would tear Momma Pearl apart."

"That doesn't make it okay."

"No, but it does make it complicated." I waved her back to the table. "Now finish your cake or I'll set you to the potatoes."

Half an hour later a gentle knock sounded at the back door and Edward's head appeared. "Hi. We thought we'd drop by and see if you need help with food for tonight."

I waved him in and turned to look at Maggie. "Told you so." She smiled and shook her head.

Edward strolled in. "What?" he asked. "What did I do now? Just being neighborly."

Sam followed sheepishly. Daphnia bounded from behind them, jumping on me and dancing on his hind legs.

I put down my spatula and bent to greet the dog. "Hello, Daphnia, how nice of you to come see me." I scratched his ears. He licked my hand and ran to greet Maggie. I embraced Edward, standing on tiptoe to kiss his slightly stubbly cheek, then turned to hug Sam. "Come, come, you're welcome. Would you like to have some lunch first? I made plenty."

At this Maggie, busy having her face licked by Daphnia, burst out laughing. She stood, hugged the two men and handed them each a potato and a peeler.

Sam looked at the peeler. "Um, you were expecting us?"

"Unless he's been out of town, Edward hasn't gone more than three days without eating a meal here in twenty years. He knows that dinner tonight is the volunteers and that showing up for that requires both envelope stuffing and pleasantries so, yes, I was expecting you." I returned to my stir-fry.

"You eat here all the time?" Sam asked.

"Gillian exaggerates, I'm sure." Edward immediately started peeling his potato, ignoring Maggie's skeptical look.

Maggie picked up her own potato. "I'm here for lunch a lot, but Edward, I think he's here most days."

"She's a good cook," Edward shrugged, "and I like the company."

"So do I." I smiled. "Lunch is almost ready so if you want to pause the peeling and wash up, that would be great."

Maggie and Edward flew into motion, organized the peeled and unpeeled potatoes into separate piles on a side table so the work could continue after lunch, wiped the table, gathered placemats, napkins, silverware and poured beverages while Sam looked on helplessly, holding Daphnia so he wouldn't get in the way.

I smiled at him. "Don't worry, you'll get the hang of it. As we said, they're here a lot."

Once we were all settled at the table, and he had convinced Daphnia to stay curled by his feet, Sam asked Edward, "Isn't it sort of mooching?"

Edward looked startled. "Am I mooching?"

I considered. "I suppose it might look that way, but I don't see how you could." I turned to Sam. "Edward's like family. We grew up together. I've known him since forever. Why wouldn't I feed him?"

Sam shrugged. "I don't know. Maybe because he's a big guy—"

"You forgot 'handsome,'" Edward interjected. "I'm a big handsome guy."

Sam gave him a long, appraising look. "Oh, don't worry, I didn't forget."

Edward blushed. Maggie and I grinned.

Sam continued, "Because he's a big handsome guy and it's expensive? I mean, doesn't it bother your husband? He doesn't seem quite as close to 'Ed.'"

I smiled softly. "Oh, I see what you mean. But what you don't know is that it's all the same money. Edward and I, and to a certain extent Jack and his mother and the children when they lived here, all live off the same pot of money. Yeah, I know it sounds odd," I continued when Sam looked perplexed. "Edward and my grandfathers were business partners and best friends."

"And probably lovers," Edward added, forking a huge bite of salad into his mouth.

"We don't know that," I cautioned, "but it certainly is a possibility; they were very close. Anyway, they owned a tool and dye company in the city, you may have heard of it, Rosenberg and Wolf? They made a lot of money and bought this land in the 1920s as a getaway."

"And built the houses together. I say that's evidence," Edward winked at Sam.

"Eventually, they sold the business and retired here," I nodded to Edward, "together. The family story is that they couldn't agree on how to apportion the profits."

Edward snorted.

I continued, "So they left it all in one big pot, a for-profit Foundation. Edward and I are the sole heirs and board members."

"I didn't know that," Maggie said, her plate almost untouched.

Edward shrugged. "We don't talk about it much. It's sort of an odd arrangement."

"And Jack has asked us not to," I added, taking a hunk of bread from the basket and passing it to Sam.

"What about your mother, Edward?" Sam took bread and passed the basket along.

Edward shrugged again. "She doesn't like it either, but Grandpa Rosenberg was my father's father. I guess that's obvious since I'm a Rosenberg. She's okay, though. Dad was a pretty successful architect and left Mom in good shape."

"He designed this place," I made a wide sweeping gesture meant to encompass the house.

Sam looked around. "It's beautiful."

"Thanks," Edward and I said together. I continued, "The last thing he designed was this kitchen, we redid it about five years ago. He died before we started construction, so I think of it as a kind of memorial."

"So if he's the Rosenberg, are you the Wolf?" Sam pointed his fork at me.

"My maiden name. It's pretty, isn't it? I had a hard time giving it up for Sach."

"And Jack," Maggie reached for the bread basket, "how does he feel about this whole thing? I always assumed he was paying the bills around here."

"That's what he wants you to think. Jack hates the Foundation." I smiled softly. "He says it makes me more married to Edward than to him. But the truth is without it he'd never have been able to afford running for Congress. I do make him buy all my Congressman's Wife clothes, the suits and shoes and things."

"Although the Foundation more than makes up for that in campaign contributions," Edward added.

I toyed with a lettuce leaf. "He's built up a great reputation by pleasing the voters." I paused and finished softly, "Especially the young pretty ones."

Edward looked at me for a long moment. He turned to Maggie. "What is it this time?"

"Hotel key," Maggie said simply.

"Can we kill him?" Edward asked.

"Not until she tells us we can." Maggie returned to her lunch.

I stared at my plate silently, swirling food around with my fork.

"What?" Sam started, but a look from Edward stopped him.

We sat silently for a moment until Sam spoke up. "This is good, Gillian, what's in the sauce?"

Maggie and Edward exchanged grateful glances as I looked up and answered.

After lunch my friends cleared the table and got back to work. Maggie and Sam sat at the table, companionably peeling, husking, chopping, dicing and slicing whatever Edward, in charge of washing, set in front of them. As soon as they had completed one task, I whisked away the products and Edward brought them another basket of washed but unprocessed food. A bin at the end of the table gradually filled with compostable waste, while Daphnia nosed around everyone's feet in search of droppings.

Maggie and Sam teach in the same department. At first they chatted about University politics but, after about an hour, Edward called from the sink, "Enough shop talk. I don't even know most of those guys and already I hate them."

Sam laughed. "I don't know why people say academics are boring."

"Because we are," Maggie scraped potato peels into the compost bin.

"Hear, hear." Edward brought a bin of fresh picked green beans to the table and sat down to clip the ends. Both Maggie and Sam made exaggerated hurt faces. He held up his hands. "Not individually, never individually, but when you get together?" He rolled his eyes. "Sheesh."

"Okay," Maggie said, "what should we talk about?"

I scooped the peppers she'd been slicing into a bowl and started back toward the stove. "Not politics," I said firmly.

"Fair enough." Maggie eyed Edward and Sam. "So, tell us a love story. How did you meet? First date, all that." She held up her hand to pause them. "Just enough details, I'm only asking to be polite."

Edward turned and smiled at Sam. "I'm not sure Sam thinks it's a love story, he's looking sort of tragic right now."

"Onions." Sam sniffed but smiled. "Other than the stinging eyes, I'm blissful."

"Soooo—" Maggie prompted.

Edward settled into his chair, the bowl of beans between his legs. He snipped off the ends and tossed clipped beans into a bowl on the table. "I don't know if you know this, but Sam wrote a book."

"That's great." "What's it about?" Maggie and I spoke at the same time.

"Bayblies," Sam replied.

"What?" I asked.

"I think he said mayflies." Maggie frowned. "Is it related to your presentation last spring?"

Sam nodded, wiping tears away with one sleeve. "Less the behavior story I told in the seminar, the book focuses on my primary research area, mayfly genetics."

"Wash your hands," I suggested. "That should help."

Maggie continued, "In the seminar he presented some weird bug stuff, get him to talk about it sometime. For instance, there are these parasites that infect male mayflies and those mayflies try to get gang banged by swarms of other mayflies, am I getting this right, Sam?"

"Uhm, sort of, what the parasites actually do is to engender female behavior in males so they eventually deposit parasite eggs in the same streams where female mayflies are ovipositing, but I suppose—"

"So anyway," Edward said, loudly, "as I was saying, Sam finished a book and his publisher needed photographs for the cover art. We agreed to a series of field trips last spring to try to photograph mayfly emergence. You've seen the swarms? They're beautiful. I was amazed."

I nodded. "Grandpa Wolf used to point them out to me. They only live for a day, right?"

"Actually, some of them live for years but they only emerge as adults for a very short time. That's where they get their name, 'Ephemeroptera,', from ephemeral," Sam said.

"So you bonded over bugs." Maggie shuddered and reached for yet another pepper.

"But mayflies are sexy," Edward protested. "They emerge for one day, they don't eat or sleep, just mate, lay eggs and die. It's quite romantic."

"In a weird, one night stand kind of way," Maggie sliced cleanly through the pepper and began scooping out the seeds. "So that was it, you made love amid the mayflies and here you are?"

"No," Edward said with exaggerated patience, "we photographed the mayflies. Making love came much later. Not until our first real date."

I scooped up Sam's sliced onions. "I'm afraid he's the kiss and tell type."

"I know," he said. "But that first date was pretty romantic. He invited me to dinner. When I got there the only lights in the house were maybe a hundred candles. He'd laid out all these little dishes of the most exquisite food, forming a path upstairs to the bedroom and—" he stopped and looked at me. "That was from you, wasn't it?" When I nodded he turned to Edward. "You used Gillian's food to seduce me."

Edward patted Sam's thigh. "Gillian's food is sexy. I doubt anything I cooked would have worked. Although," he looked at Sam from under his lashes, "you weren't exactly playing hard to get."

Sam nodded slightly. "It would have been pretty silly at that point." He turned to Maggie and me. "Edward is nothing if not direct. When he asked me to dinner, he suggested I bring my toothbrush and test results."

"So you've been seeing each other all summer?" Maggie thought for a minute. "I think you'll enjoy Amsterdam, Edward. I spent a vacation there a few years ago. It's absolutely beautiful."

"How did you know I was going with him?" Edward threw a worried glance in my direction.

"Because you'd be stupid not to." She pushed aside the slices and reached for another pepper.

"Don't worry, Edward. Sam already told me you're going and I think it's great." I kept my back to them, busy at the stove. "You'll do some great work. It'll be fun." Then I turned and smiled. "I'll be fine. Really."

"What was the name of that sculptor who visited campus last year, Luke something or other?" Maggie asked Sam.

Sam thought for a moment. "Luke Vanderwerken."

"That's it." Maggie said. "Wasn't he from Amsterdam? You should look him up."

I looked from Maggie to Sam. "Luke Vanderwerken was here? And you didn't tell me?"

Maggie shrugged. "I think you were in Washington at the time, it was maybe February. He gave a talk."

I could feel myself flush. "I love his work. It's so sexy."

Sam laughed. "If you say so. I did think his slides were interesting." He turned to Edward. "Some of the things he said made me think he might be in recovery. I'll see if I can get his contact information from Jenny Combs in the Art Department."

Edward leaned back in his chair, "Great."

I wondered if I'd ever have the nerve to cold call a famous sculptor like Vanderwerken. Edward might, though. Not a shrinking violet, my Edward.

Later, as the three sous chefs finished assembling a giant green salad and I put the last batch of brownies in the oven, we heard a car pull into the drive.

Maggie glanced out the window. "Jack."

"Shit," said Edward. "What do you want us to do?"

"Do?" I looked at him, puzzled. "Oh, you mean about the key? Nothing. I'm not ready to talk about it with him, so pretend you don't know."

"Oh, that'll be easy," Edward muttered.

"Don't worry," I reassured him. "You're always unpleasant with him. He won't know the difference."

"Thanks. Good to know." Edward turned back to the salad bowl as the kitchen door flew open.

Jack entered carrying a stack of papers. He looked startled to see the cluster in the kitchen, but quickly recovered with a big smile. "Ah, the cooking crew." He reached forward to shake hands, but Maggie, Edward and Sam all held up their wet hands and motioned, in various ways, to the salad.

"Right, sorry." He settled for a short wave. "I'll just leave you to it, then." And with a quick kiss on my cheek, he breezed out the kitchen, heading for a distant part of the house.

"So," drawled Maggie, "I think that went well."

"You want us to stay?" Edward asked me.

"God, no. Then he'd really know something's up. Finish the salad and you're free." I paused and smiled slowly. "Actually, let's split the first batch of brownies before you go. I can make another. We'll talk about pleasant things and you can help me drown my sorrows in chocolate. Coffee?"

As she was leaving, Maggie hugged me. "Call if you need me."

"I'll be fine." She smelled of shampoo and comfort.

Edward joined the hug. "Come over anytime. You know where the keys are and you're always welcome."

I squeezed them both. "Thanks."

Three

As I stepped out of the shower, I heard people arriving downstairs. Still a couple hours before dinner so I needn't hurry. Mark and Jack could entertain. I'd always hated these work parties. They weren't as bad as fundraisers, but still… In the beginning I'd swallowed hard, rolled up my sleeves and stuffed envelopes until my shoulders ached. But small talk had always exhausted me. My smile would get stuck. My mind thick, I said inane things. Everyone around me seemed so talkative, some happy, some cynical, but everyone so social.

I'd tried to explain it to Jack, but there was no way he could understand. This was the stuff that made life sing for him. Surrounded by people, he glowed. In the limelight he charmed, witty, handsome and articulate, while I stood by, dull witted, the shy, uncomfortable helpmate. So I'd escaped to the kitchen and stayed there, as campaign season after season marched on, emerging every two years like one of Sam's damn mayflies. Ephermeroptera, ephemeral, except campaigns took more than a day, much more. They started in January with fundraisers and meetings. Then the spring primary, Jack almost always ran unopposed, but there was still the Party to help. Summer brought parades, door-to-door canvassing, meetings and more meetings at the house until midnight. All followed by the Big Push to November. How many campaigns? Ten?

The children had been so small that first time, just five and nine. This life had formed them in such different ways. John, passionately leftist, eschewed Party politics for radical causes, but old ones, nothing noisy and chaotically present. More like me than like Jack. I could imagine losing myself in a dissertation about turn of the century socialists. Still, every two years, John emerged from the library to help his father's campaign. Aurora wouldn't even vote.

I dropped my towel and surveyed myself, naked, in the full-length mirror. I'd been a little thing when I married Jack, except for the bulge that would in a few months become Aurora, short, underweight, pretty in a brunette kind of way. Still short, but after two children and half a lifetime spent in the kitchen, I looked stronger although softer, more Rubens than Maxfield Parrish. I wrapped myself in a robe and went in search of clothes.

An hour later, as I was pulling a pan of chicken from the warming oven, Katy Swanson entered the kitchen. Regal Katy, tall and thin, always a touch overdressed, made everyone else look dowdy. I straightened.

"Hi, Katy."

"Oh, Gillian, doesn't that look and smell delicious?" she gushed. "You're such a wonder, how do you do it?"

"Katy, I'm tired today and I don't have it in me for this. Let's cut the crap and be real."

She recoiled in surprise. I was pretty surprised myself.

She said, "What do you mean? What happened? Did I offend you somehow?"

"Well, you slept with my husband, that's bothersome." I figured, what the hell, I'm in it now.

Katy stopped, opened her mouth, closed it. "How did you...?" Then she shook her head. "But that was years ago. I'm sorry you found out. We certainly never meant to hurt you, but why now?"

I considered her for a long moment. "I thought so. But you're not fucking him now?"

"No. I'm not f-fu… I'm not with him now. We're just friends. That was ages ago," she sputtered.

"Okay then." I handed her the tray of chicken wings. "Be careful, this is hot. Just set it on the trivets on the buffet. Oh, and you might mention to Mark that he should keep an eye on Jack. He's fucking someone, probably on the campaign, and if it slipped to the papers—"

Katy stared at me. "You wouldn't—"

"No," I shook my head tiredly, "I wouldn't. Not because of Jack, because of my children. But, if he's sloppy enough to let me know, someone else is bound to find out. Now go, before that gets cold."

Katy spun out through the kitchen door. I leaned against the counter. She won't be coming back. Good.

A few minutes later Mark poked his head in. "Um, Gillian, Katy said you wanted to see me?"

"Chicken," I said.

"It might have been about the chicken, that's what she was carrying," Mark replied.

"No, I meant she's a chicken," I said in exasperation. "Come in, come in. Don't just stand in the doorway."

Mark entered quickly, letting the door swing shut. He blushed and fidgeted. "So, what can I do for you, Gillian?"

I sighed. "Come sit down." I softened. "I'm sorry I snapped at you. It's not your fault. Please, let's sit and talk."

Mark smiled and sat.

"Jack's having another affair," I told him flatly.

"How do you—?"

"I know, trust me, I know." I produced the hotel key and laid it on the table between us. "I found this in his suit jacket. Unless you're somehow entertaining campaign donors at the Starlight Inn? Or should I say Sta-ligh- Inn, I think the sign has been missing an 'r' and a 't' for years."

Mark paled. "Shit."

"I should let him get what he deserves," I said.

Mark jerked.

"Don't worry, I won't. It would hurt the kids and Momma Pearl and I'd hate all the commotion. So I'm not going to 'out' him. But I'm tired of finding these sorts of things. I'm tired of ignoring them and I'm tired of pretending that everything's okay. I don't know what I'm going to do about it, but what you need to do is make sure I don't wake up some morning to find this all over the morning papers. Can you do that?"

Mark nodded. "I'll try. It's the sort of thing I'm good at. That's why Jack hired me. I'm excellent on defense."

I patted his hand. "I know, thanks."

Mark quickly covered my hand with his. "I'm so sorry, Gillian. Jack's an idiot."

"Thank you, Mark." I gently retrieved my hand and gave him a pat on the arm. "You're very kind."

Just then a slim young woman with long, dark hair entered. "Oh." She looked surprised.

"I'll get right on that," Mark said too loudly and stood to go.

I sighed and turned to the girl. "Hello, can I help you?" and stopped. I stared at her.

She blushed.

"Come on in," I said finally. "Mark was just leaving."

Mark nodded and slipped out the door. The girl smiled broadly. "Is there any more of that wonderful salsa? We're out."

I nodded and continued to stare. She stood, moving a little nervously from one stiletto-heeled foot to the other. She seemed tall, probably the heels. Not beautiful, but pretty, interesting in her skimpy tank top, short black skirt and striped tights, sort of artsy. The lost wax silver rose suspended by a simple chain looked lovely against her pale chest.

I finally extended my hand. "I'm Gillian, Jack's wife. I don't think we've been introduced."

"Oh." She blushed slightly then smiled brightly. "I'm Ashley Groves. I'm an intern on the campaign."

"Nice to meet you, Ashley." I opened the refrigerator, brought out a large bowl of salsa and held it out to her. "High school or college intern?"

"Oh, college. I'm a sophomore at the U." She took the salsa, still smiling.

"Thank God for small favors," I muttered.

"What was that?" Ashley looked puzzled.

"Nothing." I paused. "What a beautiful necklace. I have one very like it, a birthday present from Jack. I think it's a Montana artist. Jack picked it up on vacation earlier in the summer. It looks lovely on you."

Ashley stared at me.

I went on, "Do you think you could do me a favor, Ashley?" She nodded, her mouth slightly open and eyes wide. "Could you please tell my husband that I'm going for a swim? Tell him not to wait up. Oh, and there are brownies in that cupboard whenever people are ready for them. Maybe you could be in charge of that?"

Ashley nodded again.

"I'm sure Katy Swanson would be delighted to help." Without waiting for a response, I turned, strode out onto the deck and bounded down the steps to the dock.

I stepped into the boathouse. Quickly, I stripped off my clothes and hung them on a hook amidst the life jackets. The August night felt warm and still. I walked to the slip and looked into the deep black water. Taking a breath, I raised my hands in prayer above my head and swiftly dove. Cool and soft, the water enveloped me. I emerged outside the boathouse.

The setting sun streaked the overcast sky and lake. "Gashed gold vermillion," the Hopkins line Grandpa Rosenberg used to quote, this was it, the sky, the water a gold-vermillion gash. I started a strong, nearly silent, crawl. I swam along the shore, away from everyone, even from Edward's dock, heading in the opposite direction, far enough from shore that no one would notice me glide by. The mosquito hour. I doubted anyone would be out, not with the air still and the lake so calm.

My shoulders felt good, my legs strong. The water cradled me. I opened my eyes and let the warm tears wash away. The rhythm of stroke, stroke, breath, stroke, stroke, breath, took over and I stopped thinking, stopped visualizing Jack's hand on that poor girl's thigh, Jack's mouth pressed against her slim neck, Jack's body pressing down on her, covering her, swallowing her whole. Stroke, stroke, breath, stroke, stroke, breath.

After a while, my arms began to ache. Finding myself near one of the few remaining undeveloped lots, I swam toward shore and rested in the shallows. Finally, chilled, I started back, swimming more slowly, a gentle breaststroke I knew I could keep up all night. As I passed my own dock, I looked up at the house. The windows blazed and people crowded around the dining room table. No one would miss me.

Edward's dock sat empty. Soft light came from his second story bedroom, but the rest of the house and the boathouse were dark. I climbed the swim ladder and stepped onto his dock. I hoped the darkness covered me as I padded toward the stairs leading to the guestrooms on the second floor of his boathouse. At the top of the steps, I felt along the mantle of the door until I found the key and let myself in.

"Hello," I called softly but no one answered. A shower first to warm up, then I'd find the spare set of sweats Edward always kept in a drawer in case someone got cold swimming. Then I'd crawl in bed. Maybe things would look better in the morning.

❦ ❦ ❦

I woke with the disorienting feeling I was back in my childhood. I lay on the bed, watching sunrise through the east window. As kids, Edward and I had shared this room whenever his family visited. Why hadn't anyone worried about us sleeping together? Two unrelated, opposite sex children of the same age sharing a bed, would anyone allow that now? Of course, we'd never felt unrelated. And those few times when we satisfied our curiosity by looking and touching seemed so innocent now.

I rose slowly, muscles stiff from my long swim. One glance in the bathroom mirror confirmed my reddened, puffy eyes and wild, tangled hair. I found an ancient ponytail holder in the bathroom cabinet and pulled my hair back, straightened the bedspread and left, stepping carefully up the dirt path from the lake. Wiping my bare feet on the elegant wooden doormat, I passed through the screened porch.

Sam, engrossed in the paper, started when he saw me. Daphnia jumped from his lap and sprinted forward, dancing on his hind legs as I opened the door.

"Good morning." Sam rose to kiss my cheek.

"Morning, am I interrupting?"

"No, no, come in. Daphnia and I were just trying to think of an excuse to come over for coffee." He gestured toward the cupboards. "I'm afraid we can't offer you anything. I keep meaning to bring over a grinder, coffee, something, but it seems too…I don't know."

"Too early? Too presumptuous?" I prompted.

Sam nodded. "Something like that."

"I think you'd be fine. But don't worry. I know where you can get some coffee." I sank slowly into a chair opposite Sam. Daphnia immediately leapt onto my lap. I scratched behind his ears. "Only… I doubt Jack is up yet, but just in case, do you think you could get it? I don't want to face him right now."

Sam looked at me. "Are those your clothes? They look a little big. Or is that too personal a question?"

I looked down at my outfit. The rolled cuffs of the sweatshirt formed thick bracelets around my wrists and the crotch of the pants brushed my knees. "Oh, these are Edward's. I slept in the boathouse last night. It's a long story. I'll tell you over breakfast, but do you think you could—"

"Of course, we'd be delighted, right, Daph?" Sam stood and Daphnia jumped down. "See," Sam gestured to the dog, who stood before him, muscles tensed and head cocked expectantly, "we are at your service."

I laughed. "I'll make you a list. There are canvas bags in the second drawer, to the left of the stove. If you forage, I'll cook."

"Now, that's a deal."

I walked Sam out and sat on the porch stoop, watching him stride the old path between the two houses. I glanced up at my bedroom, no lights and the curtains still drawn. I shuddered slightly and looked out over the lake. How many times had I sat as a child, looking at the same scene? Funny how it remained unaltered, though the town had changed so much. Sam appeared carrying two full bags. He walked back with Daphnia nipping at his feet.

I opened the door for him. "Thanks."

"No problem," he answered. "I think I found everything. The kitchen's a mess by the way. I thought those folks were volunteers, don't volunteers help out?"

"I think they're used to leaving the kitchen to me. Did the food get put away?"

"I didn't see anything out that could spoil if that's what you mean." Sam looked disgusted. "I'll just leave these things here and go clean up."

"Don't. Let's wait until Jack leaves for the office, then we can all go. I'd rather not be there alone and I need to change clothes. Today's our Dragon Lady day."

"That'll be fun." Sam set the bags down and started filling the tea kettle. "Sorry I can't join you. She sounds like such a sweet person."

"Don't worry. I'm sure you'll get your chance."

"Can't wait. Edward told me he'd rather help me pack, even though it is supposed to be blistering hot this afternoon. There's a measure of joy for you."

"You're packing for Amsterdam?" I pulled the grinder, press and beans from a bag.

Sam emptied the contents of the other bag onto the kitchen counter: eggs, bread, cheese, tomatoes, peppers, and onions. "I'm packing everything. Some will go with us to Amsterdam, some into storage for the year. I'm giving up the apartment. No use paying rent when I don't have to and when we get back, well, who knows?"

"Good plan. Couldn't you save money and store everything here? Or would that be too…?"

Sam nodded. "Don't tempt fate."

The kettle whistled and I poured water over the grounds. I opened the cupboard and pulled out two cups. After a few minutes, I pushed the plunger on the coffee and poured. I handing Sam a cup. "Let's take our coffee out onto the porch. It might be a while before the Laird is ready for breakfast."

Sam and Daphnia followed me out. "So I guess you know your way around this house pretty well after all these years."

I stopped and looked at him in surprise. "I grew up here. Didn't Edward tell you?" When Sam shook his head, I continued, "No, I suppose he didn't." I sat in one of the wicker porch chairs, curling my legs underneath me, and blew on the coffee before taking a sip. I relaxed back into the chair. Sam sipped his own coffee, waiting.

"The grandfathers bought these lots in the 1920s. At that point, the only structures were the cabin I showed you yesterday and the little boathouse. They used it as a fishing getaway for years. Then came the Depression. Grandpa Rosenberg had a sort of sixth sense about business. He thought the market was getting too high, so in early 1929 he emptied their stock portfolios and paid off all the company debt. When everything came tumbling down and their competitors were closing up, the grandfathers' company was the only one left standing. They were doing pretty well through the 1920s but it was the 1930s that made them rich."

"Wow," said Sam.

"Right." I continued, "There are two competing family stories about this house. One is that the grandfathers felt badly for all the local men out of work and decided building a year-round house was the charitable thing to do. The other is that labor got so cheap by 1934 that they couldn't resist the bargain. Probably the truth lives somewhere in between. Either way, they had this house built. The Art Deco details are original. When they retired, this is where they lived. So when I came, this is where I lived, too. Except in summers, when I sometimes stayed in the cabin."

Sam stroked Daphnia, who slept in his lap. "Do you think they were lovers?"

I shrugged. "Probably. I don't know if they were physical lovers. I'm not sure I would have known, it was a different time. But what I do know is that they were family." I tapped my chest. "Deep family. You know, they died within a few months of each other. From the beginning of their relationship I don't think they ever considered life apart."

"That's an amazing love story." Sam gazed out at the lake. "Not very many people get that, gay or straight."

"They were amazing men. Edward and I were lucky children, although I was the luckiest because I got them all the time."

"I suppose he was jealous," Sam said thoughtfully.

"Dreadfully," I agreed. "But, of course, I was jealous of him, too, since the grandfathers made such a fuss whenever he arrived. It was only later that I realized they were trying to make up for Evelyn."

"I don't have a jealous bone in my body and never have." A voice boomed from the kitchen and Edward emerged holding a steaming cup of coffee. "What are you doing here this early, and in my clothes, why was there a light on in the boathouse last night, are you finally going to leave him, and what kind of lies is she telling you?" He leaned down to kiss Sam. "Thanks for the coffee." He toasted me with his coffee cup. "Does all that produce on the counter mean breakfast's coming?"

I laughed. "Which question should I start with?"

"Breakfast, of course. We'll chop, you cook and talk."

❧ ❧ ❧

"Ashley Groves?" Sam forked another bite of his omelet. "I think I had her in General Biology. Nice kid, good solid B student, not a Biology major."

"Jack's a grandfather." I sputtered. "Of three."

"He's a cad. But I'm not going to throw any stones about age differences." Edward buttered another piece of toast. "Of course, Sam, Gillian gave birth to her first child at something like eight, so she is a very young grandmother. Also, I'm much younger."

"Six months," I muttered.

"If, my dear, you continue in this vein and decide to divulge my age to this delightful young man," he dropped into a stage whisper, "he's only thirty-six for God's sake," then continued in a normal voice, "I will personally plunge you back into the lake from which you came."

Sam shrugged. "I looked you up online. You'll be forty-nine at the end of the month. It's okay." He smiled at Edward. "I like older men. They're so, I don't know, distinguished."

Edward winced.

"Stop, you two." I said. "This is serious. Jack turned fifty-three last April. Ashley's like what, twenty? His son John is older than that, Aurora's almost thirty. What is he thinking?"

"I doubt he's doing much thinking," Edward said gently. "But you're right, this is a new low, even for Jack."

"Who knows if it is," I said. "One of the reasons I had to get out of there last night is that I couldn't face going into that room and thinking that he might have fucked every woman there. I always assumed that it was only the ones who dropped away from his group, that he'd dumped them or they'd gotten tired of him and disappeared from the scene.

But there's Katy, standing by him all these years. And maybe they're all like that. Maybe they've pitied me all along. The poor kitchen drudge with the hot rabbit of a husband." I buried my face in my napkin.

He chuckled. "I doubt they're all schtupping him. You may find this hard to believe but I'm betting most of the women on his campaign actually believe in our dear congressman."

I sniffed. "God help them."

Edward scooted close and hugged me. "It will be okay."

"No it won't," I said. "But, thanks anyway. Can you guys go over there with me after breakfast?"

"Of course," Edward whispered into my hair. "If it helps, my guess is people are too busy thinking about themselves to worry too much about you."

"Maybe, but people like to gossip." I leaned against him.

His chest shook with his laugh. "I've noticed. But eventually they get bored and move on."

"Right. But I still hear stories about you and it's been, what? Ten years? I'm not ready for that yet." I pulled back to look at both of them. "Could I stay in the boathouse for a few days? I'll stay out of your way, I promise."

Edward looked at Sam. "What do you think, Sam?"

Sam was gazing sympathetically at me. He turned to Edward. "It's not my house, honey. But if it were I'd say 'Stay as long as you like Gillian, you know you're always welcome.'"

Edward smiled. "Good answer. Stay as long as you like, Gillian, you know you're always welcome." He pulled me close.

"Don't move," Sam said. "I'll clean up."

As Sam reached for his plate, Edward grabbed his hand and brought it to his lips. Daphnia leapt onto my lap, licking first my face and then Edward's. I relaxed, for just this moment I felt warm and safe, protected. It's good to have brothers, I thought.

Four

Sam and Edward cleaned my kitchen while I changed and filled an overnight bag. I packed a lunch for Sam and threw leftover chicken, salad, chips, salsa and brownies in a cooler to take to Pearl later. I left a note on the kitchen table:

> *Jack, I am staying at Edward's. I am not available to campaign this week. Will let you know when I'm coming home. I don't care what you do but do care about newspapers, so please be discreet.*
> —*Gillian.*

By eleven, Edward and I were speeding north along the interstate. I leaned into his convertible's leather seats, enjoying the push of the wind against my face and the slight flapping of my shirtsleeve. I was beginning to drift off when Edward said, "Do you think I should have worn a suit?"

I looked at him in his pressed chinos and polo shirt and laughed. "Edward, it's a hot day. Even Evelyn can't expect a suit. Don't worry. You don't look anything like yourself. She'll be delighted."

Edward gave me a weak smile. "I'm almost fifty and my mother still brings me to my knees."

I patted his leg. "Your mother brings everyone to their knees.

Momma Pearl thinks you're a saint for even visiting her."

"Momma Pearl's the saint," Edward said. "Are you sure Jack wasn't adopted?"

"Do you remember Jack's dad? He died when we were in our twenties."

He shook his head. "Maybe vaguely."

"Right, you wouldn't remember him, Pearl didn't move here until after he died." I gazed for a moment at the passing scenery. "Jack is just like his dad."

"Oh."

We were passing through the State Forest. I leaned back and watched the play of light in the treetops as we flew by and held out my right hand to feel the wind. The air felt warm and thick.

Finally I said, "Sam's great."

Edward smiled softly. "Yeah, he is."

I looked at him. "I don't think I've seen you like this before."

He raised his eyebrows. "Like what?"

I shrugged. "I don't know. Calm somehow. Always before you seemed so wound up, even with Rob, like you were afraid of saying the wrong thing and making it all disappear."

Edward thought for a moment. "Well, it always did. Rob and I were together a long time, but it was always so off and on. Even when we were together, we were never really together, you know?"

I nodded. "That's one I know well."

"Oh sorry." He glanced at me. "I wasn't thinking."

"No, it's okay. You don't have to do the eggshell thing around me. It isn't as if not talking will make it go away. Anyway, Rob, now there was a charming man."

"Yep."

"And dangerous."

"Yep," Edward agreed.

"Is he still with what's his face?"

He shrugged. "As far as I know." He paused, glancing at me. "But you know, I think, maybe leaving was the best thing he ever did for me. Otherwise I would never have met Sam and Sam is—" He shrugged again.

"Sam is perfect," I finished.

He laughed. "Nobody's perfect, Gillian. But you're right, Sam's pretty wonderful."

"You should keep him."

"I plan to."

The wind whipped my hair and I readjusted the band tying it back. "Edward? Did you ever have an affair with a married man?"

He cocked his head to one side. "Affair? No. But I slept with a lot of guys way back when. Some of them might have been married. Not Jack, if that's what you're asking."

I snorted. "I don't think you're Jack's type."

He glanced sideways at me. "Never underestimate the homophobic ones."

"I think Maggie has."

The car swerved as he turned toward me. "Maggie slept with Jack?"

"Oh, God no. He came on to her once but, no… I mean, I think Maggie had an affair with a married man."

Edward straightened the car. "Did she tell you that?"

"No, just some things she's said. And then there's Sam and his professor and you and all those guys. I feel like the slow student."

He patted my thigh. "Someone has to show the rest of us how to be faithful. Although I'm pretty sure Dad didn't sleep around and look what it got him. Speaking of which, do you want to stop at that little antique place on the way?"

"Edward, relax. All we're doing is having lunch with her. An hour, two tops. You know we don't have time to stop, you just want to avoid your mother."

"You're great for doing this with me, Gillian. Sam offered but—" He shuddered, "I don't think we're ready for that."

"Probably. But how bad could she be? Everybody loves Sam."

Edward looked at me. "This is my mother we're talking about. And I don't know if you noticed, but Sam isn't what Mom would consider a good gender for me. Although," he said thoughtfully, "if she could get past that, he'd be the girl of her dreams. He's such a good Jewish boy. You know he lights candles every Friday night?"

"Wow, we haven't had Shabbos candles since Grandpa Rosenberg died."

"Oh, Mom always lights them," Edward replied. "You've just never been there on Friday nights. She's not comfortable with the goyim at her Sabbath table."

"You're kidding, right?" I looked at him incredulously. "The reason you guys never came down until Saturday morning was because Grandpa Wolf and I weren't Jewish?"

Edward nodded. "That and she said it gave her the creeps to see her father-in-law lighting candles."

"Why?" I asked.

"Because boys don't do that, silly," Edward explained. "Mom is nothing if not careful about gender." He chuckled. "Not that it helped her much with her only child."

We traveled silently for a while. Trees gradually gave way to farmland and the rich smell of manure washed over us. After a while I said, "Hey, this morning I was remembering the summer we played I'll show you mine if you show me yours, do you remember?"

Edward laughed. "I do. That was the summer I knew I was gay. We had all that elaborate, I guess you'd call it foreplay, talking each other into it, and then you pulled down your pants and I was like, that's it?"

"Really? I was just grossed out."

Edward gave me a mock hurt look.

"What? We were ten. I thought it was some sort of slimy worm thing." I shuddered in memory. "Sorry, but I remember it as just icky."

Edward laughed. "Guess that explains my relationship problems. Maybe I had to find a biologist before anyone could love my slimy, icky, wormy thing."

"I didn't mean—"

Edward laughed harder.

I could feel myself blush and shut up. I put my feet up on the dashboard and leaned my seat back so I could watch the sky. After a while I said, "Edward, I don't think I can be single again."

The car slowed as his foot slid off the accelerator. "What do you mean?"

I wrapped my arms tightly around my stomach. "Well look at me. I'm old and fat and if I leave Jack, I'll probably turn into one of those crazy women with cats."

Edward pulled the car over to the side of the road and stopped. Once he had safely parked, he turned in his seat. "Bullshit."

"But look at me." I gestured to myself, my eyes filling.

"You're beautiful," Edward said flatly. "But that isn't important."

"What do you mean, that isn't important? Of course it's important."

"Gillian," Edward gently took my hand, "you're beautiful. You're also kind and warm, which is much more important than if you're pretty. And of course, you paint like a demented angel, all beautiful colors and enraged angles, and that makes you interesting. Not to mention that if the way to a man's heart is through his stomach well... need I say more?"

Patting my hand once again, he turned to the wheel, accelerated and eased the car into traffic before he spoke. "You deserve better than Jack, much better. You always have."

I started to protest and Edward held up his hand. "Stop. You don't get to disagree on this. Now lay back and take a nap. I don't want to hear a shmuktz out of you. We'll be there soon."

I stared at him a moment, settled into my seat and closed my eyes. I wouldn't sleep but maybe I could just rest—

❧ ❧ ❧

I opened my eyes again as we stopped at the guard house of Evelyn's gated community. I sat up, blinking. "Is it my imagination or is it actually substantially cooler here?"

"I think the heat is required to check in at the gate and only the very best heat, the kind that doesn't generate sweat, is admitted. Or alternatively," Edward gestured to the lush canopy above our heads, "it could be the trees."

"I can never believe you grew up here. I can't believe anyone grew up here. It seems so," I groped for the word, "barren."

"It is," Edward said flatly. "There are no children here, although some of the natives are short, nonverbal and wear diapers, and not just the young ones."

"Stop." I giggled. "You're not supposed to make me laugh."

"Right." Edward turned into the driveway of a large three story brick colonial. "Laughing is frowned upon." He killed the engine and sat for a moment. "God, I hate it here." He took a deep breath and looked at me. "Ready?"

"Guess so. If you're ready, I'm ready." I grabbed the door handle. "Here we go."

"One, two, two and a half,"

"Three!" I jumped from the car.

Evelyn answered the door wearing a gray silk shirtwaist and pearls. Her jet-black hair hung in a perfect bob, curled slightly inwards to accentuate her diamond stud earrings. "Eddie." She leaned forward so he could kiss her cheek. "You're only twenty minutes late, that's a new record."

"It's my fault, Evelyn," I spoke quickly. "I'm afraid I made Edward help with cleanup from Jack's gathering last night."

"Gillian dear." Evelyn extended her hand. "How lovely to see you. How nice of you to accompany Eddie on that long drive. Come in, both of you." She led us through her large white living room, decorated with giant geometric abstracts in beige and white. "I thought we'd lunch outside. So pleasant next to the water, don't you agree?" She opened the glass doors and led us across the patio. A small table next to the pool was set for lunch. "Can I get you a glass of wine? I have a nice white Bordeaux. Eddie?"

Edward smiled tightly. "No thank you, Mother. As you know, I've been sober almost ten years now."

"Admirable, admirable but are you sure you won't take just a taste? No? Gillian, surely you'll have a glass?"

I looked at Edward, who appeared to be studying the pool. "No thank you, Evelyn. I'd love some ice tea if you have it."

Edward glanced up and smiled gratefully.

"Well, then. Eddie, be a dear and get Gillian some tea. And bring the Bordeaux with you when you come back. It will go so nicely with our salad."

He inclined his head toward his mother and headed back through the open glass doors.

"Do you want some help?" I called.

"No, I'm fine," he answered softly and disappeared.

Evelyn crossed her arms and surveyed me from head to foot. "Isn't that an interesting ensemble?"

I looked down at my outfit, a red sleeveless tank and long peasant skirt. "Thank you. I bought it at the—"

"You've always been such an artistic dresser." Her eyes narrowed. "Of course, after a certain age... And I've always thought navy suited you best. It's so slimming. Ah, here's Eddie with our drinks."

I turned thankfully to Edward, who appeared carrying a tray with two poured drinks, a wine bottle and wine glass. "Don't leave me alone," I mouthed to him as I took my ice tea.

Edward set the tray on a side table, pulled a corkscrew from his pocket, expertly opened the wine bottle, poured his mother a glass, returned the bottle and corkscrew to the tray and picked up his ice tea. "L'Chaim," he toasted us, "to a lovely lunch."

"Let's sit." Evelyn led us to the patio table where three places were set with ornate silver. In the center of each place setting sat a square white plate with three leaves of romaine lettuce, two white asparagus spears and a slice of pale cheese, all drizzled in what looked like vinaigrette.

"When I heard you were coming, Gillian, I thought a summer salad would do nicely. I know how you like to watch your weight." She smiled at me then turned to Edward, "And it doesn't look like you've been spending much time at the gym lately, dear. Do be careful, the pounds creep on after fifty."

Evelyn sat and we followed her lead. "Now, Gillian, I'm sure you've been campaigning up a storm. I don't know how you do it."

I opened my mouth to reply, but Evelyn continued, "How are your children? Is Aurora pregnant again?"

"Not that I know of."

"It's a shame she didn't finish her education. And the boy, Joe?" Evelyn said, taking another sip of wine.

"John is still working on his dissertation. He's coming up in a few—"

She shrugged. "I always wanted Eddie to go to medical school, but—"

"I would have made a lousy doctor, Mother." Edward popped one of the white spears into his mouth. "And besides, you have to make it through college to get into med school and that wasn't interesting to me at the time."

"You never finished college either, did you, Gillian?" Evelyn turned back to me.

"No. But I'm not sure that a degree in Fine Arts would have helped either of us. And Edward is doing well, his photographs are very popular." I toyed with the cheese on my plate, absently wondering whether it was mozzarella or some sort of processed white stuff. Fresh mozzarella, I decided, the lunch was likely to be expensive even if it was tasteless.

Evelyn turned toward her son. "I suppose so. What have you been up to?"

"Edward's working on a book."

He gave me a warning look.

"Dragonflies, is it?" I prompted.

"Um, mayflies, actually." Edward watched his mother carefully cut her salad into small pieces. "I'm doing the cover art for a book on mayfly genetics."

"Hmm." Evelyn paused, looking at him over her fork, which held a morsel of asparagus.

"Actually, I'm leaving for Europe in a few weeks," he continued. "My agent says travel photography is hot right now and—"

Evelyn slammed down her cutlery. Both Edward and I jumped. "Haven't you shamed me enough?"

"Excuse me?" Edward asked.

"You're going to Europe with that, that man aren't you? Don't think you can fool me with travel pictures and book covers. Do you think I don't hear the rumors? Don't you know I have to sit through hours and hours of insinuation? I can't believe you would do this to me." She glared at Edward, wineglass in hand. "You wouldn't know this, Gillian, but the Jewish community is very tightly knit and I hear about everything."

I gaped at her. "But Evelyn—"

"Don't defend him, young lady." Evelyn turned toward me. "I would think you of all people would understand the need for discretion."

"What?" My stomach clenched.

"How do you think it looks for Jack that Eddie and his consorts spend so much time at your house? Don't you ever think of Jack's career?" She turned toward Edward, "Don't you? Don't you ever think of anyone but yourself?" She turned to me. "And who knows what kind of influence Eddie's fancy boys have had on your little Joe. All those mincing—" She shuddered.

"It's John, mother." Edward set down his fork. "And there wasn't very much mincing—"

"My son?" I looked at Evelyn open mouthed. "You're worried about Edward's influence on my son?"

"Well, he wasn't the manliest of boys, you must admit that." Evelyn brought her hands into her lap and looked at me. "He's always seemed, I don't know, off to me."

I stared at her until she broke the silence. "Well, all I can say is that it is a good thing your father is dead. Going off to Europe with some—" She paused then shook her head. "He would be so—"

I looked at my watch. "Oh, Evelyn, oh, Edward, I'm so sorry." I turned toward Edward apologetically. "I just remembered I'm supposed to speak at a tea this afternoon. I had completely forgotten. If we leave now we can just make it." I placed my hand on Evelyn's arm. "Evelyn, it was so wonderful of you to invite me and I'm so sorry about this. Another time, perhaps?"

"But what about lunch?" she sputtered.

Edward stood and kissed his mother's cheek. "We'll have to starve, Mother. But as you said, we could both do without the calories. Gillian, I guess we'd better hurry if we're going to get you to that speech."

We sprinted toward the door. Edward called over his shoulder, "Bye, I'll call you."

Once we had cleared the guardhouse he pulled the car over and leaned back. "Thank you, thank you, thank you, you are a goddess and I will always be in your debt."

"Oh man, was she in rare form." I leaned back too.

"Someone must have stolen her broom." After a moment he continued, "There'll be hell to pay for this, you know."

"Only if you call her. You think that kind of mother deserves your attention? And you leave for Amsterdam in what, three weeks?"

He nodded.

"Maybe it's Evelyn that you're getting a sabbatical from."

He grinned. "Maybe."

"And, Edward?" Waiting until he looked at me directly, I added, "Your dad would have been proud of you. He always was and he still would be."

Edward nodded. "Thanks for that. I miss him."

"Me too." I sat up. "We have chicken wings, salad, chips and salsa in the cooler – picnic?"

"God, yes. Is there chocolate?"

"There is, there certainly is. But let's get a long way from here before we eat."

"Right." Edward punched the accelerator and the convertible jumped forward.

"Maybe when we get back we could help Sam move." I dangled an arm out the window. "And after that we can all go to Pearl's and get some Glenda the Good witch energy."

"And then I need a meeting."

"And then you need a meeting." I opened the glove box and pulled out a tri-fold brochure. I opened it and scanned the contents. "Six at St. Mathias?'

"Sure." Edward nodded. "And if I don't make that one, I'll do the eight o'clock at the Unitarians."

We pulled off the highway at a wayside in the State Forest. I hauled the cooler from the trunk and brought it to a picnic table, while Edward rummaged in the glove compartment for paper napkins. "I'm starved. We'll have to go light on the brownies since I promised them to Pearl. But there's plenty of everything else."

"I don't know. I'm still pretty full from that asparagus stalk." Edward sat across from me. He handed me a napkin and a plastic fork and held up a spoon for himself. "Always be prepared, that's what I learned in the Boy Scouts, among other things best not discussed." He grabbed a chicken wing and bit into it. "Hmmm, this is much better than that fat-free crap Mom was serving."

"Promise me you won't go back there before you leave." I dipped my tortilla chip. "She was awful and you don't need that."

"I promise." Edward nodded. "But I might call her."

"Edward, did you hear her? Would you let anyone else say those things? Would you?" I waived my chicken wing at him.

He shrugged. "She's my mom."

"She's a viper. You're almost fifty for God's sake, why do you put up with it?" I muttered, licking the sauce from my fingers.

"Look, Gillian." Edward spoke slowly, his eyes on his food. "I appreciate that you're being a friend here, but maybe you don't want to start throwing around 'why do you put up with it?'"

I paused. "You're right. I guess I could come up with a long list of why I put up with it, but you probably could too."

He nodded. "Truce?"

I smiled at him. "Okay, truce. It's just that I love you and I hate to see you treated so badly." Edward started to reply but I held up my hand, "I know, I know, that's exactly how you feel. Point taken. Now let's finish up and go home."

∞ ∞ ∞

We found Sam standing in the kitchen of his small second floor apartment. Despite a whirling ceiling fan, the heat was thick. Sam's face and dark curly hair dripped sweat. He looked grimy, hot and irritable. Boxes lined one wall of the kitchen. I saw more cardboard boxes stacked in the living room. He held a teapot in one hand and a coffee grinder in the other and greeted us with a wan smile. "Hi."

Daphnia ran from the kitchen, jumping first on me, and then Edward, dancing on his hind legs and wagging his entire body in excitement.

"Hey, boy. Yes, we missed you." Edward bent to scratch the dog's ears. He smiled up at Sam. "Looks like we're just in time. You're almost done."

Sam nodded. "This is the hard part, figuring out what I need for the next couple weeks. How was your mother?"

"Hideous." Edward opened the refrigerator. "Ugh, this looks bad."

Sam blushed. "I guess I haven't been here much lately. Most of that can get tossed. Garbage bags are on the counter, if you're up for it."

I looked at what was left in the kitchen: one pot, a cast iron frying pan, a few plates, some silverware. I wandered into the living room, Daphnia at my heels. Along with the boxes, the living room contained a couch, two chairs and a small desk stacked with books, papers, pens and pencils. In the bedroom I found still more boxes, a suitcase, a made bed and two folded bath towels in the closet. I returned to the kitchen.

"Can you help me for a moment?" I asked Edward, who was standing at the sink dumping a carton of sour milk. "I think I left something in the car and I need your help." I turned to Sam. "Can Daphnia come with us? Do you have a leash?"

"Sure." Sam looked puzzled. "There's a leash hanging by the door. Where are you going?"

"Just outside for a minute, we'll be right back." I clipped Daphnia's leash and started down the stairs.

Edward looked puzzled, but followed. When we got outside he asked, "What was that about?"

I leaned back against the car and looked up at him. "You need to go up there and put that poor man out of his misery."

"You want me to kill Sam?"

"No. I want you to tell him to pack up everything and come live with you. He's up there trying to figure out what he'll need if he has to spend the night there before you go, does he need silverware, should he leave some furniture and all that." I smiled. "Were you planning that Sam should sleep here between now and then?"

"I hadn't thought about it but... no, I guess not."

"Okay. So tell him." I checked my watch. "Daphnia and I are going to walk down to the Minimart on Sixth and get us all something cold to drink. It should take us about half an hour. I think the Foundation should pay some nice strong movers to come finish this job. It's brutal up there."

Edward gave me a quick hug and laughing, he bounded up the stairs.

It took me forty-five minutes. When I opened the door to the apartment I found Sam freshly showered, wearing clean clothes. Edward had changed from his polo into a dark blue T shirt embellished with colorful beetles and spiders.

"Nice shirt." I handed Edward a soda. "Tight, but it suits you."

He grinned. "Biologists have the best graphics, don't they?"

I handed Sam his drink, which he instantly drained. "So you guys ready to go? I need to get to Momma Pearl's in time to deliver dinner, or what's left of it."

"Sure." Edward took Sam's empty bottle.

Sam nodded. "Let me just grab a few things." He ducked into the bedroom. I raised my eyebrows inquisitively at Edward, who grinned back and nodded.

Sam returned carrying a large suitcase and a small cardboard box into which he threw the coffee grinder, teakettle and fry pan. "Okay, let's go." He led us down the stairs and out to Edward's car.

Sam hefted the suitcase and box into the back seat of the convertible. He hoisted himself up and over to flop in next to them and grinned up at us. "I've always wanted to do that. Just like Robin and the Batmobile."

"Wow." I picked up Daphnia and plopped him in Sam's lap. "You really are a boy wonder."

Edward just smiled.

✆ ✆ ✆

As we rounded the corner of Pearl's street, we saw the two women sitting in deck chairs on the front patio. Pearl wore a broad brimmed sun hat. Her right hand lay gently on the folded walker resting against her chair. As soon as the car stopped, I jumped out and bounded up the walk. Behind me Sam sternly ordered, "Stay." Presumably to Daphnia.

"Look at you." I called to Pearl. "Did you get out here with just the walker?"

Pearl beamed. "Aziza helped, but yes, it was such a lovely day I had to get outside."

"That's wonderful." I kissed her on the cheek and hugged Aziza. "I had no idea you were moving around so well."

Aziza laughed. "She'll be dancing soon."

Edward arrived carrying the cooler. "Hello, Momma Pearl, you look wonderful. You remember Sam?"

"Of course, of course." Pearl extended her hand. "How nice of you to visit. Can we offer you ice tea?"

"I'll get chairs," Aziza offered.

"Let me help," Sam took the cooler from Edward and followed Aziza into the house.

"Such a nice young man," Pearl said, watching them go. Edward leaned down to kiss her and she patted his shoulder. "I like this one much better than that other, Rob was it?"

Edward laughed, "That shows your good judgment, Momma Pearl."

"I don't know about that, but Rob was nasty so often, wasn't he? I don't like to see that."

Aziza came back with a round of ice tea, followed by Sam carrying three folding chairs.

"And I think this one's cuter," Pearl whispered, winking at Edward.

Edward guffawed, I giggled, and Sam asked, "What?"

"I think they were talking about you behind your back," Aziza told him. "But it's okay. She likes you."

"Um, good. Thanks, I guess." Sam busied himself unfolding the chairs.

When we were all seated and tea had been handed around, Pearl asked Edward, "How was your mother?"

He blanched. "She looked well."

"She was impossible, we left early," I added.

"Maybe it's time for Evelyn to find a nice gentleman friend and move away," Pearl suggested.

Edward rolled his eyes. "That sounds unlikely."

"What about that man you worked for, Aziza, what was his name?"

Pearl turned toward Aziza.

"Mr. Greene? I worked for his wife in her last months. Difficult woman." Aziza shook her head. "But Mr. Greene was good to her. He was very sad when she died."

Edward stared at Aziza and then turned to Pearl. "You aren't actually thinking of subjecting somebody to my mother?"

Pearl shrugged. "Who knows? Some people like to have someone to push against and some people like to be pushed. I'm just thinking it might be nice for your mother to have someone." She turned to me. "Maybe we could invite him to my fundraiser. I'm sure Evelyn will come down for that." She looked at Edward, who shrugged and then nodded.

I chuckled. "Invite anyone you want, but I wouldn't hold my breath on this."

"Gillian, you really must develop a more nuanced view of people. No one is all good or bad. Evelyn is an attractive woman. And she was good to your father." Pearl took a sip of her tea. "We'll see. Now tell me all your news." She looked at Edward.

"Well." Edward tipped back in his folding chair. "The big news is that Sam and I are leaving for Amsterdam in two weeks. We'll be there through the winter."

"Amsterdam." Pearl clapped her hands. "How lovely. I've always wanted to see Europe."

"I have a brother in Rotterdam," Aziza said. "He says the Dutch are very nice."

"What will you be doing?" Pearl asked Sam.

"I'll be working with a woman who's looking for genetic markers of enzymes that allow aquatic invertebrates to tolerate low oxygen conditions." Sam must have seen our eyes glaze because he continued less boisterously, "It'll be useful for monitoring water quality. We'll be living right in Amsterdam. My colleague, Edna, has already found us a furnished apartment on a canal."

"You must take lots of pictures, Edward. How wonderful."

"Maybe you could come over for a visit," Sam suggested. He looked around at all three of us. "The apartment we're renting has a spare bedroom. You should all come."

Pearl smiled broadly. "You see, Edward, I told you he was a nice boy." She turned to Sam. "That's very kind of you, thank you."

Sam inclined his head toward her. "You're welcome and you'd be very welcome."

Edward glanced at his watch and excused himself. "I'll be back in about an hour."

As he walked away, I sipped my tea and looked around the circle of smiling faces. Maybe it was just the warm late afternoon sun, but I wanted to hold the moment, make it stretch, keep it like a blanket to wrap around myself later in the cold I knew was coming.

Five

We arrived home at dusk to find a giant bouquet of roses leaning against Edward's door. He read the card and, grimfaced, handed it to me.

Dearest Gillian,
I am so sorry. Please forgive me. I've always loved you and always will. Please come back. I love you.
Yours always, Jack.

I picked up the apricot roses, our wedding flowers and followed Edward into the house. Sam handed me his teakettle, then the men and dog left me alone. In the kitchen I carefully cut the stems and arranged the flowers in a large vase I found tucked in a high cupboard. I put on the teakettle and rummaged in the cabinets until I found a box of Earl Grey.

Waiting for the water to boil I stood on the porch and watched the sun sink behind the hill on the far side of the lake. The flowers mirrored the colors of the setting sun. Why hadn't I thought of that before? A bad omen, sunset colors for a wedding. Sunrises are what I thought of back then, nineteen and five months pregnant, my handsome groom smiling down at me, Grandpa Wolf elegant in a white tuxedo, giving my hand in marriage, swallowing his doubts.

I closed my eyes, remembering humiliation. I'd come home from college unexpectedly. The grandfathers had been so delighted. What a lovely surprise. How had I gotten away? Then I'd told them. I'd hoped the wedding would erase the memory of their faces when I said "pregnant," so shatteringly sad. Jack had seemed what… brilliant, handsome, grown-up, with a briefcase and such lofty goals. He dreamed himself champion of the downtrodden, a passionate advocate of good causes, a savior, a messiah. I'd dreamed with him, such a believing child.

The kettle whistled.

I sat, cup in hand, staring vacantly at the giant bouquet filling the center of the kitchen table, when Edward and Sam walked in. Sam lifted the kettle from the burner, the whistling stopped. He filled my cup and rustled in the cabinet for more tea bags and mugs. Edward sat beside me. Daphnia jumped onto his lap. I just stared at the flowers.

Finally Edward placed a hand gently on my arm. "Do you want us to stay or go?"

I looked up and blinked. "Stay. I'm afraid I'm not good company, but I'd still like you to stay."

He nodded and patted my arm. Sam handed him tea and quietly hoisted himself onto the kitchen counter.

After a while Edward asked, "So, are you going back?"

I looked at him, startled. "Not yet, I think not, maybe, I don't know. It's all so complicated." I propped my head in my hands and returned my gaze to the flowers.

Sam cleared his throat. "I know it is none of my business—" I looked up and he continued. "I gather this isn't the first time Jack has—" he trailed off.

I shook my head. "No, not the first time. I don't always know the details but I know he's been cheating for years."

"So," Sam spoke slowly, clearly choosing his words carefully, "why now?" When I looked puzzled, he continued, "You're thinking of leaving him, right?"

I nodded.

"It's none of my business and, of course, given my own history—" He blushed slightly. "But why now? What makes this time different?"

"It's a good question." I paused, looking again at the roses. "I've certainly thought of leaving before. I almost did once, remember, Edward?"

He nodded. "That was the first time, right?"

"Second, I think, or at least the second time I time I knew for sure. I packed the children off to Momma Pearl's and hid out here for a week. But then it all seemed so difficult, the scandal, the children, my life so—" I shrugged, "I went back."

"And you missed him," Edward added.

"And I loved him. That always pulls me back."

"And this time?" Sam prodded. "Will you go back this time?"

I thought for a while. "Maybe. Never say never, right? But—"

"But—" Edward echoed when I didn't continue.

"But something shifted when I saw that girl, Ashley. She's so young. Young enough I might have worried if John brought her home, for God's sake." I felt a wave of anger, a hot blush moving up from my chest to my cheeks. "I just thought, what a prick, what a stupid, goddamned prick. And then I had to leave." I shrugged. "It may pass eventually, but for now I'd rather not see him."

Edward leaned back in his chair, stretching his legs. "You know, honey, I'm hoping you leave him for good. Never been a big Jack fan. But you gotta do whatever makes your life work."

I blinked. "I don't know what that is."

He smiled. "Give yourself some time. You'll figure it out."

"But you'll think I'm a wimp if I go back." I lay my head in my hands on the table.

Edward's hand caressed my shoulder. "Gillian, baby, I'm the last person who gets to judge anyone. Especially not you. You've always thought better of me than I deserve. Don't you think I ought to return the favor? So, you want to toss these flowers?"

"No, they're pretty. And it isn't their fault. Besides, I'm not to the trashing point quite yet."

"So what do you want to do?" he asked gently.

I looked from Edward to Sam. I blinked back tears. "Order pizza and watch old movies?"

Sam reached for the phone as Edward said, "Comedy, thriller or romance?"

"Not romance." I groaned. "How about something with a good murder?"

An hour later the doorbell rang. Daphnia barked, Edward sprang up to answer, Sam hit the pause button on Murder on the Orient Express and I turned to see Maggie standing at the door, holding three giant pizza boxes.

"Hi all." She gestured with her boxes. "Cheese, pepperoni and that god-awful veggie-pineapple-goat cheese concoction that Edward likes."

"Maggie." I said, surprised. "Has University pay gotten so bad you need to moonlight delivering pizza?"

"Sam called." She thrust the pizza boxes at Edward.

"Sam called?" I turned to look at Sam, who smiled.

"Hey Maggie." To me he said, "I think she makes a great pizza delivery person."

"Definitely." I patted the seat next to me. "I'm so glad you're here."

Maggie settled beside me. "Me, too." She squeezed my shoulder. "Now let's have some pizza and you can catch me up on everything."

❧ ❧ ❧

I awoke again in the boathouse. Golden light streamed through the lattice windows. When was the last time I'd slept this late? The boys had gone bed after the first movie. Maggie hadn't left until we'd finished all the pizzas, another movie (something with James Cagney), a giant bowl of popcorn and some caramel chocolate frozen yogurt we found buried deep in Edward's freezer. That would explain my bloated and vaguely nauseated feeling.

I stretched, yawned and rolled out of bed. Seeing my swimsuit peeking out of my overnight bag, I stripped out of my pajamas, wiggled into the lycra and stepped out onto the boathouse balcony. Already warm, this would be another hot, hot day. The lake still calm, I could see two small fishing boats trolling along the shore to the north and another to the south, just around the point.

I stepped onto the balcony rail, paused for a moment and dove. The cool water startled as it enveloped me. I opened my eyes and, when I saw the bottom, arched so my dive leveled off. Kicking up through the water, I emerged with a gasp. Edward's house loomed high above me. I turned toward my own home, even higher on the hill. Lights on in the kitchen. My garden fence and the expanse of wild grass cascaded down to the cabin, tucked so elegantly into the hill. I swam slowly to the ladder on the far side of Edward's boathouse, hoisted myself onto the dock and into the nearest full length deck chair to let the sun dry me. As I was drifting off again, I heard footsteps and opened my eyes to see Sam holding coffee.

"Good morning. I thought this might be welcome."

"You're an angel." As I sat up Daphnia jumped into my lap.

Sam waited until the dog had finished his wiggly, licking greeting before handing me a cup. "Mind if I join you?"

"Of course not, just how late is it?" I breathed in the rich coffee scent gratefully.

He stretched out on his deckchair. "It's after nine. I'm afraid we ate already. Edward's left for a meeting with a non-profit about some images he donated. I'm meeting him downtown for lunch later."

"That's okay. I'll finish this and head back to my house. Jack should be gone by then. I think he's speaking across state this afternoon."

"Do you need help, company, anything?" Sam looked concerned.

"I'll be fine." I shifted in my chair. "Um, Sam?"

"Hmm?" He was gazing out over the lake.

"What's it like on the other side? You know, of an affair?"

He looked at me for a long moment. "Awful. And exciting. Sexy. Heartbreaking." He turned his attention back to the lake. "And lonely. I can count the number of times we spent a full night together. Mostly at scientific conferences when we could pretend we were sharing a room to save money." He smiled sadly at me. "If it helps, I think sometimes it was pretty rough on him, too. Lying to everyone is hard work."

I took a deep breath. "Thanks. I'm sorry."

"Don't be."

"Don't you have work to do?"

Sam shrugged. "I'm an academic. I always have work to do. Today I should be finishing revisions on an article. But I'd be happy to procrastinate with you if you need me."

I laughed. "Thanks, but I'll be fine. Jack's too busy to spend much time at home this time of year."

"Okay." Sam looked at his watch and stood. "I better get to work. If you need anything let me know. Come on, Daph." He snapped his fingers. The dog jumped from my lap and followed him.

"Thanks for the coffee," I called after them. Sam waved back over his shoulder.

I savored the coffee and let my hair dry in the sun. I knew it would look shaggy and unkempt, but somehow that didn't seem as important as the luxury of warm sun and a cool breeze off the lake. Eventually I stood and climbed the stairs, reluctantly changing into a T shirt, jeans and sandals, pulling my hair into a simple ponytail and allowing the day to begin.

I entered my own empty kitchen, listening carefully for any sound of habitation. The house stayed silent. A dirty bowl, coffee cup, a few glasses and some silverware cluttered the sink, coffee grounds, the sugar bowl and a box of corn flakes on the counter. Starting coffee and toast, I washed and tidied, wondering vaguely if Jack had assumed I'd be over to clean, or if he just hadn't thought of it at all. Probably the latter, I decided.

Once seated with my toast and coffee, I dialed Maggie's number. Her voice mail picked up. "It's me," I said. "I'll be in the garden all morning. Call my cell, I'm not answering the house phone. Come for lunch if you like. It's sort of spooky here, which is weird because—" the phone beeped and I finished to myself, "this is my home."

❧ ❧ ❧

The garden gate opened with its usual creak. Entering, I latched it behind me. I used to leave it open, but one day a deer wandered in through the gate while I was weeding in a far corner of the garden. We startled each other. The deer banged around, trampled a row of spinach and some tomatoes, and broke several corn stalks before bounding over the fence. After that I kept the gate latched at all times.

August is a wonderful month for gardens and mine looked lush and full. It also needed some serious weeding. Even though I'd carefully laid out the garden with raised beds separated by mulch covered walkways, the weeds always battled me for dominion. In one corner of the fence stood a small shed from which I pulled gloves and my portable radio. Cranking up the classical station, I started with the corn, and yanked up grasses and other weeds that had sprouted between the stalks. The soil felt cool and smelled rich and moist, wormy, I thought, fecund. Each plant I uprooted seemed to sigh out a long green whisper that trailed out with the roots. The loosened dirt felt soft to the touch. That would be all those shovelfuls of compost mixed into the beds last spring.

When had I first realized Jack wasn't the man I'd dreamed him to be? Was it before we married, when I caught him flirting with that redheaded cheerleader type? What was her name? Gidget? Bridget? No, Claire, that was it, Claire.

We were just talking, Jack had said.

I believed him, furious with myself for getting jealous. What's that catch phrase of Edward's? Floating down the river of Denial. In my case, that's a mighty long river. I found myself singing in my deepest, off-key voice, "Old man river, that old man river, he just keeps rollin' along."

I inspected the corn, pulling down the leaves on one cob to check the progress of the kernels. Another week, maybe, before they'd be ready. With such a cold spring, everything was late. I moved to the salad bed, a twenty-by-three, two-foot high, stone-walled bed spanning the north-east corner of the garden. This time of year chard, mustard and kale dominated, plants that grew full and shaded out everything else so there wasn't much weeding. The rainbow chard sparkled in the sun. Maybe we'd have it sautéed with fresh mustard for lunch. Soon it would be time to clear space for the fall spinach crop.

I checked the tomatoes. A few of the Early Girls were beginning to ripen. Zucchini needed picking. I pulled some weeds from around the watermelons and knocked on one of the small, yellow early varieties, deciding we could try it for lunch as well.

Grabbing a basket from the shed, I circled the tall teepees of pole beans, so many still to harvest. Starting with the dragon's tongue beans, with their mottled purple and green pods, then the vibrant purple queen pods and finally old homestead, green and harder to find, I methodically picked the mature beans, stopping to retrieve a second basket midway. I'd be freezing most of these but picking kept up production.

As I picked I tried to organize Jack's dalliances, first chronologically and then alphabetically. Not including Claire, who may or may not have been, I remembered six: Carol, Sarah, Peggy, Betsy, Katy, and now Ashley. There must be more, maybe an entire alphabet of women. Ashley, Betsy, Carol, Katy, Peggy, Sarah, the last will be first or whatever. Was it after Sarah or Peggy that I quit caring? Sarah, I think, when I came back. Aurora had started school and John was just walking. By the time Peggy came along, Jack had been elected and the children and I were alone all winter. Since then it hadn't been too bad. Before I found out about Betsy, I'd met Maggie and then Edward settled back here, sober, about the time I started suspecting Katy. And now young Ashley, good God, what was he thinking?

I sat, then lay in the pathway, suddenly drained. Looping one arm over my eyes to shield my face from the sun, I let the waves of emotion wash over. First, a single memory floated up of Aurora, fifteen, coming into the kitchen white-faced, silent, unable to look me in the eye. Instantly I'd known that she knew, she'd seen something (would that have been Betsy?), and just as quickly I'd smashed my knowing down into some dark crevasse and gone on making dinner. But I remembered now and with the memory came an anger so old and dark and awesome that it shook me. I curled up, shivering in the midmorning heat. Then the images and anger came in waves. I felt powerless beneath them.

The day I surprised him for lunch our first year back in town, opening the door to his office in the old Patterson Building, Jack kissing Carol, closing the door before they saw me, running home. Election night, Assembly that first time, the look on Sarah's face, hot, wet, expectant. Another election night, Congress, the big one, seeing Katy's face, the same. Nights alone, children asleep ("Daddy's an important man, that's why he works so late, now go to sleep, you can see him in the morning"). Remembering, watching my children find out. Watching them lie to protect me. Letting them lie. I didn't want to feel this.

Suddenly tears replaced the anger. Lying at the base of the beans sobbing, I felt paralyzingly sad. All those wasted years. Dripping tears and snot into the ground, I felt I would never stop weeping. And then, eventually, I did.

I think I slept, the ground cool beneath me, the sun warm along my flank. My cell rang. Rolling onto my back, I sat and fished it from my pocket. "Hello?" My voice sounded thick and nasal.

"Gillian, are you all right?" Maggie asked.

I laughed, but it came out more like a croak. "I guess, yeah, I'm fine."

"Look, I'm meeting with a grad student for the next hour or so, but I'll come over right after that." She paused. "Are you sure you're okay?"

"Fine, I'm just gardening. I'll start lunch soon. Come when you can." I hung up, glanced at my basket and a half of beans and rose, unsteady on my feet. I piled zucchini, chard and mustard into the half-filled basket and made three trips to the house, one for each basket and one for the small, sweet-smelling watermelon we'd open for desert.

After a shower and change of clothes I felt calmer, but still jangly, and when I poured myself a glass of water my hand trembled slightly. Food. Preparing food would help. I poured beans into the sink and turned on the radio, flipping to an oldies station, maybe that would change my mood. By the time Maggie arrived most of the beans were washed and freezing and a pan of zucchini, garlic and the stems of the chard sizzled on the stove. Chopped chard leaves and mustard sat ready for last minute inclusion.

"I think it's just us today." I returned Maggie's hug. "I could use a glass of wine, do you want one?"

"Sure." She opened the refrigerator. "I'll get it. White?"

I nodded.

Maggie poured two glasses of chardonnay, handing one to me. "Cheers. What shall we toast?"

"Honesty," I replied. "Here's to honesty and the thoroughly examined life."

Maggie raised her glass. "I'll drink to that if it's your life we're talking about. I'm not sure I want to examine mine too closely."

"Deal." I added chard leaves to the sauté. "This is almost ready, you want spicy or not so spicy?"

"If we're examining life and drinking our lunch, I'll take spicy, please." Maggie laughed and took cutlery and napkins to the table.

I added the mustard.

"Hmm, this is great," Maggie cooed over her first bite. "If I didn't love your tasty meat dishes, I could become a vegetarian. Now, what are we being honest about?"

I scooped some of the stir-fry onto a slice of whole wheat bread. "Jack's adultery."

"Were we dishonest about this before?"

"Sort of. I tend to ignore it," I answered slowly. "I had this sort of epiphanal experience in the garden. I'm not sure yet how things are going to change, but they will."

Maggie took another sip of wine. "This feels decadent. I feel almost guilty, like we're drinking behind Edward's back."

I giggled. "I doubt Edward would begrudge us a glass of wine now and then. I don't think it even bothers him to see us drink, I just never do because—" I shrugged.

"I know," Maggie replied. "So you want to talk about the epiphany?"

"I'm not sure I can." I took another sip, the bite of the wine cool in my throat. "But let's talk about what's next."

Maggie nodded, biting into zucchini. "Here's my first choice, you could leave him."

I chewed for a moment. "I could, and I may, but not yet, certainly not before the election. I know it sounds odd, but I believe in Jack's platform. Not," I protested as Maggie started to speak, "that I think he does. He believes in whatever will get him re-elected, I know. But some of what he does is good, in spite of himself. And his opponent? You want that?"

Maggie shook her head sadly. "No, I don't. I can't stand what Jack does to you but I have to admit I always vote for him, if only as the lesser of—"

"Right." I nodded. "So I can't leave him before the election. And even afterwards, the papers, tabloids, reporters—" I shuddered. "God, you've seen them, the pathetic political wives discussing their horrid marriages on talk shows. Believe me, I've made a point of noticing how it goes for them. It's always awful. I hate the idea of our private business spattered all over the morning news. And I don't even want to think about the comedians. Because what did I or the kids, or Pearl, ever do to deserve that?"

"But," Maggie put a gentle hand on my arm, "it would pass, Gillian, and then you'd have a life."

I shook my head. "Maybe, but you know it won't matter what I do, if I stand by him, kick him out, slink into obscurity or write a tell-all book, everyone will feel free to judge me and my life. I can't deal with it, I just can't."

Maggie gave my arm a squeeze and changed the subject. "Did you pick everything in here this morning?"

"No." I took a deep breath. "Not the garlic. My garlic's not ready yet. But everything else is fresh."

We ate in silence for a few minutes. I said, "John's coming home Friday. He and Jack plan to knock on doors across the district this weekend."

"Are you going to tell him?"

"God, no."

"He's a grown man, Gillian. I think he could handle it."

"Maybe," I agreed, "but should he have to?"

She shrugged. "Should you?"

"Good point," I conceded. "But I'm not going to tell him, or at least not yet."

"How are you going to manage that?"

"Potemkin, that's what we've always done," I replied. "We'll just pretend. Ready for some watermelon?"

※ ※ ※

Later that afternoon I called Mark's cell. He assured me Jack was working the other side of the district and wouldn't be home tonight.

"He's worried about you," Mark told me.

"He's worried about scandal," I replied. "Tell him his secret is safe with me. I'm not going public."

"He'll be relieved to hear that. So am I, frankly," Mark said, "although I'm not proud of myself for that."

"It's fine." I reassured him. "Protect him. It's what I want, too."

"He doesn't deserve you."

"So I've heard. Give me some notice before he comes home, will you?"

"Sure."

I called Edward and left a message, "Hi, it's me. I'm staying here alone tonight. I'll be fine. Just need time to think. Have fun without me, be romantic. You guys are great and I love you. Thanks."

I phoned Pearl, who thanked me for calling and told me they were working that thousand-piece red apple puzzle. I told her I'd be over in the morning and signed off.

Later yet, I opened another bottle of wine, curled into an overstuffed chair and watched the sun sink behind the hill across the lake, thinking, tomorrow I'll make plans and lists and resolutions, but tonight I just want to disappear.

⁂

The clock said three a.m. The house quiet; outside the lake looked calm in the moonlight. Sometime in the night I'd moved from the chair to the floor and woke with a stiff neck and headache. I felt dizzy and unsteady on my feet as I trudged upstairs to my bathroom. Turning on the light, I winced and reached for the ibuprofen bottle. When I looked in the mirror a sad old woman with wild hair and puffy eyes stared back at me. My mouth tasted dry and sour. Moving slowly, I slathered toothpaste on my toothbrush and scrubbed away the scummy feeling in my mouth. I turned the shower on full, stepped in and stretched my neck muscles, letting the hot water pound on them until they gave way. I let the water cascade over me for a long time before reaching for the shampoo and soap.

I shaved, moisturized and deodorized. I patted on the expensive eye cream guaranteed to de-puff even the baggiest bags. I blew my hair dry, trying to comb in a little style. When I finished, the woman in the mirror didn't look quite so old, although still sad, tired and bloodshot.

I pulled on a robe and walked down the stairs. Turning on the living room light, I surveyed the damage from the night before: two empty wine bottles, a crumpled bag of potato chips, and a half-empty pint of ice-cream tipped over next to a wineglass and melting onto the end table. Wadded tissues and potato chip crumbs surrounded the overstuffed chair, some apparently ground into the carpet by my head and hips. Lovely, the perfect pity-party picture.

After I'd cleaned, straightened and vacuumed, I made myself coffee and sat at the kitchen table looking out at the lake. Still quiet. Soon the birds would wake and the day would start and I'd probably have to see Jack. Or I could just go on hiding? What's that old '60s button? "Not to decide is to decide."

For me the best way to think is to cook. I started on zucchini bread with extra cinnamon and walnuts. While that baked, I mixed a batch of John's favorite chocolate chip cookies. Once those were in the oven, I made bread. Then I thought that Pearl might like a fresh bean salad and a cold gazpacho for lunch. By eight-thirty, when Edward and Sam came to check on me, I'd mixed batter for crepes and was finishing a filling choice of apple-raisin or spinach and feta.

They knocked on the lakeside door. Edward poked his head in and whistled when he saw the array of baked goods covering the kitchen table. "Rough night?"

"I don't want to talk about it," I said. "Breakfast is almost ready. Help yourselves to coffee."

Sam and Daphnia followed. "So you were expecting us again?"

I shook my head and smiled at him, bending to pet Daphnia. "This time I was just hoping. At some point it occurred to me that maybe the smells would tempt you over."

Edward poured two cups of coffee and handed one to Sam "It did start smelling good about halfway here. When did you start?" He looked again at the array of food.

"About four this morning." I shrugged. "It seemed the thing to do."

"Who's going to eat all this?" Sam asked.

"You'll eat some." I moved a rack of cookies to make room for them at the table. "And Pearl, and John, he's coming home tomorrow afternoon, and I suppose Jack, he'll be back today."

"That explains the cooking." Edward threw himself into a seat at the table and grabbed a cookie. "What are you going to do?"

"I'm not sure yet." I poured batter into my crepe pan, rolling it around the edges until it formed a paper thin layer along the bottom. "Sweet or savory?"

"Sweet." Edward took a giant bite of cookie.

"Savory," Sam said. "Can I help?"

"Here." I handed him two forks. "The napkins and some placemats are in the second drawer on the left." I pointed to the built-in cabinet in far corner of the kitchen.

"Aren't you eating?" he asked.

I grimaced, "No thanks. I'm not up to it this morning." I flipped the crepe in the pan, careful to avoid Edward's gaze.

He stood and strolled to the sink to wash his hands. Casually, he opened the recycling bin and looked in. He raised his eyebrows, put a hand on my shoulder and said gently, "That's not a solution, Gillian. Trust me on this. I really do know. It just makes things worse."

I nodded, blinking back tears. He squeezed my shoulder and took the plate I held out.

"This looks great." he said loudly, turning to Sam. "The benefit of a long friendship with Gillian, my young friend, is that you get served first."

I handed Sam a plate. "The benefit of not having an atrocious sweet tooth is that you get served best."

Sam smiled and took his plate. "Edward thinks it's his many personal assets that will keep me, but the secret is the food."

Six

A few moments after I rang the bell I heard a distinctive walker click-step-step and Pearl answered the door.

"Pearl, you're up and about. That's wonderful. Where's Aziza, is everything all right?" I leaned to kiss her cheek while balancing two large containers of salad and soup and a bag of baked goods.

"I sent her to the store." Pearl stepped back to allow me in. "It must be so confining for her, sitting all day with an old woman. So I send her out every now and then. It gives her some privacy to call her parents back in Somalia, poor dear."

I carried my burden into the kitchen. "I can't imagine how hard it must be to leave your family behind."

Pearl followed me. "You do what you have to do. After her husband and son were killed, home wasn't safe."

"And her parents?" I unpacked the contents of my bag.

Pearl shrugged, leaning on her walker. "They won't leave. She has a brother in Yemen and one with asylum status in the Netherlands. We live a blessed life, Gillian, we really do."

I nodded, lifting the plastic containers as I opened the refrigerator. "This is gazpacho soup and a bean salad for your lunch." I glanced at her sheepishly. "There might be enough for a few lunches, but you can probably freeze the soup."

Pearl surveyed the zucchini bread, yeast bread, and cookies covering the counter. She sat heavily at the kitchen table. "What's wrong? Is it Jack?"

"I'm fine," I lied. "I just couldn't sleep, probably excited because John's coming home tomorrow." I sat across from her. "Don't worry, everything is great."

Pearl watched me for a long moment. Then she patted my hand. "You're a good girl. No matter what, you'll always be my good girl." Then she straightened and said, with forced cheerfulness, "So, a cup of tea? How about a game of scrabble?"

I smiled at her, blinking back tears. "Both would be great." I jumped up to start the water as Pearl reached behind her to the shelf where she kept the deluxe wooden scrabble board Jack bought one Christmas. Preparing myself for my inevitable defeat, I cut thick slices of zucchini bread to serve with the tea.

❧ ❧ ❧

As I was leaving Pearl's, my cell phone rang. "Jack should be home around six," Mark told me.

"Thanks," I replied.

"You okay?"

"No," I said, climbing into my car. "But don't worry about it. You might want to come over tonight around," I thought for a minute, "how about around eight? There'll be some things the two of you will need to talk about."

"Anything I should know now?"

"Come tonight. It all depends on what he says."

"Let me know if I'm out of a job."

"I doubt it." I smiled. "My guess is that Jack will do anything to survive politically."

Mark chuckled. "If my job hinges on Jack's willingness to compromise, I'm safe."

❧ ❧ ❧

When Jack opened the front door I was ready. I'd changed into my Congressman's Wife clothes, in this case a navy blue linen pantsuit, and applied make-up. I still wasn't hungry, but had set the table with a light supper: salad, cheese, and homemade bread.

Seeing me standing in the hallway as he opened the door, Jack paused. "Gillian."

"Hello Jack." I inclined my head in what I hoped telegraphed condescending graciousness.

"I'm so glad you're here." He stepped forward, taking my hand. "I'm so sorry you thought, I'm so—" he looked at me, eyes filling. "I didn't let myself hope—"

"Come into the kitchen, Jack, I've made us supper." I pulled my hand away. "We need to talk."

"Can I make myself a drink first?" He moved toward the liquor cabinet.

"Of course," I answered. "But make it light, you need to pay attention to everything I say."

I sat at the table sipping ice tea as he entered, glass in hand. He'd loosened his tie and looked very much the Hollywood ideal of a dedicated politician. I've always suspected his good looks won him more votes than his politics. "Sit," I told him.

He did.

"Gillian, honey—"

I held up my hand to stop him, knowing I couldn't let him talk or smile or touch me.

"It won't work, Jack. You can't charm me. I'm finished."

He started to protest, but I rushed on. "I'm not interested in your explanations." I paused, watching the color drain from his face. I could feel the betraying tendrils of pity beginning to unfurl and hardened my voice. "I'm also not interested in seeing our personal shit, your shit, on the front page. I'm not interested in having my family embarrassed. So I'm willing to save your pathetic reputation, but only on my terms. Are you ready to listen?" I could feel my face and chest hot and flushed. I was really doing it.

Jack stared at me. He fingered the fabric of his slacks. Finally he nodded. "Go ahead."

I leaned back in my chair. "First," I held up one finger, "no more speeches. I will attend one campaign function per week. You can choose the event. I will shake hands and smile and make small talk, but I will not speak, understood?"

Jack nodded, relaxing slightly.

"Second," I held up another finger, "I will continue to cook for the campaign, but," I paused, narrowing my eyes as I looked at him, "if Ashley or Katy or any other woman you've fucked comes into my kitchen ever again all bets are off, got it?"

Jack lurched forward in his chair and sputtered, "Gillian, I've never... how could you think I'd—"

"Cut the shit, do we have a deal?" I glared at him until he sat back and nodded, more wary. "Third, you will not touch me, ever again."

He opened his mouth to speak but closed it as I continued, "On Monday after John leaves I'm moving into the cabin. I'll stay in the house when the children are home and pretend we're a family, just like always. We'll pose together for photos, we'll make nice, we'll survive the election. After that," I shrugged, "who knows, but until November we'll make a pretty facade. Agreed?"

Jack drained his glass. "Do I have a choice?"

"You always have a choice, but I don't think you'll like the alternative."

He nodded and stood. "I'm going to get another drink. You want one?"

I shook my head. "No."

"Jesus, you can be a cold bitch sometimes." He walked out of the kitchen.

I picked up an arugula leaf and bit into it, savoring the bitter tang, then buttered a thick slice of fresh homemade rye.

Jack re-entered, his glass darker amber and sat opposite me. "How long have you been planning this?"

I took a bite of the bread and chewed before answering. "I suppose since I met Ashley, your pubescent nymph."

"Ashley? She's just a girl who works on my campaign," Jack said dismissively. "You're being irrationally jealous."

I shrugged. "Maybe. I suppose I could take her picture to the day clerk at the Starlight to be sure. But don't you think that would get people talking?"

Jack blanched. "Shit."

"Right," I answered, "my thoughts exactly. You should try this bread, it's good."

Jack picked at his salad. "I should call Mark," he finally said.

"I already did, he's coming over in about an hour."

He looked up at me, surprised, "Really?"

"Yes." I put down my fork. "Jack, I don't care what you do, I really don't. But," I paused until I was sure of his full attention, "you might want to keep it in your pants. All deals are off if I wake some morning to find your dirty laundry all over the papers."

Jack blanched, started to speak, stopped and simply nodded. He sat back in his chair and watched me in silence as I ate my dinner. He finished his drink. We were both relieved when Mark rang the doorbell.

I nodded to Mark as he entered the kitchen. "Hi, make yourself at home, there's more salad in the bowl if you'd like. I'll clean up later." I turned to Jack. "Excuse me, I have work to do," and I exited out the patio door, down the steps and through the grass to the cabin. I closed the door behind me and collapsed onto the couch before I let out the first sob. The cabin air felt moist and hot, but I hugged myself close as I rocked back and forth, feeling it all crumble away.

❧ ❧ ❧

The sun streamed in the east window of the cabin. I sat up from the couch where I'd fallen asleep wrapped in an old cotton blanket the grandfathers brought back from Puerto Vallarta. My suit hung over the back of a chair. I looked around the studio. Dusty. I opened the windows and breathed deep the sweet smell of wet grass.

I spotted my old running shoes, abandoned in a corner. It took some rummaging in my paint-clothes bin until I found a pair of shorts (slightly too small) and a T shirt (way too big). I changed in to them, tied back my hair and, carrying my shoes, left the cabin and walked quietly up the steps and into my kitchen.

Impossible to tell if Jack was home but his glass from the night before sat in the sink. I moved it to the dishwasher and crept downstairs to the laundry room where I found a clean pair of socks. Out on the front stoop, in the warmth of the early morning sun, I pulled on my socks and shoes. When had I last run? At least a couple of years.

To my right, with houses scattered at discreet distances, the road wound down into town. In the other direction it climbed steeply to a cliff above the lake, and then undulated for miles along the shore, a harder path but with fewer houses and a better view. I started by walking briskly uphill. Once atop the hill, I tried jogging a few steps. Each step thudded heavily, but I kept going until my lungs hurt then walked for a few minutes until the gasping stopped. Intervals—wasn't that what I'd read?—were better than our old, run until you drop training method? I looked at my watch. Run for five minutes, walk one, run five, walk one, starting… now. I jogged. Had I always clomped so with each step? I checked my watch, forty-five seconds. Make that run for one minute, walk for one. If I make it to the Dillerman's mailbox, that's half a mile, round trip one mile. Good enough for a first day.

As I topped the crest of the hill on my way back, I remembered what I used to love about a morning run. My lungs hurt and I felt ominous twinges in my left calf, but the view from the top was worth it. Lacland, with my neighborhood, downtown, the lake, even the Pinetown Mall, spread beneath me. On Edward's front step I saw Sam stooping for the paper. He looked up. I waved and ran down the hill, allowing gravity to take me, just hoping that my feet stayed beneath me all the way. Somehow I made it and stopped in front of him.

"Morning," I panted.

Sam smiled broadly at me. "Morning." Then he ordered, "Stretch."

I smiled and obediently stepped into a runner's lunge. Sam, hitching the thighs of his jeans to give himself room, dropped beside me. "Here," he coached, "if you move your back foot you'll get a better calf stretch and let your groin muscles open at the same time." He bounced out of the stretch and crouched before me, pulling on my front foot. "Don't let your knee extend over your ankle."

I looked down at him. "So you're a personal trainer in your spare time?"

He smiled sheepishly. "I'm kind of addicted to marathons so I'm careful about injury. Now switch sides." After adjusting my stance again, he cocked his head. "When was the last time you ran?"

"I don't know." I sank into the pain of the stretch he'd maneuvered me into. "A couple years, maybe longer."

"Well, start slow," he cautioned. "No use damaging yourself. Hey, maybe you want to invite me over for some of your great coffee and we'll talk about it."

I laughed. "You're on." Then I stopped. "I don't know if Jack is—"

Sam smiled gently. "He drove off a few minutes ago."

"Great." I straightened, groaning slightly. "I guess I overdid it."

Sam laughed. "You'll be stiff tomorrow morning, I think."

I nodded. "Probably, now how about some coffee?"

Carrying coffee and a slice of toast to the kitchen table, I saw Jack's note.

> *My dearest Gillian,*
> *Last night was so painful for me I cannot tell you. I cannot imagine what I have done to lose your trust. I will always love you and I pray that we can work through this terrible time.*
> *Yours always, Jack*

I handed Sam the note and sat heavily. Suddenly my beautiful thick slice of toast, slathered with homemade raspberry jam looked vaguely distasteful. I leaned back in my chair and sipped my coffee, watching Sam peruse the note.

"So you confronted him."

"Yeah, I did," I whispered.

"How'd he take it?" Sam sat across from me.

I shrugged. "Never admit anything, even if they have pictures." I set down my coffee cup. "It was civil. We were civil. He agreed to my terms."

"Divorce terms?"

"No, too public. I mean lie to the media and his constituents terms." I closed my eyes. "It's going to be a long couple of months until the election."

"Do you have to participate?" He bit into his toast.

I shook my head. "I don't have to do anything. But I'll keep up appearances through November before I make any decisions." I paused and looked at him. "I'm going to miss you guys. I'm getting used to our coffee routine."

Sam smiled. "Me too. So you'll just have to come to Amsterdam. I hear they have coffee there too."

I looked at him, startled. "There's a thought," I said, and changed the subject by asking his advice about running.

As he was leaving, I said, "John's coming home this afternoon. I hope you get to meet him."

"I'd love to." He smiled. "Do you want to come to Shabbat dinner? I'm afraid the food won't be up to par, but we'll try to make up for it with the company."

"I haven't been to a Sabbath dinner since Grandpa Rosenberg died."

"Think about it." Sam waved and then he was gone.

⁂ ⁂ ⁂

Mark called around nine, as I finished dressing.

"Hi, um, Jack wanted me to call about scheduling." He sounded embarrassed.

"Figures. Let me get a pen." I ran downstairs, found a pen and turned over Jack's note so I could write on the back. "Okay, shoot."

He cleared his throat. "John is supposed to come home this afternoon, right?"

"Yes, I think so." I drummed the pen on the table.

"We have a meeting at seven tonight, so Jack thought he'd stop home for a drink and a short visit with John before that, say around six."

"That should minimize our time together." I drew squiggles along one side of the paper.

He cleared his throat again. "So, he has a busy morning tomorrow but hoped that you and John could meet him for a rally at the Pines Bar and Grill after lunch, around one. The rally starts at two. Um, maybe you could bring some appetizers?"

"I can do that." I wrote "appetizers" on the paper, and "one—Pines."

"Great." Mark sounded relieved. "The rally should last a couple hours. Then Jack was hoping that John would join us for a trip to the eastern side of the district. We'll probably have to spend the night over there and come back Sunday afternoon."

I laughed. "So this is Jack's creative way of splitting custody of our grown son? I wonder what he'd do if we lived in a more urban district and he had to come home every night. So I get Friday and Saturday morning, he gets Saturday night and Sunday morning. He really is the great compromiser. Hmmm, a person could take that a couple ways, couldn't they? Compromiser of the compromised."

Mark asked gently, "Are you okay, Gillian?"

"Sure." I wrote "OK" in big block letters. "Tell Jack that's all fine with me and we'll expect him at six."

Mark cleared his throat again. "Um, the Journal wants an interview with you, standard wife of the candidate stuff."

"No. No interviews. Not unless you want me to tell the truth."

"Right. I'll put them off. Can I do anything for you, Gillian?"

I shook my head even though I knew he couldn't see me. "Just keep me out of it as much as you can." I hung up the phone and frowned at my paper, covered with spiky doodles. Whatever, I thought, just whatever. I made an appointment to have my hair and nails done, might as well do the role right. Then I started on the appetizer list.

Over lunch I told Sam and Edward everything.

"Are you going to talk with John about all this?" asked Edward.

"No." I dished out pasta with Italian sausage, kale and tomato sauce.

"He's not stupid, Gillian." Edward took his plate.

"I know." I handed a plate to Sam. "He'll know something is wrong, but it won't be the first time. It isn't like he thinks his parents have a fairytale marriage."

"How's he doing?" Edward forked his pasta.

"You can see for yourself. Sam invited us to dinner."

Sam blushed. "I forgot to tell you."

Edward beamed. "That's great. Are you bringing food, too?"

I laughed. "I've already started the brisket and the challah dough is rising." I pointed toward my bread bowl on the counter.

Sam stammered, "I didn't mean you had to—"

"Yes she does," Edward interrupted him. "You haven't tasted her brisket, or her challah. When did you ask her to dinner?"

"This morning while you were sleeping. Oh, speaking of that," Sam pulled a folded sheet from his pocket. "I picked this up at school and thought you might be interested. It's a 5k run at the beginning of October." He handed me the flier.

"You're running again?" Edward raised his eyebrows.

"I don't know if I'm running again, I ran, sort of, this morning." I unfolded the flier. "Thanks Sam, this is sweet of you. I don't think I could—"

"Sure you could." Edward exclaimed. "You used to run half marathons all the time. October is ages from now. I tell you what, starting tomorrow morning I'll run with you every day until we leave, that's," he paused to think, "thirteen times. Mom said I needed more exercise. You can't be more out of shape than I am, so we'll be great partners. That way I'll arrive in Amsterdam looking gorgeous and you'll be on your way to 5k."

I laughed. "It's a deal. But you have to get up in the morning. I won't wait until nine to run, it just gets too hot."

Edward grimaced. "Okay, okay. I'll set an alarm."

Just then a squirrel ran up a tree outside the kitchen window and Daphnia erupted, running to the patio door, jumping, barking and whining. The squirrel, apparently noting that Daphnia couldn't escape the kitchen, perched on a branch and chattered down at the dog.

"Poor Daph," Sam said. "He goes on Monday to get a certificate of health from the vet along with bunches of shots. He also gets weighed and he'd better be less than fifteen pounds so he can travel in the airplane with us. Otherwise, it's a long haul in baggage."

"He gets to go with you? Won't he have to stay in quarantine?" I asked.

"Evidently not." Sam wrestled his dog back from the window. "Although it might teach him better manners."

"I doubt it." Edward leaned over to scratch Daphnia's ears. "Behaved isn't in little Daph's nature. He's a rebel, like me, right, boy?"

I rolled my eyes at Sam.

He smiled. "Yes, honey." He patted Edward's head.

⁂

John arrived in early afternoon to find me in the kitchen braiding the challah. "Hi Mom."

I wiped my hands and embraced him. "You're here early. That's wonderful."

"I drove like a madman." He laughed. "Terrified I wouldn't get here in time to swim. It's been incredibly hot down south. All I've dreamed about is the lake."

"Go." I released him. "Get in the water now. I was hoping I could take you to your grandmother's in an hour or so? I have some errands to run, but she'd love to see you."

"Sure," he said, already peeling off his shirt. "Call me when it's time to go." With that, he flew out the door. I watched him run down the steps, across the dock and leap into the water. It was only as I saw him dive that I registered he must have driven the entire trip in his swimsuit.

An hour later I parked outside of Momma Pearl's and watched John saunter up the walk. I waived to Aziza as she opened the door, waited long enough to hear Momma Pearl's squeal of joy and drove off to my Congressman's Wife beauty appointments.

That night Jack was only ten minutes late getting home. He gave John a big smile and a hearty clap on the back. "Good to see you, son. Thanks for coming up to help."

John smiled. "Sorry I can't do more, Dad."

"Drink, son?" Jack asked, going to the bar.

"Maybe I'll grab a beer." John headed to the kitchen, leaving Jack and me alone for a moment. Jack concentrated on pouring himself a drink. I watched, wondering if he'd speak before John reentered the room. He didn't.

Later, after Jack left, John asked, "Is something wrong?"

"We're fine. You know how elections are." I gathered food to take to Edward's.

John accepted the challah I handed him. "Yeah, I guess."

We carried our dinner into the street, stepping out into a warm-winded cricket symphony. John walked ahead, tall and thin in the streetlight.

Edward opened the door. "John." he roared, enveloping him, while Daphnia pawed their legs.

"Hey, Uncle Edward."

Still holding John in a half embrace, Edward pulled me into the house, kissing my cheek. Sam stood a few feet back, surveying the scene awkwardly. John squatted to pet Daphnia.

"Who's this?" he asked.

"His name is Daphnia, after some sort of crustacean. And this is his owner, Sam." Edward pulled John forward. "Sam, this is John. John's an aspiring professor, too, so you'll have lots to talk about."

Sam stepped forward and shook John's hand. "Really, what's your field?"

"History." John smiled. "But I'm not sure about the whole academia thing."

"You still have plenty of time to decide," I said, handing Edward the brisket. I turned to Sam. "John just finished his preliminary examinations and is working on his dissertation."

John shrugged as if embarrassed. "Working isn't exactly the right term. I've only spent a few hours in the library this summer. I've a summer graduate assistantship and mostly I've been digitizing old photos and records in the basement of the Historical Museum."

"That explains your pale demeanor," Edward called from the kitchen. "You'll need to bask in the sun all weekend, get a vitamin D fix."

John laughed. "I'm afraid I'll have to get my D on the run. Dad has me knocking on doors all around the district."

"It should be nice weather for canvassing." I avoided Sam's eyes. "I used to love the walking, it's just talking to people that I hate."

John shrugged. "I can't remember an election year when I didn't go door-to-door. It wouldn't feel like summer to me."

Edward emerged from the kitchen and waved us through to the screened porch. They'd brought the old oak table from the dining room and set four places, positioned so they all faced the lake. Each place was set with the bright hand painted placemats John, Aurora and I had made for Edward twenty years before. I'd sewn midnight blue batik fabric rectangles and let the children finger paint them with yellow, red and white fabric paint. The effect was only occasionally nauseating. Edward had brought out the ancient good silver and etched crystal water glasses. Grandpa Rosenberg's candlesticks dominated the table.

Sam took the challah from me and set it on a silver platter, covering the bread with a large linen cloth. He placed Daphnia on a cushion in the corner and told him to sit. To my surprise he curled up on the pillow and did just that.

"The table is beautiful," I breathed.

"Wow," John grinned. "This is amazing."

"Do you remember Shabbat with the grandfathers?" I asked him. "You were so little when they died."

John shook his head. "I think I remember sticking my fingers deep into the challah one night and getting scolded, well, sort of scolded." He smiled. "But maybe I've only heard the story."

Edward, his arm around Sam, smiled fondly at John. "I wasn't around much in those days, but when I was, it was clear those guys doted on you kids. You'd burp and they'd clap with joy. Now," he clapped his own hands, "what can I get you to drink? We have ice tea, milk, juice and some sparkly soda things. Or you could come into the kitchen and choose for yourself."

The setting sun touched the horizon as Sam bade us sit, lit the candles and covered his eyes. He sang in a beautiful, low tenor:

"Barukh atah Adonai Eloheinu, melekh ha'olam, asher kid'shanu b'mitzvotav v'tzivanu l'hadlik ner shel Shabbat." He translated. "Blessed are you, oh God, ruler of everything, who sanctifies us with your laws and commands us to light the Sabbath candles."

"You sing beautifully," I told him.

"He studied to be a Cantor," Edward said, proudly.

Sam shrugged. "That was a long time ago."

"What's a Cantor?" John asked.

Edward explained, "Sort of a singing Rabbi without the secret Rabbi powers."

Sam laughed. "Close enough. And since I'm the closest thing we have to a Rabbi, I'll lead us through the blessings. We don't have wine, so let us raise our glasses of fizzy beverage or whatever. Just smile and nod if you don't know the words." He and Edward sang the blessings for the wine and for the bread. I mumbled along with what I half remembered, and John simply watched. Sam broke off a chunk of challah and passed along the rest. When we all had a piece he declared, "L'Chaim." and bit into the bread. "That is good." He nodded in my direction.

"Thank you. It's an old family recipe," I told him. "You know, I learned to cook here. Some of my earliest memories are of sitting on a stool helping Grandpa Rosenberg braid challah."

"Grandpa cooked? What about Mrs. Myrna?" Edward asked.

"He loved to make challah every Friday, but you're right. I learned to cook from Mrs. Myrna. She was amazing. Mrs. Myrna was our housekeeper," I explained to Sam. "She lived downtown and came out every weekday. I suppose I asked her to teach me to cook so we'd have something to eat on weekends."

"She was a mountain of a woman who slapped your hand hard if you stole a cookie, but she doted on Gillian. In Mrs. Myrna's eyes, Gillian was a model child. Me, on the other hand—" Edward lifted the tray of brisket in front of him and breathed in deeply. "Gillian, we need to invite you to dinner more often."

"You are such a flatterer," I told him. "Which is why Mrs. Myrna baked all afternoon when she knew you were coming down. You know, the thing that used to fascinate me as a child was thinking about Mrs. Myrna at home with her own family. I'd get jealous, possessive, mean spirited I guess."

Sam said, "So the reason I can't cook is we didn't have a housekeeper? Maybe we should take cooking lessons from Gillian so we're not always begging her for food."

Edward shook his head. "Not me, I tried, don't have the patience." Then he brightened. "But do feel free."

"Maybe when we get back." Sam laughed.

"Are you going somewhere?" John looked from one to the other.

"Amsterdam," they said together.

Sam continued, "I'm on sabbatical next year and Edward is coming along to photograph tulips or something."

"A year in Amsterdam." John sounded wistful.

Sam considered him. "In pondering an academic career, while you're thinking about the scarcity of jobs, the long hours, low pay and high stress, don't forget sabbaticals. Taking a year off to do research every seven or so is an amazing privilege."

"Does it make up for the rest?" John asked.

"Right now it feels like it," Sam answered. "Ask me again when I'm in the middle of next year, knee deep in all the crap I avoided while I was away, and the next sabbatical feels almost mythical."

"This salad looks gorgeous." I took the bowl Edward handed me. "When I told you to take whatever you wanted from the garden, I had no idea you'd be so inventive. Is that purslane?"

"They eat it in Asia," Edward explained, "and I thought we could weed while we foraged."

I took a bite of the tiny leaf. "Hmm, not great, a little sour, but interesting."

"Try it with dressing," John suggested. "It's good. I like the dandelion flowers, the yellow is a nice contrast."

Sam smiled. "We assumed the salad would be mostly decorative." He popped a piece of roasted carrot into his mouth. "This is delicious, Gillian. My mother used to cook potatoes and carrots with her brisket, but somehow they always turned out mushy and overdone."

"The secret is in the—" I stopped and shook my head. "When you get back I'll show you."

We ate in silence, watching the sunset. Fireflies emerged, their tiny lights blinking on and off like Schrödinger's cat.

Finally, John broke the silence, a sweep of his hand encompassing the table. "So, do you believe in all this?"

"In dinner?" Edward asked.

"In God," John countered.

"It's complicated," answered Sam at the same time that Edward said, "Sort of" and I declared, "yes."

John laughed. "Well that's quite the consensus." He turned to Sam. "You just sang a beautiful prayer, you studied to be a cantor and you're a scientist, right? So, do you believe?"

Sam laid down his fork and looked thoughtfully at John. "Like I said, it's complicated. You're right. I am a biologist. I teach freshmen about the non-magical beginnings of life, about evolution through natural selection, about all the ways that life goes on without Divine assistance." He took a sip of juice. "But I'm also a practicing Jew. The two realms seem completely separate to me. Religion teaches us not to follow our own selfish, biological imperative, but to seek justice and good. For me it isn't about belief, it's about a code of behavior." He smiled apologetically. "You shouldn't ask academics complicated questions, we're trained to speak for fifty minutes nonstop, and to expect you've taken notes."

John nodded. "I get the part about religion keeping us from acting badly. But do you need God for that?"

I spoke up. "I don't know. Believing in God doesn't make you good. I've seen lots of good church goers who steal and covet and commit adultery. It seems to me that believing in God is just good for your soul. I don't care if there is a literal God, but life seems more barren without one. And," I shrugged, "since we can't know the answer, we get to pick. I pick faith because it makes my life feel better."

Edward nodded. "When I first started with A. A., I had the hardest time with the whole God thing. I fought it until someone told me I didn't need to believe in God, I just had to believe that there was a power higher than me, that I wasn't in complete control of the universe." He laughed. "It took me a while to see that I wasn't the absolute center of everything."

"Sometimes you still forget," I teased.

"Guilty." Edward nodded. "I don't know if I believe in God, but I do believe in prayer. I was a real mess. It wasn't until I prayed to have my addictions lifted that I was able to get on with my life. It worked and keeps working. So I have to believe at least in that."

"Do you miss it, Uncle Edward?" John asked. "Drinking, partying?"

Edward looked at him wide eyed. "God, no. I'd rather be tortured by fire breathing midgets than go back to puking and blackouts."

"Fire breathing midgets?" Sam asked, eyebrows raised.

"Childhood fantasy," Edward explained, taking a bite of brisket.

"So, how about you John?" I asked. "God?"

He shook his head. "I just can't. I can't see the world in terms of good or bad. I see people scrambling for money, sex, power. Right now in several parts of the world people are killing each other over all those things, not to mention nationalism or race or religion or any of the other constructs we use to divide ourselves. Where's God in all of that? And of course, as a kid I had the shining example of my dad in church every Sunday, chasing tail the rest of the week." He looked at me. "I know we're not supposed to talk about that stuff, but it really burns me."

I touched his arm. "I know it was hard on you."

"On me? What about you?" he asked.

I shrugged and stared at my plate.

None of us spoke for a few moments. John continued with a slight smile, "Guess I've spent too much time in the library and not enough with people lately. Shall I change the subject now?"

Sam smiled. "This was a perfect Shabbat table discussion. And, in good ecumenical fashion, it looks like we have a nice range of beliefs represented. Too bad we couldn't find a religious fundamentalist to round out the slate."

Edward chuckled. "Don't hold your breath." He turned to John. "It was a good topic, but it looks like your mother would like a directional change. So why don't you tell us about your research? I'm hoping I'll find it more accessible than Sam's, and better dinner conversation. I assume you're not looking at the genitals of bugs for example, or grinding things up to look at their genes?"

Sam made a face at Edward and John laughed. "Not looking at any genitals unfortunately, nor am I looking at or in anyone's jeans. Oh, sorry, Mom."

"You're old enough that I assume you have but—" I held up my hand as he started to speak. "I don't want to know the details until you're bringing someone home to dinner and even then I don't want to know."

John laughed again. "Fair enough. My dissertation is on the history of radical labor unions, in particular I'm interested in the interaction of Socialism and Anarchism in the Wobblies in Northern Idaho and Montana around the turn of the century."

I watched him grow more and more animated as he told the story of violent uprisings in silver mines and equally violent management reprisals. He seemed so grown up. And that night, his face lit by the candles and his own enthusiasm, I thought that maybe he'd turned out relatively unscathed by his parent's mistakes.

On the walk home I asked, "Have you heard from your sister?"

He stiffened slightly. "Yeah, I drove over for a weekend about a month ago and we email." He paused then continued, "She wants me to come for Thanksgiving with Pete and the girls." He stopped and put his hand on my arm. "I'm sorry, Mom, I know you're not invited. She just can't get past it all, so she goes out of her way to punish you guys."

I patted his hand. "She's not trying to hurt me. She's lashing out at your father, she's never forgiven him, may not ever forgive him, not after that last time at Kaitlin's christening. But, don't worry, she and I talk. I get down there sometimes. It's all right. I think it is lovely you're still close. You should go. Really. I don't know what we're doing for Thanksgiving, but we'll cope and it would make me happy to think of my children together."

He put an arm around me. My head hit just below his armpit. "You're sweet, Mom."

"Look at the moon." I stopped midway between the two houses and pointed. "A waning moon is an unlucky time for love."

"Isn't that half the month?" John chuckled. "Pretty cynical view if you ask me."

"Right." I checked my watch. "It's almost ten. We should get to sleep. I have food to prepare tomorrow morning."

"I'll help." John glanced at the empty drive. "Hey, shouldn't Dad be home by now?"

"I expect he's working late tonight so you can get out on the road tomorrow right after the rally."

"Sure." John looked closely at me. "That makes sense." But he didn't sound convinced.

It was close to one when Jack quietly crawled into bed. He didn't roll toward me. Carrots, celery, tomatoes, green beans and dip (sour cream, yogurt, pureed red peppers, garlic and dill) and there were tamales and dolmades in the freezer. Eventually I fell back asleep.

❧ ❧ ❧

I probably should have been able to do it alone. God knows it wasn't my first awkward public event. But I wanted support so, along with John, I showed up at Jack's rally with Edward, Sam and Maggie. We arrived just before one, loaded down with trays of food. Marty Donovan, owner of the Pines, met us at the door. I hadn't seen Marty since the last campaign, although I'd sent a condolence note when his wife, Martha, died of ovarian cancer in January. Marty, Martha and I all went to high school together back when the world was young.

"Hey Marty." I gave the big man a hug.

"Gillian, how are you? Still looking good, I see."

"Flatterer." I gestured to John. "You remember my son, John."

"Sure I do. How are you? Still working on that doctorate?" Marty shook John's hand vigorously.

John smiled. "Still working."

"Your dad sure brags about that." Marty clapped John on the back.

"He does?"

"Of course he does. Nearly all the time." Marty looked at John in astonishment. "You gotta know how proud he is."

"Thank you," John replied. "That's good to know."

Marty showed us into the banquet area behind the pub proper. Mark and his crew of college interns were setting up chairs and checking the PA system. He waved to us and pointed toward a long table, covered in white crepe paper and decorated with red and blue bunting, set along the back wall. Jack Sach for Congress signs decorated the walls. The five of us immediately started setting out food, napkins and plastic cutlery. John scattered lavender sprigs and cut flowers between the trays, giving the table a festive look.

People began arriving around one-thirty, entering in small, chatty groups. Some were party faithful, people I'd known for years, including the state senator and the assemblywoman from this district, along with the mayor and even a couple candidates for the school board. Others I didn't recognize, many of these looked nervous and out of place, newcomers to political schmoozing. John turned on the Sach smile and worked the crowd like a professional. I did my best to make people comfortable.

It was after two when Jack finally arrived. He always staged his entrances for the best effect and this was no exception. He strode into the room, followed by a gaggle of aids, including Ashley, making excuses about the traffic, shaking hands, patting shoulders and kissing cheeks, that amazing, enchanting smile lighting up the room.

After half an hour of this, the local party chair walked to the podium. "Good afternoon." she called and a number of people yelled back, "Good afternoon."

She began with the usual litany, "I'd like to thank you all for your efforts… Too many to mention by name, but I'd especially like to thank… this is an extraordinary year… A few more months…"

My mind wandered. From the back of the room I surveyed the crowd. Jack stood to one side, watching and nodding, his arms folded across his chest, legs slightly spread, master of the house. Mark sat in the last row, scribbling notes, glancing up from time to time, occasionally checking his watch. And of course, there was me, surrounded by friends, trying to disappear into the back wall.

And John. John stood in the far corner smiling down at someone. He's the best of the two of us, I thought. He's braver than me, kinder than Jack. Good looking, with my coloring and build and his father's height and eyes. He looked hip and charming talking with… I stopped. Edward saw it too and leaned into me, whispering, "I don't think Evelyn needs to worry about his sexuality."

"But I do," I whispered back. Edward followed my gaze to Jack, who was also watching John, his face rigid.

"Oh shit." Edward looked back at John and his companion. "Is that?"

"Yes, sir," I answered. "That's Ashley."

Edward suppressed a giggle. "They seem to be getting on well."

They did indeed. Ashley looked up at John, her dark eyes wide, a smile playing across her face. John gazed down at her, his charm turned way up. They whispered softly, completely oblivious to their surroundings.

I glanced over at Jack and caught his eye. He blinked, smiled tightly and turned toward the speaker, who was introducing a school board candidate. We all clapped politely, Jack, Maggie, Sam, Edward and I, and after a pause, as it came to their attention, Ashley and John.

PART TWO

Tang of Life Tomato Sauce

Home canned tomato sauce is wonderful to have on hand. Mine is simple. For every twenty tomatoes I use two onions (or one, if it's big), a clove or twenty of garlic (sliced lengthwise), and a bunch of cilantro. I sauté first the onions, then the garlic in olive oil (don't skimp on the olive oil, it's good for you). After the onions and garlic brown, I add the tomatoes (quartered but not peeled). I let that simmer for maybe twenty minutes, stirring often, until the tomatoes cook down. At the end I add the cilantro and pour the sauce into sterilized pint jars. I usually process these in a pressure cooker for twenty minutes, but you should check with your local extension agent about processing times. It's different from place to place and, while this is a very good sauce, it isn't to really die for.

Seven

"I can't believe you talked me into this," Maggie panted.

"Come on, we're half-way there." I slowed, giving her time to catch up, feeling guilty that I'd roped her into this at almost the last minute after I'd been training for a month.

"I feel like an idiot with Jack Sach plastered all over my chest."

I smiled at her. "Yeah, but it was great to have the campaign pay your entrance fee, wasn't it?"

"Is that strictly kosher?" Maggie breathed raggedly.

"I think so. I'm not really up on all that, but Jack thought it was a good idea."

"Hi, Dr. Mazzoni." yelled a petite blond woman as she streaked past.

"Hey, Jennifer," Maggie called to her back. Under her breath she said, "She's doing the ten K. This is fairly humiliating."

"We said our goal was to finish, not win," I consoled her. "And we are going to finish." I could feel the sweat trickling down my back but didn't mention it.

"I'm so out of shape." Maggie wailed. "Can we walk for a while? I'm hurting here."

"How about we run slowly?" I suggested, easing up on the pace considerably. "That way we can say we ran the whole way even if we come in sometime tonight."

"I can do this," Maggie conceded.

"This street is pretty, don't you think?" I asked, trying to get Maggie's mind off her pains. It really was quite nice, an old residential lane lined with huge oak trees. The light shone golden through the turning leaves. We jogged in silence.

Maggie finally asked, "It's Sam's fault we're here, isn't it?"

I grunted my assent.

"Have you heard from them? I've been so busy I haven't even emailed."

"It sounds like Sam's doing great. He loves the lab he's in, loves the city. They've even taken some touristy trips on weekends. Edward, on the other hand," I spread my hands, "he's having a harder time adjusting. I think he's lonely."

"Edward lonely? I can't imagine that. We can speed up now," she added as a woman who looked about seventy passed us with a wave.

"He's used to being surrounded by people and now he doesn't know anyone," I explained. "He emails me at least once and often twice a day. But it sounds like it might get better soon. Yesterday he emailed that he finally mustered the courage to contact Luke Vanderwerken, you know, the sculptor? I guess they hit it off and Vanderwerken is going to take him to some AA meetings and an artists group of some kind." I waved to a woman standing by the side of the road who appeared to be cheering me energetically. She looked vaguely familiar. I realized I'd seen her at party functions and that she was cheering for Jack's face bouncing up and down on my chest.

"Uh oh." Maggie was panting again. "I don't like the sound of 'hit it off.'"

"Not to worry." I tried to be subtle about slowing our pace. "I'm assured he's straight. Besides, Edward's seriously in love."

"Good." Maggie said emphatically, "I was afraid Sam would never find someone here, I couldn't stand it if they broke up."

"I thought you were a big proponent of the single life. Haven't you told me over and over again that I don't need a man to be happy?"

"You don't need a man to be happy. And I know you'd be better off alone than married to him." She nodded toward my T shirt. "But you're also not a gay man in a department of straight academics. I know from personal experience how hard it is to be the only single woman in the department. I figured Sam had to feel isolated."

"I don't think I'm the single type," I said. "I know, I know, how will I know if I don't try it? Hey look, I can see the finish line. Five k medal, here we come."

"Oh shit," Maggie said.

"What?"

She nodded at the figure ahead of us, the one we were about to overtake. "I'm pretty sure that's the dean. It might be politically wise if I didn't pass her. You go ahead. I'll walk the rest of the way."

I laughed. "I'll wait for you on the other side." I sprinted away, amazed I still had enough energy to push.

With a wave I passed the dean, a good party woman, who smiled at me. "Good for you Gillian."

I gave it everything I had to finish the last few yards and smack my foot hard on the rubber timing strip. The clock read thirty-nine minutes and fifty-eight seconds, hardly a world's record, but I'd finished my first race in years and felt great. I didn't even mind the requisite round of hand shaking and schmoozing ("Way to go, Mrs. Sach." "We're with him all the way." "Give our best to the Congressman."). Maggie and the dean chatted their way across the finish line, Maggie trailing little behind.

When she finally reached me, I asked, "You want to get out of here and get some coffee?"

She shook her head. "I can't. I have a lecture to write for Monday, a paper I'm supposed to get to my coauthors early next week and Karen, my marvelous grad student, just handed me a draft of her thesis chapter. I'm delighted to have it, but her timing could have been better. Still, I should get it back to her as quickly as I can. So, if I'm going to can tomato sauce tomorrow afternoon, I'd better get to work today."

"You don't have to come over tomorrow." Instant guilt washed over me for taking her time.

Maggie waved dismissively. "Are you kidding? Please, I'm counting on those tomatoes to save my sanity." She gave me a quick hug and turned to go. "Ah," she said, limping slightly, "ibuprofen, here I come."

I laughed and walked through the parking lot to my own car, getting clean and fed first on my list. I checked my watch, only nine. The day stretched before me.

On my way through the kitchen, I made a pot of coffee and a fried egg sandwich to carry down the hill. My little cabin felt warm and welcoming. I filled the old claw-foot tub with steaming water and dumped in half a box of bath salt. Setting my sandwich and coffee on the closed toilet lid, I stepped in and slowly lowered myself into the heat. I stretched my hamstrings, allowing the warm water to coax their release.

I retrieved my sandwich and lay back in the tub, balancing the plate on my chest. I let the smell of toast and egg waft over me. Then I brought the food to my mouth and took a giant bite, piercing the egg and letting the yoke roll down my chin. I smiled as I chewed. Even in the crappiest times of your life, some moments are just inherently good.

Refreshing the hot water several times, I lingered over coffee in the tub. A long list of tasks awaited me and I didn't want to get on with it, didn't want to step out of my warm cocoon and back into my life. What would I do today if I were free? Paint, read, paddle my kayak through the channel to Bear Lake. Get over yourself, how hard can your life be? I scolded myself. Most people actually work for a living. A promise is a promise and I promised to keep cooking, keep up the façade, even though he doesn't deserve it. Now why did I do that?

At least I hadn't had to sleep in the main house very often. John had been up three times to help with the campaign. Had he come up that often during the last couple campaigns? Maybe not. But, of course, he was through with class work. And didn't Maggie talk about wanting to procrastinate during her doctoral research? Maybe he was trying to get close to Jack again, weren't father-son relationships complicated and…? I grabbed a towel and pulled my pickled body out into the pleasant September morning air. This is a family built on avoiding hard questions, why stop now?

Maggie arrived in time to help carry in the two bushels of ripe tomatoes I'd harvested from the garden.

"What about all those green ones?" she asked.

"I checked the forecasts, we've got another week or so." I hoisted my bushel basket and waddled toward the house. I carried my basket into the pantry and directed Maggie to set hers in front of the kitchen sink.

She looked at the brimming basket. "Are we going to can all these tomatoes?"

"We'll start with these and see how it goes, but it should be fun." I laughed. "Don't worry, you can be excused after the first few batches. But I think you'll be happy with the tomato sauce come January."

Maggie sighed. "Okay, okay, how do we start?"

"To begin with, you wash, I'll chop. Then we can switch if you want. For the first batch we need about twenty tomatoes." I set my two largest cast iron pans on the stovetop and turned the burners on low. I flipped the back burner to high while I was at it to start heating the water in the pressure cooker I'd filled earlier in the day.

"Don't we dip these in hot water and get the skins off or something? Seems like my mother was always dipping and peeling." Maggie ran water into the sink and bent to scoop a handful of tomatoes from the basket.

"Yeah, I used to do that. But I got lazy one day and found that leaving the skins on made a better tasting sauce." I smiled at her. "See, sloth can pay off."

She shook her head. "I can't put you and sloth in the same sentence, but I'm just as glad not to scald my hands peeling tomatoes."

I took the first tomatoes she handed me and cut them in quarters. Once we'd chopped the tomatoes, I brought out the bowls of garlic and cilantro I'd prepared after breakfast, handed Maggie onions and pointed her toward the food processor. I poured olive oil into the pans, added the garlic and onions and let them sauté for a few minutes before scooping in the tomatoes.

I watched it simmer. "We're on our way. Let's start the next batch."

When we had the second batch cooking, a third batch of tomatoes and onions chopped, and the first batch secured in the pressure cooker with twenty minutes to go, we took a break. I set a timer to remind us, poured ice tea and led the way onto the patio. We flopped into the swinging chair and stretched out our legs.

One of those perfect fall days, warm but not hot. Along the shore, trees flamed with color. The dark green, glassy lake water reflected the orange, red and gold of the trees. A flock of migrating ducks paddled in the water by the boathouse. "The lake is so beautiful today," Maggie breathed, settling back into the cushions.

"Did I tell you I saw pelicans one day last week?" I tilted my face to the sun.

"Pelicans? Aren't they endangered?"

I shook my head. "That's the brown pelican, these were white. I think they're called American White pelicans and they're pretty common, just not around here."

"Hmm," said Maggie, sipping her tea. "Speaking of endangered, any news about John and what's her face, Ashley?"

I grimaced. "No news, but that isn't necessarily good news."

"Does he know? I mean have you told him?"

I shook my head. "I'm the one person who can't talk about it. I'm his mother. He's twenty-five years old. I have no right to tell him who he can and cannot date."

"But don't you think he should know about Ashley and his father?" Her mouth curled in distaste.

"Of course I think he should know," I snapped, "but I don't think I'm the person to tell him. I don't even know for sure that Ashley's the one. And anyway, don't you think she should be the one to tell him? Or Jack?"

Maggie shook her head. "Maybe. But I think you're playing with fire. I'd be nauseated to think that I'd been sleeping with the same person as—" She shuddered. "It's just icky, don't you think?"

I sighed. "Yes, I think it is icky. But I can't see what I can do about it, except hope that nothing's happening and what we saw was simply a flirtatious moment that didn't go anywhere."

"I hope so." She sounded skeptical.

"Speaking of going nowhere." I changed the subject. "Did I tell you about Pearl's matchmaking efforts?"

"Her what? Matchmaking who?"

"Evelyn and some guy that Aziza used to work for." I giggled.

Maggie looked at me wide-eyed.

"You know that every campaign Pearl hosts a fundraiser for Jack at the Pines?"

She nodded. "Doesn't she call it something corny like 'Mother knows best.'"

"That's the one," I agreed. "Anyway, this year she invited this guy, a widower named Mr. Greene, who she wanted to introduce to Evelyn."

"That's a set up for bad jokes like, it was Mr. Greene in the—" Maggie started.

"I know, I know," I cut her off. "I couldn't believe it, but the most amazing thing was that Pearl introduced them and they seemed to hit it off. Evelyn must have liked what she saw because you should have seen her. She turned it on and beamed at him. The poor man was toast. At the end of the night he kissed her hand goodbye."

"Oh my God," Maggie shook her head. "Poor guy."

I shrugged. "Pearl seems convinced they could live happily ever after. Who knows? There's no accounting—"

"You're right there." She sighed. "People make the damnedest choices."

"Like me," I murmured.

"You were young."

"For thirty years?" The buzzer went off. "Enough self-pity, back to the grindstone."

Maggie rose reluctantly and followed me into the kitchen. I looked over my shoulder at the lovely, calm lake. What the hell was I going to do?

৵ ৵ ৵

Sometime in the middle of the night I woke to rain pounding the cabin roof. I sat up. Rain streaked the windows, obscuring the view outside. I could barely see the trees swaying violently in the wind.

Suddenly the room lit up. A few moments later thunder rocked the cabin. Another lightening flash. I counted, "One, two, three," and thunder cracked again. Wrapping my blanket around me, I walked to the window to watch the storm roll through.

When I woke again it was light and my digital clock dark, power out. I looked out at the cloudy sky. The only thing it told me was that the day had dawned. I scrambled for my watch. "Shit." It was late and this was the only day of the week when it mattered. I rolled off the couch and into the bathroom, looked longingly at the tub, and settled for a quick sponge bath with a damp cloth. I brushed my teeth and worked my hair into a bun. The first pair of pantyhose I pulled on had a run, but I dug around until I found a flawless pair.

Clambering into the dark gray linen suit I'd hung on the bathroom door the night before, I tried to mentally reorganize my day. I was due at the fundraiser in an hour, but had promised Pearl I'd stop on my way. No power, no breakfast. Maybe Pearl would give me coffee if I begged, probably even if I didn't beg. I decorated myself with discrete gold hoops and a pearl necklace, slipped on the sensible-but-attractive pumps Jack bought me earlier in the summer, and ran out the door. Flying through the main house kitchen, I grabbed two jars of tomato sauce and jumped into the car before God remembered to scratch, as Grandpa Wolf used to say.

I let myself into Pearl's, calling, "Morning."

Pearl and Aziza, comfortably seated at the kitchen table working on a jigsaw, looked up startled as I whirled into the kitchen. "I can't stay long." I planted a kiss on each woman's cheek. "But I'd kill for a cup of coffee. Look, I brought tomato sauce in exchange."

"Of course, dear," Pearl said. Aziza started to get up. I waved her back down, slung the jars onto the counter and found a cup. I spoke quickly as I poured the coffee. "I woke late and I'm supposed to be at a rally in," I checked my watch, "oh, I have half an hour. I guess I can calm down, it's only a few minutes drive from here."

Pearl smiled. "Please, honey, sit down." She patted the chair beside her. "We're delighted to see you for however long you can come."

I sat down, shaking my head. "I'm sorry. I just got in such a flurry. I don't like even the idea of being late."

Pearl chuckled. "I know. It's lovely you're so responsible, even when you're doing things you hate."

I grimaced. "Does it show?"

Aziza laughed. "Even I know you don't like these political things. But you're a good wife." She patted my hand.

Pearl looked at me thoughtfully. "Aziza's right. You are a good wife. But is that always the best for you, I wonder? Does Jack appreciate you enough?"

"I'm fine," I said firmly. There were lots of uncertainties in my life, but of one thing I was sure, Jack was not a topic I wanted to discuss with his mother. "I got a note from Edward last night that you're considering a trip to Amsterdam this winter."

Pearl beamed. "Wouldn't that be lovely? Of course, I'm not sure it's possible. If Aziza could come with me, but—"

"You can't go, Aziza? Why not?" I asked.

"Last month the INS denied my application for asylum." Aziza looked down at her hands. "I am appealing. But I cannot leave the country just now."

"Oh my," I said. "Do you have a lawyer?"

"Yes." Aziza looked up. "She is very good, she helped my cousin. She is also very expensive. Pearl is helping, even though I told her not to."

Pearl fluttered her hand at Aziza. "Of course I'm helping. It's appalling."

"Why did they turn you down? Surely the fact that your husband and son—"

But Aziza shook her head. "I do not have the proper paperwork. You see," she smiled sadly, "I left rather suddenly."

"Nonsense," Pearl said sharply. "It's discrimination and I won't stand for it."

I'd never seen Pearl so passionate. "Perhaps Jack can." I stopped, realizing that Jack wouldn't risk the political fallout.

I saw Pearl thinking the same thing. She spoke briskly, "So I'll need to find someone else to travel with me to Europe." She looked at me and smiled slyly. "Amsterdam would be lovely in January, don't you think?"

"I doubt it." Then, suddenly understanding, "Oh, hmm, maybe, let me think about it." I looked down at my watch. "Oops, gotta run." I gave Pearl a quick hug and a kiss. Aziza walked me to the door.

"Are you all right?" I asked her.

She shrugged. "Al-Hamdulillah, it is in God's hands."

"I don't know what I can do to help, but if there's anything, please let me know." I squeezed her shoulder. She nodded and I sprinted to my car.

The fundraiser was held at the lavish home of one of Jack's most ardent supporters. I pulled up to the curb in time to see John stepping out of his car.

"John." I waved. "This is a surprise. Can you stay for long?"

He hugged me and smiled sheepishly. "Hi, Mom. I drove up to visit a friend over the weekend. I'll be heading back to school tonight."

"Oh," I said slowly. "Still, it's nice to see you."

John blushed. "Don't be mad. I would have come to see you before I left."

"That's all right," I said, distracted. Two middle-aged women, wearing prominently displayed Sach buttons, emerged from a blue sedan. I smiled, waved to them, and took John's arm. "Shall we go in?"

Mark met us at the door. He shook hands briefly with John then turned to me, clasping my hand in both of his. "Thanks so much for coming."

"A deal's a deal, Mark. Don't worry so much." I smiled and walked past him to greet our hostess.

"What was that about?" John whispered to me.

"Oh, you know Mark, he's such a fretter." I gave a dismissive wave. "Now put your game face on and go mingle." I gave his arm a squeeze and released him to the half-crowded room.

One of my many campaign liabilities is that I'm a terrible small talker. So over the years I've cultivated a reputation as a quiet, sweet, perhaps not very bright, but overall appropriate and pleasant wife. This allows me to shake hands and smile when required, and generally navigate through political gatherings with a few, usually poorly chosen, words. When I speak I often get blank stares or puzzled, polite smiles, so I keep quiet and try to stay busy with food or fliers or whatever else needs doing. My son, although he inherited much of my temperament, is more fluid in social gatherings. I attribute this to acclimation. John was four when his father first ran for office, his entire childhood defined by this passionate, intensely informed and sometimes artificial world. He melted into the crowd smoothly. I mumbled my way toward an aide to offer help.

From behind a stack of campaign literature on a table in the corner of the living room, I watched the crowd. Jack hadn't yet arrived, probably by design. John chatted with an old family friend, perhaps about his research but, given the atmosphere, maybe they discussed the "Issues." I heard fleeting fragments from the conversations around me, "teachers' unions," "pension funds," "seats in the State Legislature," but tuned out. As usual, Jack led in the polls and it all seemed a formality to me. But then I'd never really understood the process. How was it that much of my life revolved around something I found so uninteresting?

A flurry of activity at the door and Jack entered, aggressively cheerful and handsome, followed by a retinue of young staffers. I spotted Ashley, young and beautiful, in a clingy white sweater, short plaid skirt and tall, spike heeled boots. How did she have the time to be at a fundraiser in the middle of a weekday? Wasn't she supposed to be in school? I sounded like the matron I was. Who cared how she got here? Maybe she was taking the semester off. I looked at John. He, too, was watching Ashley, but with a soft, tender, proprietary gaze. I swore under my breath.

The aide standing next to me asked, "Excuse me?"

I blushed. "Sorry, I just remembered something I was supposed to do."

"Do you have to go?" he asked, concerned.

"No," I said, "it's too late now, but thanks."

Just then Jack swept up, reached his arm around my shoulders and kissed the top of my head. "Great crowd, eh?" he asked the aide.

"Yes, sir." The young man straightened visibly in the glow of Jack's attention.

"I should talk now, honey," he said, pulling away from me. "I'll see you later."

"Sure," I said, not quite up to the charade. "I have errands to run. I'll stay through your speech and then take off."

"Fine." Jack agreed, already distracted by his next well-wisher.

"Do you happen to have an aspirin or something?" I asked one of the interns trailing him.

"I think so, Mrs. Sach, you okay?" She dug into her purse.

"Just a headache. Thanks." I gave her what I hoped looked like a smile as she handed me two tablets. "You're a lifesaver."

"No problem." She beamed. "Hope you feel better." She turned to join the crowd.

"Me too," I said softly and wandered toward the kitchen to find some water.

When I re-emerged, the hostess was finishing a glowing introduction of Jack, the wonderful Congressman, our friend in Washington, the last great hope. He stood to hearty applause. Jack's a great speaker. He's engaging, articulate, even friendly. I've heard him hundreds of times, but I'm still amazed by his ability to connect with a crowd and hype them up to a rhetorical climax. He started with something self-deprecating that made them laugh, good naturedly kidded a few in the audience (the very influential or the very rich), then passed through his issues (check, check, check, check, done) and finished with a plea for their votes and their cash.

I cringed inside as I felt the last part coming, the one I always dreaded. Sometimes he didn't include his grand finale, but this time he did.

"And finally, I'd like to get my wife up here." All eyes turned to me.

I smiled and stepped out from behind the table.

"Come on up, honey. Let the people see you."

I walked toward him, willing a smile onto my face. Two more steps to Jack, then I turned to face the crowd, feeling my husband's arm slide around my shoulders like a snake.

And the big finish, "Elections are hard work, they take lots of people and lots of time but we will win this." Applause. "With your help, this Jack and Jill will top that hill." Scattered laughter, could there really be anyone who hadn't heard that before? Applause and finally, "Thank you Ladies and Gentlemen. Thank you for all your support." And done.

I gave Jack the requisite kiss on his cheek, shook a few more hands, found our hostess, thanked her profusely, and trotted toward the door. I grabbed John's arm and pulled him outside with me. He looked startled, but followed easily.

Once outside, I embraced him. "I didn't want to leave without saying goodbye," I said into his shoulder. "You're going straight back, aren't you."

"Pretty much." He squeezed me back.

"I love you," I said, a little gruffly. "Be safe." He looked at me quizzically. "Drive safely," I amended. "Call when you can."

With that I escaped into my car. I gave John one more cheerful wave as I drove away. In the rearview mirror I saw him watch me for a long time, then go back into the house.

I drove home without stopping, pulled the car into the garage and sat staring blankly out the windshield. Could I go on this way? Finally I shook myself. Those were not the thoughts to have sitting parked inside a closed garage. Up and out of the car, I fled to my cabin, threw off my Congressman's Wife clothes, pulled on sweats and a long-sleeved T shirt and ran to the boathouse. The dock, still wet from rain the night before, smelled strongly of cedar. Hoisting it into the water, I slipped into my kayak and within minutes paddled into the wind, toward the channel to Bear Lake.

Eight

Please join Congressman Jack Sach,
his family and friends,
for election returns
Time: After the polls close
Place: Lake of the Woods Hotel Banquet room
Dessert and cash bar
Hosted by Jack Sach for Congress

We'd done this ten times in twenty years. Jack got himself elected four times to the State Assembly, and six, going on seven, to the United States Congress. In the early years election nights were tense, anxiety filled affairs. Since the last gerrymandering of the district our anxiety was all for show. Jack hadn't had a serious opponent in ten years. This time his opponent, a twenty-year-old student with a staff of two, raised maybe a tenth of Jack's war chest. But Jack always campaigns hard. He loves the guts of it, going door-to-door shaking hands, speaking, kissing babies, everything.

Over the years we developed an election-day routine and this year, even though everything seemed different, nothing had changed. I'd bake all weekend and most of Monday. There'd be cookies, pies, fudge and a cake for the party. I'd rise early election day to work in the kitchen, cutting vegetables, making fruit plates and organizing everything for transport. Sometime in the late afternoon a couple of Jack's volunteers would arrive with a van and we'd load everything up, drive to the hotel and start setting up for the crowds.

Jack would sleep until noon, preparing for the long night ahead. Eventually he'd dress, eat and leave to rally the troops busy with last minute get-out-the vote calls and of course, loudly and publically cast his ballot. On a year like this, with no presidential election to overshadow him, Jack would place himself where he could bask in full electoral attention. I decided I had time for a run before it all began.

The cold air felt sharp and clean, a sunny late autumn morning, perfect voting weather. I slipped through the front door, paused for a few stretches and began a slow jog up the hill. It was colder than I'd thought, not quite cold enough to snow, but cold enough to make me pick up the pace. In the past few months I'd grown to love this early morning time, running along the cliff overlooking the lake. The rhythm of my feet slapping against the pavement, wind rustling the leaves, birdsong, more infrequent as the days got colder, and the distant lapping of waves formed a perfect counterbalance to whatever craziness was running through my brain. On this election morning, my mind ran faster than my feet. I had a life to plan.

Coming back, I crested the hill and breathed in the sight of my cold November town. I knew every house and store. As a child I'd known someone in every church, as an adult I'd knocked on most of these doors to visit, celebrate with, mourn, or campaign the citizens. I trotted down to my cabin to wash and change, passing my sleeping garden, where only the salad bed sprouted green. The lake sparkled, surrounded by bare trees, bereft of boats, a thin skim of ice near shore.

The light on the kitchen phone blinked as I returned. Ed from the Journal wanted an election day comment from both of us. I deleted the message and began pulling carrots and celery from the refrigerator. By the time Jack got up, I'd finished my slicing and arranging and was almost out the door.

"I'm going to visit your mother," I called to him from the front door as he entered the kitchen. "Tell your minions I'll be ready for pickup by three." I left before he could answer.

Aziza ushered me into the living room where Pearl sat knitting in an easy chair before the fire. "Gillian." She beamed. "I wasn't expecting to see you until this evening. How lovely."

"Good morning, Momma Pearl." I stooped to kiss her cheek. "So you're coming tonight?"

"Of course we're coming." Pearl said. "I haven't missed a returns party yet."

Through the archway, I could see a giant bouquet of yellow roses decorated the dining room table. "What beautiful flowers."

Pearl smiled brightly. "Jack brought those yesterday, with a special invitation to the party tonight."

Good old Jack, doesn't visit his mother for weeks, but he'll make sure she's there on display when he needs her, I thought, but smiled and said, "How nice of him."

"Take off your coat, honey. I'll make tea." Pearl started to get up.

Aziza and I simultaneously said, "No, I will." We laughed. Aziza waved me into the chair next to Pearl, and strode off to the kitchen.

Pearl watched her go with a sigh. She whispered, "Poor dear, she met with the lawyer and I don't think it's going well, but she won't say. I do hope it all works out. I've been asking around but haven't found her next assignment."

I was surprised. "You're that much better?"

Pearl fluttered her hand. "I'm fine, dear. I can sit, stand, walk, drive, and cook. I'm not ready to go dancing yet, but I certainly don't need a full time nurse. Shush, here she comes. I don't want to mention it until I've found her someplace new."

Aziza entered with a tray of cookies and two cups of spicy smelling tea, which she handed to us with a smile. "As long as Gillian is here, would you mind if I stepped out to the store for a moment? I would like to call my parents today and need to purchase a new phone card."

"Of course, take all the time as you need. We'll be fine," Pearl assured her.

Aziza glanced at me and I nodded with a smile. "Go, I can stay for an hour or so."

She smiled and with a wave she was gone.

Pearl and I sipped our tea in silence for a few minutes. Then, setting her cup down, she turned to face me directly. "Gillian, I'm glad we have this time alone. I've been wanting to talk with you."

"About what?" I asked, surprised.

She touched my arm "My dear, you've been like a daughter to me all these years, better than most daughters. I'm so grateful for you. You know how important you are to me."

I nodded, not trusting myself to speak.

She continued, "These last few months you've been so sad, much more than usual. I'm worried about you."

"More than usual?" I asked. "Am I usually sad?"

"Well," she said carefully, "you're happy sometimes. I remember how you glowed when the children were born." She paused, looking off into the distance and smiling softly. "But," she met my gaze, "I haven't seen you truly happy in a long time."

Tears were leaking out. I said softly, "I know."

She nodded. "It's Jack, isn't it?"

I paused, whispered, "Yes."

She pulled a fresh tissue from her sleeve and handed it to me. "What is it?"

Giving in, I sniffled my way through the whole sordid story, starting with that flirtatious Claire. I even told her my fears about John and Ashley, John and Jack and Ashley.

Aziza returned halfway through my story, but a nod from Pearl and she quickly withdrew to the kitchen.

Finally I stuttered to a stop, sobbing on Pearl's shoulder as she patted my back saying, "There, there" and "Oh, my poor dear" and other loving, ineffectual, but comforting murmurs.

Eventually I straightened. "I'm so sorry," I gasped.

"Why should you be sorry?" Pearl's voice held an edge. "It seems to me that my son has some explaining to do."

"Oh, don't tell him I told you." I pleaded. "It will only make things worse."

Pearl patted my knee. "Don't worry. I won't talk with him about this. I know how he can get. After all, I've known him longer than you. I had hoped… but never mind. So what will you do?"

"I'm not sure." I blew my nose. "In the short term I'm going to visit Aurora. I called her last week and told her I'd drive down after the election."

Pearl sat back. "That's a surprise. How did she sound?"

"Once I assured her that her father wouldn't be joining us she sounded fine, said the girls would love to see me and all that. I haven't seen them since last winter when Jack was in Washington. I won't stay long, they're all busy with school and work. After that," I shrugged, "I'm thinking a European vacation might be nice, visit the boys, see the world."

She clapped. "That's a wonderful idea. When would you leave?"

I smiled. "Actually, that's what I originally came to tell you. I've already bought my ticket. I leave in a week. If you're still interested in going in January and if Aziza took you to the airport and I met you, it wouldn't be like traveling alone. Oh, but Aziza might not be here—"

She clapped again. "That's a wonderful plan. If you're out of the country I can't possibly do without Aziza. After all, Jack pays her salary and he'd have to see that." She smiled. "That will give me two months to settle things for her. Excellent."

"Are you okay with my leaving?" I asked meaning, I think, are you still my mother?

"I'm so angry at my son I could spit," Pearl said. "But, given his behavior, I'd be angry with you if you didn't leave."

"Thank you," I whispered, leaning to hug her.

We sat silently for a moment then Pearl asked, "Will you divorce him?"

I shook my head. "I don't think so, at least not for now. It's all too public. But I don't feel particularly married, either. I've been living in the cabin for months."

Pearl gazed into the distance. "Jack's father was a difficult man," she said finally. "Did I ever tell you about Jacob Fritz?"

"No," I answered, startled by the conversational turn.

"Well, perhaps another time." She smiled. "Can you stay for lunch? Aziza made the most delicious cucumber soup last night and there's plenty left."

"I'd love to." I looked at my watch. "I don't need to be back for about an hour." I stood and walked toward the kitchen. Catching sight of myself in the hall mirror, I stopped.

"Oh, God, I look awful." I stared at my red nose and puffy eyes.

"What am I supposed to do about tonight?"

"I thought of that." Aziza came out of the kitchen carrying a bowl of thick green paste. "Come sit and I will cover your face with this and your eyes with these." She held up two cucumber slices.

"Thank you, Aziza, that's so sweet," I sat in the recliner. "Is this some ancient Somali remedy?"

She laughed softly, slathering cool goo across my forehead. "No, Habeebitee, this comes from an expensive American catalogue. It is guaranteed to take last night's party out of you so you'll be ready for tonight," she recited, as Pearl chuckled and I blushed.

❧ ❧ ❧

By three, when two young men came to help me load food into the van, I managed to look tired but pleasant, an acceptable spousal visage for the last day of a long campaign. The polite boys insisted on doing all the carrying. I directed the placement of long flat boxes filled with pies, stacks of cake boxes and big plastic bins of vegetables, fruit and cookies, along with a collection of platters, serving plates and utensils, a five pound bag of ground coffee, a large basket of teas and cocoa, and the five gallon carboy of freshly pressed apple cider I'd picked up at an organic farm on Sunday. We inched our way slowly downtown. The blond, Keith, drove carefully, while the other boy, Jeff, and I sat among the stacks of food and held them steady. It took us nearly a quarter of an hour to drive a mile to the hotel but everything arrived intact.

I let the young men, joined now by others, both paid staff and volunteers, carry the food through the back door and into the banquet hall. Mark met me inside, looking sweaty and nervous, wearing his lucky shamrock lapel pin.

I surveyed the half-decorated room. "You can't honestly be concerned about Jack's race."

"No," he said, "I'm worried about the fifth district state senate seat and it will be touch and go with the mayor and the sheriff's race, but Jack will be fine, even with the rumors about AHC."

"What do you mean?" I asked, but Mark moved off to supervise some bunting hangers in the far corner. I turned my attention to the white linen covered food tables and began supervising my own enthusiastic crew. I hadn't been paying attention to the other races but, gauging from the mood among the staffers and volunteers, it was likely to be a good night for the Party.

John arrived around four and immediately pitched in with my catering crew. Shortly thereafter, I saw Ashley handing red, white and blue cardboard stars to a tall young woman on a ladder. Secrets, I thought, we're choking on them.

"John." I touched his arm. "Can I talk with you a minute outside?"

"Sure, Mom." He looked startled.

We walked into the autumnal dusk. The air had turned even colder. Smells like snow, I thought. Pulling him down the walk and away from the building, I turned to face my son. "It's none of my business," I started, taking a deep breath, "but—"

John's eyebrows knit together. "Mom?" he asked when I didn't go on.

I puffed my cheeks and blew the air out forcefully. "Look, I do know this is none of my business but is there something between you and Ashley?"

His eyebrows shot up. "You know her?"

I nodded. "We've met."

He smiled softly. "Isn't she great?" When I didn't answer he said again, "Mom, is there something wrong?"

"I don't know," I said slowly, "maybe not. But I think you should ask her that."

He looked at me, puzzled.

I touched his arm. "I don't mean to be cryptic and maybe there's nothing, so I don't want to say anything in case I'm wrong, but I want you to promise to talk with her, ask her, ask her if there's anything you should know. That's all."

"Mom, this is crazy," John said in exasperation. "I don't get it. What's going on?"

"Maybe nothing, John." I reached up to cup his cheek. "Probably nothing. If she tells you there's nothing, I'll believe her and we can all go to lunch tomorrow."

John looked exasperated but nodded his assent.

I tried to smile. "Then I can get to know her and see for myself how great she is."

John's face slowly relaxed. He smiled and leaned down to kiss my forehead. "All right Mom, I don't know what you're talking about, but I'll ask her tonight. Whatever you're worried about, I'm sure it's all fine. Now let's go inside before the gossip starts."

I returned his smile, working to keep the concern from my eyes, and, arm in arm, we re-entered the hall. Ashley looked up and flashed John a brilliant smile. She saw me and her smile faded slightly, but she waved pertly before turning back to her decorating tasks. It's going to be a very, very, very long night, I thought.

Polls close at eight. Around seven, with the decorating and food preparation complete, the crew began wandering off in search of dinner. John and Ashley left in a large group of young people. His arm rested briefly along her back. She smiled up at him, and then they were swept out in the crowd. Maggie arrived with takeout Chinese. We drove to the park and sat in the car, using chopsticks to scoop beef and asparagus in black bean sauce and pork fried rice from cardboard cartons, watching the wind froth white caps across the lake.

I told her about my conversation with John. "I don't have concrete proof that Ashley's the one." I adjusted the towel I'd spread over my chest to protect my blouse. "For all I know, it was someone else entirely and Ashley is just a nice young girl who likes politics."

Maggie looked skeptical. "And the necklace?"

I shrugged. "There may be a perfectly good explanation, I can't think of it."

We ate in silence for a few minutes. Maggie asked, "When do you leave for Aurora's?"

"Tomorrow morning. I think I'll stop off in the city, it's about halfway and I'd like to spend a night or two on my own. I told Aurora I wouldn't be there until Friday, but I can always go earlier if I want to."

"It sounds like an adventure," Maggie said, wistfully. "Think of me, I'll be spending my nights this week grading tests."

"Do you ever regret the single life? I'm not sure I'm up to it."

Maggie stared at the water for a long moment. When she spoke, her voice was pensive. "After my last breakup I spent a long time thinking about what to do next. It seemed that my choices were to try again or to deliberately choose a single life with cats." She smiled ruefully. "To tell the truth, I was never very good at relationships and sex. It's not that I don't like all that, but it never seemed like such a big deal to me. So the decision wasn't difficult. It's not a bad life, really. I'm in control of my time, my money. I don't have to consult anyone about anything. I'm free."

I set aside my empty container and dug in the bag for my fortune cookie. Cracking it open, I read aloud from the little white slip, "The time for new romance, lucky numbers 2, 8 and 17." I chuckled.

Maggie looked at me thoughtfully. "I'm not sure you're ready for the single life and cats quite yet."

"Dogs are more my style," I said. "Look at my choice in men."

"Jack wasn't a choice. you were too young to be conscious. We'll judge your taste in men by the next one." Maggie packaged up our garbage.

"It's funny how love dies, don't you think?" I crumpled the fortune in my hand. "When we were first together sometimes I couldn't breathe because I was so happy. I've lived with the memory of that so long I almost didn't notice it was all gone. Aren't you going to read your fortune?"

"Nope." She put the car in gear. "Don't like them."

I rebuckled my seat belt. "The cookies or fortunes?"

"Both."

We returned in time to set up the coffee machines and start water for tea. As usual, Pearl was among the first to arrive, accompanied by an elegant Aziza. "Wow," I whispered hugging her, "you sure clean up well."

She smiled. "Shukran, Habeebitee. Thank you for inviting me. I don't get to dress up often, it's nice."

I found them chairs near the big-screen TV, so they could watch the returns in comfort. Mark rushed over and greeted them, offering to get drinks, cake, whatever they needed. Pearl smiled at him indulgently. Aziza looked down, smiling.

I turned my attention to the door, where Evelyn was making a grand entrance, accompanied by a short, plump, white haired man in a richly tailored suit.

I hurried to greet her. "Evelyn, how wonderful of you to come."

"Thank you, Gillian," she said, graciously. "I'm happy to be here. You remember my friend Syd Greene?"

"Delighted," I said, thinking, Pearl, you're amazing. "Thank you for coming."

He bent over my extended hand, his lips grazed my knuckles. "It is a pleasure to be here, Mrs. Sach. I have the greatest hopes for your husband." His East Coast accent was slightly nasal but overall quite pleasant.

"Thank you. Please, call me Gillian."

"You look nice, Gillian, have you lost some weight?" Evelyn peered at me.

"Um, maybe, thank you," I answered.

"That's good, dear. I hate to see a woman letting herself go."

"Uh, let me find you a seat." I ushered them to chairs near Pearl, who smiled jauntily and winked at me.

I found Maggie serving cake. She inclined her head toward Evelyn. "Mr. Greene, I presume?"

I nodded.

She shook her head, "Poor guy," and continued slicing.

"I'm not sure how long I'll last at this," I told her.

Maggie looked around. "No Jack yet. Maybe you can slip out after he arrives."

I nodded. "I should wait for his acceptance speech. But maybe I'll develop a headache shortly after he makes his grand entrance. Shouldn't be difficult, these events always give me one."

A few minutes later Syd Greene appeared at the cake table. As I handed him a slice with two forks he gestured over his shoulder at Evelyn. "Isn't she marvelous?" he asked, his voice hushed.

I didn't look at Maggie as I replied, "She's something else, all right."

Syd Greene beamed. "I've never met anyone so straightforward, so honest, even brutally honest. She's one of a kind."

I nodded my agreement. "That she is. Would you like some coffee, Mr. Greene?"

"Call me Syd, and no thanks, I think I'll get us wine." He toddled off, carrying his cake.

"That should help," I murmured under my breath, glancing at Maggie who stared after him slack jawed. "Pearl said it," I told her, "one person's poison is another's ambrosia."

Maggie shook her head. Together we watched him hand Evelyn the cake plate, lean down and whisper something in her ear. Evelyn erupted in laughter. He grinned down at her and turned toward the bar.

We looked at each other and laughed.

Jack arrived with a flourish, followed by his entourage, as the first returns started coming in. It looked like a landslide. John and Ashley still hadn't come back from dinner. I made my excuses and let Maggie drive me home where I changed into jeans and a sweatshirt. I finished packing my suitcase, my portable easel, and a satchel of art supplies, and carried them to the car. I made tea, wrapped myself in a throw, found my book, planted myself in an easy chair in the living room and prepared to wait.

∞ ∞ ∞

I dozed off, but woke around midnight to the sound of a key scraping the front door lock. I eased myself out of the chair and stretched. Jack was still fumbling with the lock as I opened the door and startled him.

"Gillian." he said in surprise.

"Come in, Jack, we need to talk."

He swayed in front of me.

"Look, I know you're drunk, but this can't wait. I'll make coffee."

"What's this about?" he asked, enunciating carefully.

"Sit." I steered him toward the kitchen table. I found half a cup of cold coffee on the kitchen counter and topped it off with leftovers from the pot. I'll just nuke it, I thought. He's not in any condition to savor and besides, I don't care. Within a minute I handed him the heated coffee and sat across the table.

Jack blinked a few times, took a sip of the coffee, and declared, "Sixty seven percent. I got sixty fucking seven percent of the vote. That," he dug his finger into the air in front of my face, "that is a fucking mandate. I don't care what those stupid reporters say."

"Congratulations, Jack." I looked directly into his eyes. "I'm leaving you."

"Wha—? You can't leave me, you promised—"

"I promised I'd stay through the election. It's over, you won. Now I'm going."

"But," he hammered one fist into the other, "but, you can't… what about the papers?"

"I didn't say I was divorcing you," I explained. "I said I'm leaving. You can tell people I'm on a long vacation. You can tell them I'm taking time to paint. You can tell them I'm in a sanatorium for all I care, although I wouldn't if I were you, that might be worth investigating."

"But where will you go?" He looked around the kitchen, as if finding it impossible to imagine my leaving the room.

"For the moment I'm going to see Aurora."

He looked at me blankly.

I spoke more slowly. "You know, your daughter, the mother of your grandchildren?"

"I know who Aurora is, you idiot." he roared, standing and leaning across the table. "I can't figure out why you're going to visit her. We're not on speaking terms, remember?"

"She's not speaking to you," I corrected. "She calls to talk to me every couple weeks. Of course, mostly she wants to talk about what a crappy childhood she had and her mean, distant, adulterous father, but we speak. I've even visited her while you were in Washington. So now I'm going down there for a weekend to get to know my granddaughters better. After that I'm leaving for Europe."

"Europe?" He paced back and forth across the room. "It's that fucking fag, isn't it? He finally talked you into leaving me, that son of a bitch."

"They don't even know I'm coming. I only bought the ticket yesterday. I fly to Amsterdam next week with an open round trip ticket."

"So who's the guy?" He spun to face me.

I watched him for a long moment. "There's no guy. I'm just done with you, Jack. I can't do this anymore. I don't care who you screw. You're free and so am I. Easy, no muss, no fuss. Separate domiciles, separate checking accounts, separate lives. If you want, I'll come home every couple years for campaign appearances and otherwise you're on your own."

I pulled an envelope from my pocket and set it on the table between us. "In case you don't remember this conversation in the morning, I've written you a letter."

Jack picked it up, staring blankly at the envelope.

"There's also a letter drawn up by my lawyer," I continued. "It contains a lot of legal language, but basically it says that if you mess with me or piss me off in any way I'll sue for divorce on the grounds of infidelity."

Jack looked at me, his mouth tightening. "You can't prove anything—"

"I don't need to," I interrupted him. "The press'll do that for me."

"You'd never—" Jack slowly sank into his chair.

"And, of course, there are the kids. Remember when John caught you in bed with the blond? Oh, you didn't know I knew? I bet you also thought I didn't know why Aurora cut you off. She told me and she'd tell a judge and, even more important, she'd be happy to sell her story to the Enquirer. Don't you think they'd like to know that you came on to your daughter's best friend at her wedding, which she forgave you for, until you did the same thing at each of her daughters' christenings?"

"I never—"

Again I interrupted, "You did, Jack. You really did. I'm leaving early in the morning. You go on up to bed now, I'll clean up here." I stood.

Just then the front door flew open. John roared, "You fucking asshole!"

We both looked up, startled by a disheveled John standing in the doorway. Flushed and red-eyed, he stared at his father, sniffing back tears. "You're a pig." Aurora's right. You're a sleazy, slimy, pervert who can't keep his dick in his pants. You're disgusting."

Jack reared up, "Don't talk to your father—"

"I won't." John stepped forward and, leaning with his hands braced on the table, loomed over Jack. "After I'm finished here tonight I won't talk to my father ever again."

"What is this all about?" Jack looked wildly from John to me and back again.

"This is about Ashley," John said slowly, "sexy little Ashley. I can't believe I—," he shuddered, "where you—" He turned to me. "Why didn't you stop me earlier, before…?"

"I'm so sorry. I wasn't sure. I'm so, so sorry." I reached to touch him.

He jerked away. "Well, he was and I was, so I guess we were." He looked at Jack. "You can have her. You two deserve each other." He turned and walked out the front door.

I followed, calling to him.

John stopped and stood in the front yard, the moonlight washing all color from his form. I wrapped my arms around him. He stiffened and then melted. I let him weep, his head resting on mine. When he finally quieted, I reached into my pocket and pulled out my keys.

I held them out to him. "Here, sleep in the cabin tonight." He looked at me, puzzled, and I explained, "I've sort of been living there for a while. You take it tonight. I'll stay in your room. We'll have breakfast together early."

He looked toward the house.

"He's not invited. I'll bring breakfast down and we can eat in the studio."

John nodded.

I patted his back a few times, then watched as he walked, slump shouldered, through the side yard and around the back. I took a deep breath and reentered the house.

From the empty kitchen I heard Jack thumping around the bedroom upstairs. I turned into John's light blue bedroom, just off the living room. Posters of rock bands that couldn't possibly still be popular covered the walls. Slipping out of my clothes, I slid between the dark blue flannel sheets, pulling the comforter up to my chin. I started to think about breakfast but fell asleep before I could begin my list.

PART THREE

Les Ails Escape

Using your serving soup bowls, measure water into a stock pot, one large bowl per person, and one or two for the pot. Set to boil. For each serving, clean the skins from one head of garlic (that's one whole head, not one clove,) per person. Add them to the pot and boil till they're soft to the touch, about a half hour.

    Peel, chop and sauté an onion or two. Peel a few carrots and cut into thin rounds. Any number of root veggies can be added: parsnips, yams, turnips, beets, kohlrabi, rutabaga, celery root or whatever else you have. Once the garlic has softened, blend the stock in the pot with an electric hand blender (or pour the soup in a blender, puree and return it to the pot). Add the root veggies and simmer till soft.

    Wash and chop a green vegetable: spinach, kale, chard, just about any green that's not lettuce, about a half pound per serving. Add to the soup when the root vegetables are tender and simmer until the greens wilt.

    Add salt, pepper, cayenne, olive or sesame oil, or anything you like, to taste. Stir and serve in warmed soup bowls. If you like, you can top each serving with grated cheese. You can make lots of substitutions with this soup — be creative — there are many, many ways to make this escape.

Nine

Tray balanced in one hand, I opened the cabin door. John lay still asleep, curled on the couch beneath a blanket. I crept in and softy closed the door behind me. As I set out breakfast, he spoke. "Morning."

"Good morning, honey. Did you sleep?"

"Some."

"Here, this should help." I handed him coffee and shivered. "Cold in here this morning, let me light the stove."

John sat, silently sipping his coffee, while I stoked the woodstove and lit a match. Backing away, I sat in the old yellow overstuffed chair across from the couch. We watched the fire through the little glass window in the stove door.

"So you've been living down here how long?"

I smiled an apology. "Since September. I didn't want to upset you. I think that backfired."

He snorted. "Yeah, it did."

"What happened last night?" I asked softly.

John shrugged, his eyes fixed again on the fire. "We all went to dinner at Haley's Hamburgers on Pine and everything was fine. After dinner I asked Ashley if she wanted to walk back." It's only a mile or so, you know?" He paused.

"She said that would be great. And it was, until I said something like, 'Hey, my mom asked me to ask if there was anything you needed to tell me.'" He looked at me, mouth tight. "She stopped. She wouldn't talk, wouldn't walk, just stood there. Then she started to cry, that loud, shaking, weeping little kids do." He took a sip of coffee and a deep breath. "It was awful, Mom. I didn't know what to do."

"What did you do?" I prompted.

He gave me a half smile and said, "Well, I couldn't have her howling like that in the street, so I coaxed her into the Flame, you know, that raunchy bar off Main?"

I nodded.

"I got her to a booth in the back and let her cry for a while." He made a face. "I bought her a couple of shots and a beer. That finally calmed her down."

"Did she say anything?" I asked.

He shook his head. "For the longest time she wouldn't talk. We sat there with her crying and me sitting there watching." He shivered. "It was terrible. I've never felt so powerless, so—" he struggled for the word, "so inadequate. But finally, after another beer and some nagging from me, it all came out, every hideous detail. Needless to say, I sent her home in a cab. I never want to see her again." Tears glistened on his cheeks.

I moved to the couch, put my arms around him, and patted his back.

Eventually we straightened, both of us sniffling. I found some tissues under the couch, handed one to John and blew my own nose. "He can be so difficult."

John nodded. "Yeah, but I think she hurt me more. I can't believe she didn't tell me. She said it was all over by the time she met me, but I don't believe her." His face contorted. "How could I? I bet she was screwing him whenever I wasn't around. It's disgusting. It's like some awful Greek story, or something from Jerry Springer." He covered his face. "God, I feel so, crappy, dirty, awful."

In what may be my most ridiculous motherly statement ever, I said, "Maybe some toast?"

John laughed. "Sure, toast. I suppose this is pretty bad for you, too."

"I've had better years," I rose to get our breakfast."

He followed me to the table. "How long have you known?"

"About Ashley? Until last night I didn't know anything for sure." I carried bread slices into the kitchen and slid them into the ancient toaster. "I guess I've suspected for a few months, that's when I moved down here. But really, I've known about his—" I paused, searching for the word, "proclivities for a long time. I just ignored them."

"Yeah." John leaned against the table and stared out at the lake.

"I supposed that's what I did with you, too." I avoided his eyes. "I ignored what was happening between you and Ashley. I could have told you earlier but," I shrugged, "I hoped it wasn't true and it would go away."

John stepped into the kitchen and hugged me. "It's all right, Mom. I put a lot of energy into hiding our relationship from you. Don't know why, really. Maybe some part of me knew all along." He released me as the toast popped. He slathered thick layers of butter and jam on his. I did the same, with slightly more modest portions. We sat again by the fire.

John gestured toward one of my darker paintings, propped in a corner. "That's us, as a family, all placid appearances and secret dramas."

I contemplated the image. "You're right. We've never been transparent." I leaned back in my chair. "I'm tired of it, John. I don't want to hide out anymore."

"What will you do?"

I smiled at him. "To begin with, in about an hour, I'm getting in my car and driving to your sister's, with a detour for a few days in the city."

"Really?" He sat up straight. "That's great. I mean, wow, that's wonderful. She'll be so happy to see you."

"Will she? I hope so."

"Of course she will," he crowed. "This is wonderful news. She's always saying how much she misses you, how she wishes you could spend more time with the girls, all that. That's just great."

"I miss her, too," I said. "I don't know why I haven't done this more often. I haven't seen the girls since last winter."

"I'm really pleased, Mom." He dusted toast crumbs from his

fingers. "That doesn't answer my question. What will you do?"

I shrugged. "I honestly don't know yet. For the moment my plan is to visit Aurora, Pete, and the girls, and then fly to Europe and spend some time touring, maybe with Edward, maybe alone, and figure it all out. I know it sounds cowardly, but I'm not ready to face a big public scandal right now, so I'm going to escape."

"I can see that," John said. "Frankly I'm not looking forward to having our private life discussed around the breakfast tables of America. And," he smiled at me, "avoidance is what we do best."

I nodded. "When you find something that you're good at—" We both laughed.

Later, as he helped me lock the cabin and we walked to our cars, he asked, "How long are you going to be in Europe?"

"I don't know. I've an open-ended ticket."

"Maybe I could join you over break. I'm not likely to do Christmas with him." He gestured toward the house.

"I'd like that." I hugged him. "I'll stay in touch by email."

I stopped at Maggie's office on my way out of town. Still early, sleepy students stumbled along the campus walkways. I poked my head into her tidy space. "Morning."

She looked up from her computer and smiled broadly. "Hey, so are you off?"

I nodded.

"Have a wonderful time." She came around the desk to hug me.

"I'll try." I returned her embrace. "You have a conference at John's university next week, don't you?"

She nodded.

"Do you think you could check on him while you're down there?"

"Uh oh," she said. "He found out?"

I nodded.

"Ugly?"

I nodded again.

"Sheesh." She shook her head. "I'll call and invite him to lunch."

"Thanks." I relaxed a little.

"No problem. Good excuse for me to get away from stuffy

academics." She hugged me goodbye, holding tight for a long, warm minute.

≈ ≈ ≈

It takes five hours to drive from my house to the city by the old highway. The landscape alternates between dense state-owned forests and rolling farmland. I hadn't driven this way in years, choosing instead the faster thoroughfare route. But I wasn't in a hurry and the scenic route suited my mood perfectly.

When I was a kid, farmhouses dotted this area. Now the fields seemed bigger, unbroken by habitation and the towns smaller, with more shuttered buildings and peeling paint. I stopped for lunch at a diner in a tiny village named Victor Falls. I asked the waitress the way to the falls, but she didn't know. An old man, huddled over coffee at the counter, told me that years ago there'd been a dam on the river south of town. He remembered swimming in the millpond. The dam broke sometime in the '50s and the falls disappeared. I thanked him. He suggested we'd all be forgotten some day and I agreed. The conversation ended up much more compelling than my overdone burger and greasy fries, but the apple pie tasted fresh with a light crust. The old man and I proved the only customers through most of lunch. I left a big tip and drove on.

There's no way to avoid the bleak strip mall, fast-food Americana of the last hour of the drive. Gradually the buildings got bigger and the parking spaces fewer, as downtown grew up around me. I pulled over and fumbled in my bag until I found the address of the hotel I'd booked online. Once I found the map and located myself on it, I pulled back into traffic. I could feel my back tense, my neck rigid. Had I ever driven in the city alone before? I didn't think so. Was I driving too slowly? Probably. Cars passed me. I kept glancing from the road to the map in my lap and back again. Finally, after only two wrong turns and one interminable effort to change lanes, I arrived at my destination. Looking up at the elegant hotel tower, I silently thanked the grandfathers for allowing me to make my getaway first class.

I pulled in, let the porter unload my baggage, and the valet take my car. Within minutes I was whisked to a large room overlooking the theater district. I tipped and smiled and finally everyone left and I was alone. I turned the tub faucets and emptied the little bottle of bubble bath into the rising water. Peeling off my clothes, I sunk into a lusciously hot bath. I'd booked two nights of this luxury on the way toward my angry daughter. I planned to enjoy it as much as I could.

I lay in the tub, letting the drive wash away, choosing not to think by mentally perusing my dinner choices. Jack and I had eaten in the city many times, particularly when he served in the state legislature and many times since. But I'd never stayed alone, able to decide without consultation or consideration. Thai, Ethiopian, Indian? Something ethnic, surely, something I wouldn't cook on my own. Indian, I decided, remembering an excellent curry I'd eaten a few blocks from the hotel. I'd walk, do some window shopping. Early still, maybe I could get tickets to a show, a ticket I corrected myself, and relaxed into the tub, feeling, for just a moment, a world opening around me.

The restaurant was as I'd remembered, a cavernous, inelegant spot, with plastic covering the tables, smudged and misspelled menus and tongue-biting hot vindaloo curry that mixed beautifully with creamy saag paneer. I followed it all with a warm cup of chai and sat back to ponder the evening before me. Did I have the energy to hunt out theater tickets? No. A movie? Maybe. Grab something for dessert, head back to the hotel and find an old movie on the giant television in my room? Had I come to the city to do what I could do any night at home? Give it a rest, I told myself, paid the bill and walked out into the early evening.

❧ ❧ ❧

I woke early and found the hotel gym. I surveyed my choices, stepped onto the Stairmaster and glanced at the big screen TV, tuned to a local news station. I heard "Jack Sach" with a start and then realized the anchor was reviewing election results. The only other gym patron, a middle-aged man, swam laps in the small pool. I found the controls and surfed channels until I found an original Star Trek episode. Safe from reality, I began my climb to nowhere.

I skipped breakfast in anticipation of finding a fabulous early lunch. At a small coffee house I ordered a giant latte from a pleasant young barista with a colorful snake tattoo circling her left cheek. I sat to sip my frothy coffee in a plush velvet chair, facing the window. How remarkable that the last time I'd an entire day to myself in a city, with no plans and no one to please, had been during that first college semester. I'd ditched classes one day and taken the train in to see a traveling Monet exhibit. What an earnest young woman I'd been, carrying an air of propriety around with me, even in my flowing hippy skirts and silver bangles.

All that seriousness, where did it get me? I wondered. Who would I be now if I hadn't married Jack? I remembered my first day of high school. I'd been so excited, imagining a whole new self, free of the constraints of grade school. I'd dressed carefully that morning, deciding on social butterfly for my new persona. In my mind's eye, I saw myself moving from group to group, telling funny stories. I saw the love in everyone's eyes, smiles, laughs and welcoming gestures. Of course, it didn't work out that way. I suspected that once again in my new life I'd be quiet, serious, timid Gillian. But maybe I could wear a few brightly colored clothes and tell more of my secrets.

I opened a copy of the free People's Press, an alternative paper with some social commentary, more reviews of music, theater and culture around town, and lots and lots of advertising. As I drank my coffee, I perused the theater section, noting a couple of interesting possibilities at smaller venues. I skipped the music reviews, feeling way too old to even understand that scene. I scanned the events calendar and stopped at the notice of a touring Visionary and Outsider art exhibition at the museum, a perfect way to start my day. I checked my watch. The museum, about a fifteen-minute walk, wouldn't be open for another hour. I signaled Snake Girl for another latte and settled back to read the theater reviews more carefully.

Out on the street, a cold wind whipped my face. I wrapped my scarf tightly around my neck, tucked it into the collar of my long wool coat and walked briskly toward the museum. Not yet Thanksgiving, Christmas windows already decorated the storefronts, displaying emaciated manikins in velvet and faux fur, surrounded by brightly papered packages and tinseled plastic trees. Pulling my hat down to cover my ears, I picked up the pace, thinking briefly how incongruous I must look, an oh-so-appropriately dressed middle age woman almost jogging down a respectable city street.

A delicious wave of freedom washed through me, who cares what they think? I laughed out loud. A young man bundled against the wind in a cashmere overcoat, walking quickly in the opposite direction, studiously avoided my eye as he passed. Right, amend that to a proper looking middle-aged woman, running and laughing. I laughed so hard I had to stop. Seeing myself again in the eyes of passersby—obviously I looked crazy—sent me into further spasms of laughter. Every time I looked up and saw how intently they worked to ignore the crazy, hysterical woman, sent me into another spasm.

Finally a young woman stopped and asked, "Are you okay?"

I waved her off, and struggling to control myself, continued toward the museum. Pulling a tissue from my pocket, I wiped my face and blew my nose. Laughing warmed me. I walked more slowly the last few blocks to the museum's massive main entrance.

I love the high-ceilinged elegance of the museum. When Jack was in the state legislature, I'd come down to the city for opening week and stray fundraising dinners throughout the session. In those years I spent whole days wandering the galleries. There's a Jasper Johns on the second floor that once captivated me for two solid hours. I have an old sketchbook full of careful copies of a Hopper landscape, a Manet portrait and an awkward replication of a Braque cubist piece, along with a few more complex representational sketches I made outside the Modern galleries.

Now I arrived without sketchbook and bought a ticket to the special traveling Visionary and Outsider Art show. The show included a few famous "Outsiders." A long row of Dr. Imagination figures, with large, unfocused white eyes and bottle cap dreadlocks, lined the entrance to the exhibit. There were Bill Traylor's simple, almost stick figure stories, told in primary colors on cardboard, a large Moses Tolliver wooden watermelon slice and an ornate Rick Ladd bottle-cap encrusted chair (the wall tag beside this piece thoughtfully informed us that Rick Ladd was an Outsider-informed but academy trained artist, a distinction only a critic could love).

Aside from the well-known artists, the exhibit contained hundreds of anonymous pieces, from Haitian sequin voodoo flags to slave art from the 1800's. The great wash of old and new, recycled and refinished, brightly colored, exuberant, political, personal, frightening and funny, both exhilarated and overwhelmed me. The raw spirit of art and invention, of the human soul crying out and laughing, swept me up and carried me onto the street in search of the Queen of Sheba Ethiopian cafe.

A lunch of doro wat, lentils and collard greens scooped up with spongy, delicious injera warmed me nicely. I lingered over yogurt and coffee and planned my afternoon. I wanted to take gifts to my granddaughters. The hour walk across town to an upscale toy store would be good for me. Outside the wind died and the sun broke through to warm one side of the street. I crossed to walk uptown in sunshine.

I don't know my grandchildren well enough to make buying presents easy. I walked up and down the aisles of the store. What should I get? I only see them once a year. I can't arrive without presents. On the other hand I can't come like Santa Claus, ready to buy their little hearts. I could picture Aurora's disapproving frown if I showed up with baskets of toys. But the girls deserved something special from their all too often absent grandmother.

A nice young salesman with spiky hair and a three day beard growth (how do they maintain that?), helped me select a giant stuffed rhinoceros for Kaitlin, an old fashioned doll house for Haley and an elaborate beading kit for Emma, as well as a board game and some plastic clay for us all to play with together. Guilt, fear of the children or Aurora's disapproval, mixed with excitement and something softer like longing, and I bought too much. For a little extra the store agreed to deliver my bundles to the hotel, leaving me free to walk back in the warming November afternoon.

※ ※ ※

I propped my tired feet up the wall as I lay on the bed, scanning the theater section again. Dance, I decided. Drama sounded too, well, dramatic. I wasn't up to the emotional investment required for "a family in conflict" or "a troubled marriage" or even "soldiers returning." On the other hand, I blanched at the idea of musical revivals and didn't feel up to a traveling Broadway show. I needed to escape the tyranny of story. I circled the address of a production by a small dance company where I speculated tickets wouldn't be an issue, and let myself drift off, a catnap.

According to the bedside clock I awoke again at nine-thirty. I rose groggily and wandered into the bathroom. Staring at myself in the mirror as I peed, I decided that retreat might be the better part of valor. Maybe if I slept more I'd wake as a younger, less wild-eyed self. Throwing myself on the bed, I flipped on the TV and scanned the room service menu.

Ten

Driving from the city to Aurora's, you wind through two hours of suburban and exurban sprawl and cross the state line. I'd never been sure, but I suspected they moved there to escape Jack's shadow or at least to avoid reading about him in the local news. It isn't a pretty drive. I distracted myself with "Morning Edition," then switched from classical to country, as I found my thoughts circling the awful morning after Kaitlin's christening when Aurora had stormed from the house, pulling her children and Pete behind her, shouting to her father that she would never, ever, never speak to him again. The babies cried, poor Emma looked on wide-eyed and frightened, and massive, gentle Pete tried his best to manage their escape. I stood there, an innocent bystander watching the collapse of my family.

I changed the channel again, finally finding a religious channel playing out a children's story with an obvious plot and heavy-handed morality, disturbing somehow, but at least distracting.

Better to remember way back when Aurora and Pete were teenagers. Aurora fell so hard she mooned around the house, barely able to engage in the simplest conversation. Pete had seemed stricken, too. They were each other's first, and perhaps only. They'd turned thirty this year which meant together for fifteen years, married eleven.

I felt an illicit excitement as I neared Aurora's and thought, with a jolt, this is what Jack craves. It's like I've been having an affair with my granddaughters for years, sneaking down at least once every winter, leaving home on Monday after dropping Jack at the airport on his way to Washington, always sure to be home by Thursday night in case he flew back early, calling home every couple hours to pick up messages, so I could call him on my cell phone and pretend I just stepped out. I laughed. We all have our secrets.

At their exit I descended the ramp and consulted the directions Aurora had emailed me. Passing an upscale mall, I turned onto a winding street lined with starter mansions. Probably this was once all one farm. Definitely a more prosperous neighborhood than the three bedroom ranch nearby I'd visited last winter. Pete's practice was doing well, must be lots of sickly pets around here. I stamped down hard on my sense that the old neighborhood was more fun, with swing sets in every yard and a continuous pickup basketball game crowding into the street. Why is it so difficult to remain uncritical of my children's choices? I wondered. Can I really think I'd run their lives better than I do my own?

I found Aurora's house cuddled along one side of a cul de sac. A basketball hoop hung on their neighbor's garage. The house across the street sported a giant tree house in the back yard. On a cold day like this, with cars tucked inside garages and windows shuttered tight, it was impossible to tell if anyone was home. Of course it was still early, just past one. Hailey and Emma and maybe even Kaitlin would be at school. I slowed and considered turning back toward the mini mall.

The front door opened and there stood Aurora, short like me and solid like Jack, the exact opposite of her long, lean brother. Her T shirt was sparkling clean, her jeans were pressed. . She'd cropped her light brown hair. I pulled into the driveway. The backyard erupted in barking. A small golden retriever and a fat hound dog ran out from behind Aurora to greet me.

"Niko, Huckleberry, stay, QUIET!" Aurora roared. The dogs immediately sat and the barking from the backyard ceased. She greeted me with a hug. "You made it."

"Wow," I said, "I am always impressed by how well you've trained the dogs."

Aurora shrugged. "I won't let Pete bring them home unless they're trainable."

Over Aurora's shoulder I smiled at Kaitlin. Her pictures don't do her justice. She's becoming a pretty little girl, especially with her long hair in ringlets. I waved to her behind her mother's back. She giggled and returned my wave.

Aurora pulled away and looked over her shoulder at her youngest daughter. "She just got home from half-day kindergarten. I was feeding her some lunch, you hungry?"

"What's for lunch?" I asked. "If it's soup and crackers then yes, but if it's Spagettios I'm fine, thanks."

Aurora laughed. "It's make your own sandwich and tea."

"Then I'm hungry." I turned toward the car.

"Just grab your bag and bring it into the hall. You can unpack later," she said. "I've got to get Kaitlin fed so I can take her to dance class."

At the door I squatted in front of Kaitlin. "Hello."

"Hello," she said softly, her eyes flickering from mine to the floor.

"You've grown so much since I saw you. You're getting to be such a big girl. Can I have a hug and a kiss?" She nodded and I put my arms around her, hugging her gently as she breathed a feather light kiss onto my cheek.

I released her. "I'm sorry I didn't come see you sooner"

"Why didn't you?"

"Ouch." I looked up at Aurora.

"Come on, Kaitlin." She patted her daughter's hair. "Let's get some lunch. You can ask Grandma questions later. She's had a long drive."

"Okay," Kaitlin said, obediently. She looked back over her shoulder at me. "Did you bring presents?"

I smiled and nodded as Aurora said, "Remember, honey, you're not supposed to ask that when people come to visit."

Kaitlin smiled at me, then nodded to her mother and we all entered the bright yellow kitchen.

"The new house is beautiful." I sat at the kitchen table.

"Thanks." She opened the refrigerator. "We needed the room, especially for the dogs." She gestured through the kitchen window toward the back yard, where I counted at least four dogs of varying sizes, not counting the two swirling around our feet.

"The pack seems bigger than last winter," I commented, careful not to sound critical, even though I was thinking that one dog per child ought to be enough.

Aurora smiled, putting a plate of cold cuts on the table. "You know Pete, if he had his way there'd be twice as many. You wouldn't believe how many people just drop their dogs off in front of his clinic. As I said, my rules are they have to be trainable, and he has to do most of the training, and good with kids and other dogs, otherwise they're out of here."

She shuttled condiments from refrigerator to the table. "But even so, we're already at our limit again, especially when they're all inside. You'll see. The yard goes back about two acres, all fenced, but they still need more exercise. We had a border collie mix for a while. I took it on runs and we tried, but had to send it on to the Humane Shelter. I couldn't keep up."

I watched her whirl around the kitchen getting plates, utensils, filling a Sippy cup for Kaitlin and dumping tea bags in mugs for us. "Can I help with anything?"

"Nope," she said simply. "It's easier to do it myself."

"So you're taking dance lessons?" I asked Kaitlin. "That sounds fun."

She lit up. "Madam Sue says I can be a butterfly."

"In the Holiday recital," Aurora explained, slathering peanut butter and jam on a slice of whole wheat with the crusts cut off. She set it on a plate in front of Kaitlin. "She could be in full day kindergarten but she already knows her letters and numbers and can read some simple words like—"

"Cat, C A T," Kaitlin supplied, beaming at me.

"Good job," Aurora told her. "I talked with a friend who teaches kindergarten. She said the biggest thing she teaches kids is how to get in line. I thought dance sounded like a fun way to learn that. And besides, she loves it, don't you, honey."

She nodded. "Hat, H A T." We applauded.

After lunch we drove to a two-story building, just past the minimall, with a large sign outside proclaiming, "Sutter's Dance Studio," in elegant blue lettering. "Wait here." Aurora jumped from the driver's seat, opened the back door, and unbuckled Kaitlin's car seat in one fluid motion. "I'll be right back."

I watched them disappear up the steps, wondering if my daughter had always been quite this competent. Probably I just hadn't noticed.

Back in the car, Aurora shifted into drive. "We have exactly one hour and twenty minutes. Let's get coffee and dessert."

I laughed. "At least you inherited something from me." She looked at me quizzically and I explained, "Your love of coffee and a sweet tooth."

She grinned. "Thanks for the former and maybe you should apologize for the latter."

We pulled into an espresso shop at the edge of the mall. Before approaching the counter, Aurora threw her coat over a chair in a corner, overlooking the parking lot, away from the other customers. I ordered a latte and a gooey piece of cake. She ordered a complicated drink (double something, skinny, no something, I couldn't keep up) and carrot cake.

I started to pay but she waived me off. "I have a discount card. You can take us to dinner Sunday night."

"Deal."

"I warn you," she told me, "it's likely to be an expensive meal, only the very best pizza for my kids."

"I'm good for it," I assured her.

As soon as we settled Aurora asked me, "So, have you really left him?"

"Sort of," I sighed, shaking my head. "It just seems so complicated."

"It's not complicated," she grimaced. "He's a jerk and always has been. He screws any woman who stands still long enough. Sorry," she apologized, seeing my grimace, "but it's true. You can afford to leave. I don't see any reason not to divorce him immediately, if not twenty years ago."

"You're probably right, but I just don't think I could face that." I gestured toward a newspaper on the table next to us.

"It'd be juicy news, wouldn't it?" she agreed.

"Too juicy." I sipped my coffee.

She took a sip of her own drink before continuing, "If I know you, you're worrying about how difficult it might be for us, me and John."

"And the girls and Pearl and even Pete," I finished for her.

"Well don't. I, for one, would be happy to see him exposed as the pig he is."

I sat back and blinked. "You don't really mean that. Think how embarrassing it would be for the girls, especially Emma. She's old enough to almost understand and the kids at school—" I shuddered.

Aurora nodded slowly. "It would suck. But we'd deal. Then, over time, it would become old news and no one would remember. That's how it goes, Mom. Sometimes it's crappy for a while, but then that passes and you're through it."

"Maybe you're right. But I'm not going to do anything until I get back from Europe."

"That's so cool that you're going to Europe to see Uncle Edward. He'll be thrilled to have you. He's so lonely he's been emailing me every day."

"You haven't told him I'm coming, have you?"

"No." She shook her head. "You told me it was a secret so I haven't even told Pete."

I laughed. "You can tell Pete. And I'm not sure why I haven't told Edward, except that I just want to disappear for a while. In my whole life there has never been a time when I was really alone, when no one knew where I was and what I was doing. Do you think that's silly?"

"No," she said, "as long as you don't turn up missing or something."

"I won't. I'm simply flying to some unnamed European city and staying for a few days before I surface. I'll be back in touch by next weekend."

"Promise?"

"I promise."

"Then you can go. And speaking of going," she glanced at her watch, "if we leave now you can see the end of dance class and watch your untalented but happy granddaughter."

At the top of the stairs we found a large room with hardwood floors and mirrors lined with ballet bars along the walls. A small group of parents sat in folding chairs near the door. "It's a real dance studio," I whispered to Aurora.

She nodded. "They take little kids in the afternoons. Look." She pointed to the far corner where a line of seven little kids in leotards made circles of their arms and followed as the teacher led them in a winding line around the room. Aurora pointed to two empty chairs. She softly greeted a few of the parents as we sat.

"So I didn't have to skip the dance performance after all," I whispered.

"What do you mean?" she asked.

I smiled to myself. "Nothing, never mind."

❧ ❧ ❧

We drove directly from the dance studio to Haley and Emma's grade school, a long one-story building, surrounded by brightly colored playground equipment and soft grass. We'd only waited a few minutes when the bell rang and children began pouring out. I spotted Emma first and stepped from the car.

"Grandma!" She sprinted toward me and flung herself into my arms, quickly followed by Haley.

I hugged them close. "I've missed you both so much."

When we returned to the house I handed out presents, received oohs, aahs and kisses from the girls and some slightly amused exasperation from Aurora. She let in all the dogs and sent them with the children to play in the basement. "Good socializing for everyone."

We started dinner, a soup Aurora called Les Ails Escape. "Garlic in French is 'ail,'" she explained, as we peeled clove after clove. "Escape because it keeps the vampires away."

Just as we dumped greens into the soup, Pete arrived. "Gillian." He enveloped me in a giant bear hug. "How are you?"

He looked so concerned that I answered him honestly. "Don't know. Ask me in a couple months."

He nodded and squeezed me again. "Well, it's great to have you here." He looked down at the gifts scattered around his feet. "Looks like Santa came early. I hope they thanked you properly."

"They did. They're wonderful girls."

"Thanks, I think so too."

Emma helped me set the table, laying each utensil precisely in its place and straightening the napkins that I'd flopped down. Haley and Kaitlin ran circles around us, chased by several dogs.

"It's wonderfully alive here," I told Aurora, as she produced a platter, with a loaf of homemade bread in the center surrounded by three different chunks of cheese.

She stopped a moment, looked at the running children and smiled. "I suppose. There are days, though—"

When we finally had dinner ready, Pete barked a short command and all six dogs lay in a row along one wall of the dining room, a trick that always amazed me.

During dinner, the girls tumbled over each other telling me stories of their many accomplishments. Kaitlin, of course, would soon be a butterfly. Haley placed third in the second grade spelling bee. And Emma was going to try out for the school play; she wasn't sure if she wanted to play the lead or paint sets but said she'd decide soon. Pete and Aurora discussed the weekend schedule: Haley had a soccer game and Emma's Scout group was going to the roller rink on Sunday afternoon. Emma declared she didn't want to go because of Grandma. Aurora suggested we all go, to which there were cheers and a sympathetic smile from Aurora for me.

After dinner we did the dishes, washed and jammied girls, fed dogs, played two games of Go Fish and one of Old Maid. Aurora and I led the girls upstairs to Kaitlin's room, where we all piled on the bed. I read their next chapter in the Lion, the Witch and the Wardrobe and was transported to that treacherous, wintery Narnia. Aurora smiled across the children's heads and I remembered her reading this very chapter to John as I watched, so long ago.

Back in the living room Pete had built a fire. He sat reading on one side of the couch, one dog at his feet, another curled next to him and a third, the little toy poodle named Pita, beneath his book. Huckleberry sprawled in an armchair. Two more, the golden retriever (Niko was it?) and a lab (new since my last visit), stretched in front of the fire.

Pete set down his book and smiled as we entered the room. "Evil conquered yet?"

"I'm afraid not." I flopped into a chair by the fire as Aurora sat on the other side of the couch and reached to pet the dog beside her (was that Beowulf, the mixed something or other that had been around for years?).

Pete said gently, "Aurora told me about Jack. I'm so sorry, Gillian. Is there anything we can do to help?"

"You're doing it." I smiled. "Just being here is a tonic."

"Well, you're welcome anytime."

"Hey, Mom," Aurora piped in, "why don't you come for Thanksgiving? John will be here. I wanted to invite you before but—" She shrugged. "The only rule is that Dad cannot be mentioned all day."

"Really?" I asked. "I'd always assumed the two of you spent most of Thanksgiving together complaining about him."

Aurora shook her head. "I can see why you'd think that, since I would come back from my therapist boiling over and call you. But really, for the last few years I've tried not to talk about him much at all. With varying success." She gave Pete an apologetic smile.

"Is that healthy?" I stretched my legs toward the warmth of the fire. "I mean, aren't you supposed to feel and process and all that?"

"Sure." The dog inched its head onto Aurora's lap and she stroked it. "And I do plenty of that. I just got tired of him hijacking my life, my marriage, my relationships. Haven't you noticed that whenever he's part of the conversation he sucks up everything? A few years ago, I realized that the only relationship I had with my brother involved complaining about Dad. So now every Thanksgiving we get together and Dad isn't invited, even into the spaces between us."

"It might be more difficult this year." I told them the whole saga.

"Oh shit," Aurora said when I finished. "Poor John."

"Man," Pete frowned, "that'd be a shock."

"Should I call him?" Aurora asked. "Do you think he'll mind you've told me?"

"I think it would be great if you called," I assured her. "He knows I'm here and I'm sure he assumes we'll talk."

Pete watched me, absently petting the two closest dogs. "This must be awful for you."

I stared into the fire. "It's bad. I keep thinking I should have been able to stop it, should have… I don't know."

"You're not in control of either of them, Mom. You certainly can't control Dad. He can't even control himself." Aurora touched my shoulder. "And John? What could you do?"

I shook my head. "Warn him."

"Warn him about what? 'I think maybe your father is sleeping with one of the interns so watch yourself.' Don't you think after all these years John might have guessed that? Sorry, broke my own rule, but he really is a pig."

"That's what John said," I smiled at her.

"Well, he was right."

We sat silently for a long time. Finally I said, "I'm sorry. I'm very tired. Maybe we could talk more about this tomorrow."

Aurora leapt up. "Of course, Mom, I'll show you to your room. We have a real guestroom now. You're going to love it. You don't even need to sleep surrounded by stuffed animals."

She helped me carry my bags to a small room at the far end of the house. A brightly colored vintage quilt covered the bed, the only other furniture a simple pine bureau. A painting Aurora and I had done together when she was twelve hung on the wall.

She saw me looking at it and smiled. "Normally I have an old movie poster in here and this hangs in my study, but I thought you'd like the company while you're here."

"Thanks," I whispered. "You're a great daughter."

"So, now that you're a runner—"

"I'm not a runner, I'm a jogger," I corrected.

She shrugged. "Same difference. I try to run the dogs every morning around six, you up for it?"

"I'm slow," I told her. "I'll keep you back."

She laughed. "If you're willing to hold a couple of leashes, I'm willing to go whatever pace you want. I warn you, though, it's chaotic."

"All right. Wake me if I'm not out by six."

"Great. I love you Mom." Aurora kissed my cheek. "I'm glad you're here."

"Me too."

Eleven

Sunlight filtered through a pretty window. I woke before six, pulled on my sweatpants, a T shirt and thick flannel shirt and slipped into my socks and running shoes. By the time I arrived in the kitchen, Aurora was ready with coffee.

She handed me a cup and smiled. "Are you sure you're up for this? It's a challenge. We take out four. Huckleberry and Pita aren't much for running. Normally I do half my run with two, then switch, but they'd all love more time on the trail."

"I'm delighted, as long as you don't expect me to keep up with either you or the dogs."

"We'll forgive you," she said. "Have a banana and we'll go."

Aurora took Beowolf and a graceful elderly greyhound named Sally. . She gave me Niko, the golden retriever and the lab, improbably named Herbert. "Here's the trick. You need to keep a leash in each hand. You can let them out as much as you want, these extend about fifty feet but I recommend keeping them shorter. Make sure both dogs aren't exactly the same distance from you. Otherwise they'll get tangled up, which they may anyway. I'll run ahead and you follow, we're heading up this road to a trail into the woods. Once we're away from the road we can let the dogs go and run like real people, but as long as there's chance of cars we have to keep them leashed. Okay?"

She handed me both leashes.

"I guess," I said. "What's the worst that could happen?"

"The dogs could get tangled up, run between your feet, you could fall on your face and break something." She grinned and jogged off with her two dogs trotting ahead.

"Oh, if that's all," I muttered, looking down at the two, sitting expectantly at my feet. "You guys ready?" They wagged their tails. "Ok, let's start with a brisk walk, shall we?"

As I started moving, the dogs leapt forward, instantly at the end of their leads. Each time I pushed the little button on the leash handle to let line out, the dogs strained forward and ran farther than I'd planned before I could get my thumb off the button. Finally I said, "Forget it," and let both leashes all the way out. Niko wove in behind Herbert, stopping to pee. Herbert turned to see what Niko was doing and by the time we were jogging again the ropes had hopelessly tangled. But they ran without tripping each other or me, and my pace was no challenge to either of them, so I decided not to worry.

Aurora laughed when she saw us, but I was grateful when we caught up and turned into the dense young forest. We paused to let the dogs go so they could run ahead.

"We've got about a couple miles of trail before we need to turn back," she told me. "I love it out here. It took me a while to get the dogs used to staying close, but now we come out most mornings."

She trotted ahead on the dirt trail. With the dogs loose I could focus on my surroundings. With every breath cold air filled my lungs. The woods surrounding us felt bleak and smelled slightly fungal but, even with the sound of running dogs, Aurora's footfall ahead of me, and my own ragged breath, the quiet enveloped and welcomed me.

As I'd suspected, Aurora ran much faster. I watched her retreating form. The dogs ran up the path, stopping, sniffing, peeing, then running back to meet her, a swirl of animation in the still woods. They rounded a bend and disappeared. I panted on, eventually warming enough to shed my flannel shirt and wrap it around my hips. The cold air tingled on my bare arms.

Eventually the dogs ran toward me again, followed by my swift, sturdy daughter. She passed me with a grin. I turned around and followed her out of the woods. On the way back the dogs, now calmer, pranced easily at the end of their leads. Still, I was relieved to see the opening of the cul de sac that signaled the end of our journey together. After the dogs had been fed and let out into the back yard and our muscles well stretched, we sat in Aurora's warm kitchen with fresh coffee.

"That was good," I said. "But you're right, it's chaotic."

She smiled. "Most of my life is chaotic, but in a good way. Did I tell you I'm working part time now?"

"No, where?"

She blushed. "Just at the clinic. I'm keeping the books and working the front desk a few hours each morning. It helps Pete, saves some money, and gets me out of the house." She sipped coffee. "I've missed it, you know. I know none of the jobs I had while Pete was in school were important or even good jobs, but I loved being part of something. The last few years I've felt, I don't know, kind of out of it."

"But you're such a great mom. That has to mean something."

"It means everything, are you kidding? Otherwise I wouldn't have started staying home full time as soon as we could afford it. But with Kaitlin in kindergarten mornings, I'd started to rumble around here like a crazy person." She stood and flipped on the oven. "I think I'll make muffins this morning." She half-smiled in my direction, "I guess I'm not good at the whole stillness thing."

Aurora pulled out a bowl and began piling bags of flour and sugar, baking powder, eggs, milk on the counter. She scooped out approximate measures of each, whisking the dry ingredients together before adding eggs and milk. From the freezer she retrieved a container of frozen blueberries and dumped in a generous portion.

"What, no measuring cups? Who taught you to cook?" I teased.

"A great cook once told me that you only need to measure carefully when you bake. I, of course, have spent my life trying to prove her wrong." She grinned. "It helps if the people you're cooking for have simple palates or big appetites." She lathered butter into muffin tin cups and began spooning out her mixture. "Did you ever consider going to work, Mom? I mean outside the house."

"Sure. I even started back to school when you entered kindergarten.

But then I had John, which put that on hold. By the time he started school Jack had already been elected. I started a course that first winter, but it was just too hard, between being essentially a single mom and Jack's district office, which we ran out of the house in those early years, remember?"

Aurora nodded. "But I thought Dad always had a staff."

"He did," I admitted. "I was mostly there to serve coffee and make sure everyone showed up while he was down in the Capital. Still, it seemed like a job at the time."

"Sounds like a job to me," Aurora agreed. "What about now?"

"Hmmm," I said, "I hadn't thought about it. I'm awfully old to start something new."

"Nonsense," Aurora opened the oven door and slid in the muffins. "What about your art?"

Just then Haley wandered into the kitchen. "Morning, honey," Aurora said. "Did you sleep well?"

Haley nodded and climbed into my lap. I pulled her close. She leaned into me, watching her mother sleepily.

"Guess that starts the day," Aurora declared. "Muffins in ten minutes. You want juice to start?" Again Haley nodded.

"Can I help?" I asked Aurora.

"How about this, you do the holding, kissing, and patting part of breakfast and I'll deal with food." She smiled down at her daughter. "Don't you think it'd be fair to give Grandma some of that lovin' I get from you guys all the time?"

Haley nodded and planted a soft kiss on my cheek. I squeezed her tight, loving the kid shampoo, strawberry scent of her hair.

Pete strolled into the kitchen holding Kaitlin. "Look what I found in my bed," he announced, jiggling her up and down. Kaitlin giggled.

Emma appeared last, just as the muffins emerged from the oven. She greeted us with sleepy kisses and slumped into her chair, cradling the orange juice glass her mother handed her.

Aurora looked at her thoughtfully for a moment. "You stayed up reading late last night, didn't you?"

Emma nodded. "I was at a really good part," she explained, with just a touch of whine.

"That's fine." Aurora handed her a warm muffin. "We agreed you could stay up reading if it wasn't a school night, but you might want a nap later, maybe this afternoon before Haley's game."

"I'm too old to nap," Emma complained.

"I'm not," Pete said. "Tell you what, how about if we pull the mattress off our bed and into the living room so we can all have a nap after lunch. I bet Grandma likes napping." He smiled in my direction.

"Grownups are allowed to read during nap time," Aurora explained.

"I'd love to nap." I said. "But only if you'll all three cuddle with me while we do."

Even Emma agreed to that. The muffins tasted perfect, moist and delicious. The morning flew by and we napped well. Turns out grandmas do not read during nap time, but they sometimes snore. Despite Haley's soccer team's humiliating loss and a small tussle over Monopoly late in the day, we made it through and eventually toddled off to bed.

I collapsed, exhausted. I couldn't imagine what the day would have been like without our afternoon nap. With no nap scheduled for Sunday, I guessed I'd find out. Aurora warned me that the morning would include something she called Home Sunday Schooling. I'd almost drifted off when I suddenly realized that I hadn't thought of Jack all day. Aurora's influence, I decided and tumbled down into sleep.

⁂

"So what's this about Home Sunday Schooling?" I asked Aurora as I flipped pancakes the next morning. "Have you had a religious conversion lately?"

She shook her head. "No, that's the point. Mostly this is a religion-free zone, what with my ambivalence and Pete's outright antipathy."

I raised my eyebrows.

She explained, "You know his folks, his mom is still trying to convert him in every phone call. So anyway, we've always been pretty secular. Then last summer Emma came home from a friend's house talking about God and Jesus and asking all sorts of questions. We realized that if we didn't instill our values in them, someone else might. Just a minute."

She disappeared into the dining room and came back with clean napkins and placemats. "So now we Home Sunday School the kids. Right now we're reading Bible stories and talking about the lessons we see in them. Later we're hoping to branch out into other religions, but for now we're starting with what we know."

"Sounds like a lot of work." I remembered one year when I volunteered to teach John's Sunday School class.

"I guess, but it's better than the alternatives." She set the table. "I can't deal with church and neither can Pete. Look, I know you guys did your best taking me to church every Sunday, but I could never get over the feeling that it was all part of the show."

"I suppose there's always been a component of that," I confessed. "I mean, I've always been a believer and, to tell you the truth, most of the time I enjoy church. I love that feeling of prayerfulness and the music. But there's no denying that, come the coffee hour, we were on display."

"Right." She set out glasses of milk and orange juice. "I hated that. And Dad," she shuddered, "he's the definition of hypocritical. Once I figured out that he was screwing around so much, I couldn't stand to even see him in church."

"I remember. There was a lot of yelling and door slamming on Sunday mornings in those days. You know, your brother said much the same thing."

"I'm not surprised."

I scooped pancakes out of the pan and onto a warming tray in the oven and poured in more batter. "But, back to you. You don't seem as angry now. Visiting you has sometimes been scary."

"Well, it's easier now that you're not defending him. But you're right, I'm not as angry," Aurora said, her head in the refrigerator. "I just got tired of it. He was in my head, controlling my life for such a long time." She emerged with butter and syrup for the table. "Then I started seeing this great new therapist and she helped me see my way out." She grinned. "I sound so middle aged, don't I? Turning thirty will do that to you. Anyway, one of the things I finally got was that it wasn't all bad, some of the best things in my life came out of my horrible relationship with Dad."

"Like what?"

"Like Pete." She stopped to look at me, hands on her hips. "If I hadn't been so hell bent to get out of the house, I might not have gotten serious with Pete so early, we might not have married right out of high school and we might have lost each other."

"I can't imagine that," I said, flipping another batch.

She shrugged. "Who knows. If you start playing 'what if' you don't know what could happen."

"Do you think this will be enough?" I pointed to the stack of pancakes warming in the oven.

Aurora nodded. "You want eggs?"

I nodded. "But shouldn't we call the kids before starting them?"

"Yeah, you're right." She refilled my coffee. "Let's sit a minute and rest before the onslaught."

"You know it's funny." I sat. "That's the second conversation I've had about religion recently. John brought it up at dinner with Edward and Sam a while ago."

"Sam, that's Uncle Edward's new guy?" She stirred cream into her cup. "Do you like him?"

"Very much. I've never seen Edward this happy."

"I'm so glad." Aurora sounded relieved. "Rob was truly obnoxious. Did John ever tell you that he came on to him?"

"Are you serious?"

She nodded. "Yeah, the year before they broke up."

"Wow, poor John."

"To tell you the truth I think he was flattered," she said, and when I looked shocked she laughed. "I think it's a guy thing, as long as they're not freaked out about the gay part, they just don't get traumatized by passes like we do. But it does prove one thing."

"What's that?" I asked, nervously. She had an evil look in her eye.

"You and Uncle Edward really are soul sisters. You go for the same kind of randy men."

"Ouch." I didn't see the humor. "Let's hope that for Edward, at least, that's in the past tense."

"What? Your next love is going to be a repeat of Dad?"

"I'm not going to have a next love. I'm almost fifty, a grandmother, for God's sake. And," I reminded her, "I'm still married."

She waved her hand dismissively. "Married to Dad doesn't count. I still think you should divorce him. But even if you don't, it's time for a change."

Just then Kaitlin entered and rescued me.

For Sunday Home School we sat in the living room after breakfast while Pete told a simplified and G-rated version of the story of David and Bathsheba.

"Was that right?" he asked the girls when he finished. "Should David have married Uriah's wife?"

Emma said, "She should have said no."

"Good," Aurora praised her. "I think you're right. Bathsheba should have been faithful to Uriah. But how about David?"

Haley held up her hand. "He was bad for looking at her in the bathtub. Bathtubs are private."

"Right," Pete agreed. "So how about Nathan? Should he have told his friend David that he was wrong?"

Emma spoke first again, "He should have minded his own business."

"Is that what you would do? What if Haley stole a candy bar, not," Pete hastened to add as Haley protested, "that Haley would ever do something like that. But say she did something you thought was bad, would you tell her you thought she was wrong?"

"She would, she's always telling me I'm wrong," Haley said.

"I am not," Emma protested.

"Are too," Haley countered.

"I tell Daddy when I think he's wrong." The girls looked at their mother, open mouthed. "He's hardly ever wrong, of course." Aurora batted her eyes at Pete.

The girls giggled.

"I've even told grandma I thought she was wrong."

They looked at me. I nodded. "It's true. She did it this morning."

"The point is," Pete interjected, "that it's important to tell each other what we think. And if we're wrong we can admit it, like David did."

"But don't you think," I added, "that after we talk to each other, we need to back off and let the other person do what they think is right?"

Aurora gave me a long, thoughtful look. "That's a good point, Mom. Thanks. Got that, girls? We need to respect each other's free will."

The girls nodded and Pete announced, "Now it's my favorite Sunday School time."

All three girls chimed, "Cookies!" and ran to the kitchen.

"You picked that story for me, didn't you?" I asked Pete as we followed.

"You bet," Aurora called over her shoulder.

"And your point's a fair one," Pete said. "From now on, consider us your cheering section."

"I'm not keeping my mouth shut." Aurora waved her forefinger in the air. "But I concede that it's your life."

"Generous of you."

❧ ❧ ❧

Rollerblading at a rink with your grandchildren and a Girl Scout troop turns out to not be so different from roller-skating with those children's parents and all their friends. I'm still a terrible skater. The only difference was that now I found the noise, the atmosphere, the sheer seediness of it all sort of charming and I wasn't in charge of snacks. For dinner, as promised, I bought pizza at a funky, natural food place near the mall. We ordered, predictably, plain cheese pizza for the girls, but for ourselves we chose one artichoke and feta and one with goat cheese with roasted tomatoes. We even had a dessert pizza that tasted like a chocolate cream pie.

By the time we got them home, Kaitlin slumped fast asleep in her car seat and both Haley and Emma were well on their way. We carried them to bed. Pete built a fire while Aurora made tea.

"When does your flight leave?" Aurora adjusted a dog snout and sat down.

"Tuesday morning," I stood with my back to the fire. "I thought

I'd leave here tomorrow when everyone goes off to work and school. I've booked a hotel near the airport so I won't have to get up too early before my flight. I was hoping I could leave my car here. You could use it while I'm gone. There's a bus or shuttle or something that will take me in, isn't there?"

"I can drive you," Aurora offered. "Pete can do without me for the morning."

"Thanks, that's sweet of you." I smiled at them. "I have enjoyed this visit. Thank you both so much."

"Our pleasure," Pete said. "You know you're always welcome."

"It was great getting so much time with you," Aurora grinned. "Having the weekend together made a difference. I know the girls had a great time."

"It's not just that." I sipped my tea. "This was freer somehow. It's been a long time coming, but this is the first visit in years that felt normal."

Aurora nodded. "I agree. It's like we're not hiding any more. Not tense, you know?"

"Yes." My throat tightened. "It's better. Let's not go back."

"To the future." Aurora toasted me with her tea cup.

❧ ❧ ❧

Aurora and I took the dogs out one last time Monday morning then sat with coffee before the others arose.

"Pete's going to pick up Kaitlin and take care of the girls today." I started to protest, but she waved me off. "He loves an excuse to bring them down to the clinic and they'll be excited to play with the boarding animals. S-o-o," she drew out her sentence for effect, "I thought, if it's all right with you, I'd play hooky all day, and take you to the plane after lunch."

"Of course, that would be lovely. But is anything wrong?"

She laughed. "No. I think we should go shopping."

"Shopping? What for?"

"Mom." Her voice held almost the same note of exasperation she'd used as a teenager. "Look at you."

I looked down at my running clothes. "What?"

"Not now, silly. Look at your wardrobe. We need to take you shopping."

"What's wrong with my wardrobe?"

"First," she counted on her fingers, "it screams corporate or conservative church lady or Congressman's Wife."

"Which I am," I reminded her.

"Maybe, maybe not." She grinned. "But you're also an artist and you're going to Europe." She held up another finger. "Second, you need a simpler wardrobe for traveling. Your linen pant suits will get all mussed on the plane."

"I was planning to wear wool, which should be fine."

She waved dismissively with all three fingers. "And third, and you can't argue with this, they're all too big on you.

"They are?"

She nodded. "Baggy. You've lost what, twenty pounds?"

I looked at her, startled. "I don't know."

She pulled me into the bathroom and pointed toward the scale. I stepped on gingerly. I stared at the dial, looked up at her and nodded.

"I guess running makes a difference," I said.

She rolled her eyes. "That's why most people do it." She looked at her watch. "Better start getting them up. How about if you roust them out of their beds; they're more likely to look lively for Grandma, and I'll get breakfast on the table. And then," she rubbed her hands together briskly, "we can go shopping."

The girls looked so peaceful nestled in their beds. They smelled like sleepy kid as I kissed their foreheads. "Morning, darling," I said to each in turn, "time to get up and get dressed."

Monday morning breakfast rushed more than weekends, but I'd done the routine before. All my previous visits had involved the waking, washing, dressing, feeding, the "Do you have your lunch?" "Here's your backpack," buckling in and waving goodbye ritual. The girls kissed me goodbye and I promised to see them again as soon as I could. Tearing up, I stood in the driveway waving then turned to Aurora. "I'll be ready in a few."

"Take your time. Stores don't open until nine."

❧ ❧ ❧

Big chain stores anchored the corners of Aurora's neighborhood mall. Scattered between were a variety of smaller shops, most of them also nationally known. Aurora steered me to a tiny boutique at the edge of the strip called Simply Guinevere's. Inside, the racks discretely displayed brightly colored, richly textured clothing. I held up a peasant blouse in a linen cotton blend, beautifully and unevenly died rich purple and blue. "This is beautiful." I glanced at the price tag. "Aurora, this shirt costs $125."

"So you can't afford it?" she whispered back. "Splurge, Mom, you're going to Europe, I think you should get the skirt that goes with it, too."

I looked at her skeptically. "I don't like to waste money."

She laughed. "Don't you think you should buy a few nice things so you can look spectacular on your amazing new journey?"

"When you put it that way." I grinned, holding the blouse up to my chin and looking in the mirror.

We spent an hour and a lot of money in Simply Guinevere's. Aurora took me to The Well Trod Woman, where I bought a pair of walking shoes and knee high leather boots with a sensible but elegant heel. We visited Jumping Horses, another clothing store, where I purchased an ornate, deep crimson gypsy skirt for myself and bought Aurora an azure blue silk dress that made her look lovely, royal and wise, after which we scurried back to The Well Trod Woman for strappy party shoes to match her dress. At Travelwell I bought a trunk on wheels for my art supplies, a new handbag and a travel laundry kit, just in case.

As we stumbled out to the car, arms overflowing with packages, I said, "That was the most extravagant morning I've ever spent."

She grinned. "Fun, wasn't it?"

Back at the house we dumped the bags onto the guest room bed. I looked at the profusion of colors and textures. "Are you sure all this won't make me look like a foolish old woman?"

Aurora picked up an ankle length, blue nubby cotton skirt and the mauve sweater we'd found to go with it. "You look wonderfully yourself in all of these. Much more like my mom feels than you ever looked in those pants suits."

"How am I going to fit all this into my suitcase?"

Aurora picked up my bag and overturned it on the bed. My old clothes made a navy, beige and black pile beside the newer multicolored heap. "Easy." She picked up a pair of slacks. "These go. Your choice, Goodwill, or a box in my basement?"

I looked at them. "I wore those to the election night party on Tuesday." I picked up one of the empty shopping bags and held it out. "Goodwill."

"Excellent." She dropped the pants into the bag. "This too?" She held up the matching blazer and I nodded. "How about if you keep your casual stuff, jeans, sweats, T shirts, and we'll toss the rest." She picked up a pair of gray wool slacks.

"Not those." I grabbed the pants from her.

"Mom, they don't even fit."

"I don't care. They're warm and soft and I like them." I folded them neatly, along with a matching blazer and blouse, and placed both carefully in the bottom of my empty suitcase.

Aurora laughed. "I'll let you keep those, but everything else goes."

Even without my old clothes, the suitcase barely closed when we finished. I had to move a sweatshirt, my running shoes and robe into my art supply trunk. I stuck a change of underwear, my toothbrush and a baggie of toiletries into my new handbag, along with a thick novel Aurora pressed on me, insisting, "It's not Dostoyevsky but great plane reading."

We pulled into the Airport Hilton in the early afternoon. Aurora dropped me off with a firm squeeze, a kiss and an admonition to email her as soon as I could after landing. "Have a wonderful trip, Mom. And give Uncle Edward a big kiss for me. I'm proud of you."

"I'm proud of you, too, honey." I gave her a final hug. "You've grown up into a wonderful woman, a marvel."

"Thanks," she said. "I gotta go before I start bawling. Love you."

"I love you too." I waved as she drove away.

A bellhop appeared. I looked down at my luggage, one suitcase and a rolling trunk. I started to tell him I could handle it then stopped. I'd just spent over a thousand dollars on clothes. I could certainly afford to tip this nice young man for carrying my bags. "Thanks." I smiled. Here's to the future.

Ensconced in my room, I checked my ticket, deciding I needed to check out by eight in the morning. The bedside clock said three. Children and grandchildren are tiring. I lay on the big soft bed and closed my eyes. Maybe just a little—

I woke a few hours later and ran myself a bath. Turning on the radio, I listened to James Taylor sing "I've seen fire and I've seen rain" as I lowered myself into the soothing hot water. I felt disconnected, free. No one expected me anywhere. Edward didn't even know I was coming and everyone else thought of me as already gone. I wondered why the Catholics thought of limbo as a bad thing. It felt pretty good to me.

Eventually I emerged from the bath, opened my suitcase and pulled out my new green sweater dress. Falling loosely to midcalf, it felt warm and comfortable. When I saw myself in the mirror, I realized it didn't look bad, not bad at all. I pulled on my new boots, twirled once before the floor length mirror, and left for dinner.

In the hall, the elevator discretely dinged as the door opened. I slid in and punched the button for the top floor dining room. The door slid open to reveal a panoramic view of the airport. I saw one plane landing and another taking off. A hostess, wearing the perfect little black dress, showed me to a table overlooking the United Terminal. She handed me a menu and left me alone with all those pretty lights.

"Hello," said a deep voice behind me. "Are you waiting for someone or could I join you?" I turned to see a middle-aged man in a conservative suit sitting alone at the table behind me.

He smiled. "I don't mean to be forward, but I hate eating alone."

I surveyed him, medium height, broad shoulders, the start of a paunch. He wore his hair stylishly short, graying at the temples.

I smiled and nodded. "Sure. I don't mind." Since when didn't I mind? Hadn't I just been reveling in my aloneness? But this was different, wasn't it? Eating with a stranger was a different kind of alone.

"I'm Mike." He swung into the chair across from me.

"Gillian." I extended my hand.

Manager of an office supply store in Pittsburg, in town for a convention three floors down, he spoke in a deep, melodic voice. I enjoyed watching his open face as we discussed the vagaries of business, the weather and the Steeler's prospects.

"So where are you on your way to or from?" he asked as our dinners arrived. My salmon salad looked anemic next to his thick, pink steak, until I flicked it with my fork and the salmon fell away in glorious, perfect flakes.

"I'm, um, going to visit my brother." It seemed the simplest explanation.

When he asked if I wanted a drink after dinner I thought, why not? A jazz quartet played softly in the dark hotel bar. We sat side by side in the corner table, facing the band. He ordered a bottle of Chablis and the waitress poured two glasses.

"To new found friends," he toasted.

We clinked glasses and I sipped. What the hell am I doing?

"You're a very beautiful woman, you know."

Another part of me thought, Gillian, you should shut up and listen.

"Thank you." I leaned back into the cushion, trying to relax.

"I don't usually do this." He ran a finger up my arm. I thought, sure you don't, and shivered as his hand grazed my neck.

"Are you cold?" he leaned toward my ear and whispered.

"No," I breathed.

He cupped my chin and turned my face toward his. Our mouths inches apart, he asked, "May I kiss you?"

I looked into his dark brown, impersonally warm eyes. His pupils dilated as I watched. How long had it been since anyone wanted me? His mouth was hot on mine before my "Yes" was fully spoken. His firm, warm lips opened slightly, coaxing mine. For a moment our mouths engaged completely.

He pulled away and looked at me with a slight smile. "I'm probably pushing my luck, but we could take this bottle up to my room if you like."

I took another sip of wine, picked up his hand and traced the pale ghost of skin around his ring finger. "You're married."

"Yes." He took my left hand and fingered the gold band. "Does it matter?"

I shook my head. "I guess not." I picked up my purse and stood. He looked up at me enquiringly. I ran my hand through his short brown hair. "So, let's go."

His room exactly mirrored mine. The message light blinked. "You should call her," I said. "I'll wait."

He looked at me for a moment, traced the curve of my chin and nodded. I leaned against the door while he dialed home. He turned his back to me and spoke softly into the receiver. I didn't listen, didn't need to, I'd been on the other side of those phone calls for years.

When he hung up I moved toward him slowly, pulling my dress over my head as I walked. I undid my bra and dropped it on the floor with my dress. He gasped.

"You're amazing," he said when I stopped, a few feet in front of him, clad only in dark blue lace panties and boots. We stood for a moment. I watched his eyes scan me slowly. Then he reached out and touched my face.

Later he said, simply, "Jesus," as I rolled off him.

"That was great." I scooted to the side of the bed.

"What are you doing?" he asked, as I found my dress and slid it over my naked body.

"I've got an early flight." I slipped my panties and bra into my bag, leaned over and kissed him lightly on the forehead.

"It was nice meeting you," I said from the door, looking from his open mouthed, slightly relieved face, down the length of his torso to the crinkling condom. I waved, exited, and walked unsteadily to the elevator.

Smiling, I let myself into my room, ran a bath and wrote a short note to Jack on hotel stationary. "You're right. It is great getting to know new people. Gillian." I'd mail it in the morning.

Twelve

The novel Aurora gave me held my interest through the first flight and a layover in New York. Then, still tired from the night before, I slept most of the way to London. What with the layover, the long flight and the time change, we finally landed just after midnight and shuffled in a long, groggy line through immigration, baggage claim and customs. Online I'd discovered something called the Yotel at the airport terminal. I retrieved colorful money from an ATM and found Terminal 4, where I checked in at the automated kiosk to my little pod, a sort of high tech stationary sleeper car. I ordered a sandwich from cabin service and, around two in the morning, climbed into bed and swallowed a sleeping pill. I knew I should probably find a way to check email but it could wait for the morning.

✺ ✺ ✺

At ten the next morning a discrete knock let me know I'd overstayed my booking. I climbed out of bed, washed my face, pulled toothbrush and fresh underwear from my purse, slid into yesterday's clothes and was out on the terminal floor within minutes. It took longer to find a coffee kiosk. I'd last been through Heathrow the summer I graduated high school. After thirty years, at least in the airport, the accent proved the only familiar thing. With my luggage more unwieldy than I'd hoped, I eventually found a train that delivered me to Paddington station. I took a taxi to the little bed and breakfast hotel advertised on the internet as "clean and safe, reasonable rates."

The hotel sat in the midst of a long line of white rowhouses, on a side street near Victoria Station. Glad for the taxi, I'd never have found it on my own. Pulling my luggage up the front steps, I opened the dark wooden door and stepped into a simple sitting room where two brocade couches and a leather armchair faced the fireplace. Directly before me sat a long side table stacked with tourist office brochures and a desk bell, beside which a discrete sign said, "Please ring for service."

Moments later a woman about my age with short, graying red hair appeared, dressed in dark wool slacks and a dense brown sweater.

I introduced myself.

"Welcome, I'm Mary," she said in a rich, BBC accent. "You must be exhausted from your flight."

"Some," I agreed. "But not too bad, I slept in one of those funny cabin things at the airport."

"Oh, I've heard of those. Never tried one, of course, but I hear they're not awful." She led me up a short flight of stairs. "It's lucky we had a room for you, last minute cancelation. It's down this hall. I'm afraid the only thing we have is a family room with two beds, a tad more dear, but there you go." She opened the door to a small, clean room. Two full sized beds engulfed most of the space, leaving just room enough for a large wardrobe. A single armchair faced a curtained window with a view to the street below. On the wall hung an idyllic English countryside watercolor reminiscent of Constable.

"This is perfect, thanks." I loved the unforced coziness of the room.

"Brilliant." She pointed. "Bath down the hall this way, shared with two other rooms, a nice couple from Australia and a young French girl taking a term off to travel around. Towels are in the wardrobe, as well as extra blankets if you're chilled. We serve a full English breakfast between seven and nine each morning. If you need anything just ask and I'll do what I can."

"Actually, I'd like directions to an internet cafe and maybe suggestions for a curry lunch."

"Right." She handed me the key. "Leave your bags and come back downstairs. I'll give you a map."

Map and directions in hand, I set out for the internet cafe, which consisted of a single room lined with computers, the central station manned by an anemic, rather hostile looking young man who nodded toward an open computer in the corner. I logged into my email, intending to send a quick note to Aurora before scouting lunch. Instead I found thirty-six emails from Edward with headings like "Where are you?" "What's happening?" and "What the fuck?" The most recent email heading simply said, "Okay". That's the one I clicked.

> Dear Gillian,
> Finally wore Maggie down. So you're over here somewhere. Good. Call me when you're ready. Better be before Thanksgiving. We're going to Crete – you should be there. By the way, I'm still hurt but I get it so I'm kind of hoping you don't read the other things I sent – especially the last five. Oh shit, that means you're going to read those for sure, doesn't it? I was pretty angry. I'm over it. Love you. Call soon. E

I replied simply, "Love you too, I'll call soon. Sorry. G."

I deleted the other emails before I could think about it, wiped my eyes, wrote Aurora my reassurance, and left to find a phone. Everyone in London carried a cell phone pressed to their ear but I had to walk several blocks before spotting a classic red telephone box.

"Hi," I said when he answered.

"Gillian!" he exclaimed. "It's Gillian!" I heard Sam's whoop in the background. A wave of guilt almost knocked me over.

"Sorry," I said. "Somehow it sounded like a great idea to surprise you."

"It was a great idea," Edward roared. "You just should have told me you were going to do it." He laughed and everything was all right. "So where are you, Woman of Mystery?"

"London. Between Victoria station and Hyde Park, to be precise."

"That's wonderful, just a minute." I heard a muffled conversation. Edward returned. "How about if I come down to London and we travel back here together on Friday?"

"Can you do that?"

"Sure, Sam's working all week. He'd be glad to have me out from under foot. I'll check the flights, but at the very least I can take some kind of combination of train and ferry and be there by morning. Where are you staying?"

I gave him the number of the hotel and rang off. Finally, I went in search of lunch. Back at the hotel, I explained to a skeptical Mary that, although he'd be staying with me, the guy who left the phone message saying he'd meet me at Victoria Station around eight tonight was just a friend.

"I'm not your mum," she said. "Just don't make anyone uncomfortable and you can do what you like. It'll cost extra for another breakfast."

I nodded.

She continued, "I suggested you meet by the clock tower, Little Ben on Victoria Street. The Station's a bit crowded for finding each other."

"Right, thanks."

Edward showed up only fifteen minutes late, looking very European in his long trench coat, a leather overnight bag slung over one shoulder and camera case over the other. His face lit when he spotted me. He almost ran the last half block and grabbed me up in a twirling embrace. "You look great." he exclaimed. "I can't believe you're here, it's so good to see you." He let me down. "I'm starving and I want to hear all. Where are we going for dinner?"

"Thai?" I asked. "I passed a little place on the way that smelled wonderful."

"Excellent, lead on."

We wedged into a table along one wall of the restaurant, Edward's bags crowding our feet, and ordered spring roll appetizers and Thai iced tea. He turned his attention to me. "So?"

"So much has happened. I've been afraid to email you because, well, you know how those things get out. Actually, I don't know how they get out, I mean, isn't it all supposed to be password protected and—"

"Gillian," Edward said firmly, "Jack, you, what happened?"

I sighed. "It's a long story."

Edward looked at his watch. "Let's see I have, um, about three days. Will that do?"

I smiled. "I think the whole thing with John and Ashley tipped me over the edge."

"Wait, John and Ashley? You mean that was real? And Jack and Ashley?" His eyes opened wide.

"Both." I told him everything. We finished the spring rolls and ordered Phad Thai, fried shrimp with curry powder, and beef and bean red curry. I talked almost nonstop through dinner, with Edward throwing in the occasional question to keep me on track. We were finishing with khanom buang, a crisp dessert pancake covered in coconut cream, coconut flakes and coriander leaves, by the time I got to my encounter with Mike.

"Wait," Edward said. "You had a one night stand with a married guy in the airport hotel?"

"We used a condom," I said defensively.

"So you essentially doubled your life list of sex partners, what, yesterday? And you waited until dessert to tell me?"

"That's not true, I made out with Marty Donovan in tenth grade. And I probably would have gone farther if he hadn't dumped me for Martha, which if you ask me, he only did because of the name thing," I said defensively. "Although I guess it worked out. Except that she died, of course."

Edward laughed. "I love you, Gillian. So now that you're vastly more sexually experienced, what are you going to do?"

"About my marriage or my sex life?"

"Both, I guess."

I thought about it. "I'm hoping that being over here and away from it all for a while will bring some sort of revelation about my marriage. As for sex?" I shrugged. "Dunno. Mike was nice and I had a good time, but I think I'd rather not do that again. Maybe I'll be a nun, shouldn't be that different from marriage, just without the headache."

Edward smiled. "Maybe, but I don't think you'd like the food."

"Good point." I licked coconut cream from my fingers.

Back at the hotel Edward surveyed our little room happily. "I get the bed nearest the window."

"Suits me," I said. "That way I won't have to stumble over the suitcases on my way out to pee."

"It is crowded in here, isn't it?" He flopped onto the bed. "Just how long are you planning to stay?"

"My reservation runs through Wednesday, but she said I could extend it an extra day. Guess no one's coming in until the weekend." I rummaged in my bag for a bathrobe.

"I mean, over here. Looks like you brought everything you own." He gestured to my trunk and suitcase. "I take it this isn't a two-week visit."

"Open ticket." I grinned. "I thought you guys might need a cook."

"I think we do." He grinned back. "I'll call Sam and tell him." He whipped out his cell phone.

I grabbed my pajamas, robe and toilet bag. "I'm off to the bathroom. Give Sam my love."

I took my time changing and brushing my teeth. Then I heard a door opening in the hallway and, remembering the shared nature of the "loo," I scuttled back to the room.

Edward, relaxed in sweats and T shirt, lay stretched out on his bed, reading a brightly colored magazine. "There's a modernized version of Oedipus that looks interesting for tomorrow night. And one of those depressing but relevant and moving musicals that make 'musical comedy' an elusive term."

"Either sounds good," I said. "Last time I was here I was intent on avoiding all the trite tourist stops. I'm older and less cool now, so do you think we could visit the Tower? And maybe Buckingham Palace for the changing of the guards?"

"Whatever you like." Edward laid down his magazine and reached for the light. "I'm just along for the company."

"So what's this about Thanksgiving?"

"We're going to Crete and you're coming," he said firmly.

"Who's we?"

"You, me, Sam, Sam's colleague Edna, her husband and kids and I'm trying to talk Luke into coming with us." Edward sounded sleepy.

"Luke?"

"Yeah, you remember the sculptor everyone kept saying I should contact? He's great. We've been kind of hanging out. He's doing an installation in Paris right now, but I'm hoping he'll be done in time to meet us in Crete."

"You mean Luke Vanderwerken?" I swallowed hard.

"Uh huh."

"Wow."

"He's not like that, not scary at all. Really, you'll enjoy him. I told him all about you. Now go to sleep."

"Goodnight," I said, snuggling into bed. "I'm glad you're here."

"Me too." He patted the bed beside my knee. "This is like when we were kids."

"You're going to show me yours again?" I asked. "Really, it's okay, you don't have to."

"No, silly, when we were seven and eight-year-old kids. Remember when we'd get tucked in together in the boathouse and spend the night scaring each other with ghost stories and wild flashlight shows?"

"I do," I said. "And then we'd run up to the house and fall asleep on the couch in the living room with the lights on. Life stretched out so long before us then."

"Still does, darling," Edward said, sleepily, "maybe even more now."

I lay awake a long time, but fell asleep remembering the creaking and rocking of the boathouse, little Edward's hand latched firmly into mine.

Thirteen

I barely had time to unpack and settle into the apartment in Amsterdam before Edward was urging me to "Pack up, we're off to Crete."

A three-hour flight from Amsterdam brought us to Athens where we changed to a plane with no more than a dozen seats that carried us out over the Mediterranean. Landing in Iraklion an hour later, we stepped out into the relatively warm afternoon sun. I shrugged off my coat, glad I'd thought to tuck a sweater in my handbag. The sky really was a different blue.

Edward picked up the keys to the two compact cars we'd rented. I agreed to drive with Sam's colleague Edna and her two boys Casper, eight, and Peer, ten, while her husband Kevin rode ahead with Sam in Edward's car. Peer complained in Danish about riding in the girls' car.

Edna translated then admonished him, "Speak English, Peer. This is a good opportunity for you to practice."

Casper stared at me with the same shy intensity he'd had since we first met. Edward and I consulted the maps, agreeing that the inland road through Perema looked like the shortest route to our rented villa in Rethymnon. I followed him out of the airport and into the chaos of the Cretan road.

"It keeps you awake, doesn't it?" I asked Edna, after a particularly close encounter with a careening delivery truck. She simply nodded and leaned between our seats to check on the boys.

"I'm so glad you're driving, not me," she said after we made it through a roundabout with minimal signage.

I smiled. I didn't want to admit how much I was enjoying the adrenalin rush. "So what are you and Sam are working on?"

"My work involves biomonitoring, using aquatic insects as indicators of water quality." She looked to see if I was following.

I nodded. I wasn't particularly, but the road took all my concentration and I was glad for her to talk.

"I have been looking for genetic markers, specific DNA sequences, that indicate whether an animal has the ability to live in polluted waters, for example in low oxygen conditions." She stopped, perhaps noticing my lack of attention.

"Is it going well?"

She nodded. "Quite well. Sam's expertise in mayfly genetics is very useful to my work, so ours is a very productive collaboration. We're hoping he can try these techniques on your continent when he goes home."

"My continent." I smiled. "Funny to think of it that way."

She smiled. "Of course, you're American, so we could say your world, but that is a more political discussion."

The last thing I wanted was a political discussion, so I said, "And Kevin, what does he do?"

She laughed. "Kevin, now he is a more famous scientist. You see he chose a sexier field. He is a climate modeler and, of course, climate change is very important to the Netherlands."

"I suppose," I said, distracted by a large truck coming toward me that looked too wide for the road, or at least too wide for its lane.

"Most of Holland shouldn't exist. If the seas rise we might very well disappear."

"That's a grim thought," I said.

She nodded then was distracted by Peer and Casper jostling in the back seat.

Although we traveled across a good chunk of North Central Crete, we arrived at the villa in just over an hour. I'd seen the photos posted at the booking site on the web, but they didn't prepare me for the spectacular view from the patio. We could see a vast swath of the Mediterranean, the cove around the city of Rethymnon stretching off to the East.

Shouting something in Dutch, Peer streaked past me toward the swimming pool, Casper in hot pursuit.

"This is gorgeous." Kevin put an arm around his wife. "Thank God for these Americans and their quaint Thanksgiving rituals. Who else would come to Crete in November?"

"It's quite warm, though," Edna said. "If it's like this tomorrow we might even be able to swim."

Edward piped up, "Guidebooks say it's quiet here this time of year and that alone makes it worth the journey, provided you can live with some chance of rain."

Sam looked wistfully into the gardens ringing the terrace. "Daphnia would have liked it here."

Edward looped his arm around him. "He'll be just as happy hanging out with the dog sitter. She looked the type to slip him extra treats."

Sam smiled. "I know. That's why I hired her."

"Let's get settled so we can eat." Edward clapped his hands, picked up his bag and entered the villa. "Six bedrooms, it said, a master suite on each side of the house." He turned to Kevin and Edna. "East or West wing?"

"East for the sunrise," Kevin said firmly, then backpedaled. "That is, if you don't mind."

"God no," Edward groaned. "Sam doesn't need any more incentive to get up early." He turned to Sam. "Go west, young man, go west."

Sam rolled his eyes.

Edward looked at Peer and Casper, "That puts you in the smaller rooms down that hall." He pointed toward the eastern wing. Slinging an arm around my shoulder, he steered me toward the opposite hall. "Since we don't have children and Daphnia isn't here to require his own room, you and Luke get the small rooms over here. If he gets here, that is."

As we walked down the hall together, I whispered, "Edward, I don't know if I'm comfortable sleeping next to some strange guy."

He looked at me and guffawed. "That's right, sleeping wasn't on your agenda last time."

"No, I mean, it's not like that. This is Luke Vanderwerken we're talking about," I stuttered.

Edward grinned. "Should I send you over to sleep with Peer or Casper instead?" He squeezed my shoulder. "You will be sleeping in the next room from him, not in bed with him. But I suppose I could make him sleep on the couch if it will make you more comfortable."

"Sorry, guess I'm nervous about meeting him."

"The work is not the man," Edward said, sonorously.

"What the hell does that mean?" I pushed open the door to my room.

"No idea, but it sounded good, didn't it? Don't worry, he's probably not coming and if he does, he won't be here until Friday, so relax." Edward patted my back and opened his own door. Over his shoulder I glimpsed a large suite with an ocean view.

I stepped into my own whitewashed room, decorated with yellow wicker furniture and blue upholstery. A double bed graced one wall, covered in a deep blue bedspread and laden with yellow and blue striped pillows. A white curtain hung across the far wall. I opened it to find floor to ceiling glass, interrupted by a sliding door that led to an enclosed courtyard.

A small metal table surrounded by four matching chairs sat under a Plane tree in the middle of the courtyard, the flower beds stark, except for two large rosemary bushes. Surrounded by a shoulder-high brick wall, and completely separated from the outside world and the rest of the house, the courtyard sported three entrances, one in the wall for gardeners, one to my room and one, wouldn't you know it, to the room next door.

❦ ❦ ❦

I woke at dawn to a quiet house and, grabbing my sketchbook for company, found the kitchen. We'd discovered a small grocery on our way to dinner the night before and stocked up on coffee, tea, a cardboard box of olives, a huge chunk of feta cheese, apples, oranges and pomegranates (Edward proclaimed one could not come to Greece in winter without eating at least three pomegranate seeds, in honor of Persephone), cereal and milk for the boys, and bread, an oblong crusty loaf of whole wheat as well as a round olive bread with sprigs of rosemary peaking through the crust.

The kitchen opened onto the main patio. I found some cushions for the metal chairs, grabbed a throw from the living room sofa and my coffee, and stepped out into the cool morning air. Before me, blue sky graded into an even bluer ocean. In the East, the sun sat just above the horizon, shining a swath of gold across the ocean ripples. Homer's rosy fingered dawn. The town obscured my view of the shore, but even up here the air smelled of fish.

Just as I completed a sketch of the old harbor, Sam appeared, cup in hand. "Mind if I join you?"

I glanced up with a smile. "Please do, just give me a minute."

He sat quietly, watching the water while I finished roughing in the lighthouse.

I lay down the book, open to let the sketch set, and turned to Sam. "Morning. I wondered when we'd get back into our routine."

He smiled apologetically. "I'm sorry, I'd gotten used to going in to the lab early. I'm afraid I've been neglecting you."

"Nonsense, it took me most of the week to get my internal clock reset. So things are working out well with Edna?"

Sam nodded enthusiastically. "You should see her lab. She has an incredibly dedicated and smart group of students and post docs. It's a great place to be." He paused. "I'm afraid it hasn't been as fun for Edward. I've tried to carve out enough time but," he shrugged, "you know academics, we can get preoccupied. Until he met Luke and started going to local AA meetings, I'm afraid he was going a little stir crazy. That's another reason I'm glad you're here."

"I'm glad, too. This seems a world away from home, which I guess it is. But what I mean is, I can go whole hours without thinking about all that crap, well, maybe not hours, but certainly minutes."

"It's been bad, hasn't it?" He stared into his cup.

I nodded. "God awful, most of it, especially seeing John in pain. I think that's been the worst of it."

Sam grunted consolingly.

"But you know, it hasn't been all bad. I can't remember a better visit with Aurora. And there's also this odd feeling of freedom." I took a sip. I could feel Sam waiting for me to continue. "I feel lighter in here." I tapped my chest. "Maybe because, at least within my family, I'm not hiding it all, trying to keep everything together. It's all fallen apart and a part of me is glad. Is that awful?"

"No." Sam shook his head. "It sounds pretty healthy to me. It's like," he paused, looking out over the ocean, "it's like when I finally came out to my parents." He continued, still facing away from me. "They were great parents, good liberals even. But some part of me knew that it wasn't going to be good when they found out." He looked at me, smiling ruefully. "Always trust your intuition."

"They didn't take it well?"

"No," he snorted, "not well at all. Mom ran out of the room weeping and locked herself in the bathroom. My father just sat and stared at me. I was twenty-five, one year into my PhD program, but that night I felt like a naughty five-year-old. I left and haven't been back since."

"Oh, I'm so sorry, that's terrible," I said, thinking of my own children. "Maybe they're over it now."

Sam shook his head. "I send them a card every Rosh Hashanah, just in case. No response yet." He scuffed his shoe against the flagstone for a moment. "But the point is, that was a crappy time in my life and if I had it to do all over again, I would have gotten it over sooner. Having the family meltdown was less horrible than all that weird dancing around we'd done before. I love my folks, but that was the first honest day I'd had with them since eighth grade."

I looked at him, a successful, handsome, self-confident man, and thought about the fourteen-year-old terrified boy he'd been. Reaching over and patting his arm, I felt a wave of maternal sorrow for both man and boy. "Your parents are fools. Too bad they've missed seeing the great guy you are now."

"Thanks," he said. "Now that's enough or we might both start crying, which is not the way to start a vacation."

I laughed. "No, but it is the way I traditionally start Thanksgiving."

Sam grinned. "There's a tradition worth breaking. I'm starving, let's go put together a Mediterranean Diet breakfast."

Halfway through the morning we finally had everyone up, dressed and fed. We decided it was too late in the day to drive back toward Iraklion and see the ruins of Knossos Palace. Sunny and already warming, the day seemed to lend itself to wandering. We decided to explore the old city and eat a late Thanksgiving lunch on the waterfront.

We walked down our hill to the Four Martyrs Square, named after the almost Spanish looking church it fronted, past a seventeenth century minaret and through the Porta Guora or Great Gate, as Kevin, reading from a guide book, patiently explained first in Dutch to Peer and Casper, and then English to the rest of us.

In fair English, Peer said, "It does not look great to me. It is an old wall up high between two houses."

"He's going to love the ruins," Edward whispered in my ear, and I shushed him.

"Originally built by the Venetians, Rethymnon was destroyed by invaders in 1571 and almost entirely rebuilt by Greeks and Venetians at the end of the 16th century." Kevin read on, "The Turks conquered and lived here from the middle of the seventeen century until almost 1900."

"That would explain the mosques." Edna gestured to a domed red stone and brick building with gracefully pointed open arches at the entrance.

"Actually, that started out as a convent," Kevin told her. "If we turn here we should end up at a place with some serious religious history, first it was a church, then a mosque, then a church again."

"Why are we walking in the street?" Peer asked.

"No cars allowed in the old city." His mother took his hand in hers. "And, this late in the year there aren't many people either."

"Where's the harbor?" I asked. "It looked beautiful from above."

Kevin consulted his guidebook. "It's supposed to be essentially unchanged since the 1300s and," he looked around him, "if I'm right, there should be a little alley up ahead which will take us there."

The harbor stopped my breath. An old fortified wall circled back from the lighthouse I'd seen from the villa, creating a calm harbor in which floated ancient and new fishing boats, as well as three modern yachts. Two and three story medieval buildings extended along the walkway. At one edge of the harbor I could see an extension of the fortifications, the Fortezza, Kevin called it.

Most of the businesses looked closed for the season, but I thought I saw life in a cafe at the far end of the walkway. The boys jumped up and down, begging to see the fort. Sam and Edward wanted to walk out to the lighthouse. All I wanted was to find someplace to sit and draw the harbor. So we split into four and two and one, and agreed to meet at the cafe whenever our wanderings were complete.

❧ ❧ ❧

"From now on I'm making souvalaki, Greek potatoes and dolmades every Thanksgiving," I said to the group assembled for a late lunch at the harbor cafe.

"I've always felt uncomfortable about Thanksgiving." Edward dipped his dolmades into an egg-lemon sauce and bit into the grape leaf wrapped meat and rice. "I think it might be the wholesale slaughter of indigenous people or something. But I like celebrating it here, away from the pilgrims."

Peer looked up at his mother. "What does he mean?"

She smiled down at him. "Edward is making one of his odd American jokes."

Kevin interjected, "But you're right, I suppose. I mean I can't imagine celebrating the day whites invaded South Africa or anything like that."

"Oh, let's not start," Edna chided him. "It's such a lovely meal, why spoil it with politics?"

Sam reached across Edward for the souvlaki platter. "In my family," he said, once he'd secured the meat, "we used to go around the table every Thanksgiving and say something we were thankful for. So I'm going to start and you all can join in if you like." He paused and looked around the table. "I have so much to be thankful for this year, it is unbelievable. Edna, I love working with you. You have such a great team and I'm learning so much, thank you." He lifted his water glass to toast her. "And your amazing family," he added, toasting each of the boys and Kevin in turn. Turning to me he said, "Our new friendship has been a special treat I definitely didn't see coming and I'm so glad you're finally over here." He toasted me.

I tipped my own glass in return.

Settling his arm around Edward's shoulder, Sam said, "I'll save most of this for later, but you may very well be a reason to believe in God." He kissed him gently on the cheek. We all murmured appropriately. Edward just blinked and smiled.

"Oh my," Edna said, "that was lovely. You prepared, didn't you?"

Sam nodded.

"Well, I didn't, but I'm certainly glad to be here and that you're all here and Sam, it's great to work with you as well. Boys, anything you're thankful for?"

But they were busy throwing bread chunks at each other and laughing gleefully.

Kevin said, "I'm certainly grateful for well-mannered children. I do wish I had some."

My turn. I looked around the group and lifted my glass. "This," I swept my hand to take in the group, the food, the harbor, "is a miracle." My hand hit something soft. I heard "Oof" just as I noticed that someone had come up beside me.

"Oh, I'm so sorry." I looked up, expecting the waiter. Instead I found a short, barrel-chested man with graying red tufts of hair and an enormous nose, rubbing his upper thigh.

"Good thing you're not a better shot," he said with a smile.

"Luke." Edward jumped up to hug him, followed quickly by Sam. "You're here. I thought you couldn't make it until tomorrow. How'd you find us?"

"Got away early. You weren't hard to find, as far as I can tell you're the only tourists in town. Mind if I sit?" Luke Vanderwerken said, his accent only slightly colored by Dutch. He grabbed a chair from the next table and swung it in beside me. "You must be Gillian. Edward has told me a great deal about you." Before I could answer, he was introducing himself to Edna, Kevin and the boys.

"So, what's a miracle?" he asked once we were all settled.

I could feel the blush creeping up my face but answered anyway.

"Everything right now feels miraculous."

He looked at me for a long minute, nodded and turned away. The conversation moved on to a discussion of whether the afternoon would prove warm enough to swim. We finally decided it was warm enough for children to splash in the ocean and grownups to beachcomb. So we wound our way out of the old city, back to the present, up to our villa and, after packing towels and snacks in the basket conveniently provided by our landlords, we piled into cars and drove away from town to a long, deserted beach lined with modern luxury hotels.

Kevin and the boys stripped down to their suits and ran, howling, into the waves. Edward stretched out on a towel and pulled his cap over his eyes. Sam pulled out a chess board and looked quizzically at Edna.

Luke turned to me. "It looks like everyone else is entertained, shall we walk?"

I looked down the stretch of beach, golden in the late afternoon sun. "I'd love to."

We walked a few minutes in silence. Finally I spoke, "This is probably going to sound silly and girlish, but I have to get it out of the way."

He raised his eyebrows but nodded.

I took a deep breath and rushed on. "I love your work. I've seen lots of photos in art magazines, but only a few pieces in person, the 'Gulls' sculpture in the park in Chicago and, of course, 'Peace In Our Time' in D.C. They left me breathless. And I'm having a hard time getting past that to relate to you as just someone else here on Edward's Thanksgiving picnic."

Luke stopped and faced me. "Thank you." He held my gaze. "As a matter of fact, I like your work as well."

"My work?"

He nodded and turned to walk on.

I followed.

"I haven't seen much of it, only a few pieces Edward brought over with him, but I like what I've seen. You have an original eye. Gutsy. Is that the right word?"

I laughed. "Maybe, yeah, I could see that."

He stooped to examine a washed up jellyfish. "Have you ever seen photos of jellies at night in the deep ocean?"

I shook my head.

"If they're disturbed, for example if they're hit by the bow of a small boat, they're bioluminescent, that means they light up around the edges, blue or green. It's wild, really beautiful." He walked on. "Where do you show?"

"I don't."

"Why not?"

"It's complicated."

He looked at the sun and then down the beach. "I think it would be possible to walk for several miles down this beach, and we have nothing more to do this afternoon. I think this might be the right place for a complicated story."

I smiled and told him first about Congressman Jack and my fear of ending up a novelty, on display for all the wrong reasons. But once I started talking about Jack and my fears, I found I couldn't stop and I told him the whole awful story. He asked a few questions but mostly listened, eventually turning around and heading us back. I sputtered to a finish while we were still some distance from the group. We stopped.

He offered a rag from his pocket, apologizing for the clay crusting one corner.

I blew my nose, wiped my eyes, started to hand him back the rag but thought better of it. "I'll rinse this and get it back to you."

He smiled and said softly, "As you wish. That's quite a story you're living. I'm very sorry. When you are on the other side, we'll talk about getting you a show, okay?"

I nodded, feeling incredibly stupid for dumping the whole story out on this poor man who only wanted to talk about art. He must have seen something in my face because he placed a hand on my arm. "I'm glad you told me. It will help to have talked it out, I think. Now, come here." He grabbed my hand and pulled me toward the shore and out into the surf.

"What?" I asked, as my shoes went in and the cool water hit my legs. He dove forward into the wake, pulling me with him. The cold hit my face with a shock and I came up sputtering. "What?"

He wiped the water from his face and blinked at me, smiling widely. "Now there is a reason for your red eyes."

I stared at him a moment and then laughed. "You're crazy."

He nodded. "But I think it's better that our friends think we're crazy than sad, don't you?"

We dripped and laughed our way back to the group.

Sam held out towels for us. "What happened?"

"Artistic differences," Luke said. "Simplest way to tell her she was all wet."

Everyone laughed except Edward who looked worried.

"I'm fine," I mouthed and he relaxed.

That night we ate at a restaurant high on the hill, overlooking the lights of Rethymnon. Luke and Edward talked Edna, Kevin, Sam and me into buying a bottle of retsina, then laughed when we all grimaced at the first sip.

"What's in this?" I gasped, while Peer and Casper pointed and giggled.

"Turpentine," Edward told me. "They used to make it in pine barrels, but now they just add the turpentine after."

"That's awful." Sam set down his glass.

"Your faces are the best argument I've had for sobriety in a long time," Luke said, toasting us with his water glass.

We all ordered water the next time the waiter came by.

Fourteen

I woke to another beautifully blue morning and grabbed my sketch book. In the kitchen I found a pot of coffee already brewed. Pouring myself a cup, I opened the door to the patio. Luke sat at the table hunched over a portfolio sized sketchpad, his hands flying across the page.

"Coffee?" I asked. He growled something and waved me away. I ducked back inside, took my coffee into the living room and setting aside my sketchbook, picked up a magazine. Sam arrived shortly with his own cup. He settled into a chair across from me, a book propped on his knees.

After about an hour Luke joined us, carrying a full pot of coffee, with which he refilled our cups. "Sorry I was so gruff," he apologized. "I'm afraid I can be fairly single minded."

"No need to apologize," I said. "Actually, I'm envious. I've never been able to put my work first like that."

His eyes fell on the sketchbook beside me. "You were coming out to work."

I shrugged, surprised at the angry look on his face.

"Don't do that," he said so sharply that Sam looked up from his book. "Don't let anyone get in the way of your work. Not even another artist." Seeing my expression, he continued more gently, "You've got to be terribly selfish, Gillian."

I smiled, embarrassed. "But I'm just an amateur—"

Luke cut me off. "Bullshit. Either you're an artist or you're not."

I could see Sam smiling out of the corner of my eye. I ignored him, said briskly, "So, shall I make breakfast?" and brushed past Luke into the kitchen.

He followed me and watched for a moment as I took down a large platter and began removing things from the little refrigerator. "I've hurt your feelings," he said after a while. "What a brute I am this morning." He ran a hand through his bristly tufts of hair. "First I chase you off the patio and then blow up at you for going. Please accept my apologies, I'm not housebroken you see."

I smiled in spite of myself and he said, "Let me help you with that."

I nodded, "Apology accepted," and passed him the olive carton. "Can you put these on one side of the platter, please?"

"Of course, may I also put out this cheese?" He held a large chunk of feta.

"Sure," I said, my back to him as I slipped bread slices into the toaster and eggs into a pot to hard-boil. By the time I looked back, he had constructed a wonderful, stair stepped, off kilter tower of the olives and cheese. I smiled, quickly sliced an apple and passed him the slices.

"For color," I suggested. He beamed and added the apple slices, rind side out, to his creation.

Sam came into the kitchen as we finished the platter. "Wow. That's breakfast? It's too beautiful to eat."

"Transitory art, think of it as one of Goldsworthy's leaf and stick arrangements." Luke glanced at me. "Perhaps presumptuous, but I like it, don't you?"

I smiled.

He turned back to Sam. "Or if you like, a sand sculpture built at low tide."

Sam shook his head. "I have no idea what you're talking about, but I'm getting Edward and his camera. Don't anyone touch this until everyone has seen it."

"Seen what?" A groggy Edward scratched his chest as he entered the kitchen.

"Our collaborative breakfast sculpture." I watched his eyes widen as he noted the arrangement of fruit, cheese, olives, eggs and toast on the kitchen table.

"And I thought you couldn't get more creative in the kitchen," he said. "It gives a whole new meaning to the word 'presentation.'"

Once everyone appeared, it took far less time to dismantle our sculpture than it had to build it, but the glow of collective praise carried me through packing a giant picnic basket for lunch and organizing the drive to Knossos, the ancient Greek palace where Daedalus may or may not have built a labyrinth to house the mighty Minotaur.

Following the blue highway signs in Greek and English, and doubling back a few times, we finally found the site, drove past the private pay lots and parked free near the west entrance, beneath a giant cypress. We shared the lot with a handful of other cars and one tour bus.

"You can't get anywhere near this place during the summer." Luke climbed out the back of Edward's car. "Absolutely crammed."

The boys bounded out of my car and, chattering loudly in Dutch, ran toward the tree-lined entrance walkway. We followed them and finally reached an open stone courtyard from which we could see the ruins of the palace entrance. Kevin squatted on a broken bit of wall and called to the boys. He pulled a small blue book from his coat pocket and, once they were seated, began reading in Dutch.

"He's telling the story of the Minotaur," Edna said. "Shall I translate?"

"Please," I said, "my Greek mythology's rusty."

"Now he is telling of the evil King Minos, whose palace we are about to enter, and how he used to make Athens send girls and boys to be sacrificed to the Minotaur, a half-man, half-bull monster who lived in a labyrinth in this very palace." She paused as Kevin paused, allowing the boys to look around at the crumbled stones.

Kevin started again and Edna followed. "Theseus, the son of Athen's king was the greatest hero Athens had ever seen, so one year he sailed here as one of the doomed boys. But really he came to slay the Minotaur so Athens would never again need to send its children to death. Theseus was very handsome and King Minos's daughter Ariadne fell in love with him at first sight."

Peer and Casper giggled and Edna said, "I'm afraid my boys are not romantics yet." Then, as Kevin spoke again, her voice shadowed his. "Ariadne loved Theseus so much she did not want him to die. She gave him a ball of string, so that after he killed the Minotaur he could find his way back."

Kevin shut the book and pulled a ball of string from his pocket. He spoke to the boys and they leapt up, chattering excitedly in Dutch. The three of them hurried toward the Palace entrance. "He has told them it is time to find the labyrinth." Edna smiled. "Shall we go?"

The five remaining adults turned to enter the palace.

"Didn't it all end badly, though?" Edward asked. "Something about black sails?"

Edna nodded. "And faithlessness. Theseus had promised to take Ariadne away with him, but instead he abandoned her on an island. She cursed him to forget to change his sails from black to white, the signal to his father that he was alive. His father, seeing the returning ship with black sails, believed his son dead, and he threw himself into the sea."

"Betrayal." I scanned the ruined walls. "Potent stuff."

Edna nodded.

We paid the fee and once inside we all wandered in different directions, agreeing to meet for lunch in the central court near the throne room. I found myself drawn to an open space named the Piano Nobile, where I could look down on both partially restored and unrestored rooms and walkways, and try to imagine the palace as it had once been. Beyond the ruins the hills rolled out, dotted with scrub, olive and cypress trees. A cool breeze made me glad I'd brought my jacket. I found a warm spot of broken wall, sat, and sketchbook in hand, began trying to capture the feel of ruin and renewal.

I'd just finished the rough outlines of a white trumpet flower growing from between two pavement stones when I heard Luke's voice over my shoulder,

"Nice," he said, "sad but beautiful."

"You startled me." I straightened from my hunched position.

"Sorry, may I join you? If I'm interrupting I can go."

"No, please sit," I told him, thinking, what if this is a test and I'm supposed to prove I'm a real artist by sending him away?

But he smiled and took a pad, somewhat smaller than my own, out of his bag. He also produced two black charcoals and handed me one. "There's a game we used to play in art school. It goes like this. We look at the same scene and each draw for about a minute, then trade and you finish mine, I'll finish yours. What do you say?"

"That it sounds intimidating." I accepted the charcoal.

"Nonsense, if we don't like them we toss them. It's just a game. Let's see," he scanned the horizon, "how about the scene to the left of that pillar?"

"Including the pillar or not?"

He shrugged. "I think it makes a better composition with, what do you think."

I looked. "Only if we cut the scene before we get to the end of wall."

He nodded. "Good. Let's begin."

I sketched the broad contours first, trying to capture the starkness of the midmorning sun juxtaposed against the softness I saw in the hills beyond. I was just getting to the fine, internal lines when Luke said, "Time." He smiled at me as we traded. "You see, even when I'm pleasant I can be arbitrary."

"It's all right. That was a good stopping place for me." I took his pad and looked at his vision of the same spot. His lines were stronger, more architectural. He'd tilted much of the scene, giving it a playful cartoonishness. I saw where I could do something interesting by bringing in a minor note. We finished at about the same time and looked at our completed sketches.

"Wow." I looked at the whimsical notes he'd invented along my column and hidden in the vegetation in the distant background.

He held my completion of his sketch. "Wow is right. You've added complexity, that's interesting. It never worked out this well when I was in art school. Can I keep this?"

"I'll trade you," I said. "But I don't have anything to fix with, they'll smudge."

He pulled a can of hairspray from his bag. "Never leave home without it." He grinned. We sprayed and lay the drawings on the courtyard to dry. He leaned back and looked around. "When I was here before there were so many tourists you couldn't enjoy it like this. But there were also little lizards on all the rocks, basking in the hot sun. Now, we've lost the hot sun and the lizards."

"Sam will be disappointed," I said. "Peer and Casper, too. But I think I'm fine without tourists, heat or lizards." Just then we heard the sound of someone speaking through a megaphone in a language I didn't recognize.

"You spoke too soon." Luke moved the drawings to an out-of-the-way spot as a large group of Asian tourists invaded our courtyard, led by a smartly dressed young woman in platform shoes that looked like a sprained ankle to me. We watched the group and listened to the foreign patter, then tucked our dried drawings deep into our sketchpads and braved the labyrinth in search of our own noisy group.

Over lunch Kevin and Luke argued amicably about whether the eighteenth century archeologist who excavated Knossos had destroyed antiquities (Kevin's position) or created art (Luke's position) when he recreated parts of the palace, building wooden columns and repainting frescos. Edna allowed that it might not matter since everyone, King Minos and the archeologist were dead. Edward said he thought the spruced up parts made a nice change from rubble, but mostly he spent lunch previewing the digital images he'd taken over the course of the morning.

We stayed so long amongst the ruins that we decided to stop for dinner at an Irakilos restaurant before heading back to the villa. By the time we got home everyone was ready to retire to their own rooms. I made a pot of tea and carried it out to my private courtyard table. Although the day had been warm, without the sun the air cooled sharply. I wrapped myself in a blanket stripped from my bed and pulled one of the chairs out from under the cypress tree so I could watch the stars. I wasn't surprised when Luke joined me, pouring himself a cup from my teapot.

"This is such a beautiful island," I said. "When were you here before?"

"Years ago." He wrapped his own blanket tight, tipped his head and watched the sky. "With my wife on our honeymoon."

"You're married?" I tried to remember what I'd read about his personal life.

"Widowed."

"Oh, I'm so sorry."

"Me, too. I can't even tell you I was a brave and good husband, because I wasn't. But I do I think I started out well, or at least that's what I'm remembering today." He looked over at me. "Don't look so concerned, she died about fifteen years ago. Cancer, of course."

"You don't have to talk about this if you don't—"

He shook his head and looked back up at the sky. "You told me your secrets, maybe if I tell you mine, we can be friends, isn't that how it is for women?"

I laughed. "Certainly for little girls, maybe for grown women, too."

"Yes, I think it is." He leaned on the back legs of his chair. "Magda was beautiful, a dancer from Brazil. We met in London around the time of my first show." He played with the edge of his blanket. "I was something of a phenomenon back then, both for my art and for my bad behavior." He gave me a wry smile. "You may have heard about it?"

I nodded.

"So I married Magda and we came down here on our honeymoon. That may have been the last good time we had." He sat up abruptly, threw off his blanket and began pacing the courtyard. "It was my fault. Magda had a temper, oh could she fight." He smiled at the memory. "But then, I gave her plenty of reasons. What is it Edward says? 'Everyone's a slut when they're drunk.' I don't know if that's true for everyone, but it was for me. I drank, I screwed, and drugs, well, if you followed the art news you probably read about some of that."

He looked at me and I nodded.

"I would like to tell you that Magda's cancer got me sober, but it didn't. I left, couldn't handle it. I wasn't even there when she died. I drank shamefully through the funeral and checked myself into treatment the next day." He shrugged. "It wasn't my first attempt at the cure, as they used to call it, but somehow it stuck. I guess I'd hit bottom."

"I'm so, so sorry."

He shrugged again and sat next to me. "Her death was her last gift to me. Without it, I am convinced I'd be dead now. Instead, I'm still here, still making art and still going to meetings." He picked up his cup from the flagstone. "Good tea. Anyway, now we are even, so we must be friends."

I leaned over and hugged him. "We don't have to slit our hands and do the whole blood brother thing that guys do for friendship now, do we?"

He shuddered. "Ick. No." We finished our tea and, blankets firmly wrapped around our shoulders, said good night from our respective doorways.

❧ ❧ ❧

I woke to rain pounding the courtyard. In the kitchen I found Luke at the table with toast and coffee, a suitcase and shoulder bag at his feet. He smiled as I entered. "Good, you're up. I hoped I'd get to say goodbye. I have to leave, the owner of the piece I installed last week called to tell me that some idiot hit it with a car when they were leaving a party last night and he needs it repaired right away." He shrugged. "He's paying for my flight and my time so I can't say no. Besides, no one else can really make it right."

"Oh. Well, it was very nice meeting you." A sudden wave of emptiness washed over me.

He smiled. "It was nice to meet you, too. I was thinking that if you're free on Thursday, I could finally make good on my promise to take Edward on an art tour of Amsterdam. Maybe you could join us?"

"I'd love to," I said, a little too enthusiastically.

"Good, then it's settled." He looked at his watch and stood to rinse his dish. "Now I need to go. Tell everyone I'm sorry I missed the end of the party." After a quick kiss to my cheek, he was gone.

Later, while Edna, Kevin and the boys played a board game on the bed in their room, and Sam drove into town to check his email, Edward made a fire in the living room and we cuddled on the couch watching the flames.

"How're you doing?" he asked after a few minutes.

"Up and down," I answered. "Glad I'm here."

"Me too." After a long pause he asked, "So what do you think of Luke?"

"I like him. I think I could learn a lot from him and I'm flattered to death that artistically he takes me seriously."

Edward sighed in audible relief. "I'm so glad. I think he's terrific and I was nervous you wouldn't like him. He's been great to us, just great."

"I like him fine," I said. "Did I tell you he's taking us on some sort of art tour on Thursday?"

"He is?" Edward pulled away to look at me. "Wow, you must have done some serious arm twisting. I've been trying to get him to take me museum hopping for months."

"No, it was his idea. Guess he figured you'd waited long enough." I relaxed back into the cushions.

"I guess," Edward said slowly.

Just then the door opened and Sam burst in, holding a small cardboard box. He flopped onto the couch on the other side of Edward, opened it with a flourish and announced triumphantly, "Bakery."

"What are these crinkly, donut-like things?" Edward pulled a glistening pastry out of the box.

"She called them diples or something." Sam bit one. "Good, but very sweet, hand me your tea."

Edward handed Sam his cup, still examining his own diple. "These are wild looking. Where's the bakery? Do you think she'd let me take some shots?"

Sam shrugged. "You can try. It's right downtown. She's not busy. I think I might have been her only customer today. She doesn't speak much English," he warned. "Oh, I almost forgot, Pearl wrote that she's trying to talk John into bringing her over here after Christmas, while he's still on break."

"Great." I bit into my baklava, savoring the sweet honey walnut mix and ignoring the flakes of crust falling on my chest. "But I thought she wasn't coming until January. I hope everything's all right at home."

Sam handed me the email. "Doesn't sound like anything. Maybe she's simply accommodating John's schedule. We've only the two bedrooms, I'm not quite sure where we'll put them, but—"

I licked my fingers. "She can sleep with me and maybe John on the couch or in Edward's study? It will be cozy, but they won't stay long—" I trailed off. "Look at me, always the planner, here I am a guest in your house, mooching off your hospitality and figuring out how to move in my relatives."

Edward grinned. "Of all the Gillians I know, that's my favorite, the one with chutzpah. Besides, we're paying a fortune for the apartment and it isn't all coming out of my photographic sales or Sam's reduced sabbatical pay. We should have a Foundation meeting soon to sort it out."

Sam smiled. "Even if you weren't helping with the rent it'd be fine with me. I can always escape to the lab, which is probably why Edward is so delighted to have company."

"Give me back my tea, Abandoner." Edward engulfed the rest of his diple, gulped the last of the tea, wrapped one arm around each of us and leaned back on the couch. "Sam already did all that God talk at dinner the other night, but I think this is as close to heaven as I'm ever going to get, my best friend and my beshert both here by a roaring fire on a rainy day in a villa in Crete. In my dreams I couldn't have written it better."

"What's a beshert?" I asked.

Sam kissed Edward's cheek. "Your true love, the other half of your soul."

Edward took over. "The story is that our souls get torn in half when we come to earth, so that one soul ends up as two people. Of course, the rabbis thought in terms of a man and a woman, but it's a big system, mix-ups are bound to happen. Anyway, we don't feel complete until we find our other half." He squeezed my shoulder. "Yours is out there somewhere, looking for you."

My eyes filled. "I'm through with all that. Just doesn't work out for some people."

"He'll be sorry to hear that," Sam mumbled, eyes closed, his head resting on Edward's chest.

"Who?" I asked.

"Your beshert."

Fifteen

Back in Amsterdam life settled into a predictable pattern. Our small, extravagant, and beautiful apartment in the canal district encompassed two long narrow floors of a 17th century building. Just fifteen feet wide, the rooms stacked together like pop beads. On our first floor a large living room overlooked the street and canal in front, and the kitchen-dining area opened onto a balcony over a lovely little garden in back, with a bathroom and stairs nestled into the hallway between. Upstairs, Sam and Edward's bedroom fronted the street while the area over the kitchen split into two very narrow bedrooms, one Edward had turned into his office and the other I made my own.

I loved the proportions of my room. It was so narrow that a tall man could probably lie with his head touching one wall and his feet the other, which made the length, maybe 30 feet, seem even longer. When I arrived, the simple furnishings, a bed, desk and bureau, were clustered by the tall leaded window looking out over the back garden. I immediately moved them around so I had space for my easel by the window. I covered the ancient wood floor with a canvas drop cloth and gave my afternoons over to painting.

Mornings I fixed breakfast for everyone in the brilliantly updated, compact but satisfying kitchen. Usually Sam left early for the lab and

Daphnia and I had an hour or so to ourselves before Edward appeared. On warm days I sat on the tiny balcony. Most days dawned cool and bleak. We woke to frost one morning but by midday it was gone. Some of the time Edward left early, intent on catching the light, but mostly he rose late for a leisurely breakfast. Having him watch me putter around the kitchen, baking bread or preparing the next meal, made me feel like something out of a 1950s sitcom, except of course I've never worn heels and pearls while cooking. But then he'd smash that image by dusting or vacuuming or cleaning the bathroom and mopping the kitchen floor.

Eventually I'd stuff a sketchpad and some shopping bags into my backpack, click Daphnia onto his leash and descend to the street. I was grateful the boys had chosen to live in the canal district, heart of the old city. Stepping out the front door, I found myself on a boulevard where the canal formed a giant meridian and the streets narrow one-way passages with tiny sidewalks. Parked cars and trees lined the canal edge. Boats moored along the concrete sides of the canal. The air smelled wet and fresh even when it wasn't raining.

We lived on a residential street, but busier areas were just around the corners. A few blocks walk to the Nieuwmarkt brought me organic produce on Saturdays and on Dam Square I found a giant upscale food plaza and a view of the Royal Palace. So mornings we shopped, usually stopping at a street cafe to rest, read, sketch, or enjoy a coffee, Daphnia curled happily at my feet.

Although we emailed nearly every day, I felt adrift from my family and friends back home. The days graded into each other in a way I hadn't known since childhood. The only distinguishing points were Fridays, when Sam lit candles, and Thursdays, when Luke educated Edward and me about Dutch art. He made us promise not to go to art museums without him, although he allowed we could visit any other type of exhibit on our own. In the first three weeks of December we circled Museum square, visiting Mondrian at the Stedelijk, Vermeer at the Rijksmuseum and, of course, Van Gogh at his own museum. We didn't stroll through the galleries like tourists. Instead Luke pulled us from room to room, steering us toward particular works.

Later, at a café, we engaged in comparisons of light, texture and composition. Afterwards I felt energized, images and connections tumbling around inside me so intensely that after our first Thursday, when poor Sam and Edward endured a half-burnt, half-raw dinner, I started cooking Thursday's meal ahead. Christmas Eve (coincidentally the last night of Chanukah) was scheduled to fall between our third and fourth outings.

As we studied the Potato Eaters at the Van Gogh, Edward turned to Luke. "Speaking of eating, are you free on Christmas Eve?"

Luke stayed silent a long moment. He looked at me and I said quickly, "If you're busy, we understand. I mean, we'd love to have you, but you know, if you have somewhere else to be, then—"

He raised his eyebrows, and I stopped, took a deep breath, told myself to quit babbling and let the poor man speak.

"As it happens, I'm free," he said finally. "And I'd love to come, if it isn't an inconvenience."

"No, no inconvenience" and "We'd love to have you," Edward and I gushed.

Luke smiled, asked if he could bring anything, thanked us, and turned back to the painting. "What do you think he's feeling?" Luke pointed to the tall young man on the left. "Do you think she wants him or is she afraid? I feel the painting leaves us wanting to know. Let's move on."

Christmas Eve day, I recruited Edward to carry my shopping so that when I saw the large, fat goose in a butcher's window I couldn't stop myself. Then I found chestnuts, endive, fresh pomegranates, mangos and blood oranges and the meal began to take shape. We had to stop and rest a few times on our walk back from the market, but as I surveyed the ingredients strewn across the kitchen, I knew it would be worth it.

I baked bread I envisioned as a cross between a challah and Greek Christmas bread with bits of anise and orange poking from the braids. By early afternoon, the rich smell of roasting goose, mixed with a sharp note from the pomegranate sauce simmering on the stove, filled the apartment. Daphnia circled the kitchen, sniffing and licking the floor in search of dropped scraps. Edward entered, his eyes widening when he saw the spread, and the mess.

"Maybe I could help with clean up and setting the table?"

"Can we move the table into the living room?" I asked. "We'll have more room and it's prettier at night."

"Sure. Good idea. We can set the Chanukah candles in the front window like the rabbis tell us we should."

I helped him move the table then hurried back to the kitchen, while he rummaged for a tablecloth. After a while, he returned and began scrubbing pots. When dinner was finally at a resting point, I went to change.

I paused on my way upstairs. "The table is beautiful, Edward, thank you." He'd found a bright, flowered cloth and set out four coordinated, but mismatched napkins and the best cutlery and glasses our rented digs provided.

"I doubt it is up to the meal." He looked at the settings critically. "Could use some crystal, but we have what we have."

Upstairs, I changed into the deep purple linen blouse and skirt Aurora had persuaded me to buy. Looking in the mirror, I first pulled my hair back in a bun, decided that looked too matronly, tried pinning the sides with a clip, too girlish, and finally gave up and let my hair flow down my back, gray streaks and all. The doorbell rang as I slipped into a pair of ornate Chinese slippers. As I descended the stair, I saw Luke and Edward standing in the hallway, Luke bent over Daphnia, rubbing his ears. He looked up and froze.

Edward turned, following Luke's gaze. "Wow."

"It's too much, isn't it?" I said. "Aurora talked me into this and—"

Luke interrupted me. "You look beautiful. That color on you, it's amazing."

"Thank you." I felt a blush heat my face and neck.

Luke laughed. "That color's nice, too."

I excused myself into the kitchen. I threw on an apron, determined not to leave the kitchen until Sam's arrival forced me out. I felt foolish. I should never have let Aurora talk me into the clothes. Parading around like some idiot peacock. I stirred the pomegranate sauce, basted the goose, and checked to make sure the sorbet had set properly. I heard Daphnia's bark then Sam's voice as Edward swung into the kitchen.

"What are you doing?" he asked.

"What does it look like I'm doing? I'm cooking."

"You're almost crying." He held my shoulders. "What's wrong?"

"Don't. Don't be nice to me or I'll cry."

He pulled a tissue from his pocket. "Too late." He handed it to me. "You want to tell me what this is about?"

"Oh, Edward, I feel so foolish. Aurora talked me into this outfit and now I look like— like—"

"You look hot," he said flatly. "You stopped a man dead in his tracks. Is there a problem with that?"

"He was just embarrassed for me." I fought back the edges of a sob.

Edward guffawed. "If that's what embarrassed for someone looks like, I need to get out there and do some stupid looking things. Honey," he said more gently, "I love you but you might be the stupidest person I know. Now dry your eyes and think about something comforting. I know, imagine an impotent Jack." He jiggled his eyebrows until I laughed.

"If anyone asks, I had to cut a few last minute onions."

He nodded and left me to compose myself.

❧ ❧ ❧

Sam sang the blessing in his lilting tenor as he lit the Chanukah candles. We sat in silence for a few moments, watching the flicker of flames across the full Menorah.

"On this last night of Chanukah, I have something for everyone, but you all need to open together." Edward pulled out three packages.

"But you've already been so generous." Sam blushed then turned to Luke. "I mean Gillian and I have had presents every night."

Luke smiled. "Good, I like the idea of a long giving season. And I'm flexible. After all, here in Holland Santa has no reindeer, but instead comes on a steam boat with a helper in black face."

"What?" I asked.

"We're not always as enlightened as you imagine, but we're working on it."

Edward passed out the presents. "Now on three. One, two, three, rip."

I opened my package and looked at the close up of Luke and me with our heads together, downturned faces solemn, concentrating. "When did you take this?"

"At Knossos," he said proudly. "Can't you see the red column in the background?"

"I love this," Luke said quietly. "Are they all the same?"

"You and Gillian have the same image. Sam's is the group picture we had the waiter take after dinner that last night," Edward explained.

"Thank you." I avoided looking at Luke as I stood to kiss Edward's forehead. "It's wonderful. I have something for all of you as well." I retrieved the bag I'd hidden behind the drapes and felt suddenly shy. "I made them all small. So if you don't like them they won't take up much space." I brought out the wrapped miniatures.

"That's encouraging," Edward teased.

"I'm not going to make you count." I read tags and handed the gifts around. "Open them whenever you like." I watched as they pulled off the paper. Edward grinned, Sam looked delighted and Luke looked... thoughtful. Shit.

"You look just like this sometimes." Edward showed Sam the little portrait.

"She caught that look you get." Sam held his up next to Edward's face and considered. Looking at me, he said, "This is wonderful, how it looks like him without really looking like him."

"Thank you." I glanced nervously at Luke, still considering his portrait.

Finally he looked up and caught my eye. "I don't spend enough time with a mirror to know if I look like this, but it's how I often feel. I didn't know it showed. Thank you." He held my gaze for a long moment. "It happens I brought little presents as well." He disappeared into the hallway and came back carrying his satchel.

"First, to the magnificent Edward and long-suffering Sam, something to grace your doorpost." He handed Sam a small, oblong box wrapped in shiny blue paper.

Sam held it out questioningly to Edward, but Edward shook his head, smiling. "You're the long suffering one, you open it."

Sam carefully unwrapped the box and gasped. He looked at Luke wide eyed. "You made us a Mezuzah?"

"I made a Mezuzah box for your doorpost. You'll have to find your own prayer for the inside," Luke corrected.

"Look ,Edward," Sam held out a small metal box decorated with ornate scrolls. Tiny figures seemed to dance in and out of the scrolls.

Edward took it. "Wow. This is gorgeous." He looked up, tears welling. "Luke, this is amazing."

"You're welcome." Luke turned and walked slowly toward me, pulling a square box wrapped in deep crimson paper from his bag. Sitting on the arm of my chair, he handed it to me. "And this is for the incomparable Gillian."

I looked down at the box. "I'm afraid to open it."

"Don't be," he said softly.

I undid the tape, careful not to rip the paper. Opening the lid, I slid my hand into the shredded newspaper. I touched something cold and pulled out a bronze, slightly larger than my hand. I looked closely at the abstract figure, perhaps a dancing woman or a flame, smooth, beautiful, but somehow disturbing.

"It's magnificent." I twisted it in my hand to watch the play of light across the polished surface.

"You see," Luke said, "we had the same thought, to give the other a mirror."

I looked at him. "This is me? This is how you see me?"

He brushed a strand of hair from my face. "This is who you are."

Sam coughed apologetically. "I'm way out of my league. I brought chocolates."

Dinner tasted delicious, everything perfectly done. But it felt like an afterthought.

✠ ✠ ✠

Luke called Christmas morning to arrange our Thursday outing.

"My mother-in-law and son fly in Wednesday," I told him.

"Ah," he replied, "the place I was going to take you has too many stairs for your mother-in-law. Do you think they'd like the Rembrandt exhibit at the Rijksmuseum?"

And so it was settled, we'd meet for lunch and Luke would show us the Master. Perhaps it was the result of too much goose fat the night before, but I felt suddenly queasy.

Sixteen

I paced the waiting room outside Customs until I finally spotted John's dark hair bobbing above the crowd. A moment later he saw me and waved. The crowd parted and I saw Pearl grinning at me from a wheelchair. My stomach dropped. I ran forward. "What happened?"

They looked confused, then Pearl's face cleared. "Oh, you mean the chair. It seemed easier and faster for traveling. My walking is much better than when you left, really. You want me to show you?" She started to stand, but I waved her back down.

"Later. I'm sorry I panicked. I've missed you." I leaned to hug her. Straightening, I pulled in my long limbed son. "Both of you."

"I missed you too, Mom." He squeezed me. "I know it's been only a month, but it seems like a long time."

"Amen," said Pearl. "So where to next?"

"Here, Mom, you take Grandma. I left our bags with a nice guy from the flight. I should go rescue them and him." John spun the wheelchair into my hand and ran back to get the bags.

"He's a wonderful traveling companion," Pearl said, watching him go. "You did a good job with that boy. Now tell me everything. How's Edward? Sam? What do you do all day?"

I laughed. "You'll see soon enough. Here comes John with your bags. Is this chair yours or the airlines?"

"Ours for the duration." John strode up, one bag slung over his shoulder, another wheeled behind and Pearl's folded walker tucked under his arm. "We're ready, lead on."

We rode the train to the Central Station and grabbed a cab from there. The cabdriver stared open mouthed when Pearl ignored the chair he held out to her and walked up to the front door. "She walks. It's a miracle," John whispered to me.

Edward opened the door holding a huge bouquet in one hand and Daphnia in the other. He bowed to Pearl, handing her the flowers. "Welcome, Momma Pearl, our house is yours." Daphnia strained toward Pearl, his whole body wiggling in Edward's arms.

"Thank you, Edward." She buried her nose in the bouquet. "How lovely, you're a thoughtful young man."

"And Johnny, you look great, especially for a man from a lagging time zone." Edward bearhugged John, squeezing the poor dog between them.

"Thanks for having us, Uncle Edward." John's voice came out muffled through Edward's shirt. Daphnia licked both men's faces.

Once we'd divided the luggage, with John in Edward's study, Pearl with me and the wheelchair in a closet, I brought Pearl and John to the kitchen for tea. I asked about the flight, we talked about Thanksgiving at Aurora's, the new job Pearl found Aziza and circled around until finally I asked, "How's Jack?"

Pearl took a deep breath. "There's been some talk about that Health Conglomerate, what is it called?" She turned to John.

"AHC," he replied grimly, scratching Daphnia's ears as the dog lay curled in his lap.

"AHC? Is that the company that had something to do with Jack's subcommittee?"

Pearl nodded. "It seems there may have been some… impropriety. It's probably nothing, of course, but it has been worrisome."

I looked at John. He nodded, tight lipped.

"Well," I said, "I'm sure it will all work out." There was a long silence. I stood. "Maybe you'd both like to clean up before supper?

I know you're tired, but the trick is to stay awake until evening. Sam should be home soon and we'll have an early supper so you can get to sleep."

※ ※ ※

Later I cornered John alone. "How are you really?"

He shrugged. "Some days are good, some bad. This is a good day."

"Are you still seeing Ashley?"

"God, no. I'm sure she's a great kid, just a little twisted, which," he grinned, "I might not mind under normal circumstances." His face shut down. "But these are not normal circumstances. And I don't know if Dad's still seeing her, if you were going to ask."

"I wasn't. Are you in contact with him?"

John shook his head. "Not yet. Aurora and I had a nice talk, the Friday after Thanksgiving, of course. We both agree we'll need to get past all this with him at some point, but neither of us is there yet."

I hugged him. "Give yourself the time you need."

※ ※ ※

Luke proved an idyllic docent of the Rembrandts. He took us on a slow tour of one gallery. Gone was the frenetic art teacher and critic Edward and I had enjoyed, replaced by a gentle, charming art historian. Pearl and John were clearly captivated. Edward and I exchanged glances, but I had to admit Luke was hitting all the right notes to enthrall his audience. He declined to join us for tea after the museum, proffering as excuse an unexpected meeting.

Later, as Pearl and I lay in bed, she said, "I like that young man very much."

"Luke? Me too," I said sleepily.

"Did I ever tell you about Jacob Fritz?"

I sat up. "I think you started to before I left."

Pearl sighed. "You remember Jack's father. He could be difficult."

"I remember."

"Jacob Fritz taught in the classroom next to mine. I was teaching second graders in those days, what a wonderful age. Jacob taught the next year up." Pearl was silent for a while. I thought she'd fallen asleep when she continued, "My husband was starting in business then. He was gone a lot. Jacob and I used to eat dinner downtown together occasionally after parent teacher conferences or if faculty meetings went too late. Jacob was single and Jack— Jack Junior, your Jack— wasn't born yet. Well, one thing led to another and—" again she was silent.

"Did you love him?" I asked.

She sighed. "I was crazy about him. He wanted me to run away with him, such a romantic. But, well, you didn't do things like that in those days, think of the scandal. When I look back—"

"You know you made the right choice," I finished for her.

"Oh no, dear," she said, sharply. "It's my one great regret. I should have walked out on Jack Senior years ago. And I certainly shouldn't have let what people might think get in the way of being with the man I loved. I looked for him after my husband died but, of course, it was too late by then, he'd made his family with someone else."

We were silent again. Just as I thought she'd drifted off, Pearl said, "I do like your young man Luke."

"He's not my young man," I told her.

She didn't reply.

❧ ❧ ❧

Friday dawned clear and unseasonably warm. Perfect weather for visitors, but I had to admit I'd begun to think of the rainy winter weather as vaguely romantic, like Wuthering Heights. John got up at dawn, probably still jet lagged. While I sliced bread for his toast, he asked, "Hey Mom, are you sleeping with that guy Luke?"

The knife slipped. "Ouch." I popped my nicked finger into my mouth. I shook my head at John as I reached for a paper towel to wrap my wound.

"'Cause it would be all right if you were." John picked up the knife and finished slicing the bread. "He's cool. I called Aurora last night and she googled him while we were talking. Did you know he's a really famous sculptor?"

I wrapped my finger in paper towel, pressing against the small cut to stop the bleeding. "Is googled a verb? And yes, I know he's well known and no, I'm not sleeping with him. We're friends." Taking a few slices from John I dropped them in the toaster. "Since when are you impressed by fame? You've met plenty of famous people."

John grinned. "Not artists. And none of them looked at my mom like that."

I blushed. "We're just friends. Why does everyone keep jumping to conclusions?"

"Friends are good." Sam sauntered into the kitchen followed by Daphnia, who immediately jumped into John's lap. Sam poured himself coffee, leaned against the counter and turned to John. "If you want to come to the Institute with me this morning, you're welcome. I'll hand you over to the grad students and they can show you around. Fridays are always slow and I'm sure they'd be glad of a break."

"Wow, I'd love it." John quickly turned toward me. "If that's okay with you."

I kissed his head. "We'll be bereft, but it might be a good excuse to do things you'd hate, like china shopping or whatnot."

"Don't do the stuff I want to do, like the Anne Frank house or the red-light district." John handed a plate of toast to Sam, his other hand stroking Daphnia's back.

"Interesting combination," I said. "Perhaps we could visit those places on two different days?"

Just then Pearl walked in, already dressed, her purse in hand. "I've been reading about tulips. It's a fascinating history. There's a museum where we can learn about political corruption and speculation in the tulip scandals."

"Count me in." John said. "But today I'm going to go meet hot Dutch chicks at Sam's work."

"Are there any?" I asked Sam.

"You're asking me? It's true that Edna's lab has more women than men, not all of them Dutch, most are hard-working, clean and pleasant. I've never felt I had the right to ask more than that of any woman." He bit into his toast. "This is good, baking fresh bread is, of course, a plus, but I can't tell you whether any of Edna's students bake."

Pearl smiled serenely at Sam. "I wish there were more men like you."

"Be a problem for continuation of the species," John said.

"Oh, there are too many people anyway." Pearl sat down beside John and accepted a cup of coffee.

Sam started coughing, apparently having inhaled some toast.

Edward strode into the kitchen. "How's a man to sleep through all this racket?"

"Ever the gracious host." Sam handed him coffee.

"I just checked my email." Edward sipped thoughtfully. "Apparently my mother married Mr. Greene, either in or out of the ballroom with a knife. Actually, they eloped."

"Oh, I forgot." Pearl rummaged in her bag. "I was supposed to bring you this. She dropped it by the morning before we left, evidently on her way to Florida." She pulled out a small, neatly wrapped package.

Edward opened it, looking for a long moment at the picture in a simple silver frame. He held it up to the rest of us, revealing a headshot of the smiling couple. They both wore tailored navy. He sported a single rose boutonniere, she a large orchid corsage. "Poor bastard," he muttered, setting the frame on the kitchen counter.

"Now Edward," Pearl admonished, "you of all people should know that taste is an individual thing. Mr. Greene happens to find certain kinds of women challenging. I think they'll be very happy."

"You're absolutely right. Florida, huh?" He brightened. "Let's toast the happy couple." We all raised our mugs and he continued, "What's that Fiddler on the Roof prayer? Ah yes, let me paraphrase. May the Lord and Mr. Greene bless and keep my mother…far away from us."

"Have you met her?" John asked Sam as we all drank.

Sam shook his head.

John smirked. "Clearly you are a darling in the eyes of God."

"Oh stop it," Pearl chided. "It's true Evelyn can be difficult but," she held up her hand to stop our chatter, "she, like everyone else, deserves happiness."

"You completely engineered this," I accused Pearl, pulling muesli and bowls from the cupboard.

She blushed. "Perhaps I encouraged the match." She gave Edward a small grin. "Consider it a belated Christmas present."

Edward engulfed her gently. "On behalf of my mother and myself, I thank you." He planted a solemn kiss on the top of her head.

"Oh, speaking of celebrations—" Sam took the stack of cereal bowls I handed him and set them on the table. "Edna has invited us all to their house for New Year's Eve. Evidently they do a big bash every year."

"Awesome." John dumped Daphnia off his lap and started pulling out spoons, butter knives and napkins from the sideboard. Daphnia sniffed the floor, searching for dropped toast and cereal. "And with the time change, we'll ring in the New Year way ahead of the folks at home."

Pearl frowned. "Oh dear, I'm afraid I didn't bring any fancy clothes."

"Clearly we must shop." Edward transferred the fruit bowl from sideboard to table. "And you need something new, too, Gillian."

"I just bought new clothes," I protested. "Why is everyone trying to dress me?"

"Because I'm afraid you've gotten into a rut, dear," Pearl said.

"I can't believe you're siding with him," I told her, but she and Edward were already discussing the day.

"I know just the place." He slid into a chair and picked up the cereal box. "I've passed it on Prinsengracht. Oh, this will be fun." He looked up at me. "Really, I'll help. I'm good with women's clothes."

"I bet that's a sight," John snorted.

Edward turned to him. "I said I'm good with women's clothes, not in them. I'm a photographer, remember?"

"You're a nature photographer," Sam said softly.

"I'm a photographer, and in the past, I produced my share of portraits for aspiring models and yes," he looked around at our skeptical faces, "some of them were women. Anyway," he scooped up a large spoonful of cereal, "you need me to carry."

Life without a car can be challenging, but with Pearl in her wheelchair and Edward along to carry packages, we managed our way to the dress shop on foot, stopping only twice along the way for more mundane items, first oranges and later yogurt and cheese.

As we neared the street, Edward scouted ahead. "Found it," he called and sprinted across the street.

"Perhaps we should cross at the intersection." Pearl eyed the traffic. I nodded and wheeled her up, across and back to where Edward paced impatiently.

I relaxed when I saw the window of the vintage store. "Actually, this might be fun."

"Of course it will be." He took charge of Pearl's chair. "I'm thinking the '30s were your decade, Momma Pearl, and Gillian will make an excellent flapper."

"And you?" I asked.

He smiled. "Do you suppose they have a top hat? I've always wanted a top hat."

In the end, Pearl chose a white rayon suit with black velvet trim that the saleswoman assured us came from just before the war. She looked quite elegant once we added faux pearls and a little black pillbox hat, complete with veil. Edward found his top hat, a brocade suit vest and pinstriped pants.

He held up a gangster suit and spats. "Sam?"

We giggled, nodded and searched until we'd found a 1940s era letter sweater and watch cap for John. I pawed through the racks, growing increasingly discouraged.

"I don't think there's anything for me."

"How about this?" Edward asked, holding up a simple but slinky, dark blue bias cut silk dress.

"Does that thing have a back?" I asked. When he shook his head I said, "I'd freeze." He grinned and pointed to the huge embroidered shawl Pearl held for me to consider.

"It's you," he declared.

"I'm too old and fat," I protested.

"Just try it on," he cajoled and Pearl nodded enthusiastically.

I sighed and took the garment into the tiny, curtained dressing room. Stripping to my underpants, I slid on the cool silk. I had to admit it fit. Perfectly.

I twisted to see how the dress draped, exposing my back, falling into soft folds above my dimples. I looked at my back critically.

Not bad for nearly fifty, but I'd better cover it in the presence of the young.

I stepped out of the dressing room. Pearl beamed.

Edward said, "Jesus, you look like Myrna Loy."

"Is that good?"

"Very good," Pearl said. "Perfect."

"I'm still too old and fat."

Edward snorted. "Now you're fishing. Here try these on." He held out a pair of dangling rhinestone earrings. "I'll look for shoes."

❧ ❧ ❧

Our costumes were a hit. Edna and Kevin lived in a beautiful three-bedroom apartment in Borneo Sporenburg, the new sustainable development in the Eastern Docklands. We crossed the most amazing rolling red pedestrian bridge to get there. The apartment itself abutted the river. Parties spilled from other apartments into the central patio in a joyous, somewhat tipsy, revelrous chaos. Kids, including Peer and Casper, thundered up and down stairways throughout the complex.

Edna introduced Pearl to her own mother, a ninety-year-old bridge fanatic who spoke perfect schoolbook English. The two women settled into opposite chairs at a card table in the corner and were soon the center of their age group. Similarly, the graduate students engulfed John and swept him away immediately. By the time I spotted him again, a pretty Asian woman had appropriated his cap and pulled him onto the small dance floor that had transformed the patio.

I drifted between Sam, ensconced with a clutch of academics holding forth in one corner, Edward surrounded by a small group that looked to be the only entirely sober kernel in the room, and the kitchen, where I helped whenever Edna allowed. Finally, I came to rest by the large plate glass window overlooking the river and watched the lit up boats glide by.

Luke arrived, out of breath, at about ten minutes to twelve. From across the room I saw him apologize to Edward. "Sorry I'm late." He checked his watch. "It's still last year, isn't it?"

Edward laughed, clapped him on the back, turned him around and pointed toward where I stood. As I watched him approach, I realized how much I'd hoped he'd come. We smiled. I pulled my shawl more tightly around my shoulders, shivering as his eyes traveled the length of me.

"Hi," I said.

"Hi."

Just as he reached me the crowd began to count. "Ten, nine, eight—" Why hadn't I ever noticed those flecks of gold in the green of his irises? "Six, five, four—" He took my hand and pulled me toward him. I realized with a jolt that we must be exactly the same height. "Three, two, one." Our lips met in the sweetest, most tender kiss I'd ever imagined.

He pulled away. His hand cupped my face. "That's all I've thought of today and then the cab got stopped in traffic and I thought I'd missed it."

I smiled. "Do it again."

This time his mouth pressed harder, insistent rather than tender. Finally we broke and he pulled me close. My eyes focused and over his shoulder I saw Pearl and Sam both smiling.

"When does your family leave?" His voice rasped in my ear, his breath on my neck made me shiver.

"Next Tuesday morning."

"Have lunch with me Tuesday," he said.

"You don't have time on Tuesday," I protested. "Thursday's the only day you're free."

He brushed the hollow of my neck with his lips. "I'll make time. Please. Gillian, don't make me wait."

"I can't be casual," I warned.

"I'll wear a tux." He pulled back enough for me to see his eyes. "I don't feel casual. Say you'll have lunch with me on Tuesday. We'll do anything you like, we can talk or visit art museums or—" he wound his hand under my shawl and ran a finger up my spine, "or whatever."

"Okay." I breathed. "But for now you have to stop that."

He smiled and kissed me once more, softly. "Ok, I'll stop…for now." He stepped away and took a few deep breaths before crooking his arm for me. "Shall we go mingle now?"

After an excruciating cab ride home in which I felt the weight of my companions' unuttered interrogations, I climbed the stairs, slipped quickly into my pajamas and bed without even washing my face. When Pearl climbed in and settled into her own side, I pretended to be asleep. She turned off the light and rolled away from me. After a long moment of silence she said, "What a nice man."

I didn't answer. I couldn't articulate my thoughts but felt pretty sure they had nothing to do with nice.

Seventeen

We all avoided the subject of Luke for the next few days. I didn't trust myself to voice what I was feeling and whatever it was, I wanted to hold it close, terrified it might disappear. The others made vague, feeler forays into regions where his name might logically arise. I either changed the subject or left the room and eventually the queries stopped. Perhaps I remained silent in fear of disapproval. To be fair, I never sensed any, only curiosity, and from Sam and Edward, joy.

Sam returned to work shortly after New Years. Everyone else bundled up and Edward and I played tour guide, visiting places we'd not yet seen ourselves. John found the red light district a fascinating sociological study in legalized prostitution. I thought too much of it might put a girl off sex for good. Pearl just smiled. The tulip museum sparked an interesting discussion about free trade. The Jewish museum, first opened before the war and reopened after, with the population it described gone, made me weep.

John purchased an English edition of Anne Frank's diary and read to us the morning before we visited. The inscription over the exit stopped us all. "In spite of everything I still believe people are good at heart." That's about as inspiring as it gets, I thought. John argued that her idealism would have faded with age.

"Don't speak ill of the dead," Edward snapped, then apologized and said maybe he should walk home alone.

Alone was the last thing I wanted to be. As we walked along the streets around the museum neighborhood, I kept envisioning Anne and Margot arriving, dressed in all their clothes, to entomb themselves in the tiny attic and wait.

The next day I let Edward take John and Pearl to the Van Gogh museum, begging off with a headache, unwilling to let them know it felt disloyal to go without Luke. I stayed in my room. Daphnia slept peacefully on the bed while I painted until I'd leached out the angry sadness clinging to me like cobwebs from any other attic. I stepped back to see what I'd done. That vision, that's the disturbing stuff Luke sees. My hand sought and found the bronze he'd made. Caressing it, I turned the easel to the wall so it couldn't infect my dreams.

Tuesday morning came.

Luke called early. I picked up the hall phone.

"When can I see you?" he asked.

"I'm taking Pearl and John to the airport at ten. I can meet you around noon."

"I could come to the airport."

"No, I'll meet you in front of the Central Station, under the clock. I'll give you my cell number."

"I'm not good at waiting, Gillian. But I'll work on it." He took my number and rang off.

I took a deep breath and hung up the phone. Turning, I found Sam carrying two coffee cups. He handed one to me. "Luke?"

I nodded.

He smiled. "Shall we wait dinner?"

I looked at him helplessly. "I don't know, maybe not."

He smiled and gave my shoulder a quick squeeze. "Take your toothbrush, just in case."

❧ ❧ ❧

I was shaking by the time I exited the station. Luke must have seen me before I saw him. He bounded up, engulfed me in a forceful embrace and kissed me passionately. I pulled away, glancing around. No one paid any attention.

He smiled, stroked my face. "This is Amsterdam. You can see much better shows than this just a few blocks away." I blushed and he laughed. "I love the way you blush, you're so American. Come, you're a food person, let me feed you. I'll take you to a little place where they know how to do dim sum the likes of which I've only had in Hong Kong."

He took me to a large chaotic restaurant that smelled of hot oil and fish. We found a somewhat secluded table. I let him fill out the card. After all, I'd never been to Hong Kong. Soon the waitress transferred little plates from her cart to our table. I picked up my chopsticks.

Luke smiled. "Here, let me." He expertly plucked up a dough wrapped bundle and brought it to my lips. I bit in, tasting the warm, savory filling and felt it drip down my chin. Luke popped the other half in his own mouth while I wiped my face.

"We're not going to make it through lunch if you keep that up," I warned.

He smiled. "I'm ok with that, although it's good to take one's time."

"Should we talk about this?" I scooped up a portion of seaweed salad.

He chewed for a moment and took another bite. "We should." His eyes held mine. "First, I wasn't being flippant the other night. I'm hoping we end up in bed soon, and that is very much on my mind, but this is real for me. If it isn't real for you then we'll just have lunch and I'll do my very best to let things go back the way they were." He stopped, watching me closely.

I had trouble breathing. It took a long time before I could say, "I'm terrified. I've had so much emotional turmoil in the last few months. I wasn't expecting this. I didn't think I even knew how to feel anymore and I know I've never felt this. The last time I fell in love I was eighteen and stupid. As you know that didn't work out so well. Oh, God, I'm talking too much. This is what, like a first date? I've just alluded to my ex, well not really ex, husband and I know you're not supposed to say the L word on the first date, are you? See, I'm way out of touch, and I'm babbling."

Luke took my hand. "It's okay. You get to say whatever is honest for you. Just so you know, from my point of view, you're moving in the right direction." He leaned forward and kissed me, a gentle, tender kiss that almost brought me to tears. "So, are we agreed that we wouldn't be averse to moving into L territory?"

I laughed and nodded. "And I'm good with the bed soon idea, too."

His grin broadened. "Good girl. I like your spirit. Here, eat, you need to keep up your strength. Try the chicken."

We ate in silence. He dipped a meatball into sauce, "There's something else. It's not very romantic, but perhaps we could stop by the clinic on our way home?" Stooping over his plate to bite, he looked at me from under his eyebrows.

"Clinic?" I asked. "You mean…? I've only been with two men and one was very, very careful."

He nodded, dipped another ball and touched it to my lips. "And Jack. You're sure about all his partners?"

"Good point." I bit into the meatball.

He kissed me again, our lips slippery with sesame oil and pork. Pulling back, he said, "And I don't think you should have to worry about my behavior either. Haven't you had enough of men asking you to trust them?"

"I suppose," I said. "So I guess we'll have to postpone that whole bed thing for today."

"Are you kidding? This is Amsterdam." He checked his watch. "I bet we're lovers by three. Oh, I do love that blush."

֎ ֎ ֎

I'd never been anonymously, or otherwise, tested before. We took our numbers, a nice young woman drew blood, and we sat in orange plastic chairs to wait. I read the condom posters, some scary, some funny, festooning the walls.

"This is not the sexiest thing I've done recently," I whispered to Luke.

His lips caressed my neck as he ran a finger up my arm. "Think of it as twenty-first century foreplay."

"It's getting sexier," I admitted.

He chuckled.

My phone rang. "Hi Edward."

"Gillian, you have to come home."

"What happened?" I looked at Luke, who'd stopped what he'd been doing and watched me. "Can't it wait? I'm sort of busy now."

Edward snorted. "I bet you are." Serious again, he said, "Come home. Bring Luke. It's important. Mark just called. Jack's been arrested and there's a warrant out for you."

"Shit."

The woman called our numbers. Luke took my slip from my lap and went to retrieve our results.

∞ ∞ ∞

"Mark wanted to book you on a flight out tonight," Edward greeted us, holding Daphnia. "But I told him you'd driven up to Groningen and wouldn't make it back in time. So you leave tomorrow morning."

"Thank you."

"Who's Mark?" Luke asked.

"My husband's campaign manager," I said automatically and flinched when I felt him stiffen. "It's his job to clean up Jack's messes."

Edward ushered us into the living room. "Maybe he should get another job."

Sam appeared, holding a tea tray. He set it down and put his arms around me. "I'm so sorry."

"Rotten timing." I sniffed back tears. Luke led me to the couch where I curled against him and accepted the tea Sam offered. "So, what happened?"

Edward shrugged. "I don't know all that much but evidently the FBI has been investigating Jack's connections to AHC for months. Yesterday they appeared with search warrants for both his office and the house. They found money hidden in various places. This morning they arrested him."

"He's in jail?" I tried to process what I was hearing.

Edward shook his head. "Are you kidding? He's a United States Congressman. They read him his rights, he called an attorney, and they released him on his own recognizance."

"So why do I have to go?"

"Warrant. They need to question you," Edward explained gently. "They found some of the money in the house and," he paused, fingering his cup, "there was a stash of money in the cabin. Her studio," he told Luke. "You have to go back and cooperate."

"The cabin? He went into my cabin?" My stomach churned.

Luke held me closer. "I'll go with you,"

I shook my head. "No, God no. The reporters will descend like vultures as soon as I get off the plane. You don't need that." I pulled his arms around me more tightly. "We don't need that."

"She's right," Edward said. "There's no way around it. It's going to be ugly. I'll go, they already know me as a 'close friend of the family.' Don't worry. I'll take care of her."

Luke, quiet for a long time, finally grunted assent.

Edward looked at his watch. "John and Pearl should land in about an hour. Aurora's meeting them so they can drive up together. I think she's taking your car. I've booked us through to the regional airport. I wasn't sure what the scene would be like at the house and whether the kids could get away, so I called Maggie. She'll meet us."

I nodded, numb.

"Are you hungry?" Sam asked.

I shook my head. "I should pack."

"I'll help." His hand on my back, Luke pushed me up. I nodded and climbed the stairs. He followed. I could feel Sam and Edward watching and worrying. I had to give them something to do.

"Maybe we could eat in a couple hours?" I called down to them. Immediately I heard their footsteps, hurrying toward the kitchen.

Once in my room I sat on the bed. Luke sat next to me, cradling my hand.

"This isn't what I pictured for the afternoon," I told him.

He snorted. "Nor me. Although I suppose technically I am in, or at least on, bed with you."

"I don't know what I'm up for, but will you stay tonight anyway?"

"I'm not leaving you until I have to." He pulled me down on the bed beside him, holding me close, stroking my hair, letting me cry.

Eventually I rose and opened my closet to start packing, fingering all the bright, flowing clothes I'd purchased in the last few months. "Forget it. I have a closet full of clothes back there. I'll just pack a toothbrush."

I heard Luke's long exhale. I turned to see him wiping his eyes with his sleeve. "Are you all right?"

He cleared his throat. "You're planning to come back."

I looked at him, then around the room, contemplated the ready easel and my paintings propped against one wall. When was the last time I'd painted this much? Years ago. I turned again toward him, solid and kind, slightly flushed, his hair tufted out on one side, flattened against his head on the other. "I hadn't thought about it, really, but it feels like I'm leaving home, not going there."

He smiled. "Good."

There was a discrete knock on the door.

"Come in," I said.

Edward poked his head around the doorstop. "If you're hungry there's food."

We followed him down to the kitchen. They'd made a salad and laid out bread, cheese and olives, as well as small bowls of heated leftovers.

Sam shrugged apologetically as we entered. "It isn't much, but I didn't think anyone would be very hungry."

I placed my hand on his arm. "Thanks, Sam. This is perfect."

I picked at my food. Luke asked questions about Mark, Maggie, Aurora, Jack, every name he'd heard in the living room. I let Edward and Sam fill him in. "You'll like Aurora," I added. "She's very straightforward."

"I look forward to meeting her," Luke said, and I caught the smile in the glance Sam and Edward exchanged.

After dinner, we resumed our positions in the living room. Daphnia jumped onto my lap, his fur warm beneath my hand. It felt like fog had descended over my brain. I let Luke enfold me and drifted in and out of the conversation. I kept trying to jolt myself back by thinking, "arrested" and "bribery" and "warrant," but my thoughts skittered away again, like worms in my compost when I lift the lid.

Finally Edward stood, saying he needed to pack. Sam kissed my forehead, scooped up Daphnia and followed. "I'm ruining their honeymoon," I said softly.

"You're not ruining anything," Luke whispered. "Don't take on what isn't yours."

"Let go and let God?"

"Something like that." He pulled me closer. "And besides, I think Edward and Sam will have many honeymoons. Just think how happy they'll be together when you both come back."

I closed my eyes, sinking back into his warmth. "I can't see that far right now. I can't get past tomorrow and the image of camera flashes."

"Been there, done that as they say." He twirled a strand of my hair. "I wish I could make it disappear, but between the drugs and the drunks, I tried that and it only made things worse. The only thing you can do is push through and remember that it will end. Shall we go up and try to sleep?"

I nodded and followed him up the stairs. I pointed to the bathroom. "I think there's a spare toothbrush in the cabinet if you like."

He nodded and disappeared into the bathroom.

When he opened the bedroom door I was standing in the center of the room, looking at the bed. "Is something wrong?" he asked.

I looked at him and blushed. "I don't know what to wear."

"To the airport?"

I shook my head. "To bed."

He smiled. "What do you usually wear?"

"It depends on the weather, I suppose, but maybe a T shirt, maybe nothing. I have some flannel pajamas, but nothing sexy or even attractive."

"Nothing is a provocative image, very Dutch. Wear a T shirt. Here wear mine if you like." He sloughed off his shirt and pulled a white, paint-stained T over his head and threw it to me.

It felt warm. Reflexively I brought it to my face and inhaled. I heard his sharp intake of breath and looked up. He blinked and looked away.

"I'll go change and wash my face," I told him. He nodded.

In the bathroom I looked in the mirror. What a contradiction, my eyes rimmed red and a flush creeping up my neck. I felt hollowed out, yet some part of me hummed.

Luke squatted by the window, his feet and chest bare. It took me a moment to register that he had turned my canvases around and was examining them. He looked up when I closed the door. "This is what you've done here?"

I nodded, feeling my knees soften beneath me.

He turned back to the images. "Why don't you sign them?"

"I never sign my work."

"Why not? Don't tell me you're one of those perfectionists who's never done."

"No, it isn't that." I stood behind him, looking down at my rendition of the back garden. "These are finished. I just haven't ever known what to write."

He looked at me over his shoulder. "Traditionally one signs one's name."

I smiled. "I know. But what name? Gillian Sach, Jack Sach's wife? Just Gillian? G.S.? And since only my friends hang them, signing seems pointless."

"Hmmm." He turned back to the stack of canvasses and pulled out an abstract portrait of Daphnia on the bed. "You have such a strong female voice. Your work is a beautiful juxtaposition between soft domesticity and hard edges. You should sign these. They should not only be hanging on your friends' walls. Call yourself whatever you like, Just Gillian, Spider woman, anything. What was your maiden name?"

"Wolf."

He stared at me. "And you don't know what to sign? It seems to me the only question is G. Wolf or Gillian Wolf. I'd choose Gillian Wolf because it mirrors your work, but either would be fine." He propped the canvasses side by side, stopping for a long time before the painting I'd made after visiting the Anne Frank house. "You can be terrifying. That's good for your art, must be difficult to live inside though."

"You should talk. Remember, I've seen 'Peace in our Time,'" I said.

He laughed, cut a long strip of canvass from a roll in the corner, rummaged amongst my supplies and produced a thin brush. "It would have been better if you'd done this before you cleaned your brushes, but that can't be helped. We'll do the best matches we can." He spread the canvas strip across my work table and handed me the brush. "Practice a few to get the hang of it."

"You're railroading me."

"I'm pushing you, that's different. Acrylic, right? I'll get you some water." He grabbed a paint encrusted jar and strode from the room.

It was well after midnight when we finished. A small signature, Gillian Wolf, graced the corner of everything I'd painted since arriving in Amsterdam.

Luke surveyed the canvasses with satisfaction. "I'll have them photographed while you're gone. I'll need slides if I'm going to interest any dealers. While you're home, sign whatever you have stashed in your studio. Edward can photograph them. It will give you both something to do."

I looked at the line of paintings, rubbing paint from my fingers. "Do you really think I'm ready?"

He shrugged. "I do. We'll have to see if the art world will bite. I think I can get your slides seen. Then it's up to the work."

Turning off the light, we climbed under the covers. I reached for him. He clasped my hand in both his and brought it to his lips, kissing each finger in turn.

"What would you have done if I'd tested positive?" I asked.

"Taken you to a physician." He caressed the inside of my arm. "It would have made a complicated situation more difficult, don't you think? But I'd like to think that at the end of the day I would still have been right here."

I moved toward him, laying my body full against his. He brushed the hair from my face, watching me with gentle eyes. "How are you feeling?"

"Confused, sad, hopeful, scared, excited, should I keep going?"

"Let's pause for a time on excited." He ran a finger across my lips. "But don't let me railroad you into this as well. I've wanted you from that first night, when you almost hit me in the balls." He rubbed his hand along my belly, strong, sculptor's hands molding my flesh.

"You're a most amazing, beautiful, sexy woman. I need to taste you, feel you, know you. I want to make love with you over and over."

"That feels good," I said. "I can sleep on the plane."

Later we rested. I held his hand in front of my face, looking at it in the vague light cast by the city outside. I ran my fingers along the calluses. "Working hands," I said.

"That's what Vanderwerken means; roughly translated it means 'of the workers.' That's how I've always seen myself, as a worker."

"There's so much I don't know about you." I laced my fingers between his.

"You can know anything."

"How old are you?" I asked.

"Fifty-six last August."

"Children?"

"No, unless you count the sculptural ones. I do have some assistants who see me as a father figure, but that's all."

"Parents?"

"My mother is alive but not remembering. She lives with my brother in Rotterdam. I visit them maybe once a month. My father died three years ago."

"I'm sorry."

"Don't be. He lived a full life and died a happy man. What more could any of us ask?"

"Siblings?"

"Just my brother in Rotterdam. He has almost forgiven me for my years of disrepute and for the fact he has to take care of mother. He's divorced. I have three nephews I don't see often enough, some of which is my fault, some his."

"Do you do this often?" I tried to slip the question in with the rest.

"If by this you mean talking about myself, no. If you mean, lie in bed with a beautiful woman, watching my heart break because she's leaving in the morning, no. If you simply mean sex, not so often in recent years. As you may have noticed I'm not good looking—"

"You're very handsome," I protested.

He kissed my forehead. "You're sweet but I know your eyes are better than that. If you like the way I look it is not because you're seeing through these." He kissed each eyelid softly. "Anyway, as I was saying, despite my appearance, opportunities arise, probably for the wrong reasons. I have sometimes taken those opportunities, also probably for the wrong reasons."

I lay silent, trying to formulate the question. Before I could find the right words, he answered it. "I am by nature a faithful man, or at least sober that's true. I won't betray you, Gillian. We will be what we will be, but as long as we are this," he ran his hand down my torso, resting it gently against my pubic bone, "I will be only with you."

I didn't notice the tears until he kissed them away.

❧ ❧ ❧

Luke and Sam rode the train to the airport with us. Edward carried an overnight bag and his camera case. I'd crammed a few things into my purse: a toothbrush and underwear in case we got stranded, Luke's T shirt, the framed photo of us, and the bronze he'd made me.

At security, Sam hugged me tightly. "This too shall pass," he whispered.

"Walk with me a minute," Luke said. "You have time." We left Edward and Sam near the security line and found a secluded alcove. Leaning against the wall, he brought my hand to his lips. "Just so you know, I'm not letting you go, not really."

"I know."

"We'll meet in New York next month?" I nodded.

His eyes were steady on mine. "Remember what I said last night. Think of this as a cleansing. Believe me, I know something of scandal. It's going to be awful, really awful, but then it will be over. And you'll be free." He pulled me close and kissed me passionately. "I've waited a long time for you, Gillian. I will wait longer if you promise you'll come back."

"I promise."

"Ik hou van jou."

"What?" I asked.

"Nothing. Go, you'll be late for your flight."

Eighteen

Edward gave me the window seat. I stared out at the runway, blankly watching as men in yellow slickers serviced the plane. The luggage tractor circled round and out of habit I looked for my bag, but of course I hadn't brought one. Edward patted my knee. I looked down at his hand, almost not recognizing my lap in grey wool Congressman's Wife slacks. I covered his hand with mine, smiling at a crust of ochre paint caked in my index fingernail.

"Do you know what 'Ik hou van jou' means in Dutch?" I asked him.

"No. Did Luke say it to you?"

I nodded.

"Then it probably means have a nice day or eat your soup or something else that might be difficult to say early in a relationship."

"Oh." The engines started and I could already feel my stomach dip.

"It's like I can't get away." I pulled a tissue from my pocket and dabbed my eyes. "I run halfway around the world, try to look different, be different. I meet someone wonderful and I get sucked back in. Jack's a damned whirlpool or vortex or something."

Edward put an arm around me and squeezed. "You're already free, Gillian. This is just clean up." He handed me a stick of gum. "Better flex your ear canals, I have a feeling you've got many transatlantic flights in your future."

"Argh," I groaned. "How the hell am I supposed to work that out? Who knows if he'll even still be there when I come back? Maybe he'll find someone else. Men do, you know."

"He'll never find anyone like you," Edward said. "Unlike your ungrateful husband, Luke actually knows that."

"I wish I was as sure as you."

"No, you wish you were as handsome and young as me, but you'll have to live with that envy, darling."

The steward leaned toward us. "Can I get you something to drink?"

"Got Hemlock?" I asked.

"Hmmm, let me check. I know I have Absolut."

"I'll have water," I said, and Edward giggled.

⁂

Maggie had managed to talk security into escorting her into the Customs area so she could meet us.

I hugged her. "How did you get in here? You're amazing."

She laughed. "'Member of the Congressman's staff' works wonders."

She hugged us both, asked if we'd gotten any sleep on the plane (we hadn't), if we'd eaten (we had), and steered us to an espresso bar so we could tank up before greeting the cameras.

"He's home. It's absolute chaos, reporters everywhere. Karen, my grad student, is parked outside baggage claim. I'll call her when we get near so she can have the car ready. Edward, your job is to hold Gillian's arm and steer her. We plow through. No comment. Say it for me, 'no comment.'"

"No comment," we dutifully repeated.

"Be firm. I've been watching newsreels to figure out the best effect. Smile, but don't catch their eye. Graciously say you have no comment. You've done nothing wrong. Your picture is already all over the paper, so you might as well smile and wave. Here's my comb." She held it out and opened a compact so I could see to straighten up.

I did what I could.

She appraised the results. "Ready?"

I took a deep breath and nodded. Edward gripped my elbow. Maggie flanked me on the other side and called Karen to alert her we were on the way. "Lights, camera, action." She swung open the security doors.

At first I thought it might be anticlimactic. Maybe they'd all gone home. Then someone shouted, "There she is!" and the flashes began. We pushed through. I smiled, waved and only occasionally made eye contact.

"Mrs. Sach, how do you feel about your husband's arrest?"

"No comment."

"Mrs. Sach, did he do it?"

"No comment."

"Gillian, where have you been?"

"Hi, Ed, no comment."

"Mrs. Sach, is he making a deal with the prosecutor?"

"No comment."

Maggie opened the back door. Edward pushed me in and followed. Maggie slammed the door, hopped into the front, and told the young woman behind the wheel, "Go!"

I sank back into the seat. "Holy shit. That was not fun."

"It'll be the same thing at your house." Maggie pointed to our young driver. "This is Karen, I stole her away from the lab for the afternoon. Karen, meet Gillian and Edward."

"I'm taking you away from your work," I apologized.

Karen laughed. "Are you kidding? I volunteered. Maggie arrived at work this morning and announced, 'I need someone to drive a getaway car.' Every hand in the place shot up, but my bench is nearest the door."

"And she's just puttering around waiting for things to incubate," Maggie said.

I looked out the window. "Snow, I'd forgotten there'd be snow by now. No wonder I'm cold."

"What's the plan?" Edward asked. "I have to tell you that I'm dead tired, and as you can tell from her ramblings about the weather, Gillian's barely coherent. I don't think either of us has slept much lately."

"Well, you're not going to get to sleep quite yet. Sorry," Maggie said. "There really is a warrant out for you, Gillian. The only way I could talk the FBI out of coming to meet you themselves was if I promised to deliver you into their hands. So we're meeting them at my house in a few minutes."

I wanted to crawl in bed, but tried to pull myself together. "Do I need a lawyer? I don't think I want that guy from Jack's campaign. Maybe we should call Morrie Jakobitz, the Foundation trustee."

"Already did," Maggie told me. "He recommended a criminal lawyer named Peggy Spitz. We're picking her up on the way."

"I love you, Maggie."

"I love you too, Gillian. And I missed you, and I want to hear about everything very soon. Turn here, Karen, there she is." Maggie pointed to a small blond woman in a long black coat. We pulled over and Peggy Spitz crawled in beside me.

"Hi." She introduced herself. "How was your flight?"

"Long and I didn't sleep much. I'm not at my best."

"I'm sorry about that, but I'm afraid it can't be helped." She pulled a legal pad and pen from her briefcase. "I wanted Maggie to pick me up so we'd have a few minutes together before you talk with the FBI. First, should we find somewhere more confidential to chat?"

Maggie said, "I've told Karen that if anything said in this car ends up in the papers she can kiss her grant money goodbye. I think we're safe."

Karen shrugged. "You would have been anyway, but the threat is certainly an incentive."

"You feel comfortable talking?" Peggy asked me.

"Of course, I'm not sure I have any secrets." I felt empty and tired.

Peggy checked her notes. "So what did you know about Jack's dealings with AHC?"

"Nothing."

"Nothing?"

"I asked him about a newspaper account at one point last summer.

He told me not to worry about it and I didn't." I leaned back in the seat, suddenly very, very tired. "I've been preoccupied with other things. You should know I haven't seen or talked with my husband since the election and we essentially separated at the end of the summer."

"Separated, meaning…?" she asked.

"Meaning I moved into the studio, but kept up a pretense until after the election. Then I left town."

"Why did you separate?"

"Is it important?"

She nodded. "So I don't end up blindsided by something someone else knows that I should. Whether you need to tell the police will depend on what it is."

"My husband was having an affair with one of his staff members. And it wasn't the first. He's had quite a number of them during our marriage. I finally got fed up."

Peggy whistled softly. "I'm sorry. This could get ugly. I have to tell you that it is very unlikely that something won't come out, particularly given the media attention. Can you handle that?"

I shrugged. "I guess I'll have to."

She nodded. "So, you don't know anything and he hasn't talked to you about this and you have no connection to the money?" She raised her eyebrows, and I nodded. "Gillian, it is very important I know the truth, no matter what it is. Anything you want to tell me?"

I thought for a minute. "I don't know if it's important to anyone but me, but as of yesterday, I'm having an affair myself."

"You are?" Maggie asked. Peggy shot her a look.

"One night stand type affair or something that's likely to continue?" asked Peggy.

"Oh, I had one of those, too. But he wouldn't even know my name and besides, he has his own reasons to keep secrets, so that's not going to be an issue. But this new affair, yes, I think it will continue."

Maggie was staring at me open mouthed.

Edward grinned at her and confirmed, "I'd bet on that."

"Who?" Maggie asked.

"Luke Vanderwerken."

"The artist?" Peggy and Maggie asked simultaneously.

I nodded.

"Oh my, this could get interesting. Here's my advice," Peggy said after a moment. "You're not guilty of anything illegal, so you might as well tell the truth. Don't volunteer the affairs, yours or his, but if you're asked, answer truthfully. It isn't illegal and the FBI isn't interested in broadcasting to the media. What you want to avoid is looking guilty. And feeling guilty, even if it is just about adultery, will make you look guilty. Got it?"

We pulled into the driveway of Maggie's two-story Victorian. Two cars, one from the local police, idled in front of her house. I took a deep breath. "Yes, I think so."

"If you need to talk to me at any time while they're questioning you, just say so, and we'll talk. If I tell you to quit talking, quit talking. Got it?"

I nodded.

She opened the door. "Showtime."

Maggie lifted her eyebrows at me.

I said, "I couldn't very well have told you in an email. Later, I'll tell you everything later."

She grinned. "That's so cool." She opened her door and stepped out.

Edward squeezed my shoulder. "You okay?" I nodded, and he helped me out of the car.

When you are the wife of a congressman representing the rural district where you grew up, you know almost everyone. So it didn't surprise me when Dan Osborne, who'd been a year ahead of me in school, and Kim Schmidt, whose husband had been fixing my cars for years, stepped out of the patrol car. I smiled at them and they nodded a greeting.

Two men I didn't know climbed from the unmarked car. They introduced themselves as Agent Morrow and Agent White from the FBI. Evidently they didn't have first names.

Maggie led us into her warm, cluttered living room. Looking at the grim-faced FBI agents, I breathed a little easier when Dan and Kim followed us into the house and stationed themselves near the door. I remembered a much younger Dan— Danny it was then— staring down the playground bullies.

I settled onto one end of the couch, next to a stack of papers. Probably, if my past experience in this house was any gauge, somebody's thesis. Something deep in me immediately relaxed in this familiar, safe place. Maggie'd been smart to set it up this way. I felt much better.

Edward started to sit next to me, but Agent White said, "I'd like to speak with Gillian alone if you wouldn't mind."

"I'll be all right, Edward. But do you think you could find me a cup of coffee or tea or anything with caffeine?"

He squeezed my hand and followed Maggie into the kitchen. They'd be listening at the door, I thought, but didn't tell the FBI.

Peggy sat beside me on the couch. I introduced her but she seemed to already know everyone. Agents Morrow and White took the armchairs facing us.

Agent White spoke first. "We need to ask a few questions. You know that your husband has been arrested on suspicion of accepting bribes, along with some corollary offenses?"

I nodded. "I know he's been arrested. I don't know the charges. I only heard about it last night, or whatever time that would have been here." I looked at my watch, which said it should be eight in the evening, but of course it would be much earlier here. I needed to focus.

Agent White said something.

"I'm sorry," I said, "could you repeat the question?"

"When was the last time you communicated with your husband?"

I thought back. "Election night, I think, although I might have spoken with him the next morning, I can't really remember."

"And not since then?"

"No."

Agent White looked at Agent Morrow, who nodded. They must have been confirming what they already knew from phone records and that sort of thing. Of course, it was possible that real FBI didn't do all the stuff they did on TV but—

Agent White asked, "What do you know about AHC?"

"Nothing. I think it stands for American Health something, but that's about it."

"Mrs. Sach, you have a small cabin that you use as a studio, is that correct?"

"Yes, it was my grandfather's fishing cabin."

"Do you spend a great deal of time there?"

I shrugged. "When I can."

"Are you aware that agents searched your studio and found a great deal of cash?"

It physically hurt to think of Jack in my cabin. "Someone told me you found money in my studio. Where was it?"

"Inside the woodstove."

I raised my eyebrows. "That's a daring spot."

"Why?"

"The woodstove is the only way to heat the cabin. Someone could have burned it up."

"Not if everyone knew not to light a fire," he said, watching me. "Who has keys?"

I thought about it. "I do. And there's a key hanging in the kitchen with all the others. I think John made a copy when he was in high school, at least I think it was John. I used to find used condoms in the trash. But, of course, that was years ago."

Peggy shot me a look. I shut up.

"When was the last time you were there?"

"The morning after the election. I've been out of town since then."

"You've been in Europe?" He checked his notes.

"Great Britain and Amsterdam," I confirmed. "Oh, and a long weekend in Greece."

"Odd time for a world tour, don't you think?" he asked.

"I needed to get away." I immediately regretted my word choice.

"From what?"

I took a deep breath, glanced at Peggy, who nodded. "My marriage hasn't been good for a very long time, Agent White. I promised Jack I'd stay with him through the election. I left as soon afterwards as I could."

Agent White nodded thoughtfully. "Mrs. Sach, I'm sure you can see my problem here. I'd like to believe you. But a European vacation in the middle of a bribery scandal, well, you can see how it looks. We have no way of knowing how much cash your husband actually accepted. Do you see where I'm going?"

Edward's head popped through the kitchen door. He held out a coffee cup and gestured toward me. Dan took the cup and shooed Edward back into the kitchen before bringing it to me. I sipped, thinking.

"I can probably produce credit card receipts for most of my expenses," I said after a minute. "But I'm not sure that's the point. I don't need the money, Agent White. You must know that, it's public knowledge."

He nodded. "We know you inherited money. But money has its own allure. Perhaps you wanted more."

"I didn't. I've never had to worry about money and, strange as it sounds, I don't care about it much. We don't spend all the interest on the money we have. I'm glad for it but… How much did you find?"

He checked his notes. "Around a half million dollars, a lot of money."

"That is a lot of money, but it wouldn't change things for me. The Foundation holding my inheritance generates an income of something over two million a year. We give away a big chunk of that, use much of it and reinvest the rest. I don't need to scurry around in darkness doing illegal things for money I wouldn't even use."

"Then why would your husband accept bribes?"

"I don't know if my husband accepted bribes. I don't know anything about it. But to answer your real question, he has no control over my money."

"But you said 'we.'"

"Oh, right. It's complicated. I can give you the estate lawyer's number and he can tell you all the details. The other half of the "we" is Edward, the man who came in with me."

"Oh, I see." Agent White made a note on the pad. "And is this Edward the reason your marriage hasn't been good lately?"

Dan snorted in the corner, but quickly recovered when the two FBI agents looked at him. I smiled at Dan. "No. You can think of Edward as my sort of brother. You should talk with Morrie Jakobitz, our trustee."

"So what has been the problem in your marriage?"

"Do we really have to talk about this?"

"I'm afraid so."

"My husband's had an affair," I said simply.

"Do you know with whom?"

"Lately, a young woman named Ashley Groves. She worked on his campaign."

The two agents exchanged glances.

"I'm sorry," I said. "I'm tired. I've been up something over thirty-six hours. Could we continue this all later?"

Agent White nodded. "We appreciate your cooperation. You should know you're still under suspicion and it would be unwise to leave the area."

"I need to be in New York for an art show in February." When he looked skeptical, I added, "I just flew half way around the world to answer your questions. I think you can trust me to New York and back."

He cracked his first smile. "Just let us know where you'll be."

After they left Maggie asked, "Do you want me to fix a late lunch?"

"Lunch," I said. "Is it only lunch time?"

Maggie handed me another cup of coffee. "Try to stay awake as long as possible to adjust to the time change."

Peggy also accepted coffee. "I think that went pretty well."

"Do you think they believed me?"

She shrugged. "Hard to tell, but you convinced me. They'll probably be back for more. Make sure to call so I can be there if you talk with them." She sipped her coffee and checked notes. "I'd also suggest you contact Morrie Jakobitz and tell him to disclose your financial information to the FBI, otherwise he's bound by client privilege."

I looked at Edward, who nodded.

Peggy continued, "The fact you don't need the money is a convincing argument. You don't seem like the gaming type, so they're going to have a hard time making a case for you taking bribes you don't need."

Edward smiled at me. "See, I knew that money would come in handy sometime."

Peggy said she needed to get back to the office. Maggie handed Edward her car keys and asked him to drive Peggy back downtown. She sat me down at the kitchen table while she pulled salad ingredients from the refrigerator.

"So your insurance salesman—"

"Office supplies," I corrected her, playing with my coffee cup.

"Right, office supplies. So what was that like?"

I shrugged. "The sex was great. But, I don't know, it didn't feel right. I don't mean morally, although that's probably true too. But I felt, I don't know, disconnected."

"And Luke? By the way, I can't believe you slept with Luke Vanderwerken." She looked up from slicing tomatoes. "He doesn't seem the Casanova type."

I smiled. "That's an understatement." I picked at some crumbs on the table. "I'm married to Casanova. And Luke, he's...well if sex with Mike, the office guy, was disconnected, sex with Luke is hyperconnected." I paused, thinking. "That's not about his technique or anything, I think, more about us. I don't know. I'm not making sense."

"You're making sense," Maggie said quietly. "And if he's this way about you, I think Edward's right."

"What did Edward say?"

"That I'd better update my passport because we'll be visiting you in Amsterdam."

Edward returned with the news of reporters still camped at the house. Maggie served the salad, apologetically setting out several bottled dressings. I wasn't hungry anyway.

"Hang out here for today so you can recover from the flight and the time change," she suggested. "We'll call this an early dinner, play a few rounds of pinochle or something and you can make it an early night. Gillian can take the extra bedroom and if you want to stay, Edward, the couch pulls out."

"I think it'll probably be safe for me to go home," he said. "I'm just the neighbor. But I'll stay here for a while longer in case I can be useful."

I leaned forward and settled my elbows on the table. "Maybe you could talk to Morrie about letting the FBI see Foundation records? Call him from here in case he needs to talk to me."

Edward nodded and Maggie handed him the phone.

I used my cell to call the house.

Aurora answered. "Hi Mom, where are you?"

"I'm at Maggie's. I hear it's crazy over there."

"It's nuts. I found some guy crawling in the shrubs." She sounded cheerful.

"That's less surprising than that you're answering the phone."

I could hear the smile in her voice as she said, "My therapist suggested this as an opportunity for healing. I think she might be right."

"How's John?"

"He's holed up with Grandma Pearl. He says they're still recovering from jet lag, but I think he's just not ready to face Dad. Are you coming home?"

Home, I thought, where the hell is that? But I said, "I'll come by in the morning, I'm not up to it today."

"You might want to stop by the grocery on your way. It's like being under siege here, once you're inside you don't want to brave the onslaught."

"Can I bring you anything?"

"Chocolate would be good. And maybe some fresh vegetables. It seems like Dad's been living out of the freezer and take-out since you left."

"How is he?"

"Denying everything and drinking too much, so pretty much like always. Mark's practically living here, and I let him keep Dad company most of the time."

"Who'd have thought you'd turn into Cordelia in the end?"

Aurora laughed. "I don't know about that, I'm not raising an army for him quite yet."

Edward called from the other room and I signed off, telling her I'd be by first thing in the morning. Handing me the phone, he mouthed, "Morrie."

I took the receiver and heard the comforting voice of the old man who'd managed the Foundation since the beginning. I supposed someday he'd retire and we'd have to find someone new, but for now he knew more than anyone, probably more than Edward and I did, about our financial lives.

"Gillian," he said warmly, "I'm so sorry about all this. How are you?"

"Mostly numb and tired right now, but thank you."

"Did you have a nice time in Europe?"

"It was lovely."

"Edward said something about—" Morrie trailed off.

"About telling the FBI whatever they want to know," I finished for him.

"That's right. I just wanted to make sure. I'll send a courier over with some papers to confirm."

I called John at Pearl's to let them know I'd arrived. She told me he'd gone to the store, but she'd let him know I called.

"He doesn't need to return my call," I said. "Just tell him I love him."

※ ※ ※

"I hate this tired, buzzy, stupid feeling," I told Maggie later, after we'd finally convinced Edward he could go home.

"I kind of like it in you." She placed her scrabble tiles. "These are some of the easiest wins ever."

"Is it bedtime yet?"

She checked her watch. "It's five. How about one more game?"

"Don't you have work to do?"

"Sure, and I'll do it after I tuck you in."

"If I promise to stay up for another hour, can I use your computer to check my email?"

"Tell him I said hi."

Cool in Maggie's study, I found a lap quilt and wrapped it around me as I logged on. I hadn't checked email in a few days so I faced a full inbox. First I deleted all the trash then read a joke that was making the rounds. Emma'd sent me a long chatty note before all this happened. I wrote her back something I hoped sounded upbeat.

Finally, Luke's message read:

> Darling Gillian, It's only been an hour and I miss you. I wish I was there or you were here. Imagine me holding you now.
> Luke.

I wrapped Maggie's quilt tight around me, typing myself across the ocean to him. Then, at six on the button, said goodnight to Maggie, found my bed, slipped into Luke's T shirt, crawled in and slept.

Nineteen

Predictably, I woke insanely early. The bedside clock read 3:48 a.m. but my watch, still on Amsterdam time, told me I'd slept late. I crept to the study and logged onto the computer, afraid of how Luke might have responded to my long rambling note of the night before.

> Amazing Gillian,
> Thank you for writing. If I could not wake this morning holding you, at least I can hold your words. Your ordeal sounds like something out of an American TV program, it must seem very unreal. I should be there with you. I've decided to start a new piece for the group show next month. They want three from me. I put together a series but now don't like the third. If I start today it should be finished in time. I miss you. Write me again. Twice a day if you like. More even if you can.
> Yours, Luke

I smiled. "We can think of this as an extended conversation with long pauses," I wrote. "Tell me about your day, where and how do you live? Everything. I'm going to the house this morning. Don't know what I'll find or how I'll feel. My world is very different now."

I first signed it "Love, Gillian," erased that, tried "Cheers G.," "Fondly Gillian," and finally decided to mirror him with, "Yours, Gillian."

On a hunch I called Edward. He answered brightly on the second ring. "Couldn't sleep either, eh?"

"Actually, I feel like I slept in. I'll be dragging later," I told him. "Can you come pick me up? I'll go crazy sitting here waiting for Maggie to wake."

"Sure. I'll be right over."

"Can you bring a pair of sweats and maybe a sweatshirt or something? Maggie's clothes will all be too small and I can't deal with my Congressman's Wife suit at this hour."

I changed the sheets on her spare bed and wrote Maggie a note. By the time Edward arrived, I was pacing the living room floor in T shirt, clean underwear, pumps and coat, my suit slung over a chair. As soon as I saw his car round the corner, I grabbed my things and ran outside.

He opened the door so I could slide in. "Nice outfit." He threw a bag into my lap. I pulled out dark blue sweats and a matching sweatshirt.

Wiggling into them I said, "These must be Sam's, they almost fit."

Edward smiled. "So where are we going in fleece and heels?"

"I think I have to go home now, don't you?"

"Probably. At least you're not likely to get ambushed by the press at five in the morning." He pulled away from the curb.

"Don't be too sure. How about if we pull into your driveway, I'll borrow some boots and tramp over on the back path." I sat forward, peering out at the snowy landscape. "Edward? I don't want to be here. I think we should be back in the canal district."

He smiled. "Me too. I was thinking about that while I was staring at the ceiling this morning. I know this isn't what you meant, but something in me clamped up as we came back through Customs. These last few months, it's been amazing living in a place where gay or straight is just another way people are. Did you know that the Netherlands was the first country to recognize gay marriage? Gay is probably not accepted all over the Netherlands, or in every Dutch kitchen, but in Amsterdam?" He patted my knee. "We'll get back there soon enough, just a few things to tidy up first."

I squeezed his hand. "I hope so."

Thank God for automatic door openers, I thought, as we slid undetected into his garage. Stashing my suit and shoes in the hall closet, I slid into an oversized pair of boots. I gave Edward Aurora's grocery list, promised him breakfast if he'd shop, and climbed down the back steps to the path.

The frozen, snow-covered lake rolled out before me. The winter landscape, in the moonlight so much more monochromatic than in summer, caught my breath. Snow crunched beneath my feet as I trudged the dark path toward the light in my kitchen.

Aurora looked up, startled, as I came through the back door. Her face brightened. "Mom." She jumped up to hug me. "I'm so glad you're here."

"I'm so amazed you're here." I held her tight. "I'm not sure I understand it but I'm very glad to see you."

She squeezed me, then pulled away, grabbed a cup, filled it with coffee and handed it to me. "I'm not sure I understand it exactly either, but coming seemed the right thing to do. But since I've been here I feel my anger falling away."

"That's magnanimous of you." I dropped into a kitchen chair.

She shrugged. "Not really, everyone else is beating up on him so badly I don't have to. I think the thing that's always made me nuts was that no one else saw it." She sat across from me, sipping her own coffee. "Now they do. Besides, he's not doing anything to me. It's harder on John, I think. After all, it's been a long time since I was a Sach. Hardly anyone of my acquaintance knows who he is or that we're related. But John, he has to see his name splattered all over the national papers."

"How's he doing?"

"I haven't seen him since he got back, but he sounds bitter on the phone."

"How about Pete and the girls?"

"Pete's Pete, unflappable. The girls are too young to even get it. They think I'm visiting you. They'll be fine. For that matter, John will be fine, too. He just doesn't know it yet. So how are you?"

I took a deep breath. "I don't know. Sort of numb, I guess. Maybe relieved, like something I've been dreading for years finally happened.

And nobody died. There's also a feeling of displacement. Day before yesterday I was in Amsterdam in a Chinese restaurant eating dim sum, and today here I am having been questioned by the FBI. I'm still disoriented."

Aurora looked down at the table. "Speaking of Amsterdam, John mentioned something about a sculptor? He says you adamantly denied any involvement but he thought you might be—"

"Do you really want to have this conversation? Don't children usually want to avoid talking about their parent's love life?"

"I don't know about love, but I've certainly known about my father's sex life since I was something like twelve. Whatever you're doing, it can't be more disillusioning than that. Besides, I'm a big girl. I know how babies are made, even made some myself, so come on, talk."

I laughed. "When John left we weren't involved. But since then—" I shrugged.

"Since then? As in 'what a difference a day makes?'" Aurora asked incredulously.

"Huh, I guess it was only a day. Seems longer, probably the travel."

"Wow." She stared at our reflections in the dark window. "So, pretty much this is really bad timing for you."

I nodded. "Pretty much."

"And it's too early to say if I get a stepdad."

I laughed, almost snorting coffee through my nose.

She grinned. "When can I meet him?"

"You want to meet him?"

"Sure. John got to." She sounded about two years old. Then she smiled. "He says this guy, is it Luke?"

I nodded.

"He says that Luke is perfect and you're happy around him and that even Grandma thinks you should jump him."

"Pearl thinks I should jump him?"

She grinned. "I believe John was paraphrasing there. Anyway, so when do I get to meet him?"

"I don't know. He's coming to New York for a group show the first week in February."

Just then Edward opened the back door. Aurora jumped up. "Uncle Edward."

He stepped into the kitchen, set down two large grocery bags and held his arms wide. "It's my little Borealis." He twirled her around. "I haven't seen you in much too long."

"I know." She nestled into his chest like she had as a little girl. "More of Dad's collateral damage."

"Breakfast?" I asked.

"Yes, ma'am, flim flam spaghetti man," they both sang and laughed at the old joke.

We unpacked the bags and I dribbled blueberry pancake batter into animal and flower shapes, as if this were a summer Sunday morning when the children were small. Aurora bubbled to Edward about her life, her girls and Pete, as he fed her questions and made her laugh. This is how life would be without Jack, I thought.

By seven the sky outside had begun to brighten. Color bled into the horizon. Too late in the year for birds, but the reporters woke, peppering someone with questions as the front door opened. Mark entered, throwing a few "no comments" over his shoulder.

He saw the three of us at the kitchen table and smiled, entering with hand outstretched to greet each in turn. "Morning Aurora. Mr. Rosenberg, nice to see you. Gillian, did you have a nice trip? I'm so glad you're home."

"Hi, Mark, I had a very nice time, thank you." I gently extricated my hand from his. "Can I get you coffee, something to eat?"

"I ate already," he said, "but I'll take a cup of coffee."

"It looks like you had to run the gauntlet." Edward gestured to an empty chair as I poured coffee.

Mark slumped into the chair with a sigh. "You get used to it. They're only doing their jobs, I suppose."

"He's done a number on your career with this, hasn't he?" I handed him a cup.

He shrugged. "Maybe it's a good thing. Over the Moon Ice Cream is for sale, you know. My brother's been bothering me for months to go in with him on it. I'm thinking when this is all over I might take him up on it and give my ulcers a rest."

"I loved Over the Moon when I was a kid," Aurora said. "That's the best ice cream ever."

Mark smiled. "I know. We used to go there all the time as kids, too. My brother even proposed to his wife in a corner booth. It might be nice to do something that wouldn't change the world but could make someone happy."

"I don't think restaurants are stress-free work places," Edward warned.

"Believe me, after this," Mark nodded back toward the door and I couldn't tell if he was referring to the reporters or Jack, "anything would be stress free."

"Good point," Edward agreed.

Just then I heard movement upstairs. I looked at Edward and Aurora. "I'm not ready for Jack yet. Let's go down to the cabin." When they nodded, I turned to Mark. "I'm afraid we're abandoning you. I'll be up later to talk with him, just not yet."

Mark stood and started cutting bread for toast. "That's probably a good plan. He's not exactly gracious in the morning these days."

The cabin felt warm and looked lived in, the last embers from a fire glowed in the woodstove. Aurora apologized as we entered. "I'm afraid I've been staying here. I couldn't sleep in the house."

I patted her shoulder. "I'm glad. I like thinking of you here and safe." I looked around, trying to see evidence of either Jack's rummaging or the FBI search.

Seeing me scan the place, Aurora said, "They said they tried to replace everything as they searched. I couldn't tell in the house either."

I walked around touching paint tubes, brushes, pausing to flip through a stack of finished pieces. "It feels like such a violation that he came in here to hide his secrets. Do you suppose he's always done that?"

Aurora shrugged. "Who knows. He's never respected personal boundaries before."

I looked at her for a long moment. "You're right, of course. But I never thought of him coming in here, into my refuge."

Edward put an arm around me. "I doubt he came in here much before. He'd have had no reason to. Wouldn't make a good hiding place when you were around and there's nothing else here he's ever expressed interest in."

That stung a little, but it was true. "I'll call a locksmith," I said. "Should have kept better control over who had a key all along."

"I'll move up to the house, Mom, if you want to stay here," Aurora offered.

Edward jumped in. "Nonsense, come stay with me. It's close enough that you'll be right there for all the drama, but far enough away you can sleep at night." He smiled and wiggled his eyebrows at her. "Trust me, that's a formula I know. Besides, I'm not used to living alone anymore and the house feels cavernous."

"The house is cavernous." Aurora laughed. "I'd love to stay with you."

They packed her things and left to trek across the yard, promising to be back soon. I turned on my studio computer and read,

> Dearest Gillian, I love your name Gillian, Gillian, Gillian. I loved your questions. We will use this time to get to know each other so that once we are together again we won't need to talk and can stay in bed all day. I think this is a very good plan. Where do I live? Mostly I live in my studio, a converted warehouse in the Eastern Docklands, not so far from where we first kissed. But I'm a true Dutchman, I sleep on a boat moored nearby. There are perhaps too many spiders and the kitchen is cramped, but it is lovely to have the water rock you to sleep. How do I live? I eat (this morning yogurt with a banana) and I sleep alone in my rocking bed. I am hoping some of this will change soon. I work all day in the studio with several young helpers, some are artists, some helpers, but all will be nice to you, I promise. It will be in their job description. What did I do today? I found myself moving from place to place caressing every smooth surface, thinking of you. Kissing you, Luke.

I wrote him about the conversations of my morning and how it felt to enter my violated studio. "It all feels so different," I wrote, "the house, the place. I don't know if the difference is me or you or the FBI, but I do know I miss you terribly. G."

I sent the email, found some jeans and a sweater, along with my own boots, and changed. Again I knelt by my stack of finished paintings, this time paging through them more slowly, reabsorbing my earlier self. I placed one on my easel, turning it to the morning light, and began mixing tiny dabs of paint to find the right color for a signature.

❧ ❧ ❧

The FBI showed up right after the locksmith, who evidently passed out business cards to all the reporters on his way in. Edward, Aurora and I sat by the woodstove, sipping more coffee and chatting in that way people do at wakes, funerals and hospital bedsides.

"We'd like to ask you a few more questions, Mrs. Sach." Agent White looked huge and out of place my little cabin.

"Do I need my attorney?"

"It's up to you, of course." He looked around, his face expressionless.

I reached for the phone. "I'll call her, just in case."

"As you wish."

Peggy said she'd be over in ten minutes. Aurora offered the agents coffee. Agent White declined but Agent Morrow agreed to a cup. Edward offered to wait at the house and escort Peggy down. When she arrived, Agent White looked at my companions.

I told Aurora and Edward, "I'll be fine. You guys can go on up to the house and start lunch if you like."

Reluctantly they left. Agent White looked at his notes, "We talked with Mr. Jakobitz yesterday and confirmed everything you said about your financial status." He looked at me for a moment. "One of the reasons people with money take money they shouldn't, bribes, embezzlement, that sort of thing, is that they're being blackmailed and don't want to leave a paper trail. So, Mrs. Sach, was someone blackmailing you?"

"Me?" I asked, startled. "Who would blackmail me and for what?"

"There's nothing you wouldn't want people to find out?"

"I suppose there are all sorts of things I'd rather not have other people know, but nothing worthy of blackmail."

"You're very close to Mr. Rosenberg, perhaps something in his past?"

"How is that relevant?" Peggy asked.

"With potential blackmail cases everything is relevant, Ms. Spitz."

I said, "Edward? He's an independently wealthy freelance photographer who's been completely open about his sexuality since about fifteen. Nothing to blackmail."

Agent White cleared his throat. "He has something of a past, evidently."

I nodded agreement. "He has an absolutely outrageous past. But he's been clean and sober for years now, is actively in recovery and, as far as I know, he's apologized for his sins to everyone, several times. He says doing whatever step that is, is the stuff of miracles. You can't blackmail someone who thrives on mea culpa."

Agent White checked his notes and changed gears. "You mentioned that you thought your husband might be having an affair with Ashley Groves." He looked up for my confirmation. "Did Miss Groves say something to you that made you think that?"

I shook my head. "I knew he was having an affair because I found a hotel key, and it wasn't the first time. Ashley was just my best guess."

"Have you seen the morning papers?" he asked.

"No, is there something I should know?"

Peggy gave me a sympathetic glance and a shrug. "I told you this might happen," her looked seemed to say.

Agent White cleared his throat. "A number of women have come forward in the press alleging," he paused, "inappropriate behavior on your husband's part."

"Oh shit," I said. "I was afraid that might happen someday."

"Afraid enough to pay blackmail?" he asked.

I stared at him. "You think I would pay someone to keep my husband's secrets? Hmmm, I guess it makes sense. I stayed in a crappy marriage to keep the secrets. Why not pay? Do you mind if I get myself more coffee?"

He shook his head.

I stood and walked to the coffee pot, poured myself a cup, gestured to Peggy and the two officers, who declined. I walked over to the window.

Sun glinted on the snow-covered lake, a wide white expanse.

Finally I turned. "Are you married, Agent White?"

He looked surprised then shook his head. "Divorced."

"Occupational hazard," I speculated, and he nodded. "Then you know about bad marriages. They have momentum, don't they? You just keep on keepin' on because it's harder to stop or because changing direction seems so scary or because a million little things. Then one day something, could be something unimportant that you'd usually gloss right over, something tips you over the line and things change. You might not even know it at the time, but that's when a bad marriage ends."

I crossed to the woodstove. "That's what Ashley did for me. She didn't say anything. It wasn't even anything she did. But the fact that I thought my husband might be sleeping with a girl ten years younger than his own daughter flipped that switch. She didn't blackmail me. If she had I don't know what I'd have done, but I bet I would have told her to go ahead and hand him over to whichever of Dante's circles of hell he's spinning in right now."

Both agents continued to watch me as I put another log in the stove and sat down. "You think Ashley was blackmailing him, don't you?"

Agent White said, "I'm not at liberty to discuss our investigation. What I can tell you, because you'll probably read it in the New York Times tomorrow morning, is that Ashley Groves is listed as an employee of AHC." He watched for my reaction.

I stared at him. "What an idiot. I'm sorry, Agent White. You have succeeded in helping me hate my husband, which may or may not have been by design. And I'd love to help you with your case. But I really don't know anything. Sorry."

"No, I'm sorry." He stood and extended his hand. "I'm sorry for what you're going through and for any way that I've added to your troubles." He released my hand. "You're free to go wherever you like. I doubt we'll have more questions, but leave a number where you can be reached in case we do."

Agent White glanced at Peggy. "You didn't ask for my advice, so take this for what it's worth. I've seen a number of media frenzies in my time. He won't be arraigned for at least a month and a trial isn't likely this year. If I were you I'd stay low for the next week or so. By that time the press will be bored and gone. If you don't come back from your trip to New York in February, it will be a long time before anyone notices and by then you may not care." He handed me his card. "Let us know if you see anything you think we should know. Good luck, Mrs. Sach." He inclined his head toward Peggy. "Ms. Spitz." And he and the silent Agent Morrow left.

Peggy turned to me. "I think you should feel relieved."

"I guess. It's going to take a while for everything to sink in."

Edward and Aurora must have been watching at the kitchen window. They arrived immediately with a tray of sandwiches.

"So?" Edward asked.

"So they wanted to know if someone was blackmailing me to keep your deep dark secrets," I told him.

"You have to be kidding."

"No, it gets worse." I turned to Aurora. "I'm so sorry for giving you such a crappy father. We're in for a bloody media mess."

Twenty

Feeling like James Bond, I called Pearl on Edward's cell, just in case there was a trace on mine. "Can you and John meet us at the diner behind Joe's grocery in about an hour? Don't tell anyone where you're going."

"Are we outsmarting those pushy media people?" she asked.

"I hope so."

Edward walked back to his house, planning to leave from there after a suitable wait. Aurora and I grabbed some shopping bags and my Congressman's Wife suit and walked out the front door. Three reporters met us immediately.

I smiled into one of the TV cameras. "Hi guys," I said. "My daughter and I are running a few errands. We're going first to the dry cleaners then the grocery and we might stop by a video store on the way home. You're welcome to come along, but I warn you, we have no comment and won't be picking up any comments along the way. Sorry."

The reporters laughed and the little light on the TV camera went off.

Aurora and I climbed into my car and pulled out the driveway. One enterprising car followed us and waited patiently as we dropped off the dry cleaning but kept going when we pulled into the grocery parking lot and stepped out, shopping bags in hand. We strolled through the grocery aisles, picking up some fruit, vegetables and eggs, then checked out, and walked out the back door and across the street to the Rise and Shine diner, a downtown original since 1903. Pearl, John and Edward had commandeered a back table.

I quickly filled everyone in on my visit with the FBI. "I thought you all should know before the full storm hits."

"Poor guy," Aurora said, "talk about chickens coming home to roost."

I watched John, his face and body tense, his expression a mixture of sadness, rage and disgust. "Poor guy?" he exploded. "Sick guy is more like it. And Ashley. I can't believe I… God, I'm going to be sick." He pushed out of the booth and ran to the men's room.

Edward looked at me. I nodded and motioned for him to follow. John could use an uncle.

Pearl sat, staring at her hands cupped around a mug. I put my hand on her arm. She looked up. Tears fell freely down her soft cheeks. "You okay?" I asked.

She shook her head. "No. But I will be. Poor, poor John, poor Jack, it's like something out of a tragedy. The sins of the father. Or the sins of the mother."

"You couldn't have done anything about this," I told her.

"I could have married a different man."

"That's what I've been thinking, too," I told her, then smiled at Aurora. "But if either of us had married anyone different, these two wonderful people wouldn't exist and that would be a tragedy."

Edward and John returned from the bathroom, John looking pale but steadier.

"So what are we going to do?" Edward asked.

"I'm through with the bastard," John said. "I'm sorry, Grandma, but he's beyond description. He's sick and twisted. I've had enough. I hope he rots in jail." He picked up his coat. "Uncle Edward, can you take Grandma home? I'm going back to school. I can't take any more of this." We all clustered around him, hugging him and making him promise to stay in touch. Finally we let him go and watched as he slouched out of the diner.

The four of us sat back down. Aurora spoke first, "It's still a fair question, what are we going to do?"

I nodded and told them Agent White's advice. "But I don't see a reason for you to stay, Aurora. Pete and the girls need you more than we do."

She nodded. "I'll stay tonight and leave in the morning. When I first heard the news, I thought maybe I should be up here on suicide watch or something, but there's no way he's going to hurt himself. Maybe everyone else, but he's going to do everything he can to weasel his way out of this."

"I agree," Edward said. "Jack may have a taste for self destruction but he's not the suicide type."

Pearl toyed with her cup. "I'm his mother. It's my job to stay by him until the end. That's what you sign on for. It's what either of you would do for your children. But I think you should go soon, too, Gillian. You don't deserve this and you never did. You're the daughter I always wanted and I'm proud as punch of you. I won't have you sticking around to get beaten up by the press."

"Pearl's right," Edward said. "Sooner or later he's going to have a press conference and there will be talk about whether you are or aren't there, by his side. Easier to duck the question by being out of town."

I shook my head. "I'm not staying around for long and I'm certainly not standing by him at a press conference, but I also don't want my leaving to be big news. I'll take the FBI's advice and stick around until Luke's show. It will take me that long to pack up my studio anyway."

"Where will you go?" Aurora asked.

"Back to Amsterdam for now," I glanced at Edward, "if you'll have me. I like the idea of being out of the country through most of this."

Edward grinned. "We'd love to have you back."

"So many difficulties." Pearl shook her head. "First Aziza and now Jack."

"What about Aziza?" I asked.

Edward drummed his fingers on the table. "We were talking about her before you came. Homeland security denied her asylum status. She has to leave the country within thirty days."

"Where will she go?"

Pearl shook her head. "That's the problem. She doesn't have anywhere else. I think she might go illegal. What a shame."

"It seems like everything is all upside down." I glanced around the diner, where nothing had changed in years. "Just a few months ago things were going along like always and boom—"

"You'd better get back." Edward checked his watch. "Your reporters will be wondering."

We said our goodbyes, walked through the grocery store and climbed in the car. We drove home in silence and waved to the reporters in our driveway as we carried groceries into the house. After we'd put everything away, Aurora curled up in the living room with a phone to check in on her family and I walked down to the cabin.

Checking my email I found:

> Dearest, I'm so sorry about your studio and about the chaos you're enduring. I should be with you. The new piece is coming along well. I worked half the night and was up at dawn again, pounding away. I wasn't sure I could get something done that quickly but this is pouring out like liquid fire. I may finish it within the next week. That would give me some time I didn't expect. My friend Edward invited me to stay if I was ever in the States. Do you think I should? All my heart, Luke.

My heart raced, sweat started along my arms. It felt like I was melting. I typed "Yes," then erased it. "No, it's too dangerous," erased that. "I don't know," erased that. "Yes." Finally, "yes, yes, yes, please."

ঞ ঞ ঞ

I napped before dinner, setting the alarm so I wouldn't oversleep. I'd need to deal with Jack sooner or later and sooner was probably the wisest course. From my cedar chest in the studio I excavated the thick blue African cotton shawl, embroidered in bright reds and greens, that Grandpa Rosenberg gave me for my seventeenth birthday. I wrapped it around my shoulders and climbed the hill to the main house. Opening the back door, I heard Mark and Jack talking in the den. Aurora was nowhere to be seen, probably at Edward's.

I turned on the kitchen light and opened the refrigerator. What dish goes best with emotional turmoil? Something comforting but light, I thought, and began choosing vegetables to roast (red peppers, zucchini, asparagus) and to mash (potatoes and garlic). Slicing vegetables and peeling potatoes, I felt grounded for the first time since landing in the U.S., maybe earlier. The solidity of food and repetitiveness of the tasks relaxed me, made me feel loose limbed and confident.

Eventually the smell of roasting vegetables must have permeated the house because the door opened and Jack entered, Mark trailing behind. Jack looked pretty ragged around the edges. His red rimmed eyes and pink nose reflected the highball in his hand. He wore torn sweatpants and hadn't shaved or combed his hair.

Guess the press conference won't be tonight, I thought.

"Hello Jack, Mark, I've made dinner. Are you hungry? I made plenty in case Aurora and Edward show up."

Mark smiled and nodded behind Jack's back, but Jack just stared at me. "What the hell are you wearing?" he finally asked.

I laughed. "Have you looked at yourself in the mirror lately, Romeo?" I pulled the veggies from the oven and began scooping them onto three plates, each with a side of mashed potatoes. I handed both of them a plate, fork and napkin and nodded toward the table.

Jack took his plate dully and sat down. Mark thanked me profusely and sat beside him. I sat with my own plate across from Jack in the chair I'd occupied for years. We looked at each other for a very long moment.

"Are you back?" he asked.

"No. We made a bargain, remember. If you kept it out of the papers I'd stay." I shrugged. "This isn't exactly out of the papers."

He hung his head, shaking it slowly back and forth. "I tried, Gillian. You wouldn't believe what I did to try and spare you and the children all of this."

I forked a large bite of garlic mashed potatoes, heavy on the cream and butter, into my mouth. "No, you didn't do anything to spare us. But you did do a lot of stupid things to spare yourself. And I suspect you'll do some more."

Jack stirred his potatoes. "I've always loved you, Gillian, you must know that."

"I don't know that I do know that, Jack." The roasted red peppers tasted really good. "But I don't think you loved anyone else either, except maybe yourself."

"That's a cruel thing to say," he protested. I noticed Mark trying to make himself invisible while enjoying both the food and the conversation.

"I don't think you get to decide how cruel I can be," I told him. "You do know that they played you?"

"I don't know what you're talking about." Jack puffed himself up and took a swig of his drink.

"Don't be ridiculous. I'm not some constituent you can game. Let's see if I can reconstruct it for you." I took another bite. "You hired this pretty young intern who gushed all over about what an amazing man you are and how good you are for the country, while coming on in an unsubtle, but youthfully charming way. Am I getting this right?"

Jack stared at me, stone-faced.

"So of course, you fucked her. Maybe she took pictures or better yet, for the sucker factor, had you take them yourself. Getting warmer?" Another bite, chew, swallow, the potatoes were excellent. "Time went by and then, boom, the pictures show up. I bet it wasn't Ashley herself who blackmailed you. I bet it was someone else entirely. And then, just in time, AHC came along to help you out of your difficulties…and you're skewered and screwed."

"The thing about you, Gillian," Jack said through clenched teeth, "is that you're so imaginative."

"Give it up, Jack. The FBI knows it all, and what they don't know they can guess. Why else would Ashley be on the AHC payroll?"

The color drained from his face.

"You didn't know? You're even more of an idiot than I thought." He glared at me.

"John's gone," I told him. "He's not coming back, maybe not ever. Aurora's leaving in the morning. I'll stay around long enough to pack. You're really on your own. I think your mother still loves you, though you don't deserve her. You need to put a plan together, plea bargain or whatever, and do your fucking press conference so they'll all go home."

"I should take suggestions on political strategy from you? The woman who can't even make a goddamned speech to the League of Women Voters?" His face reddened.

"I'd say relying on your own thinking hasn't done you much good. But you can do whatever you want with the advice. It was freely given, like this food, like most of what you've had from me." I finished the last couple of bites, picked up my plate and rinsed it in the sink. "I plan to file for divorce before I leave town, sometime in the next couple of weeks."

He leaned forward and reached for my arm. "But the press, how will it look if you abandon me now? It could hurt my case. I need you by my side."

I jerked away. "I don't care how it looks, Jack. I'm quitting politics, this was my farewell banquet."

I stacked the leftovers onto a tray, kicked open the back door and retraced my morning steps along the path to Edward's. I found Edward and Aurora chatting over tea at the kitchen table. They were delighted to have food delivered.

That night my email read:

> My Gillian, today I worked harder than ever. It will be worth it if I can see you, speak with you, touch you, be with you even a day earlier. I want to see where you live, know your people and places, so I can know who you were before we met. I have nothing to tell you about my day other than that I worked. Tell me about yours instead.

I told him everything, about John, Aziza, Aurora, Jack. It took more than an hour to describe the day. When I finished I felt lonely for him all over again so I started organizing my belongings to pack.

PART FOUR

Start Again With Pasta

You'll need to have Tang of Life Tomato Sauce already on hand. Slice about a head's worth of garlic (simple longitudinal slices will do) and one onion into rings. Sauté these in olive oil (use a heavy cast iron pan, it really does make a difference in how things brown). Boil water in a saucepan for the pasta. Grate reggiano (regular parmesan will work). Wait until the sauce is done before you start the pasta. I like angel hair, it's delicate and gentle and perfect if you're starting over — but any pasta will do. Just follow the directions on the package. Don't overcook it. If you want to throw noodles on your ceiling, go ahead. Drain, add the sauce, mix it up, ladle onto plates and top with cheese.

    I like to serve this with warmed sourdough and a roasted garlic spread. To make the spread, I place garlic heads in one of those tiny cast iron pans that you might use to melt butter (one head per person) and roast them in the oven at 350° F for about an hour. Lots of people cut the tops off and drizzle olive oil on the heads, but I don't. I prefer the rich, clean squish of naked garlic on my bread.

Twenty-One

At about two p.m., a week before Luke's show, Edward appeared at my door. "Come for tea."

I stopped crating paintings and followed him along the path. A light snow fell, clinging to our hair and clothing. As we reached the back door he said, "Go on in. I need to check on the pump in the boathouse," and sprinted down the steps.

I pushed open the door, stamping the snow off my boots before stepping into the warm kitchen. As I shook snow from my coat and threw it over a chair, I heard, "You really are beautiful," and looked up to find Luke leaning against the stove, watching me.

"I didn't think you were coming until tomorrow." I rushed to him.

"I misled you." He buried his face in my hair, his arms tight around me. "I thought it might be all right to surprise you."

"It's a wonderful surprise." I pulled back enough so that I could find his mouth. Our lips touched, lightly, briefly, and then again.

We pulled apart as the door opened. Edward beamed at us, bouncing slightly on his toes. I smiled at him. "This is a great surprise, Edward. Thank you."

"Wish Sam could have gotten away and come with me," Luke said.

"Me, too, but I'm thrilled their work is going so well," Edward said. "Can I get either of you tea or coffee or anything?"

"I'd like to take Luke off to bed, if you don't mind," I said. "He must be very tired from the trip."

Edward raised his eyebrows at Luke, who shrugged and smiled. Edward said, "I think that's probably a good idea."

"Can I bring dinner over later?" I asked.

"That's a relief. I thought I'd have to starve. I'll set the table, you come whenever you want."

"Call Maggie, she'll kill us if we don't invite her." I kissed Edward on the cheek, took Luke's hand and pulled him out the door and onto the path between the houses.

He stopped, looking out over the lake, the boathouses and the evergreens along the point. "It's even more beautiful here than I expected."

"I know. We've been so lucky." I walked him toward the cabin.

Inside, he moved around the space, touching and looking. He smiled as he caressed the computer key pad, picked up Edward's photograph of us and petted the bronze flame woman he'd made. I watched him finger my tubes of paint and brushes, stacked in a cardboard box, a roll of canvass and the crate of paintings. He looked for a long time out the window at the lake. I built up the fire.

Finally he came to where I stood by the couch, watching him. He stopped short of me and ran his eyes around my face. His hand caressed my cheek. "I've missed you. It's too early for long separations. Let's not do that again for a while."

I nodded, stepped into his arms and pulled him down on the couch, our whole bodies pressed against each other. He slid his hand under my sweatshirt. I felt his strong, calloused hands against my skin and kissed him hard.

Later we lay like spoons, naked under a blanket on the narrow couch. I felt his breath in my ear. "You're packing."

I nodded.

"You're moving."

I nodded again. "The movers come on Wednesday."

"Are you by any chance planning an extended visit to the Netherlands?"

I nodded and nestled into him.

"Will you stay with Edward and Sam?"

"Probably. Later I might get a better offer."

He kissed my neck. I shivered, and he pulled the blanket more tightly around us. "I'm hard to live with," he said softly into my back. "I'm driven, messy, sometimes I get up in the middle of the night to work. Other times I forget what I'm doing and leave dirty dishes and whatnot around. I can be obsessive. For example, right now I am fascinated by these three freckles on your neck."

"I have freckles on my neck?"

"Yes, one here, and here and here." He planted small kisses in a jagged line down the back of my neck. "We don't know each other well and it is probably too soon and unwise, but I want you completely in my life, in my bed every night. I want the scent of you on my clothes, towels, everything. That probably isn't a better offer, but it's the best I can make."

I rolled toward him. "Thank you, but not yet. Maybe I'll give a different answer later but for now… Let me catch my breath first." I kissed him.

He settled his face in my neck. "But you're coming back to Amsterdam?"

I nodded and could feel him smile.

"Gillian?" he said after a while.

"Hmmm?"

"Is it too early to tell you that I love you?"

"I thought you already did. What is it, 'Ik hou van jou'?"

His breath caught, "Do you think you could try that again, only with je, not jou at the end."

"Because jou is for a woman?"

He whispered, "Yes."

"Ik hou van je," I said softly, looking into his eyes.

"Ahh, that was good. We'll work on your accent later." His mouth covered mine again.

At about five we showered. Luke looked exhausted, but when I'd offered to let him sleep he shook his head. "Keep me awake until after dinner."

Dressing, I said, "Here's what I've learned from all this scandal. I'm not doing secrets any more. I don't care if it ends up in the papers or if people gossip, I need to live in the open."

He smiled, buttoning his shirt. "I'm very glad you said that. It takes quite a load off my mind. I wasn't sure about something, but now I feel much better."

"What?" I asked.

He just smiled. "You'll see."

In the kitchen I gave Luke the task of slicing garlic while I packed a canvas bag with things we could prepare at Edward's, like angel hair pasta and the loaf of fresh sourdough I'd baked that morning. "We'll do most of our cooking here because the kitchen is better," I explained.

I placed four heads of garlic in a small cast iron pan, set them in the oven to roast and a large saucepan on the burner to heat. I turned to see how Luke was doing with his garlic and saw the thin slices I'd asked for transformed into fantastical shapes. He saw me look and shrugged. "I can't help it."

"They're truly wonderful." I handed him an onion to peel and slice. "But maybe you'll want to slice this into rings."

While chopping cilantro, I heard Jack clambering down the steps. Within moments he was standing, large and slightly drunk, in the doorway. At least he'd shaved and changed his clothes.

"Where's Mark?" I asked.

"Gone to get pizza," Jack said, his eyes never leaving Luke. "But if you're cooking—"

"We're eating at Edward's. Just using the kitchen. We'll be out of your way in no time." I slammed my knife into the cilantro.

"I'm Jack Sach." Jack stepped toward Luke with an extended hand.

My stomach flipped at the thought of Jack touching Luke, so I grabbed Luke's hand between both of mine.

"This is my lover, Luke Vanderwerken," I told Jack. "Luke, meet my philandering husband Jack."

"Who's philandering?" Jack lowered his hand. "I'm not the one with a lover in the kitchen." He gave Luke a long appraising look then turned to me. "This is the man you're leaving me for? You're an attractive woman. You could have done much better than that."

I started to speak. Luke squeezed my hand, let go, leaned back against the counter facing Jack and crossed his arms. Looking into Jack's eyes, he said, "I'm sure she could do better. I can also see she's done much worse." Jack started to speak. Luke cut him off, "You see, my friend, I have a few strokes on you. For one thing, I don't reek of, what is that? Smells like Glenlivet, no, not that smooth, maybe Johnny Walker Red. I'm also not facing possible jail time and I haven't been in the scandal pages in years."

"You little—" Jack's fists clenched.

Luke's stance shifted ever so slightly so that he looked relaxed but ready.

"Stop." I waved my knife for emphasis. "That's enough. I do not find the thought of men fighting over me the least bit sexy. We'll finish up at Edward's but Jack, right now I want you out of my kitchen."

Jack glared at Luke and stormed out. "Here." I handed Luke the half-packed canvas bag. "Hold this open." I grabbed three plastic containers and scooped the lovely garlic creations into one, the onion slices into another and the poor, mangled cilantro into a third. I threw these into the bag, along with a jar of my canned tomatoes and a slab of Reggiano. Gloving my hands in oven mitts, I opened the oven, pulled out the pan of roasting garlic, placed it in the sauté pan for easy transportation, made sure everything was turned off and led Luke out the back door and across to Edward's kitchen, muttering under my breath the entire time.

Edward sat at the kitchen table with a novel as we entered. He looked up, startled.

"Jack," Luke said simply.

I slammed the pans down on the stove and began my sauce again. I only made it as far as opening the oven door and sliding the garlic in to roast before Edward took my arm and sat me down at the table.

"Breathe," he said. "I'd hate to have you burn dinner because of Jack. Tell me what happened."

With Luke's help, I recounted the conversation.

Edward smiled. "That was good, man," he said, patting Luke on the back. "Those are the kinds of lines I only think of after it's all over."

Luke smiled at him grimly. "It was stupid and oafish to provoke him like that. But to tell the truth, I'd rather have decked him."

"Still wish I'd been there to see it." Edward rubbed his hands together so gleefully that both Luke and I laughed. He continued, "Now you can cook. Maggie will be here in about an hour."

I unpacked the ingredients and began sautéing the garlic (which Edward insisted on photographing first) and onions. As soon as they browned, I poured in the canned tomatoes and left the sauce to simmer. I boiled water for the pasta, sliced some the bread to toast and grated cheese so that everything was ready to finish when Maggie arrived.

She strode into the kitchen, introducing herself immediately. Luke shook her hand. "You look familiar."

"I saw your talk here last year," she told him.

"And you just saw a picture of the two of us next to my computer," I added.

"Ah," he said, "you're that Maggie."

Over dinner, after we'd recounted and dissected the conversation with Jack, we got around to talking about our immediate plans.

"John is picking us up at the airport in the city Thursday so we can all drive to Aurora's for the weekend," I told them. "Luke needs to be in New York on Sunday to work on the installation. I'll fly out the next day for the opening Tuesday."

Maggie pointed her fork at Luke. "Tell us about the show."

"It's not a big deal, a group show, there are ten of us. I'm only contributing three pieces. One is new." He smiled at me. "I'm excited for you to see it, Gillian. I'm hoping you'll enjoy it."

"What does it look like?" Maggie asked.

"It's hard to describe. I'll send you a picture after the show. Now it is your turn, tell me what you do."

After dinner Luke stood. "Edward and I will clean up. You two can have coffee in another room."

"You're kicking us out?" I handed him my empty plate.

"Yes." He kissed my hair as he took it. "I need to vent and to say things about your husband that it wouldn't be right for me to say to you. I can't say these things to Maggie since I am trying to make a good impression. But Edward will listen and tell me all the right things about letting go, and turning it over, and I will feel much better."

"Like what things?" Maggie asked.

"Like that he's a rat bastard," Luke said. "But Gillian knows that better than I and between us, those are things for her to say, not me. Now go, I'll bring coffee." He shooed us through the door and into the living room.

We settled on the couch. Maggie giggled. "I like him."

"Me, too."

"If someone looked at me the way he looks at you, I'd think about relationship."

"He wants me to move in with him."

"Wow, that's fast. But I suppose transcontinental dating is difficult. Are you going to?"

I shrugged. "I don't know, maybe eventually. After all, I have to go somewhere. It's not like I can stay here, at least not right now. For now I can live with Edward and Sam but later—"

"What will you do about the house?"

I shrugged. "I suppose Jack will stay there until the divorce is final or he goes to jail, whichever comes first. Then we'll see."

She thought for a moment. "We have a visiting scientist coming from Malaysia with her family next fall. Maybe they could rent. It would give you an extra year to come up with a plan."

"That might work, we'll see what happens. I can't plan past the immediate future right now."

Luke appeared with two cups of coffee. "Edward says we're serving decaf and that Gillian likes hers black while Maggie prefers some milk, is that right?"

"Perfect, thank you," I told him.

When he'd gone Maggie said, "I agree, he is perfect for you."

"Nobody's perfect, but he is pretty wonderful."

"Either way, you can keep him."

"Thanks." I laughed. "I'd like that."

※ ※ ※

"Must we sleep on the couch or do you own a bed?" Luke asked as we entered the cabin.

"I have a bed. I never use it because the couch is closer to the fire." I led him into the small bedroom. Together we moved the boxes I'd piled on the bed and stacked them in a corner.

As soon as we'd settled the last box, Luke threw off his clothes and climbed under the covers.

"We'll have to stay close for warmth." He yawned. By the time I returned from brushing my teeth he was fast asleep. I crawled in next to him and watched the rise and fall of his chest until I slept myself.

It was still dark when I woke to Luke's hand caressing the length of my belly. "Good morning."

"Good morning. I don't know why people complain about jet lag."

We awoke again in daylight, snow falling heavily out the window. I made coffee in the tiny cabin kitchen and brought it back to bed.

"Good idea." Luke accepted the cup. "Maybe if we have hot liquids in our hands we can talk without me stopping to ravish you."

"Ravishing is nice." I sipped my coffee.

"So is conversation. I enjoyed your conversation long before I had a chance to know your wonderful body."

"What should we talk about?"

"Tell me about your daughter. I like John very much. Is she like him?"

So I told him about Aurora, her battles with her father, her early marriage, Peter, the girls, who she had become. "She was always the black sheep, but now I think she might be the healthiest of us all."

He smiled. "And John, do you think he will forgive his father?"

"Not for a long time if he does. Would you?"

Luke looked out the window, watching the snow fall. "Almost anything is forgivable but not without restitution, making amends, something on the part of the one to be forgiven. So maybe if Jack—"

"Jack will never make amends to John, he is constitutionally incapable of admitting he's wrong."

"I hope that isn't true. It will make it much harder for John to let him go." He took my hand. "And you, will you forgive him?"

"Ask me again after all this has died down. Right now it's hard to envision letting go of my anger. On the other hand, I don't want to carry him around any longer than I have to. But I can't know now. It's all too fresh."

He smiled softly. "It would have been better for you if we'd happened later. Good things can be confusing, too."

"I don't know, you're certainly a nice distraction. Do you think I'd be happier wallowing in my anger all the time?"

He laughed. "So now I'm a petty diversion. In that case, what's for breakfast? I'm a hungry, petulant, petty diversion and I need to be fed."

I jumped out of bed then stopped. "Shit. I am not up to facing Jack in the kitchen this morning."

"Edward's?"

I looked at the clock, just before seven. "No good, he's still sleeping."

"We could go out?"

I shook my head. "The reporters have gone home, but I'm not up to town gossips either. Wait, I know." I picked up the phone and called Pearl. She answered on the third ring. "Hi, Momma Pearl. I know it's early, but could we come over and make breakfast? Luke and I. Yes, he got in last night. Great, we'll be right over."

Momma Pearl must have been waiting by the door, because when we rang the bell it flew open. She ushered us into the warm kitchen. "Come in, come in. I've made coffee." She gestured to the pot. "You know where everything is, Gillian, make what you like. Here, Luke, sit. I'm so glad to see you."

"You're walking well, Mrs. Sach."

"Oh, please, call me Pearl or Momma Pearl, everyone does." She poured coffee into three cups. "Walking is easier at home. I don't know quite why, but it is." She brought him a cup and one for herself and sat down across from him. "So, tell me. What brings you here?"

He looked at me helplessly, so I said, "Luke and I have become lovers, Momma Pearl. Just as you suggested."

"Oh, I'm so glad." She clapped her hands and beamed at us.

Luke looked from one to the other, confused. "Did I miss something?" he asked finally. "You are her mother-in-law, aren't you? Jack's mother?"

She sighed. "I suppose it is confusing. It's just that you remind me so much of Jacob."

"Jack's father?" he asked.

"Oh no, at least I don't think so," she said. "Perhaps you'd like something to tide you over until Gillian gets breakfast?"

"Uh, yes, that would be nice," he said, accepting what looked like an oatmeal raisin cookie.

"Are you hungry, Momma Pearl?" I asked.

"I had some toast earlier, but I'll admit that when you called I decided to postpone my breakfast."

I opened the refrigerator she always keeps too full. Eventually I found enough vegetables, eggs and cheese to make a nice scramble. She still had half the loaf of whole wheat I'd brought earlier in the week and some raspberry jam she'd put up over the summer, so I had breakfast on the table within minutes.

"This is delicious." Luke took another bite of omelet. "Is your food always this good?"

"Gillian's the best cook I know," Pearl crowed.

"Clearly there is a God," Luke said solemnly, tasting the toast.

"Speaking of God," I said, "were you able to find out if Aziza can immigrate to the Netherlands to be with her brother?"

"Oh, thank you for bringing that up." Luke brightened. "I may have a solution. She can't immigrate for her brother but she can come in to work, as long as an employer will vouch for her. Then, eventually, she can apply for naturalization. It is all more difficult now that we're part of the EU but still, as long as she has work she'll be fine." He beamed at us, expectantly.

"But how can she find work there?" I asked.

"With me, of course. I talked with my brother and he got very excited about having her come take care of Mother, as long as I pay, of course." He turned to Pearl. "My mother has Alzheimer's. She isn't sick but needs constant watching. It wouldn't be a wonderful job, and she may not want to take it but it would get her into the country." He shrugged. "Do you think I could meet her to talk about it?"

I was already dialing the number of her new employer. Aziza agreed to come right away.

As soon as she entered the kitchen, she greeted me with a strong embrace. "I'm so sorry for all you're going through, Habeebeti. I wanted to tell you so earlier, but I've been afraid that if I contacted you someone would notice me. I'm not legal now, you know."

"I know," I told her. "I'm so sorry about that for you. You've been happy here and it's terrible you can't stay." I introduced her to Luke.

He shook her hand. "I'm so glad to meet you. Gillian speaks highly of you."

Aziza looked from Luke to me. "This is your new man?"

I nodded.

She turned back to him and smiled. "Gillian has been sad for so long. I hope you can make her very happy."

"Come, sit." Pearl herded us back to the table. I poured Aziza coffee and refilled everyone's cups.

"I hear you have a brother in Rotterdam. I do, too." Luke explained his proposition to her.

She listened without interrupting until he was done. "You are kind. Of course I will accept. And forgive me, but when your mother passes, will I be able to stay?"

Luke nodded. "My brother and I talked about that already. We'll find you something. No matter what, I'll sponsor you until you can stay on your own, either because you naturalize or you meet some nice Dutch person and marry."

Aziza smiled. "Can I leave right away?"

"As soon as you can book a flight," he told her.

Aziza's face darkened. "I cannot afford to fly."

"I'll pay," I said. "It would be my pleasure. I'm moving there myself and could use a friend."

Her eyebrows shot up. "Really? When?"

"Next week, I'm moving in with Edward and Sam after Luke's New York show."

Pearl gasped. I looked at her. Tears hung in her eyes. "So soon. I knew you were leaving but—" She smiled. "Really I'm glad, Gillian. Perhaps I can come visit again?"

"Of course." I covered her hand with mine.

"I must get ready to go." Aziza jumped up. She hugged me then

Luke. "Shukran," she told me.

"Afwan," I responded.

"Thank you," she told Luke.

"Believe me, you are doing me a huge favor," he said. "And don't thank me yet, Mother won't be easy."

❧ ❧ ❧

After breakfast we returned to the cabin. "I need to get on with packing," I told Luke as he stood behind me, nuzzling my neck while I tried to get my key in the lock.

"Right." He pulled back. "You've got me thinking like a seventeen year old. Put me to work, it's the only cure."

"It's overwhelming. I haven't moved in twenty years." I looked around my little cabin. "I love this space. But I don't love my life here."

He looked around. "Maybe you could visit sometimes?"

"You mean, like a summer home?"

"What do the Russians call them, a dacha? This could be our North American dacha."

"That's how it started for the grandfathers."

"I've heard you use that term before, 'the grandfathers,' it sounds epic. What does it mean?"

"While we work, I'll tell you a love story. You sort through my art supplies and see what you think is worth carting over. I'm looking for that fine balance between paying twice what it's worth to ship the masking tape and spending my first month buying and schlepping art supplies. Here's a box. I'll figure out which of my clothes I need for the next week and what can go with movers."

He asked a lot of questions and I followed tangents, so by the time I'd finished telling Luke about the grandfathers, Rosenberg and Wolf Tool and Die, Edward and the lake houses, it was almost noon.

He glanced up from sorting paint brushes. "So this Foundation of yours and Edward's, it means you won't suffer financially in the divorce?"

"It means I won't suffer financially, ever. Edward and I are, we're, well, I guess you'd say we're rich."

He stared at me a moment then went back to packing the art supplies. "And you cook."

We heard footsteps outside the cabin and a discrete knock. I opened the door.

Mark stood blushing on the doorstep. Inviting him in, I introduced the two men. He cleared his throat. "Jack is going to his lawyer at one-thirty this afternoon to start negotiating a plea bargain. He wants to know if you'd like to come along."

"Why would I want to do that?" I asked.

He cleared his throat. "If he gets the details worked out they'll have a press conference. It would look good for him if you were there."

I stared. "No. No press conferences. I told him that. I don't care how it looks. Frankly, I don't care what happens. Please tell him that in this case, 'no' really does mean no."

Mark nodded curtly and turned to go. He must have suddenly noticed the boxes. "You're going?"

"Yes."

"Oh." He looked at Luke, then back at me, his eyes sad. "Good luck."

"Thank you." I gently closed the door behind him and collapsed against it.

"For twenty years I've dreaded that press conference," I told Luke. "And now all I can think of is that Jack will be out of the house for the afternoon, so we can pack up the rest of my things."

Luke smiled. "Sometimes by the time the thing we dread arrives, we're already gone."

I called Edward and then Maggie, told them to meet at the house at one-thirty. "We're packing up the bedroom. Stealth packing, if you will."

Luke made sandwiches while I finished packing my clothes. He handed me something that smelled like turkey and swiss.

I bit into the sandwich, good, lots of mustard. "I'll get the movers to do as much as possible, but I don't want to end up having to ship back some of Jack's things."

He ran his hand gently through my hair. "Just keep reminding yourself that this part will end. I'll do what I can to make your new life better."

Edward and Maggie arrived promptly. We climbed the stairs, boxes and bags in hand. I stopped at the top, looking around. Between clothes, bottles and plates of half-eaten food, the place was a mess. I saw Luke and Edward exchange glances, but they didn't say anything.

Taking a deep breath, I handed Maggie and Edward garbage bags and pointed them toward the closet. "I moved the clothes I like down to the cabin last summer. That's what's left. I'm only taking one Congressman's Wife outfit with me. You guys pick which one, but make sure the shoes match. Everything else goes to charity."

"You hold the bag," Maggie told Edward. "Getting rid of this crap is something I've dreamt of for years."

I pulled Luke over to the bookcase. "You can pack up almost everything here. If it's about policy or politics or American history, leave it. Otherwise, most of these are mine, particularly the fiction. Jack says he prefers reality."

"Clearly." Luke tapped an empty scotch bottle with his foot.

I opened the bottom drawer of my bureau and began transferring old photos, letters and the children's report cards into a cardboard box. "Should I leave some of these for Jack, do you think?"

"Maybe a couple," Maggie suggested. "He can take them along for company in jail."

Edward said, "Leave him those awful Christmas card portraits you had done each year. Everyone looks so fake-happy in them, he's the only one who'd like to be reminded."

"Good plan." I began pulling out eight by ten studio portraits and stacking them on the floor beside the box.

Between the four of us, stripping me out from the room took about an hour. As we carried the last load down, I looked at the large, sort of sexy, landscape hanging above the bed. I turned to Maggie. "You want that? I painted it when we were first married. It's always going to mean that time to me, but it doesn't have to mean that to you if you like it."

"I've always loved that piece." She took it down. "Thank you. Don't you think it would look beautiful on the south wall of my living room?"

It took another hour to pack my books from the living room and study. We piled all the boxes in John's old room so they'd be ready for the movers, and the garbage bags for charity in Aurora's. I served my helpers cookies and hot chocolate in the kitchen and glanced into my pantry, lined with jars of last summer's produce. "Maggie, since you're the only one who's staying, perhaps you want the canned goods and the chest freezer, which is mostly full of berries and peppers from the garden?"

"Am I glad I came today. I won't be able to fit everything in my car."

"If you want them I'll get the movers to pack up the food and move it to your house, certainly easier than moving canned goods across the ocean." I looked out the window at my garden. "I'll miss it, though."

"The canned goods?" Luke asked.

"My garden."

"You garden?" Luke asked.

"More like she truckfarms." Edward gestured out the window.

Luke sat thoughtfully for a moment. "There are roof gardens all over the place in Amsterdam. We're into sustainability."

Twenty-Two

On Thursday morning Maggie drove the three of us to the airport. Edward flew with us from the regional airport to the city, where he transferred to an international flight. "I'd love to see your show," he told Luke. "But I need to get home."

"Believe me, I understand." Luke hugged him goodbye. "I'd do the same."

"Thank you staying with me," I said. "You're the best friend a girl could want."

"As are you." He kissed my forehead and sprinted off, calling over his shoulder, "See you over there."

Luke turned to me. "Are you nervous about these next few days with Aurora?"

"Some," I admitted. "I want you to like them and them to like you and everyone to finally be happy. That last part may be unrealistic. What do you think?"

"I think I'm finally happy." He pulled me close. "And that's miraculous, so who knows what else might happen?"

John waved to us as we exited the secure area.

"He looks happy," Luke said.

"Don't worry, it's temporary," I told him.
"Everything's temporary," he corrected.

※ ※ ※

I gave Luke the front seat so I could stretch out and nap in the back. I felt washed through, exhausted. Every muscle ached from packing and hauling. The movers had finally finished and drove off just before midnight. Fortunately, Jack spent most of the day downtown with his lawyers. It was evidently harder to work out a plea bargain than he'd expected.

"He probably thought he could walk in with a list of demands and everyone would fall in line," I told Luke when the promised press conference failed to materialize. I dozed through the ride, catching phrases of their conversation. I paid attention for a little while when I heard John mention his father.

"I can't get over it," he said. "I don't know if I'm just stuck in yuck, or if I'm somehow still hung up on Ashley, or betrayed by her or what. It's so Oedipal."

"Give yourself time," Luke advised. "You don't have to work it all out now."

"I guess. I get sick every time I think about it."

"I know. I had a complicated relationship with my dad, too. Not as complicated as yours, of course."

I could see Luke smiling at John.

"But it wasn't easy, he had a temper. I was angry for a long time. That may simply be the way it is between fathers and sons. But I learned a lot from him. If he hadn't been so hard on me, I might not have turned out such a contrarian. Then where would I be? My best work is essentially about defiance, always has been."

"Yeah, but I'm no artist," John said, sulkily.

"Even so, you may find it useful to know how to stand apart from the crowd. This will pass soon enough. Meanwhile, write your dissertation and get on with your life. Just because he's your father doesn't mean you have to let him define you." Luke patted John's shoulder, and I slipped back to sleep.

Aurora, Kaitlin and the dogs greeted us warmly. "Did she warn you about the chaos here?" Aurora asked Luke.

"No one can adequately warn about the chaos here." John swept a laughing Kaitlin into his arms and twirled her.

"I like good chaos," Luke said. "Happy families are often chaotic, or at least that's what it has always looked like to me."

"From the outside?" Aurora asked him.

"So far," he told her.

When Pete drove up we all poured outside again. Haley and Emma leapt from the car. "Grandma, Uncle John," they yelled, throwing themselves into our arms. After they'd all been kissed by me and twirled by John, they stood before Luke. Kaitlin joined them.

"Hello." Emma extended her hand. "I'm Emma. This is my sister Haley. You probably already met Kaitlin. Momma says you might be our new grandfather, but we're not supposed to talk about it. Is it true?"

Luke shook all three girls' hands solemnly. "It's a little early to tell for certain, but I'd be honored. I've never been a grandfather before. Do you suppose you could teach me?"

"Grandpa Bell just watches football," Haley said. "Emma's the only one who remembers Grandpa Sach and she says he yelled."

"I don't like football or yelling," Luke told her. "Perhaps I could start out as an uncle. I know how to do that. Maybe later I could grow up into a grandpapa. Would that suit?"

All three girls nodded enthusiastically. John beamed, it was evident they thought well of uncles.

Pete introduced himself. "Sorry about my girls. They tend to be forthright, don't know where they get that from." He shot a look at Aurora, who smiled and shrugged.

"It's all right, I like forthright women," Luke told him as we all trooped back inside.

Aurora whispered to me, "I like him." She corralled the girls toward homework.

⁂

"Wait, listen to this," Pete said, turning up the TV and bringing us all into the living room on Saturday afternoon. Jack's picture hung in the space beside the news announcer's face.

"That's Grandpa," shouted Emma.

"So it is. Now let's go finish our castle." Luke led them back to Emma's room, where they'd been building all day.

The announcer intoned, "Congressman Jack Sach plead guilty to two counts of conspiracy to commit bribery and one of tax evasion. He has been sentenced to five years in a minimum security prison and fined the estimated value of the gifts he received and back taxes on those gifts. In addition to the bribery case, we've been covering reports of Congressman Sach's involvement in a number of illicit affairs. He is expected to address all these issues at this press conference. Jean Fillipo is there, covering this story for us. Jean?"

"Hi, Ed, the case of Congressman Jack Sach is another in a long line of scandals involving improper behavior on the part of public officials. Behind me you can see the press preparing to hear his statement. Given that infidelity is also a part of this case, it will be interesting to note whether his wife joins him on the platform. We have reports that she will not be present today and may have filed for divorce. Here comes the congressman and it doesn't look like his wife is with him. We'll go live to Congressman Sach now."

Jack appeared, flanked by lawyers. He looked tired and sad, but just as clean cut and handsome as ever. I couldn't quite focus on his speech and caught only a few phrases, "betray public trust," "grave errors in judgment" and "inappropriate behavior."

"Good, the bastard's resigning immediately," John muttered.

Pete said, "I suppose it's possible the governor could appoint you to his seat."

John snorted. "I wouldn't want it. But even if I did, my father has just made J. Sach the last name any governor would want to be associated with."

I stood and walked to the kitchen. Aurora followed and put a hand on my arm. "How do you feel?"

"Numb. Sad. I know there will be more talk about my absence from the podium. Maybe we could go somewhere, a park or something, so we don't have to hear?"

"Sure. Let's leave the kids and men here and take the dogs for a long walk. We could all use the exercise."

I found Luke and the girls in Emma's room. Their "castle," made from pillows, boards, chairs, blankets, blocks, dishes, and pots and pans filled most of the space, with little rooms and cubby holes on at least three different levels.

"Ok," Luke was saying as I entered, "we have the underlying structure. Now we need to decorate." He handed the girls the neckties, socks, belts and shoes they'd begged from each of us earlier. A box in the corner held the Christmas decorations Aurora had donated once the four builders had sworn they'd clean up after.

Luke saw me and smiled. "Here to help, Grandma?"

"No." I ignored the expectant looks on my granddaughters' faces. "Aurora and I are taking the dogs for a walk, will you all be okay?"

"What do you think, girls? Can we entertain ourselves?"

They giggled and nodded.

Aurora and I grabbed coats. Pulling on my boots, I asked John, "You want to come?"

He shook his head, his eyes glued to CNN.

"Sure?" I asked. "They're not going to tell you anything you don't know."

"I know," he said, softening, "but I want to know what they say."

I shrugged on my coat. "It doesn't matter what they say, honey."

"Have a nice walk, Mom."

Aurora handed me three leashes and took three herself. "I'm not up to running," I told her. "The ice scares me."

"We'll walk. Even Huckleberry and Pita like to walk. The dogs can run by themselves once we get to the woods."

It took twice as long to reach the path into the woods walking. Just below freezing, the air smelled fresh. Snow barely crunched beneath our feet.

"It's so quiet," I said.

"I love this time of year," Aurora said. "The real winter."

"I'll miss it," I told her. "I'm moving to Amsterdam."

"We figured you would." She didn't break stride.

"We?"

"Pete, John and I. You told me that's where you were going as soon as the reporters left. Then John told me how happy you looked around Luke. We all realized you were bound to end up there permanently." She kicked a rock out of the road. "It'll be hard to see you go, but you'll still come back to visit, won't you?"

"At least as often as I have in recent years. And maybe you could all come over next summer, my treat?"

"That would be great. But do you think the girls are old enough to get anything out of a big trip like that?"

I laughed. "If they aren't, we'll have to bring them back next year."

We turned off the road and onto the snow covered path where we'd run a few months before, when my world had been so very different.

※ ※ ※

On Sunday afternoon John drove back through the city on his way home to University, dropping Luke off at the airport. The girls spent much of the morning dismantling their castle in what Aurora called a Home Sunday School clean up lesson. They cried when the two men left. We consoled them with a trip to the movies and pizza. By the time we got home everyone was ready for bed. I slept alone for the first time in over a week. I was, frankly, glad for the sleep, but my body felt cold, achy and empty without him.

Monday morning Aurora fed, dressed and deposited the girls at their various schools, while I packed and changed the spare bedroom sheets. We piled my gear into the car and Aurora drove straight to Simply Guinevere's so I could find something to wear to the opening. This time I didn't protest.

"What's the right look for a middle aged paramour?" I flipped through the dress rack.

"Sexy," she said.

"Black?" I held up a slinky rayon version of the perfect cocktail dress.

"I don't think so. It's hard to stand out in New York in black. But not too bright, either, you don't want to risk looking like a rube." She held up an iridescent blue shift.

I shook my head. "I think I'd feel exposed in that and I'd probably get cold. What do you think of this? In the right light it might look black without being black." I held up a burgundy satin dress with a shawl collar and button sleeves.

This time Aurora objected. "It looks like something an American Girl doll would wear. Here, I found it." She handed me a simple black velvet dress, scoop necked, with blood red ribbon trim.

I cocked my head. "Do you think it's too fancy?"

"Depends on how you accessorize. Now try it on."

I slipped it over my head. The dress felt exquisite. As it fell in soft folds along my body, I realized I didn't care how I looked, in this fabric I felt beautiful.

Aurora clapped as I stepped out of the dressing room. "Yes. Now let's find you some funky jewelry and a pair of boots to dress it down."

"I love shopping with you," I told her. "Why haven't we done more of this? All I remember from the past is battling over the length of your skirts and how much belly you showed as a teenager."

She laughed. "Who wants to go shopping for boring clothes? You're right, this is fun, but I don't think I'd have liked, 'do you like the serge or the linen?' and 'navy or beige?'"

"I see what you mean. The clothes weren't any more fun than the life." I took my new dress to the counter to pay.

೫ ೫ ೫

"Just three months since you dropped me off here last," I told Aurora, as she pulled into the airport. "Seems like so much longer."

"I didn't drop you here. I left you off at the hotel," she corrected.

"Ah, yes, that's right. This is much better, don't you think?"

"You're taking an afternoon flight to New York," she said, puzzled. "Why would you need to stay in the hotel?"

"Like I said, this is better." I jumped out and began pulling my overstuffed bag from her car.

She helped me hoist it onto the sidewalk. I hugged her. "Thank you, wonderful daughter. Figure out your schedule and we'll make plans for June."

"I love you, Mom." She wiped a tear from my face. "I'm happy for you. Forget about all this crap with Dad. Walk off with your prince. You deserve it."

"Take care of your brother," I told her. "He's going to need lots of reassurance in the next few months."

She nodded, hugged me again, and sprinted back to her car, waving as she pulled away. I stood for a moment on the sidewalk watching, before walking inside to catch my plane.

❧ ❧ ❧

Luke's face brightened as he spotted me by the baggage carousel. He sprinted over, panting. "Sorry I'm late, I went to the wrong terminal, preoccupied, I guess." Embracing me, he whispered, "I missed you last night. Although, I have to admit, I needed the sleep."

I laughed. "That's exactly how I felt."

"Oh God," he groaned, looking over my shoulder. "I forgot about the monster bag."

"We should have packed in two bags," I agreed. "But it seemed a good idea at the time."

"It will certainly make the subway trip adventurous." He helped me heft it off the carousel.

When we'd finally settled onto the train, he wrapped an arm around my shoulder. "We're staying with an old friend of mine in Manhattan, Barbara Lowe. Actually she's a dealer with a small gallery in the East Village. I showed her your slides."

"You showed her my slides? What did she think?"

He smiled. "You can ask her yourself."

"What kind of old friend?" I asked after a silence.

"The kind who's conveniently forgotten we slept together once in the '70s. Don't worry. She's in a committed relationship— I think her name is Iris— and so am I." He gazed at me for a long moment. "I won't lie to you, Gillian. I can't have a dishonest relationship. But my truth is sometimes messy. It may not always be easy for you to hear."

"I can see that." I watched the buildings fly by. "But I've already been protected from the truth and I think I'd rather be uncomfortable."

We watched the landscape for a few more minutes. "You were wonderful with the girls," I told him.

"Oh, they're great kids, really inventive. I liked them. Liked their parents too. I'm not sure how I feel about being a grandpapa but I do like the feel of their grandmamma." He kissed my forehead.

❧ ❧ ❧

Barbara Lowe lived in a beautifully renovated two-bedroom apartment in midtown Manhattan. Tall and thin, dressed in black from head to toe, her wild curly gray hair half-heartedly tied back, she looked like she'd stepped directly from the Beat era. "So you're Gillian Wolf. Come in, come in."

She served a lovely Mediterranean dinner, after which Luke excused himself to run back to the gallery and check the installation. Take-out is much better in New York, I thought, as I helped clean up and saw the cartons.

Barbara saw my surprise and laughed. "Amazing, seemed like homemade food, didn't it? Luke says you're a cook. I've never had the patience. Most nights I eat cereal or sandwiches. Let's make some decaf and we'll talk." In her living room we settled into soft white pillow chairs.

"Luke showed me slides." She smiled. "He's very enthusiastic."

"I'm afraid he might be biased."

"No." She shook her head. "I don't think so. He's more likely to be brutally honest than to flatter. And I liked what I saw as well. Every spring I do a group show introducing new artists. I'd like to include a couple of your pieces this year. What do you think?"

"Yeah," I said. "That would be great, I guess. Showing? Um, yes. That's exciting. Of course I'd like you to include me."

She laughed. "Interesting answer. All right, you're in. We'll talk details later, but everything's pretty standard. There's chocolate cake in the fridge, shall we celebrate?"

Luke arrived as we licked the last crumbs from our forks. "I'm afraid I only had two pieces," Barbara told him, carrying her plate to the sink. "But feel free to eat whatever else you find in the kitchen." She opened the closet and pulled out a coat. "Sorry to run out on you, but I'm heading off to Iris's. I haven't seen her since Saturday and you could probably use the privacy. You've got my spare key, right, Luke? Help yourself to whatever you can find for breakfast. I'm afraid I'll miss your opening, but I'll try to catch the show sometime next week." She kissed each of us on the cheek and blew out the door.

"She's amazing," I said.

"A force of nature," Luke agreed. "What did she say about your slides?"

"She wants to include me in her new artists' show."

"That's great." He hugged me. "That's a great place to start. An amazing place, actually. Most people have to play the hinterlands first."

"Thank you."

"Don't thank me, I simply showed her the slides. It's your work that got the show." His lips brushed my neck.

"It helps to have friends."

He nodded, nuzzling my hair. "I have to give you that. Nobody said the art world was fair. But the work still has to stand on its own. Now, about that dessert—"

ॐ ॐ ॐ

In the morning we discovered that there was nothing a person would want for breakfast in Barbara's kitchen. We walked to a corner diner.

"I always expect the coffee to be better in New York." I grimaced at the bitter taste.

"What, you don't like Chock Full of Nuts?" he asked. "Native New Yorkers go crazy for the stuff but I agree. It's pretty bad."

"So what's the plan for today?" I dipped toast into my egg yolk.

"I'm free until late afternoon when the ten of us are gathering at the gallery for a bite before the opening." He chewed his own toast and looked at me apologetically. "I'm afraid significant others aren't invited. It was Charlie Willow's idea. I think he's going to burn some sage and 'smudge' all of us and the work. Anyway, maybe you could show up half an hour early for the opening?"

"Sure," I said. "I'm not good with groups. It's the thing I hated most about campaigns."

"Oh but this will be quite different. You don't have to convince anyone of anything. If you make a fool of yourself it might even help your career."

I laughed. "As long as you don't call me Jill I'll be fine."

"Jill? No, I won't call you Jill. I love your name. Although Gilly has a certain ring to it, doesn't it?" He took an enormous bite of his omelet, chewed, and swallowed. "So Gilly, what do you say we do some gallery hopping of our own today, maybe stroll through Chelsea and see what everyone else is up to?"

❦ ❦ ❦

At five thirty-five I stood outside the gallery, which looked to be a series of small, art-filled rooms. I could see someone bustling around a long table in the back of the first room, probably setting out wine. A group of people clustered in an alcove. I spotted Luke before he saw me. He smiled and strode to the door.

"You're so beautiful." He pulled me into the gallery. One arm encircling my shoulder, he whispered, "Don't be scared. They already love you."

The group watched us cross the room. I was vaguely aware of, but couldn't focus on, the art around me. There'll be time later, I thought, doing my best not to trip, blush or anything else embarrassing.

When we got close, Luke announced, "I'd like to introduce you all to Gillian, Gillian Wolf."

"So you're Gillian." One woman took my hand warmly.

"Gillian Wolf, oh Luke, you're too funny," said a man in bright yellow pajama pants.

"He finished it so quickly, you must be quite the inspiration," said another, smiling at me.

I flushed. "I don't understand."

"I'm sorry, this is my fault," Luke said to me, and then to the group, "She hasn't seen it yet." He pulled me into one of the small gallery rooms. "I shouldn't have surprised you," he whispered. "Now

I've embarrassed you and that's the last thing I wanted. Let me show you the new piece."

He brought me to a shoulder high sculpture in one corner of the room. Black distressed lumber formed something of a box or cage. Cracked over a large rock, the box broke in several places, open to the sky. Jagged glass covered the bottom. A dozen or so beautifully formed bronze wolves emerged from the cracks, their bodies sleek and their expressions exuberant. Luke stood close behind me.

"It's beautiful," I whispered

"It's called Gillian's wolves."

"Oh."

"Usually I don't talk about my process." Arms wrapped around me, he spoke softly into my ear. "But I want you to know what I was thinking, so you understand. I love your name, Gillian Wolf. It made me lie awake at night, thinking about wolves. Wolves are social, loyal animals, somewhat shy, devoted to their packs. They're also very beautiful. I thought about wolves in those horrid zoos you find sometimes in out of the way places, how they pace and pace back and forth. It could take a strong force to break the cage apart, ordinary events wouldn't do it. But something catastrophic might and then the wolves could climb to freedom."

"And the glass?"

"Oh, you see, this is why I never talk about my process. The images may hang together but the story isn't always consistent. The piece needed something else, a note to bring out sympathy for the wolves. So I thought of wolves in fairy tales. That led me to thinking about the Littlest Mermaid, the real Hans Christian Anderson story, where she traded her tongue for the love of an undeserving prince and her every step felt like walking on broken glass. I thought that fit in this piece as well."

I leaned against him, pulling his arms more tightly around me. I'd never felt so naked or so loved. "And what do the wolves do when they're free?"

"I believe they mate for life."

"With their beshert." I turned so we stood eye to eye and mouth to mouth, an exact fit, a matched pair.

I heard a giggle from the other room. "I think she likes it."

I pulled back. "I love the piece. I love you for seeing me, creating me like this. But, I can't help myself, I still hate these events."

"Maybe you'll grow to like them."

"Maybe. I haven't yet."

"You don't have to come to mine, you know. You're not a possession. I don't need to display you," he glanced at the sculpture, "or at least, not in person. Of course, your own shows—" He shrugged. "Nothing's free, Gillian."

"I know." I could smell the thick scent of burnt sage. My new life and my old life, filled with whispers and gossip and podiums on which I would or wouldn't stand. I kissed Luke again, then watched as the gallery door opened and people entered, blowing on cold hands and knocking snow from their shoes.

Acknowledgments

I would not have written this without the bolstering encouragement and critical input of my first and best reader, Laurie Cheeley. My mother, Idaho State Senator Mary Lou Reed, taught me everything I know about campaigning and my father, Scott Reed, exemplifies the perfect supportive political spouse. Their love and faithfulness is proof that politics do not always make for strange bedfellows. From my brother, Bruce Reed, I learned that politics can be hilarious. My sister in law, Bonnie LePard, is a better hostess than Gillian could ever dream of becoming. Their children, Julia and Nelson, along with my lovely daughters, Sarah and Anna, give me hope for the future.

For their feedback and support I am eternally indebted to my early readers: Sarah Andersen, Shelley Arnott, Janet Fischer, Jean Kaplan, Jen Klug, Judy Malamud, Nate Nibbelink, Judith Roth, Beth Sanderson, Terry Schwartz, Willa Schmidt, Pat Shepard, Marsha Stella, Janet Taliaferro, Beth Tornes, Jane Yaris, Katherine Webster and Kim Wensaut. If I have forgotten anyone, please forgive me. I am especially grateful to my editor, Heidi Thomas. Any errors remaining in the text are entirely due to my own bad behavior. Pat Bickner's cover and interior designs are simply amazing, don't you think?

Along the way I have had wonderful writing teachers, including Lou Archer, Chana Bloch, Laura Bloxham, Rachel Guido DeVrie and Leonard Oakland. Steve Carpenter once told me that I should write a novel featuring a limnologist. Here you go Steve, I finally got around to it.

I also wish to thank my long-suffering husband and my dog, both of whom kept me happy, healthy and well-fed throughout the telling of this story. Thank you for helping me live my best love story.

CPSIA information can be obtained at www.ICGtesting.com
235343LV00004B/172/P